Dirty Job

Dirty Job

A Cauldron Of Stars
Book 2

Felix R. Savage

Knights Hill Publishing

Cover design by Jamie Glover
Photography by Andrew Dobell
Published by Knights Hill Publishing

ISBN 978-1-937396-37-4

Typesetting services by BOOKOW.COM

1

On a humid August morning when I should have been at the office, I crouched with my business partner, Dolph, in a thicket on the old helioba plantation in the Slumps. This was the edge of Shiftertown, formerly agricultural, now mostly slums. We were watching a couple of hundred RVs circle at walking pace around a vast muddy field. Only one of the RVs interested us. The one with a satellite dish on top, screen doors on both sides, and a rubber skirt over the wheels. That was the one which belonged to Timmy Akhatli, the Ek who owed me 30 KGCs.

I distractedly scratched the half-healed gash on the inside of my left arm. I'd got it breaking into the house of Buzz Parsec, my erstwhile rival, to rescue my daughter. It seemed like a lifetime ago, but it had only been a couple of weeks … the longest weeks of my life.

Insects circled us and landed on our neck and arms. We were already as bit as bit can be, having left my truck on Outback Avenue and bushwhacked through the woods to get here. Our phones were back in the truck—I had an emergency burner in my pocket. The comprehensive surveillance apparatus of Ponce de Leon thought we were driving around the Slumps, appraising properties. Dolph had laid a phone trail in advance to suggest he was house-hunting. The sun rose higher in the brash summer sky. I fingered the sap-stained blade of the machete lying at my feet. Dolph scraped soil up with his fingernails and embellished the streaks of dirt on his face and mine. Proof against facial recognition technology.

At last, just before noon, Akhatli's RV randomly veered towards us and trundled alongside the thicket.

I rose to my feet, still hidden by the bushes, and raised the machete.

Dolph ambled out of the thicket directly in front of the RV. It braked, and tried to go around him. Dolph moved in front of it again.

The prime imperative of any self-driving vehicle is not to run over people. Therefore, you can stop them by simply standing in front of them. Where would we be without advanced technology? This is the way kids in Smith's End steal cars, and this is how we were going to pay the Ek an unexpected, and doubtless unwanted, visit.

I took a couple of quick steps to catch up with the RV, and swung the machete at the screen door facing me. It gave way with a satisfying ripping noise. I leapt into the vehicle. Dolph dashed around, jumped in after me, and slammed both the side panels shut.

Timmy Akhatli backed away from us and tripped over a low table. I kicked his legs out from under him. He went down with a screech, hitting his head on the lockers that lined one side of the RV.

I dropped the machete, whipped my Machina .22 out of my waistband, and pointed it at Akhatli. The Ek now lay full length on his back, all four of his arms folded over his chest. The vehicle had tinted windows. No one could see us from outside. Dolph yanked a roll of duct tape out of his backpack and squatted to tape the Ek's treetrunk ankles.

Ekschelatans are the *other* powerful interstellar species in the Cluster. Some say they're more intelligent than humans. This one was not acting like it at the moment. His yellow eyes rolled, circular with terror. An absolutely putrid smell filled the RV—the smell of Ek, plus the more familiar smells of dirty laundry and reheated fast food. Dolph finished Akhatli's ankles and moved on to his four thick wrists.

I have nothing against Eks in general, but this one was a bad guy. We had been looking for him ever since Founding Day. He had been hard to find. Living in an RV is a good way to hide among the teeming but comprehensively surveillled millions of Mag-Ingat. The trailer throng moves around all the time, splitting up and reforming, driven by the flocking behavior of automotive AIs set to avoid getting tickets. To make matters worse, all the RVs look the damn same. We had narrowly missed Akhatli in a downtown parking lot, lost him again on the wharves, and finally caught up with him here, on the edge of Shiftertown, acting on a tip from a friend of Irene's. The whole independent shipping industry, or what was left of it, wanted this guy gone.

"You were hiding from the cops," I said, stooping to double-check the duct tape around Akhatli's ankles. "Too bad for you, it's us that caught you. We're more motivated."

Akhatli's blue, pebbly skin felt clammy to the touch, despite the stifling heat in the RV. Eks like it hot. This one was about to find out just how hot it gets when you conspire to commit genocide on one of humanity's Heartworlds.

"Is this rustbucket spoofed?" I said. Spoofing an automotive AI—constantly bouncing its signal around, so that it can't be tracked—is pro-level hacking, as well as being illegal. But the fact that the police hadn't found Akhatli yet suggested that he had spoofed his RV to evade surveillance.

"Yes!" Akhatli had an unexpectedly high, squeaky voice.

"Good." I sat down on the bench seat and plonked my feet on the low table. It was littered with rubbish, computer equipment, and holocards. "Why do you live here, anyway?"

"I—I—we are a nomadic species." I knew this to be true. Eks do not do planetary colonization like we humans do, preferring to build deep-space habitats that they can move around at will. But Akhatli's fat black tongue flickered over his lips. His gaze slewed to the underside of the table.

I felt underneath it. Ripped velcro free, brought out a plastic bottle and a reusable injector. "Well, well."

"What's that? Shabu?" Dolph said.

"Where have you been? These days, pezka it is called." Akhatli tittered nervously. His eyes followed the gear as I tossed it on the bench seat.

"If that don't beat all," I said. "An alien junkie." So *that's* why he lived in the trailer throng. Easy access to drugs. "Guess it's stressful, huh? Living on a human planet. Dealing with people like us. And Buzz Parsec. And Pamela Kingsolver." I gave him my ex-wife's alias, watching for a reaction. He just moaned in misery. "You were neck-deep in the Founding Day plot. Why the hell are you still here?"

"I am a shipping agent! Shipments for clients, I arrange! I knew nothing—"

"That was Buzz Parsec's defense. It didn't save him, and it won't save you."

"Typical junkie," Dolph said coldly. "No sense of perspective. Or self-preservation."

I got up and went forward to see if I could turn the air-conditioning on. The driver's seat was a cushiony, Ek-sized throne. I perched on its edge, found the A/C, and dicked with the steering to make sure I could control the vehicle. We were looping through the center of the trailer throng. Off to our left I saw a mobile shop surrounded by denizens of the throng: normies in disposable clothes past their dispose-by date, legs splashed with mud from the puddles that dotted the field. How did I know they were normies? Because of all the dogs running around. Shifters don't keep pets. And Shifters would rather live in a squalid shack, or in a one-room walkup in Smith's End, than in their vehicles. We like to live *somewhere.*

I steered the RV towards the far side of the field. The wheel twitched sluggishly under my hands as the AI course-corrected to avoid other vehicles. The A/C was kicking in. The sweat dried on my face. I listened to Dolph questioning Akhatli about Pippa Khratz. The Ek denied that he had ever heard of her.

I softly slapped the wheel in frustration. Pippa was the exiled heiress of Old Gessyria, a sweet sixteen-year-old girl whose political enemies had hated her so much that they were willing to take out an entire Heartworld to destroy her. And they had ended up destroying my life. *Why?* There was a big-ass missing piece in there. Akhatli had to know *something.*

The field was surrounded on three sides by the woods, which were swiftly taking it back. Most helioba cultivation had moved out to Cascaville and beyond, as Shiftertown sprawled further and further inland. Mill Creek, a stagnant brown waterway, bounded the fourth side of the field. I drove the RV over the dead stems of last season's crop, through some weeds, and into the water.

It was an amphibious RV. On land, it rolled; on water, it floated. The nose splashed into the water, throwing a muddy wave over the windshield, and rose up as a flotation field expanded beneath the vehicle. I clicked the wipers on, off.

"You should have run," Dolph said, in the back, "like your buddy Evan Zhang did." Actually, we had paid Evan Zhang to leave the planet.

"Yes, yes! Run, I will! Just don't hurt me!"

"That's not good enough. You haven't told us everything."

"I know nothing! Nothing …"

I pointed the RV's nose downstream and started the inboard engine. The helioba plantation slid away around the curve of the creek. Trees cast green shadows on the dusty water. It was a beautiful summer day. I leant my forearms on the wheel, feeling sadness open up inside me like a trapdoor. I should have been chilling on the beach with my daughter, or taking her to the zoo, instead of abducting an alien criminal.

The bridge appeared ahead of us. This was where Outback Avenue humped over the creek to become the Cascaville road. I took manual control and guided the RV towards the bank.

As we passed into the shadow of the bridge, I spotted a slender figure crouching in the bushes with a rifle. Irene, my weapons officer, had been stationed here in case Akhatli escaped us and tried to flee down the creek. I popped the sun-roof, our signal that we'd been successful. She lowered the rifle, picked up her backpack, and slid down to the water's edge. I brought the RV in along the bank and backed towards her. The bank was higher here, so Irene could get one knee up on the roof, lie flat, and roll in under the edge of the sun-roof.

I pointed the RV back into the current, got up, and went back to the living area. Irene stood on the bench seat where Dolph was sitting. "Yo," he said, looking up her slim legs to her hiking shorts and blouse, and the sniper's rifle she carried on a military surplus sling with extra ammo pockets.

"He talk?" she said.

"That's a negative," Dolph said. "He don't know nothing, he was never told anything, he just took their money."

"Yeah, right," Irene said. "You guys just don't know how to do this kind of thing. Here, hold this."

She gave her rifle to Dolph, stepped off the bench seat, and placed one boot on Akhatli's bound arms. He looked up at her fearfully. Quick as thought, she pulled a knife out of her boot and sliced one of Akhatli's ears off.

2

Eks have very small ears. They're just little mushroom-like knobs on the sides of their necks, and I think they work differently from ours. Convergent evolution ain't all that convergent. Still, the wound bled like a son of a bitch, and the blood was as red as ours, soaking into the filthy carpet of the living area. Akhatli went silent. He seemed to be paralyzed. Only his eyes strained, yellow and huge.

Dolph reflexively swept a hand through the clutter on the table, looking for something to stanch the blood with.

"No." Irene squatted. Blood squelched up from the carpet around the toes of her boots. She leaned forward and held the scrap of blue flesh above Akhatli's face. "I'm going to make you eat it. And then the other one. And then, maybe your dick."

The inside of the RV was dead silent.

"Oh, I forgot, you don't have a dick. You're not a man. You're a fucking alien."

Technically, to the best of my understanding, Akhatli did have a penis. And a vagina, too. Eks are neither and both at the same time. When they live on human planets, they typically choose human monikers that align with one sex or the other, so that dirtsiders won't have to wrap their heads around the xim / xe / xis business. Akhatli seemed more human than most Eks, so it was easy to think of him as *him*.

Irene lifted the drawstring waistband of Akhatli's shorts with the point of her knife. "OK, well, you asked for it," she said.

I coughed, breaking the horrified fascination that had held me leaning against the wall with my arms folded. Irene looked around and flickered me a wink. It was all an act, of course. Not one I had ever seen from her before … shocking in its intensity … but still, an act. Irene's sneering, sadistic pose masked her trademark steadiness of purpose. I had to be equally steady.

"The files, Timmy," I said. "Give us your customer files, and you can leave Ponce de Leon with your … whatever … intact."

"Why do you want my files?" Akhatli said in a breathy, scarcely audible voice.

"You don't need to know that." If he didn't know, he couldn't rat us out later.

"Everything I will tell you," Akhatli wailed. "I'll tell you about Pamela Kingsolver!"

My ex-wife. I went still. "Yeah, why don't you tell us about her?" As I spoke, I felt a pang of dread that some further hideous revelation was about to come out. Sophia—my ex's real name—had been the brains behind the Founding Day attack. Wasn't that bad enough? An undercover Traveller, she'd been hired by Rafael Ijiuto, princeling of the Gessyrias, to wipe out his exiled rival … and she didn't care if the entire population of Mag-Ingat died, too, just so she could get the job done. She had fled the planet after we foiled the attack. I assumed she had vanished back into the Core of the Cluster, where the Travellers hang out in their heavily shielded motherships.

"Helped her to escape, I did!" Akhatli babbled. "She wanted to get off the planet quickly and quietly … so she came to me! She knew that I have contacts in the shipping industry, the work of many years, a deep pool of contacts …"

"Yeah, yeah. Go on."

"A seat on an orbital shuttle departing from a private launch pad, and a temporary berth on an Ek freighter, I found for her! I do not work for free, of course. She paid me ... *very* well, in the region of 80 KGCs, not including the cost of the shuttle ticket ..."

"Where did she get the money?" Dolph said.

"The cops have Ijiuto," I said. "Let them work that out. Where did she go?"

"Valdivia," Akhatli squeaked.

"Valdivia?"

A Farmworld, twenty light years Corewards from here. I couldn't think of anything there Sophia would want. Maybe that was the only destination she could get on short notice ... Then I remembered that Ijiuto had asked me to take *him* to Valdivia. It must have been their fallback rendezvous.

"Where did she go from there?" I shouted. "Where is she now? What did she tell you?"

Akhatli's only response was wordless ululating, a creepy, alien noise.

"Oh, dear," Irene said. "Maybe we frightened him too much. Or maybe we haven't frightened him enough." She threw Akhatli's severed ear in the air and tried to catch it on the point of her knife. "Maybe he's more frightened of Sophia than he is of us. That would be a mistake."

I went back to the driver's seat and buried my face in my hands. I had more questions than before, and still no answers. Akhatli's cries scraped my nerves raw. I took my hands away from my face and looked out at where we were.

Thick woods enfolded the creek on both sides. We'd drifted down into Millhaven, the old industrial town that lies in between Harborside and Shiftertown. The odd factory roof reared out of the trees, but no other boats or amphibious vehicles disturbed the serene, almost rural view. Mill Creek is not used for transport—not of legal goods, anyway—and there are no fish in it that humans can eat.

This would be a good place for us to get off.

I went back to the living area.

Akhatli was quiet now, his eyes closed. Irene sat on the bench seat, toying with her knife, looking pissed-off. Dolph slumped beside her, gazing at Akhatli's gear. I didn't like his expression. He used to have a problem with that stuff. He hadn't touched it for years, but it was not good for him to be around it. I waved a hand in front of his face.

"What?"

"Time to finish this." I picked my way around Akhatli's legs and started to collect all the computer equipment I could see. Holocubes, a reader that hooked up to a holobook, the holobook itself, everything went in my backpack. This was not ideal. I had wanted Akhatli to open up his customer files for us himself. Without his help, we might have trouble getting into the files, much less finding the one we needed. But we clearly weren't going to get anything more out of the Ek. There are many reasons torture is banned by all mature civilizations, but one of them is that it doesn't really work.

Stepping over Akhatli's head, I looked down at the blood still seeping from the side of his neck. Worry burned in my gut. How were we going to get away with this? Was it really plausible to expect that Akhatli would say nothing about it to anyone, ever? I felt a spike of anger at Irene. She could have asked me before she started cutting pieces off of him …

Akhatli rose up under me and headbutted me in the stomach. I stumbled back, flailing for balance, and fell on my ass near the door.

The Ek surged to his feet, roaring in his own language, his eyes yellow slits of fire. He burst the duct tape around his wrists with one wrench. The tape fell in wet gray spirals. I had time to think that looked wrong. Then one of the Ek's windmilling fists caught Dolph on the side of the head, throwing him sideways. Irene jumped up on the bench seat and swung her rifle butt at the Ek. The space was too confined. She didn't have room to put her weight into it. Akhatli soaked up the blow, grabbed the rifle by the barrel, and grabbed Irene with his other two arms.

Dolph picked up the table and rammed it at the Ek, knocking him away from Irene.

Struggling to my feet, I tripped over something.

My machete.

Without a pause for thought, I snatched it up and lunged at the Ek. Akhatli blocked the machete with the rifle barrel, knocking the blade upwards, but I was still moving forward. And even at six foot one, I was a lot shorter than the Ek. My momentum drove the blade into his throat.

Blood jetted all over the inside of the RV. It spurted into my face, blinding me. I fell on top of Akhatli and rolled away. The Ek thrashed. Lying half on the bench seat and half on the floor, he clutched his throat with all four hands. After a subjective eternity, the hands fell away, uncurling limply. The fountain of blood slowed to a red freshet. Akhatli's feet twitched, and then stopped twitching.

I wiped my face with my t-shirt, which only smeared the blood around. I kicked one massive leg.

Like kicking a fallen tree.

"Dead," I said.

Dolph toed the curls of duct tape on the floor. Hoarsely, he said, "Their sweat has solvent qualities. Dissolved the adhesive on the tape. Forgot all about that."

"Well, fuck," Irene said.

There was a moment's silence. Then I forced my mind to start working again. Someone had to take charge. That would be me. "It's all right. It's gonna be OK. We'll sink the vehicle."

"Where?" Irene said.

The RV was still drifting downstream. The current had carried us close to the south bank of the creek. "Right here." I glanced around the gore-soaked interior of the vehicle. "Take anything that belongs to us." I picked up the machete, and put on my backpack. "Irene, can you do the honors?"

"On it." She moved forward to the driver's seat.

I checked again to make sure there were no other boats or amphibious vehicles on the river. I took a deep breath and threw open the side door.

Then I jumped.

I can't swim.

I sank. My mouth was closed but my eyes were open. I let go of the machete, and it sank. Through the murky water, I saw the bottom of the RV moving away like a spaceship, and then sunlight struck down, illuminating all the drifting leaves and twigs and bits of garbage in the water. Bubbles sparkled in a slow-moving blizzard, reminding me of how the stars of the Cluster look at FTL speed. That is the most beautiful sight I know. I'd always thought I would like it to be the last sight I ever saw.

We all have to die sooner or later. Sooner … or …

I thought of Lucy, and began to kick like crazy. All it seemed to do was push me further away from the sunlight. I swallowed water. My backpack was dragging me down, but panic had me in its grip now, and I couldn't remember how to take the damn thing off.

The sleek form of a dolphin dived under me and thrashed its powerful tail, swimming upwards with my body draped across its back. When we broke the surface, I spat out water, gasped for air, and flailed so wildly that the dolphin said, around the backpack it gripped in its mouth, "For fuck's sake! Stop panicking!" Dolph's voice always sounded higher and squeakier in dolphin form.

He swam to the north bank of the creek with me on his back. Tree branches overhung the high, undercut bank, dipping down almost to the water. I grabbed a branch that bowed under my weight, got my feet on some exposed roots, and hauled myself up to dry land. On hands and knees, I dropped my head and vomited. I was just as glad to return the water I'd swallowed back to where it came from. Mill Creek is none too clean.

Dolph climbed up the tree roots, naked, with his backpack over his shoulder. I thought about saying something about his clothes—maybe he should dive for them, maybe they would tie us to the scene—but then I didn't bother. The water would wash away any DNA evidence, and he'd been wearing generic gear. Printed on the cheap; you get one, two washes out of that stuff, then recycle it. Shifters seldom manage to hang onto their clothes much longer than that, anyway.

I wiped my mouth and spat. Then I took off my own wet clothes. The day was hot, the air heavy. We squatted, naked, in the undergrowth, and stared through the branches at the RV, which was still drifting down the river.

A faint *pop-pop* came from the vehicle. It started to sink.

Irene threw the side panel open and jumped into the creek. She didn't need to Shift to swim. She'd grown up in Shiftertown, a few blocks from the sea. Her head moved slowly towards us, blonde hair darkened by the water.

"Hard, fucking, core," Dolph said.

"Yup," I said. "She's all in."

I angled a glance at Dolph. I knew *he* wasn't all in. He had been ambivalent about this job, even before we killed the Ekschelatan.

Killed him.

In the middle of freaking Millhaven.

That wasn't in the plan.

"Nothing like getting a job off to a good start," Dolph said gloomily.

Not only was he my oldest friend, he was the person I most trusted at my back. Of course, I trusted Irene, too. But I knew Dolph wouldn't suddenly do shit like cutting off alien ears. And I knew he could keep a secret. "I went to the hospital this morning," I said.

Dolph went still. He had been nagging me to go and get a follow-up test. "And?"

"It wasn't a mistake. Dr. Zeb did a brain scan. There were signs of folding. I've got IVK."

The words were as hard to get out as they had been to hear in Dr. Zeb's office this morning. I forced the rest of it out in a rush.

"The average prognosis for survival is five years. Symptoms generally start to present within six months."

"Six months?"

"Initial symptoms include tremors, tics, and bouts of acute nausea." Dr. Zeb's words were engraved in my brain. "The tremors gradually become uncontrollable, while digestion also suffers to the point that patients are unable to keep food down. Bottom line, by next summer, I'll be a twitching, puking cripple. Lucy won't recognize me anymore."

"Does Dr. Zeb know you have Chimera Syndrome?" Dolph said suddenly.

"Huh? I don't have it. I *had* it. I've recovered."

"You don't recover from CS. You just learn to live with it."

"That's what Dr. Zeb said." As a child, I had battled Chimera Syndrome, a genetic disease that occurs in one out of 1,000 Shifters. It's virtually unknown for patients to live past the age of 12 … not in human form, anyway. I was the one in a million who had made it out the other side. I generally kept my survivor status a secret, as CS carries a stigma, but I'd had to tell Dr. Zeb about it after he scanned my brain.

"CS scars could look like the initial stages of IVK," Dolph said.

"Yeah. But he said that even taking that into account, there were unmistakable signs of folding. It's not a misdiagnosis."

After a moment's silence, Dolph repeated, *"Six months."*

"Yup. So I have less time than I thought to find the scum responsible, and throw them into the M4 black hole."

"You could do that," Dolph said, "and you'd just be that much closer to dying."

"True," I said. "I want to do it, anyway."

Dolph let out a bitter laugh. "So why the fuck are we chasing Timmy Akhatli's lousy thirty-KGC Hurtworlds run?"

"Because you're right. Revenge is a shitty goal." Emotion cracked my voice. It wasn't a delayed reaction to killing the Ek, although maybe there was some of that in there, too. It was me trying to be a better person, now that it was almost too late. "Lucy's going to lose her father. I can't do anything about that. But maybe I can find out *why* this is happening. Maybe we can find out the truth."

"This is so fucked-up." Dolph rubbed his face. "I always expected to go before you."

Irene was getting closer to the bank.

"Not a word to her," I whispered urgently. "I don't want anyone to know."

"How are they not gonna find out?"

"Not *now.* Please, Dolph. I'm begging you. Let's just focus on the job."

"You mean MF's latest power fantasy?"

I produced a rictus smile. "What, you don't believe in the crown jewels of the Darkworlds?"

3

I wasn't sure I believed in the crown jewels of the Darkworlds, either. That's what Rafael Ijiuto had called the little pendant, knife-shaped, diamond-studded, a few centimeters long, that he had worn around his neck. Pippa had had one, too. Our ship's bot, Mechanical Failure, said he had seen ones like those before. He claimed they were Urush technology. MF himself was an Urush bot, 1,214 years old, built by the mysteriously vanished race that had been the first to colonize the Cluster. He was way too cranky to be worth anything, even had we been minded to sell him, which we weren't. But even dumb Urush artefacts were known to command high prices. *How* much? MF had said it would depend if the item was in working order, but anyway, we were talking about fuck-you money.

If MF was right.

Irene believed he was. In her mind, we were already selling the crown jewels on the Techworlds. The first thing she said when she reached the bank was, "You *did* get the Ek's customer files?"

"Right here." My backpack was waterproof. I opened it and checked, anyway, to make sure the holocubes hadn't got wet, while Irene climbed out of the water, hauling her rifle and backpack. Her wet clothes clung fetchingly to her body. She had a trim figure, the slight sag of her stomach the only sign that she was a mother of two. I caught Dolph looking as she stripped off.

"It took me a while to figure out how to sink the thing," she said. "In the end I shot out the AI. That killed the flotation field."

In the shadows of the far bank, the RV settled deeper, taking Akhatli's corpse with it. When it stopped sinking, the top of the RV's sun-roof was still poking out of the water.

"Darn," Irene said. "Should've scuttled it in the middle of the creek."

"No, this is fine," I said. "It's spoofed, anyway. Time it's found, all the DNA will be gone."

"That's right," Dolph said, waggling his eyebrows. He was working too hard to cover up his shock at the news I had shared with him. "You didn't get bit by the piranhas?"

"Piranhas are an urban myth," Irene said. "All there is in that river is snakes."

"Speaking of snakes," I said, "we better get in touch with ol' python." I was referring to Martin, my engineer. "Need him to bring MF out to have a look at this stuff."

"Just take it out to the spaceport and he can look at it on the ship," Dolph said.

"It's stolen goods," I said. "Stolen from a guy we just murdered." I corrected myself: "That *I* just murdered."

"So?" Irene said. Her eyes were very blue.

"So I'm not taking that through customs," I said, deliberately missing the point. She was telling me the murder was no big deal. Because what, Akhatli was an alien? Or just because? She was wrong, though. It was one thing killing aliens—*or* humans—out in the Fringeworlds, light years from the nearest cop. It was another thing right here in our own backyard. I pushed away the rising tide of anxiety. "Better if we get MF to come out to us."

"OK," Irene said. "But you can't call them from here." Even though I was carrying a burner, it would be risky to use it so close to the crime scene.

"Right." I dropped my hands to the ground, hunched my back, and Shifted into a wolf. When I could speak again, I said. "Hike downstream. Get as far away as possible."

Dolph Shifted into his other animal form, a black-backed jackal. Irene Shifted into her black panther. We trotted along the riverbank, taking turns carrying Irene's rifle by its sling in our jaws.

The woods on Ponce de Leon are a slow-motion biological arms race between invasive species and the hardiest, fastest-growing, most poisonous survivors of the planet's original biome. We slid like furry ghosts through pufferplants, saberthorns, and upside-down trees, all fighting for the sunlight that trickled down through the canopies of murder oaks filigreed with strangler vines. Narcosloths croaked and birds trilled overhead. We could hear the sound of traffic on Millhaven Road, but for all we could see of it, we might have been a thousand miles from civilization.

We left Irene's rifle under a bush, and clawed the vines over it. She was sore at leaving it, but she knew we couldn't walk out onto Millhaven Road with that. I said we could come back for it another day. In my heart, I never planned to come anywhere near here again.

I reckoned we covered at least three kilometers before the undergrowth thinned out. We stopped to Shift back and get dressed. We all had spare, dry clothes in our backpacks. Preparedness.

Human again, we walked out of the forest into the parking lot of a seedy, sunbleached strip mall. Cybernetic implants, print-your-own clothes, instant prescriptions. Several of the shops had gone out of business. Holo graffiti tags defaced their shutters. I remembered what Dr. Zeb had said about no one reining in the small-time criminals anymore, now that Parsec was off the scene. Looked like they had the run of this place. Millhaven ain't Shiftertown, but it's close, and coming closer all the time. Shoot a gun north from the other side of Outback Avenue, you would hit a tree, but if you didn't, you would hit someone in Smith's End.

I turned my phone on and called Martin.

"Got the data," I said. That was all I could say. You have to assume that phone conversations are monitored. "But I need MF to have a look at it. Can you bring him out here?"

"I'm at the spaceport." Martin's voice betrayed his excitement. "We'll be there as soon as we can. Where are you?"

I peered up at the defunct holo sign, just a 2D substrate in the sunlight, above the strip mall. "Millhaven Shopping Center."

"Oh oh. Maybe not a good place to hang out."

"No choice," I said. "Waiting for my truck."

"You know you're only 'bout a stone's throw from Grizzly's."

Grizzly's Bar & Grill was the favorite hangout of Buzz Parsec's crew. The bears drank there, plotted, schemed, and got into bearish brawls, while consuming preposterous amounts of seafood.

"We're not that near," I said. Grizzly's was also on Millhaven Road, but farther up, nearer to Shiftertown. "It'll be fine. Just hurry."

Hurry.

Six months.

Hurry.

I lit a cigarette and eyed the kids loitering outside a tattoo parlor at the other end of the strip mall. But it was OK, they were normies, not bears. How could I tell? They had tattoos. Shifters can't get ink. It would go away when you Shift.

"They saw us come out of the woods," Dolph said.

"It's fine," I said. "Where's my damn truck?"

Irene was impatient, too, gazing up and down the road like her head was on a swivel. "I need to get home," she said. "I have to help Mia pack."

I groaned. "I have to help Lucy pack, too."

Our daughters had both been selected for the Shiftertown school district's annual summer camp. It was competitive: kids had to test in the top ten percent of their grade to get in. Lucy and Mia had both qualified for the first time this year. Was I pleased? I was just about bursting with pride. But right now, the reminder only ratcheted up my anxiety. Summer camp started tonight. This should have been my last day with Lucy. And I was hanging out in Millhaven, with a dead alien on my conscience.

At last a low-slung muscle bike zoomed up the road. Martin crouched over the handlebars, bulky in midnight-blue leathers. Behind him clung an unusual passenger: Mechanical Failure. Our ship's bot had all his grippers extended, clinging to Martin and to the bike's frame. His bendy neck was tucked down, sensor covers squeezed shut. It was fortunate that his chassis resembled a four-foot steel suitcase.

He toppled unsteadily off the bike. "Never again," he croaked. "Martin, I kept telling you to slow down!"

"This from a bot that's spent most of the last millennium travelling at faster than light speed," Martin said.

"It's different when you can see the ground." MF tentatively cracked his sensor covers open and regarded the strip mall. "Ooh la la." He had spotted the female members of the gang outside the tattoo parlor. They were not what I'd call attractive, but MF wasn't picky. His sensors extended in their direction as if on stalks.

"Work first, ogle later," I said.

Mercifully, my truck had arrived while we were waiting. We all clambered into the back. Squatting on the blankets I kept to cushion cargoes, I took out the holocubes and cube reader.

"This technology is ancient," MF complained.

Compared to him, it was young, of course. But the Urush knew things we don't. Show me the human-built bot that's still working after twelve centuries. "Eks are conservative," I said. "Can you read it?"

"Of course." MF powered up the reader. Ek script scribbled across the dimness, flickering faster than our eyes could follow, even if we could understand the Ek language. MF could understand it, of course.

I'd guess he knew every language in the Cluster. Two minutes and three holocubes later, he said, "Here it is."

"Machine parts for Mittel Trevoyvox," I said, "thirty KGCs up front, thirty on the back end?"

"I am not sure if this actually means machine parts. But yes, the cargo is going to Mittel Trevoyvox."

Martin fist-bumped Irene. "It's on!"

The Hurtworlds lie between 51 to 58 light years from Ponce de Leon, near the Core of the Cluster. It's a long journey, and there are other reasons why few people ever go there. The Hurtworlds are living hells. Leper colonies of the fourth millennium, they have nothing to offer to interstellar trade …

… but we had to go there.

Because that's where Pippa was.

But Dolph was right about one thing, it was a gamble, and my habitual financial caution hadn't deserted me. I couldn't go into the hole to fund the trip, even if I wanted to.

So we needed someone to *pay* us to make the trip, such as—

"Total Research Solutions," MF translated, "838 Millhaven Road."

"Perfect," I said. "That's just down the road a stretch."

"Let's go over there now, then. Get it over with," Dolph said.

"You want me to come?" Irene was kneeling at the back of the truck, one steely eye glued to the crack in the tailgate. "It sometimes helps to have a woman along, to make a softer impression."

Dolph suddenly laughed. "A softer impression," he cackled. "A softer impression!" His laughter was infectious. I joined in, and finally Irene did too, folding onto her haunches, laughing at herself.

"Well, OK, guys. Hope they don't call the cops on you looking like that."

Still smiling, Dolph looked down at his weathered Fish Folk t-shirt and holey jeans. "This kind of customer, looking like shit will be a plus."

Something struck the side of the truck. Clattered like a stone.

Martin flipped the bolt of the tailgate and bounded out into the sunlight. I was right behind him.

The kids outside the tattoo parlor were laughing.

"They threw something at the truck," I said.

"Goddamn normies," Martin said. "If they touch my bike ..."

But I was thinking: They noticed us. They'll remember us when Akhatli's body is found in Mill Creek.

"Let's go," I said, all laughter wiped off my face. "Marty, can you take MF back to the spaceport? We'll take the truck."

Squeezing into the cab of the truck, Dolph, Irene and I drove up Millhaven Road to No. 838. I wouldn't have known where it was without the GPS. There was no sign, only a narrow drive winding into the trees.

We were now so close to Grizzly's that when the truck stopped, I could hear faint music drifting through the woods.

"Sounds like the bears are partying," Irene said.

"There's a game today," Dolph said. He checked his phone. "Oh, look at that, they're losing. To the Sea Lions. Heh."

Irene's husband, Rex, also played rugby, Shiftertown's favorite sport. He was on the Wolves, even though his preferred animal form was a lion, because there weren't enough lion Shifters to make up a team. He had taken their kids and Lucy to watch the game today. After that, we were supposed to pack Lucy and Mia's bags and take them to summer camp for a six o'clock check-in. It was gonna be tight.

"Irene, can you stay in the truck?" I said "There isn't time for you to get all the way up to 90th Street and then for the truck to come back again."

"And also, you might need to make a quick getaway," Irene said.

"And also that."

"OK. Let's see if I can get cloudwhale chants on this thing." She started fiddling with the stereo. As we got out, she was folding her legs into lotus position. Meditation was Irene's way of coping with the kind of things we did. I guess it beat my own preferred coping method of bourbon, drunk neat.

Dolph and I walked up the drive into the trees.

The Total Research Solutions building looked about a hundred years old. This was standard for Millhaven. The town was dying by degrees, squeezed by Harborside to the south and Shiftertown to the north. But the vehicles in the overgrown parking lot told a different story. Shiny little floaters, minicars, and a segway or two—the transport options favored by trend-setting youth. On top of that, the place was surrounded by a high fence, and security cameras roosted under the eaves.

After considering the view for a moment, Dolph said, "Sketchy as fuck."

"Agreed." If the customer had gone through Akhatli to make their shipping arrangements, there was probably a reason for that.

All the same, I was not expecting a pudgy, scruffy boy with cybernetic eyes to step out of the gate with a shotgun. "No trespassing!" he yelled, pointing the weapon at us.

4

I looked down the barrels of the shotgun. It was a salutary reminder that you can die at any time, even in Millhaven on a customer call. I raised my hands away from my sides, without actually putting them in the air.

"I think there's some misunderstanding." I cued up my best customer-facing smile. "We're here about the cargo?"

"What cargo?"

"For Mittel Trevoyvox. Didn't Timmy Akhatli tell you we were coming?" I put on a confused face. "Uni-Ex Shipping."

"Wait." Cyborg boy vanished back inside, locking the gate after him. A few minutes later he was back with an elderly gentleman, who struck me as potentially more receptive. He had unruly white hair and wore a pair of imaging goggles around his neck, instead of having the hardware built into his face.

"Looks like our signals got crossed," I said, moving forward, hands out, unthreatening. "Dr. Tierney?"

This had been the contact name in Akhatli's files. I was just guessing, but I was right. "Call me Jim." The elderly gent shook my hand. "And you are?"

"Mike Starrunner, and this is my business partner, Dolph Hardlander."

"With names like those ..." Tierney chuckled, spreading creases around his piercing blue eyes. "You must be Shifters."

"Got us," I said with a grin. Shifters are physically indistinguishable from normies in human form, but to locals, names like ours are as big a giveaway as fur and flippers. Starrunner and Hardlander are the kind of moniker that Shifters choose when they no longer want to be associated with all the other Wildes, Foxes, de Leons, Waterses, and Wolfes. If I had it to do over again I would pick something like Smith.

"I can always tell," Tierney said, thumping his chest proudly.

"You must be from around here."

"That's right. Born in Millhaven, way back before the neighborhood went to hell." Tierney threw a dark glance in the direction of the music drifting through the woods.

"They been giving you trouble?" Dolph said.

Tierney scrutinized him. Dolph braced his thumbs in the pockets of his jeans, unsmiling. I intervened, "Let me give you my card." I tapped my phone, and a holo card flew through the air, heading for the phone in Tierney's pocket. He stalled it with a gesture, read the words: *Uni-Ex Shipping. Delivery Guaranteed. Discretion Assured.* Our certifications and licenses unfolded from the card like a bouquet of semi-translucent flowers. Tierney looked from the official, holo-sealed documents, to me, and back again.

"Where'd you get my name?"

"Timmy Akhatli. He decided to pass on this cargo at this time." I went out on a limb, implying that I knew what their "machine parts" actually were. In reality, I didn't have a clue. "According to him, your items are too … *hot.*"

Tierney gazed narrowly at me. As Irene had pointed out, neither Dolph nor I presented a very professional image. Dolph had a graze on his cheek where Akhatli had punched him. He had a strung-out aura, as if he lived on coffee and cigarettes, although his leanness was all muscle. I usually presented a more clean-cut image than Dolph, but not today. I had not been eating or sleeping properly, but I'd been making up for it with liquid nutrition, and it showed. Stubble, red-veined eyes, and a paint-splattered Wally's Seafood t-shirt completed the picture of a hard case with one foot in space and the other in the gutter.

But as I had been banking on, that's exactly what Tierney was looking for.

"Well, all right," he said grumpily. "Eks, Shifters, it's all the same to me."

He led us inside, while cyborg boy lagged behind and suspiciously read the small print of our landing license. I could have grabbed the shotgun off him at any time while he was doing that. They were paranoid, but they weren't professionals—at least when it came to violence.

"Cargo's been ready to go for two weeks," Tierney shouted, as he opened an inner door. "Hope you boys can fly on short notice."

He had to shout over the noise. Machinery whirred, whooshed, and hummed, and something was going thump-*thump,* thump-*thump,* like an overloaded washing machine. It was almost as bad as being on board a spaceship. Unlike a spaceship, however, the A/C was set so low that my skin goosebumped. Pitiless bright light flooded a cavernous room. It was a complete contrast with the dilapidated exterior of the building. The noise came from giant fridges, freezers, and other battered, cabinet-sized tools with screens displaying cryptic readouts. Close-set plywood shelves spilled boxes, bottles, vials, binders, and office supplies onto work surfaces. Individual workstations were tucked in wherever they'd fit. There was a strong smell of stinky socks, with overtones of lemonade.

"This a lab?" I said.

"Ding dong, you win the prize," cyborg boy said.

Fifteen or twenty young employees, many with cybernetic augmentations, stood in groups, chatting and talking to the AI assistants on their computers. It was the kind of behavior you see at creative offices, where work takes the form of hanging out and waiting for inspiration to strike. I could feel the energy in the air, all of it now bending like electricity to Tierney, as our entrance caused a momentary hush in the midst of the noise.

Tierney held up one arm and yelled, "Shipping company. I'm just gonna show them around."

He led us to a desk cluttered with screens, kitschy knick-knacks, and 3D models of molecules. Cyborg boy set out folding chairs. Tierney plonked himself into his executive ergochair. "Welcome to the future."

"So what you're producing here is … what, exactly?" I said.

"Genetic rewriting agents." Tierney held my gaze, challenging me to flinch. I just about managed not to. "Total Research Solutions is the name of our company, and that's what we sell, total solutions, so we ship autoclaves, centrifuges, photospectrometers, all the other tools used in lab work. We're a reseller for those devices, and officially, that's what this company does. So 99% of the tonnage will be off-the-shelf medical devices, but the other 1% is our own unique products. That's the reagents, crisper genes, and rewriter viruses which we make right here. Obviously, those items will not appear on the manifest."

"Obviously," I murmured. Those items were illegal. Maybe not to produce, but to export? Oh hell yes.

I wondered what drove an apparently successful scientist like Tierney to risk his career on exporting genetic engineering materials—to the Hurtworlds, of all places! It couldn't be money. The answer stood out for me in the faces of the young people grouped around us. They were grim-faced, bright-eyed true believers. They clearly saw themselves as warriors for one of humanity's most unpopular causes.

"We are saving lives," Tierney said, perceiving hesitation in my and Dolph's silence. "In the years since we left Earth, humanity has encountered *thousands* of alien bugs, viruses, every kind of disease. Some of them came near to wiping colonial populations out. But in the vast majority of cases, we have beaten these diseases back, thanks to genetic engineering. It's an ongoing war, made unfortunately more challenging by opposition to our methods."

"At my daughter's school," I said, "they teach them that genetic modification is unethical, because the only truly valuable and unique thing we have is our humanity."

"And I agree. But there are two distinct schools of gene-modding. *Germline* gene-modding alters entire populations, as was done in the past, with consequences that we are living with right now. That is no longer considered ethical. *Somatic* gene-modding is a medical technology that we all benefit from every time we go to the doctor. It's very unfortunate that the public is consistently unable to understand the distinction."

"Yeah," I said, "but it's the same technology, right? Once it gets out there, how do you know what people are going to do with it?"

"Saving lives," Tierney repeated. "Much as we may like to think it, Ponce de Leon isn't the center of the universe. Our fellow humans on other planets should have the right to do their own life-saving research."

"Our fellow humans on Mittel Trevoyvox?" I rubbed my temples. "Have you ever been there?"

"Have you?"

"I have."

"Good. I told Akhatli to get me someone with experience flying to the Hurtworlds."

I forced a laugh, remembering how we had left Akhatli's mutilated body in Mill Creek. Tierney didn't have a clue what had just walked into his lab. But that cut both ways: we hadn't had a clue what we were walking into. I picked up one of the models of human RNA and turned it in my hands.

The truth is, no Shifter can think about genetic modification without acute ambivalence. We're all too aware of how many thousands of lives were lost to pernicious mutations during the Big Shift. Some of those mutations—such as Chimera Syndrome—are still with us.

If not for germline genetic modification, we wouldn't exist … and yet, would I want gene-modding to take off again on a population-wide scale? Oh hell no. There are too many kinds of alt-humans already. We don't need the competition.

"I could name you a hundred diseases that we've licked with somatic gene-modding," Tierney said. "But there's still a lot of work to be done. For instance, I'm sure you remember the scare we had last month. Interstellar variant kuru?"

My gut hollowed out. The reaction was involuntary and internal. I put down the RNA model on Tierney's desk to hide a sudden shudder.

"Yeah," Dolph said, leaning forward. "What about IVK?"

"A challenge," Tierney said. I had already got the picture that when he said something was challenging he meant it was impossible, but he refused to use that word on principle. "Prion diseases are a toughie, and IVK is the most challenging of all. I shouldn't say this, but I almost wish the terrorists had succeeded. Then we might finally get some funding." He laughed, cyborg boy laughed, they all laughed.

"Excuse me," I said. "Be right back."

Dolph followed me outside. So did cyborg boy and a couple of the other youngsters. They stood by the gate in the fence. Cyborg boy held the shotgun. Dolph and I walked off a ways into the weeds and lit cigarettes. Was this place being watched? I looked up at the trees outside the fence. Blowsy summer foliage hung over the roof of the factory, hiding the facility from satellite or drone surveillance.

"Fuck it," I said. "I wish it was anything but gene-modding."

"We don't have to do it."

"Yes, we do."

"Mike, we are not gonna find Pippa. She was deported to Yesanyase Skont. That planet has a population of millions. How do we trace her? And if we do, then what? We rescue her? That's a felony."

"So's murder," I muttered.

"Two wrongs don't make a right. We fucked up, but we aren't going to improve the situation by taking a cargo of genetic engineering materials for sixty KGCs. Thirty down, and thirty on the back end? That's hardly enough to cover our costs."

"It ain't about the money," I said. It never was about the money for Dolph. He was just saying that because he knew me. He himself had higher ideals. That seems odd to say about a certified gun nut and adrenaline addict, but he did.

"It's all about the money for Irene and Marty." Dolph's lips twisted. The Hurtworlds job had brought out a crass side in our crewmates—Irene, Martin, and even MF—that he didn't like.

"I know." I shared Dolph's skepticism about the crown jewels. That's why I had a secret backup plan to cover our asses financially. But I couldn't tell him about that. Not yet. "Anyway, who said thirty?" I smiled crookedly and trod my cigarette out. "Bet I can get them up to seventy."

"Old man Tierney won't go over fifty."

"Seventy, at least. Loser buys the drinks."

We went back inside. I heard Dolph say to cyborg boy with an unpleasant laugh, "I met another cyborg recently. Shot his six-figure metal hand off." Dolph was not a fan of cyborgs. He saw augmentation as a crime against humanity—the same way, indeed, that many normies saw us.

But Tierney did not, and for that I liked him. We found him at his desk, and bashed out the details of the contract. I haggled him up to sixty down, and felt kind of bad about it. But business is business, and as I pointed out, he was not likely to find anyone else to take his cargo. The capacity crunch resulting from the collapse of Parsec Freight had temporarily created a seller's market. No one was gonna take a cargo for the Hurtworlds when there were other, safer jobs available.

No one except me.

Tierney walked us outside. "You boys got a ride?"

"Left my truck on the road," I said.

The afternoon was waning. Honey-colored light bathed the parking-lot. The music from Grizzly's had gotten louder. "They been bothering you?" Dolph said.

"Nothing too bad. Couple of my employees got mugged last week. Lost their electronics, their wheels."

"I'm sorry to hear that," Dolph said. "Shifters aren't supposed to act that way."

Tierney cocked a curious eye at us. "I might be wrong, but you boys don't sound like you're from around here."

He'd picked up on our San Damiano accents. "We aren't," I said. "We're from San D. But this is our home now, and we want to be good neighbors."

"I always wanted to visit San Damiano," Tierney said. "See the Big Shift memorial. A professional pilgrimage."

"So, you're the expert," I said. "What do you think of the Big Shift? Was it a big mistake? Is what you're dealing with now, this crap, is it the logical outcome of a huge ethical blunder?"

"A blunder?" Tierney grinned. "Son, my own profession would crucify me for saying this … but the only trouble with the Big Shift was it didn't go far *enough.*"

"What do you mean?"

He pointed his index fingers at me and Dolph. "Y'all are the pinnacle of biotechnology, products of the greatest genetic engineering experiment in human history. Every one of you is a walking miracle wrapped up inside a quantum-mechanical triumph over Newtonian physics. That don't mean anything to you, do it?" Smiling, he placed a hand on each of our shoulders, fatherly-like. "You've been genetically gifted with the power to manipulate reality itself. That is spooky shit. And yet you still piss around flying spaceships, shitting in people's back yards, and carjacking harmless strangers. *That's* what I mean."

"Gotta love humanity," Dolph said ruefully.

"But was it unethical?" I said. "From your point of view?"

Tierney's smile faded. "Oh yes. Unethical as all get-out. And I wish to heck they hadn't destroyed their research."

There's a monument on San Damiano, part of the Big Shift Memorial. It's a fifty-foot bronze portraying victims in their agony, but in the base of the statue is the debris of about a hundred supercomputers. They actually piled up the fucking things and set 'em alight.

Dolph nodded. "They locked in the Shifting ability and then threw away the key. Trashed the archives, wiped the files."

"It was a tragedy," Tierney agreed. "But the real tragedy is that to this day, the entire field is tainted with suspicion and burdened by onerous regulations." He sighed. "Well, maybe the next generation will do better. In the meantime, all we can do is to keep on doing the right thing. Right? It's been nice chatting with you boys."

Dolph slung a look at cyborg boy, who was standing in front of the factory, cuddling his shotgun.

"Slim can be a little over-protective," Tierney said. "It's the importance of the work. We live every day in fear that this will be our last. But I feel a lot better knowing that our products will be in safe hands. That Ek was a flake, I'm telling you."

He unlocked the front gate for us. As we walked along the drive, I looked back. Tierney waved. I lifted my hand in response. The trees hid his solid, white-haired figure.

"Nice old guy," Dolph said. "Ego the size of the freaking Cluster."

"Of course," I said. "He believes he's saving humanity."

"You owe me a beer."

"Hey, sixty ain't peanuts."

We reached the road. My truck wasn't there.

"That's funny," I said. "Maybe Irene decided to drive around."

"Call her."

I did. She didn't pick up. I connected with my truck and displayed its location on a map of the area.

"Oh, shit," I howled.

My truck was parked out front of Grizzly's.

5

Dolph and I jogged and walked along the shoulder, through the verdant needles of the native Ponce de Leon plant we call grass. Around the next curve, we came in sight of Grizzly's, a freestanding building with a pagoda roof squatting at the near end of another down-at-heel strip mall. The grill on the verandah billowed smoke. In the parking lot, about a hundred Bruins supporters were holding a tailgate party. The noise of the game, broadcast from a dozen car stereos, mingled with thumping music.

My truck stood on the verge of the road, this side of the narrow drainage ditch that bounded the parking lot.

Irene stood with her back pressed to the cab, aiming a handgun at Larry Kodiak.

The Kodiak twins, Larry and Gary, had been Buzz Parsec's chief enforcers. Used to be you couldn't tell them apart. But last month I had gotten into it with Gary K. Broke a couple of his ribs, clawed his face. He was left with a disfiguring red scar on his cheek and jaw. This hulking six-and-a-half-footer, his belly rounding out an XXL Bruins jersey, had no scar, so I knew it wasn't Gary K. It was his brother, Larry.

The gun in Irene's hands, a snub-nosed pistol, pointed unwaveringly at Larry K's stomach. I didn't know she was carrying that. But it shouldn't have surprised me. Out on jobs, Irene seldom went anywhere with only one gun … and although this was our home territory, I realized with a jolt, it was no longer any safer than anywhere else.

One of the guys with Larry saw us coming. He tugged on Larry's sleeve. I knew this bear, too: Hokkaido, Parsec's former engineer. He was squat and muscular, with broad shoulders that compensated for his soft middle.

The noise died down as Dolph and I crossed in front of Grizzly's, although the rugby commentary and the music kept going, annoying every normie within earshot. Larry swung to face us, turning his back on Irene. *I* wouldn't have done that. "Well, well, it's Starrunner and Hardlander," he gloated. "Only one missing is the snake."

I knew that the bears hated us. We had put Parsec in jail. But surely they wouldn't do anything dumb. Especially not in public. Dolph and I stopped a few meters from the knot of bears around the truck.

"I got no beef with you, Kodiak. What's going on here?" I looked at Irene.

"You can't say a friendly hello to these bears without getting threatened." Her voice was spiky.

Why had it occurred to her to say a friendly hello to the bears in the first place? I let that go for now. "You done? Because we got places to be."

"You framed the boss," Larry snarled suddenly, rounding on Irene. "You're not getting away with that!"

My blood ran cold. The fact was, Irene had faked evidence against Parsec to make sure he went down for smuggling bio-weapons. Oh, he'd been neck deep in the Founding Day plot—but he hadn't actually left himself open to criminal charges. Buzz Parsec was too smart for that. In the end, though, Irene had outsmarted him.

And the bears knew it.

Well, of course they did. *Parsec* knew he was innocent of the specific charges laid against him. And he had a pretty good idea that Irene had framed him.

But he couldn't prove it, and neither could Larry Kodiak. "Parsec is in jail," I said, "where he belongs, and that's where he'll be staying for the next ten, fifteen years. So you might as well get over it and start job-hunting."

"We're working for *Mrs.* Parsec now," Hokkaido blurted.

Cecilia Parsec was a normie. I had some respect for her, and I would have hoped she had cut these lowlife ursines loose. But it wasn't my business. "Good for you. Give her my best wishes." I sliced a glance at Dolph and began to move forward, through the bears.

They fell back, muttering insults. But Larry K blocked me with an ugly smile. "The boss doesn't forget anyone that betrayed his friendship."

"What are you talking about?" I said. "Parsec and I were never friends. I have standards."

Behind me, bears jostled Dolph. Dolph pushed back. The crowd hooted, "Shift! Shift!" They wanted us to Shift and fight. That's what passes for entertainment in this part of town. I felt a sense of weary disgust. What the hell were we doing here? I pushed Larry K in the chest with an open hand. "Out of my way."

He grabbed my shirt. Irene pointed her weapon at his face and yelled, "You need a hole in your head to help you think about this?!" Wrenching free, I threw the truck door open and vaulted up. Dolph twisted out of a knot of bears. He scrambled in and pulled Irene up into the cab as I started the engine.

I U-turned across traffic. Cars braked, AIs screamed, and horns blared. I gunned it towards Harborside.

"Well, that was fun," Dolph said. "What possessed you to go over there, Irene?"

"Like I said, I got tired of waiting for you guys. Went over there to say hello. Thought maybe I could smooth things over with them."

Dolph shook his head, looking as bemused as I felt. "Why bother? They're finished. The Kodiaks are coasting on Parsec's coattails, but that's gonna end when the money runs out. Cecilia can't keep paying them to sit on their asses forever." He snorted. "Parsec already sold the *Great Bear.*" That had been Parsec's freighter. "He sold his other businesses, some of his real estate … he's still got his spread at Ville Verde, but you figure they'll have to sell that, too. The city hit him with a civil lawsuit on top of the criminal charges."

"The bears can still bite, though," I said. "I don't want any trouble with them."

"Nor do I," Irene said. "That's why I went over there."

"Larry K said something about betraying Parsec's friendship," I recalled.

Irene nodded. "I used to work with Parsec, although I couldn't say we were friends."

I hadn't forgotten that. Before Irene joined my crew, she and Rex had been freelances. Not to put too fine a point on it, they'd been professional thieves. In that capacity, they had worked with Parsec a few times. But that was ancient history. Even before I met them, they had gone (mostly) straight for their children's sake. And I did not doubt Irene's loyalty to me … after all, she'd framed Parsec so that I could walk free.

"They've been nuisance-calling me," Irene said. "Threatening dire retribution."

"So you went over there to threaten them back." Although I believed she had made a mistake in escalating it to a face-to-face confrontation, I had to admire her guts.

"You should have told us," Dolph said.

"I'm telling you now."

"We'd have come with you."

"That's why I didn't tell you before."

"What," Dolph said, grinning, "you think we would have bit their throats out or something?" The confrontation with the bears had cheered him up. This kind of thing was more manageable than exiled princesses, priceless Urush technology, and IVK.

I turned onto his street in Smith's End. Turds and gnawed bones littered the sidewalk. Mama tigers and wolves sprawled on their stoops, watching their half-naked children play in the street. The truck autobraked to avoid a hyena strolling across the street, talking into a custom phone headset and wearing diamanté jewelry over its fur. "Dolph," I said, "how about moving?"

The fact he'd suggested house-hunting as a diversionary activity made me think he was at least open to the idea.

"Meh. I'm used to it here," he said. "I don't even smell the recycling plant anymore."

He got out and vanished into the chaos like my machete vanishing into the water when I dropped it. I drove through to Creek Avenue and turned north.

"Well, the traffic's not too bad," Irene said. "Looks like we'll only be half an hour late to drop the girls off."

6

"DADDY!" Lucy hurtled down the steps and jumped me as I climbed out of the truck. "We won!"

"Who's *we,* sweetiepie?" I swung her around, wondering how much longer I could count on having the strength in my arms to pick her up.

"The Sea Lions, of course! We had to cheer for them, because the Wolves weren't playing."

"At least they got Lions in their name," Rex said ruefully. He stood on the porch, a majestic lion surrounded by backpacks and suitcases. "Got all the packing done. Don't blame me that they want to take the whole house."

Code-switching. When you're a parent, you have to learn how to do it. This afternoon, we had murdered an alien. Half an hour ago, we'd been confronting hostile bears. Now, what I wanted more than anything was a drink. Instead, I had to think about underwear, socks, and nametags on towels. I found to my relief that Lucy had packed everything on the camp's list. I could thank Rex for that. He might be an ex-thug with a chequered past, but I could think of no one I'd rather have living upstairs.

I boosted Lucy's luggage into the back of the truck, feeling a pang at the parting which was yet to come. We had spent the last two weeks solidly in each other's company—painting the apartment, window-shopping, eating out, going to the beach. It was not too much to say that the joys, and the responsibilities, of dadhood had saved my life in the days after my diagnosis. Some evenings, Lucy had been the only thing that stood between me and a bottle of Cristo Rey. Some nights, her sleeping presence down the hall had been the only thing that stopped me from putting my .22 in my mouth.

Now, while I thought back nostalgically over our days together, she chirped, "Are you looking forward to camp, Mia?"

"Yes!" said Irene's blonde, sprite-like daughter. "Are you looking forward to camp, Lucy?"

"Yes! Are *you* looking forward to—"

"I think we get the picture," I said, smiling indulgently. The girls bounced up and down with excitement as we drove south along the Strip. The ShifterKids Summer Experience!! was located at the Lagos del Mar Resort, at the south end of Shiftertown. In some obscure deal with the city, the mass-market beach resort had opened its facilities to a couple hundred Shifter schoolkids. I pitied the management.

We drove all the way along the Strip, through the slumbering red-light district, and on through a tangle of little streets, out to the spit where Mill Creek oozes into the sea. Ten acres of reclaimed land. Private beach. Outside the walls, Smith's End; inside, manicured greenery. They had flying shuttles for the guests, so no one would have to see the slums. We arrived by the dirtsider entrance, at a drop-off circle in front of a pink colonial-style building. A reptile with spikes along its head and back, like a miniature dinosaur, was hopping across the forecourt. "Chupacabra alert!" I said. It was about the size of a wallaby and it moved like one, too. An entourage of Shifter kids followed it, whispering and pointing like it was royalty. Of course, it was just a native Ponce de Leon animal. But most of these kids had never been out of the city … and my daughter was no exception. The furthest I'd ever taken her was the zoo.

She clung to my arm as I got her luggage out of the back. Insecurity suddenly dimmed her mood. "Is it gonna be OK for me to stay here?"

"It's just an animal," I said. "They're herbivorous, and I would bet that one's been declawed."

"No. They're all looking at me."

Of course. She wasn't worried about the chupacabra. She was worried about the other kids.

"Sweetheart, it's OK. They aren't looking at you. Everyone's forgotten, anyway."

Lucy's kidnapping two weeks ago had made the news. My friend Jose-Maria d'Alencon, a Ponce de Leon cop, had personally ensured that her name was kept out of the media. Nevertheless, I'd had to inform her school about it. Lucy had been a seven days' wonder in the playground. She hadn't enjoyed the attention. Like father, like daughter—she preferred to fly under the radar.

"Most of these kids aren't even from your school," I reassured her. "There's practically no one here from Shoreside Elementary except you and Mia."

That was because the ShifterKids Summer Experience!! wasn't free. It cost 5 KGCs a week. Poorer Shifter families received financial aid, but we in the "good" end of Shiftertown didn't qualify, so we were out of luck. In fact, I had quietly insisted on paying Mia's fees, so that she and Lucy could go to camp together.

We crossed through the lobby into a landscaped garden, and walked along a path that circled ponds and humped over tiny bridges. Another stucco building shimmered through the trees. We followed kid noise to an inner courtyard where camp counselors manned folding tables beside a swimming pool. There were more kids in the pool than water, and at least one chupacabra was wallowing around with them. Mia's face lit up. She wanted to get in that pool right now. Irene said something sharp to her I couldn't catch over the noise.

We lined up at the L through S table.

My heart clenched like a fist.

I almost forgot to breathe.

The counselor checking kids in at our table was Christy Day.

Christy's gaudy t-shirt and shorts could not hide her beauty. Her cinnamon hair was tied back in a braid. I watched her animated face as she greeted campers, and remembered how soft those lips had felt on mine, how irresistible her body had looked under me. I'd been trying to forget our night together. Good luck with that.

We reached the head of the line.

Christy's boilerplate breezy greeting died. We held each other's eyes for an instant. Then she rallied. She was at work, after all. "Hi, Mr. Starrunner, hi, Mrs. Seagrave! It's great to see some Shoreside Elementary families here."

Christy worked at Lucy and Mia's school. That's how we had met. Of course, school was out for the summer. *Of course,* she had taken a summer job as a camp counselor.

"Hi, Lucy and Mia," Christy went on. "Are you looking forward to camp?"

"Yes!" Mia shouted. But Lucy looked less certain. She was clinging to my arm again.

"Go on, Lucy," I urged her. "Say hello to Ms. Day."

"I just don't know if it's OK for me to be here," Lucy mumbled.

Christy hesitated. As we had rolled up late, there was no one waiting in line behind us. "Well, it looks like most folks are checked in now, so Mrs. Seagrave, can I hand you over to Amanda, here? I think maybe Lucy needs a minute."

"Sure, fine with me," Irene said. Keeping Mia close, she zeroed in on the hapless Amanda and began to fire questions at her.

Christy, Lucy, and I walked out of the building, back into the garden. Christy's hand brushed my arm. An instant, electric jolt of desire took me off guard.

I moved away, putting Lucy between us. I needed to focus on my daughter right now. "Sweetie, why do you think you shouldn't be here?

You scored in the top ten percent. Actually, in the top five." I winked at Christy. "Who me, a proud dad?"

"You have every right, Mike," Christy said. "Lucy, your results were fantastic. The camp director thinks you show a lot of promise. It's going to be a great summer. And ... you don't have to worry about anything bad happening here." She gestured around. "The whole resort has a force field perimeter. There are armed guards." To keep out the *other* Shifters, I thought. Christy pointed up. "And see those?" White, hawk-like objects drifted in the darkening sky. "Security drones."

"Nice," I said.

"So no bad guys could ever get in."

"Unless they came in a spaceship," Lucy said.

"If they came in a spaceship," I said, "they wouldn't even be able to start their de-orbit burn before the Fleet blew them to dust. So Christy's right. This place is one hundred percent safe."

The sound of rushing water drew us out of the trees. We had reached part of Lagos del Mar's famous water obstacle course, a stretch of artificial rapids between high banks. The water came from Mill Creek but it had been cleansed of all impurities. It foamed over fake rocks. Guests in lifevests—and a few daring souls without—swam and tumbled through the rapids, helped along by dolphins and seals. That was the resort's selling point: many of the staff were Shifters, who worked in animal form.

Lucy fidgeted with the rope strung along the path. "The trouble is ... the trouble is ... all the other kids are *real* Shifters. What if they find out I'm not?"

So *that's* what was on her mind.

"Not a real Shifter?" Christy said, confused. She didn't know my ex-wife was a mainstream human. Didn't know anything about Sophia at all.

I forced a smile. "You know what, Christy, I think we'll be OK by ourselves for a while. Thanks for everything."

Hurt flashed in her eyes. Then she gave Lucy a quick hug. "OK, doll, see you back at the dorm." Without looking at me again, she walked back the way we'd come.

I led Lucy to a wooden bench overlooking the rapids. "Let's get one thing straight. You *are* a real Shifter. The genes are dominant. Even with only one Shifter parent, you're as much a Shifter as any of those kids back there, and in fact more so, because they don't know sh—crap about our culture."

"But what if I'm not?" Lucy said, kicking the bench with her heels. "What if I turn out like *her?*"

Her was Sophia. Cecilia Parsec had told Lucy as much as she thought she needed to know about her mother, which was a damn sight more than I ever had. She'd showed Lucy old vids of Sophia, and given her Sophia's Traveller coat. The overall effect had left Lucy scared of this woman, this Traveller who had tried to kidnap her, who'd hurt so many people … and yet, in a way, Lucy was fascinated by her.

This, *this* was why I had to find out more about Sophia's atrocities. This was why I had to go to the Hurtworlds.

But right now, I had to work with what I'd got.

"She's not all bad, sweetheart. She wasn't always bad."

"Really?"

Against my instincts, I nodded. The truth is always complicated, and this was the truth, too. I had not told Lucy anything about her mother for bad reasons as well as good. I didn't want to give Lucy a chance to *like* the woman who had abandoned us.

But now … now I was trying to be a better person. A better dad, for as long as I had left. And right now, that meant rising above my own bitterness and humanizing Sophia for my daughter, so she could see her as a person who had made bad choices, not a boogeyman.

"She grew up on Montemayor …"

Lucy listened, open-mouthed, as I told her what I knew about Sophia's past. My ex-wife had been an only child, like me. But unlike me, she had grown up on a wealthy, privileged planet, one of humanity's three Heartworlds in the Cluster. Exotic pets, private tutors, off-world holidays, you name it, she had it. Her father was a Montemayor senator, her mother a lawyer. She had never introduced me to them. Her excuse was that she was estranged from them, but that very fact should have been a red flag, because they had given her everything. "They had a summer house on Diaz de Solis. She went to a private school with music lessons, horseback-riding lessons, a world-class ballet studio, everything. Then college and graduate school." This in an era when college admissions are ruthlessly meritocratic. A place like Montemayor University, only a fraction of a percent of people get in. "She got a doctorate in AI studies, *and* a master's degree in philosophy."

"I could never get into college," Lucy said.

"You scored in the top five percent, remember?" I poked her. "I'm not saying higher education is necessarily a good thing. Our graduate schools turn out two types of people, politicians and Travellers, in about equal numbers. But you could definitely get in if you wanted."

Lucy screwed up her face "I like the other school she went to. With music lessons and horseback-riding, and … and everything."

Rashly, I said, "You *will* go to a school like that. You know St. Anne's, out on Cape Silvestre? They have all that stuff. Listen. Camp lasts six weeks, and then I'll be back. But you don't have to go back to Shoreside Elementary in September. You'll be going to St. Anne's."

I probably shouldn't have revealed my secret plan, but Lucy didn't ask where I was going to find the money for it. She hugged me. "You are the *best* dad!"

We sat and talked some more about St. Anne's, while the dolphin Shifters gave people rides through the rapids. It was a humiliating, exploitative way to make a living, and it made it worse that they agreed to be exploited, because jobs for Shifters don't exactly grow on trees. But Lucy would not fall into that trap. I would boost her out of the Shiftertown gravity well, if it was the last thing I did.

"No more of this mess," I muttered.

"What mess?"

"Oh …" I gestured at the dolphins. "That."

"Why is that a mess?"

"It's the mess the Big Shift scientists made. We're just living in it."

"But it's great being a Shifter." To their credit, her school did try to make the kids feel good about themselves. "Isn't it?"

"Of course it is," I said. "It's awesome."

"Poor Dad," she said suddenly, laying her head against my upper arm, and patting my knee. "Poor, poor Dad."

"Why poor Dad?"

"You have to go far away. I wish you could stay here with me."

Christy Day's white limbs flashed through my mind. "So do I."

"But it will be OK," Lucy said. I had started out reassuring her, and now she was reassuring me. "You'll be back soon, and in the meantime I am going to have fun here! I feel OK about it now." She laced her fingers through mine. "Come on. Let's go back and find Ms. Day."

I swear, I didn't deserve this child. She was enough to make me believe in a God of unaccountable blessings, who knew all the bad shit I had done and nevertheless, inexplicably, rewarded me like this.

7

Back at the ShifterKids Summer Experience!! building, we found Christy waiting for us with Irene and Mia. There seemed to be an odd froideur between them. Christy said, "Come on, Lucy, I'll show you your room, and your dad can see it, too."

The three of us went upstairs, along high-ceilinged passages filled with kids running and chasing each other. Lucy would be bunking with seven other girls. They were unpacking under the direction of—guess what?—a tubby humanoid robot, very similar to Lucy's former caregiver, Nanny B. I saw Lucy relax. The robot, to her, said safety.

Christy and I went back downstairs. At the edge of the courtyard, she said, "I've moved."

"Yeah? Where to?"

"Further downtown. I'll give you my new address." She sent it to my phone. There was a moment's silence, and then we both started to speak at once. I gestured for her to go first. "I called you."

"I know." I hadn't picked up. Because I had IVK. We had no future together, because *I* had no future. "Sorry."

"Mike!" Irene shouted. "Come *on!*"

"I'll let you go," Christy said, and walked away.

Irene had hold of Mia's hand. Mia was weeping. "Huh?"

"Mia is coming home with us," Irene said. "You might want to reconsider letting Lucy stay, as well."

"What the heck? Is something wrong?"

"It depends if you consider government interference wrong."

"Christ, Irene. It's funded by the government, run by the government, that's not a secret."

I was frazzled by parting from Lucy and the awkward moment with Christy. I strode back to the entrance, summoning my truck. Irene dragged Mia along. The little girl was sobbing pitifully. "Stop that. I'm not having them brainwashing you."

I almost hit a chupacabra as I pulled out. It was getting dark. The headlights sliced across the ruthlessly pruned greenery. "All right, I'll bite. How is it brainwashing?"

"I talked to that counselor. There will be discernment exercises."

"They do those at school, too." Discernment, in the education ministry's parlance, means helping Shifter children to learn about various animals, in preparation for choosing one at the age of twelve, when they start to Shift.

"Yes, but did you see that place? Water, water everywhere. The Shifter employees? All marine mammals. Dolphins, seals, sea lions, a couple of walruses, they've even got an orca. These are the people who'll be instructing the kids. So what kind of *discernment* do you think they're going to do? They're openly, blatantly pushing their agenda on our children. Sorry about the five K," Irene added. "We'll pay it back."

"It doesn't matter," I said. "This 'agenda.' What is it? Enlighten me."

"Rex and I think they're breeding up marine Shifters for a reason. Remember Tech Duinn?"

"How could I forget?"

"Shifters won that war for humanity. And you have to figure that was not lost on the Fleet. Now they're looking to recycle the same template, but this time, it's not wolves and tigers they want. It's dolphins and seals."

"We aren't at war with anyone."

"I'm aware of that, smartass. But sooner or later, we will be. There's always another war on the horizon, somewhere in the Cluster. And this time, they want our kids to fight it." Irene pulled Mia onto her lap. "Well, they're not getting my daughter."

Lost for words, I wove through traffic on the Strip. "And Rex is on board with this conspiracy theory?"

"Conspiracy theory? Sure, you can call it that if you want. We can't prove anything. That doesn't mean it's not happening."

I considered myself a contender in the paranoia stakes. But when it came to conspiracy theories, Irene and Rex left me in the dust. I could not decide if they were more sophisticated than me, or more credulous. "So let me get this straight," I said. "The ShifterKids Summer Experience, don't forget the two exclamation marks, is part of a long-term plan to expand the recruiting pool for a marine Shifter unit to be formed ten to fifteen years in the future to fight a marine species we haven't even heard of yet?"

"You know what, we'll walk," Irene said. The truck was stopped at a red light. She actually started to open the door

"Jesus, Irene. I'm just saying—"

"Well, don't," she snapped, smoothing Mia's hair.

As we drove back in silence to 90th Street, I thought about friendship. I considered it a sacred value, just one notch down from family. I was furious with Irene for splitting Lucy and Mia up. What is childhood without a best friend? I literally wouldn't have made it through childhood without my best friend, Dolph. One of my touchstone memories was the time I got de facto banned from the sixth grade half-marathon. I was still having Chimera Syndrome episodes, and the school forbade me to participate in sports. Then Dolph, the most popular boy in our class, had announced that he wasn't entering the half-marathon, either, unless they gave me a chance.

Then he had trained with me day after day until I was able to complete the course.

Holding my shoulders, picking me up when I fell over, holding onto me even when his hands went right through my bones.

I shuddered, and pushed the memory away as I turned onto 90th Street.

The leaves of the gravelnut in front of our building hung in a verdigris halo around the streetlight. The evening was humid and still. Mia scrambled out of the truck with a cry of "Dad," and that was when I saw the man sitting on our front porch. Rex reverted to human form so seldom that his thuggish vibe, complete with broken nose, always came as a surprise.

"Aw baby." He held out his arms to Mia. "I'm sorry you couldn't stay." Irene must have discussed it with him on the phone when I wasn't there. "We just can't let them take our baby girl away from us. You understand that, right?"

"It is *not fair,*" Mia howled. "I wanted to stay!"

"Kit?" Irene said.

"Upstairs with Nanny B."

Irene started towards their front door. The two front doors opened off the porch, side by side. About to turn the doorknob, she froze. "What's that?"

Rex sighed. "Yeah. I was about to ask you, Mike. You got any solvent?"

The porch lights were off, and if he hadn't said anything, I might not have noticed it.

A word or words had been spray-painted across both front doors in letters a meter high. The paint was gone; what remained was the shadow where it had been. I pushed past Rex, trying to decipher the dull marks.

"Happened while you were out," Rex said. "I was upstairs. Thought I heard something. I come down and there's Nunak, spray-painting the porch. In broad freaking daylight."

"Nunak?"

"A bear," Irene said. "He used to work with Parsec, but they fell out a while back."

"He's more brain than brawn," Rex said. "Parsec never did appreciate competition."

But now Parsec was off the scene.

"He had someone waiting for him in a car. Minute I opened the door, they hightailed it. I tried to get the paint off while it was wet. Used that magic eraser stuff, but you can still see it."

SNITCH.

That's what the shadows said.

Snitch.

There's no worse word in the Shifter vocabulary. Shifters do not squeal on other Shifters. That's basically the whole of our unwritten law. But we had squealed on Parsec, and the bears knew it. OK, you could argue that framing a guy isn't the same as snitching on him, but I would not expect the Bad-News Bears to appreciate that rhetorical point.

"Guess Larry K wasn't kidding around," Irene breathed.

Instinctively, I swung around to see if any of our neighbors were out on the street. At the same time, righteous indignation boiled up. Irene had framed Parsec to save *me.* If anyone had squealed to the cops, it was *me.* And yet she was taking the brunt of the bears' wrath.

"Solvent isn't gonna help," I said. "You already damaged the original paint. The only thing to do is repaint it."

"Repaint it?" Rex said. "Damn."

"Start with scraping and sanding it down."

"Guess we should do that tonight, before the neighbors—"

A scream seeped out from the second floor balcony. Irene said, "That's Kit." She dashed upstairs.

"I'll come down and borrow your paint scraper later," Rex said.

I followed them upstairs. I felt like I owed them an apology.

The door at the top of the stairs opened directly onto their kitchen, a cozy, chaotic room with two pink walls and two orange ones. Nanny B sat beside the kitchen table, pawing at an inhuman, writhing, screaming knot of limbs. A scaly foot turned into a shaggy wing and slid through her grippers. "If you calm down, you may have a cookie, Kit," she quacked.

Irene and Rex bowled the nanny bot aside. They knelt over the thrashing, Shifting form of their son, telling him they loved him, pleading with him to stop it.

I leaned against the door jamb, feeling sick. Kit kept screaming. I knew that he could not hear a word that Nanny B or his parents were saying to him right now. He was having a Chimera Syndrome episode.

"When did this start?" I said.

"About a week ago," Rex said. "Figure it was the Founding Day thing that set him off."

"And then you had to go and take him to the game," Irene said.

"Yeah, guess that didn't help."

"But no, actually, why shouldn't you have?" Irene reached for Kit, and jerked back as his body melted under her hand. "Why can't we—just—be—normal?"

As if in response, Kit screamed louder. His forelimbs bifurcated, and white fur flowed over them.

"C'mere, Kitster. It's OK, It's OK." Rex tried to pull Kit onto his lap. Kit slid bonelessly off in a puddle of fur that was already turning into iridescent feathers.

I had known for a while that Kit had Chimera Syndrome, just like me. He was a little young, at five years old, to start having episodes. They might have expected to have another good year with him. But as Rex said, the children had all gone through a stressful time lately. Irene and Rex were trying to speak to him in calm, soothing voices, but I could hear their barely-concealed panic. In fact, I felt a touch of panic myself, suddenly confronted with this nightmare vision from my past.

Feathers melted into sleek black skin. A tail whipped Irene in the face, making her cry out. For a moment Kit was a snake with feet. Then the feet elongated into clawed legs, and he became a naked canine with a pig's snout. All the animals he had obsessively studied since he was old enough to talk were blending together in unnatural hybrids … *chimeras.*

I could have told them that he was under the table because he wanted to be in a dark, quiet place. I could have told them that talking at him would do no good. The only thing that would help was holding onto him.

But if I said that, Irene and Rex would want to know why my advice contradicted the advice they'd got from the doctor and the internet. I didn't want to tell them that *I* had Chimera Syndrome. That I'd lived through this myself. Survival rates are vanishingly low, and I didn't want to give them false hope. Honestly, the chances were a thousand to one that Kit would not make it. That sometime—not tonight, not this year, but in another few years—he would start to Shift like this … and get stuck as a snake-dog-chicken, or a wolf-seal-bat. For the rest of his probably-short life.

Mia crouched in the bathroom door, white with fear. Nanny B wrapped a gripper around her. I squatted down in front of them. "Mia. Next time your brother does this, see if you can get him inside a closet, or under a bed. It helps."

She just stared at me woefully. It had to be as tough for her as it was for her parents.

All at once, Kit's screams ceased. His coat of spotted fur melted into little-boy skin, he had the right number of limbs again, and his big dark eyes gazed confusedly up at his parents. They were not even wet. Those horrifying screams had come from his head, not his heart.

"You may have a cookie, Kit," Nanny B quacked, "as your reward for calming down."

"Awesome," Kit coughed, struggling to his feet.

Then Mia started to cry. "It's not fair! He gets everything he wants! I never get anything *I* want!"

Irene and Rex reached for her, assuring her that they loved both children equally. "You can have a cookie, too," Irene said, sitting Mia on her lap. She rested her cheek on top of her daughter's head. Their blonde hair mingled. "Heck, you might as well have three. No one's going to get supper at this rate."

I cleared my throat. Rex looked up at me. "So you see how it is, Mike," he rumbled.

I nodded, understanding what he meant. They would now need to start buying Kit horrendously expensive anti-seizure meds. Then after a while, they'd need to provide round-the-clock care. Eventually he would need to go to hospice.

At least I could reassure Rex on one point. "We got the Mittel Trevoyvox cargo."

That brought a smile to his tired face. "Way to go."

"They want us to fly immediately."

"Mommy's going away again," Mia wept through a mouthful of cookie. "Mommy's going away."

Irene placed her hands on Rex's shoulders, and lowered her forehead to touch his, with the two children in between them. "This'll be the last time, Mia," she muttered. "We're gonna be rich. We'll have a car. A big house on the Cape. Heck—heck, if you really want it, we'll even have a swimming pool." Tears glistened on her eyelashes.

I backed out and closed the door quietly behind me.

8

BACK downstairs, I wandered through my empty apartment. It was *really* empty—no carpets, no curtains, no appliances, no furniture except the kitchen table and chairs. Nothing left for me to hang my humanity on. Lucy and I had begun redecorating, but we hadn't got far. I smiled sadly at the smeary hot pink and turquoise paint job she had inflicted on her bedroom walls. I missed her already.

I collected my infrared paint stripper and sander from the living-room. In my bedroom, I reloaded my .22 and stuck it into my waistband. In the kitchen, I splashed bourbon into a mug that still held an inch of this morning's coffee. Sitting at the kitchen table, I called Robbie.

"Yessir?" Holo signs shimmered behind his crewcut head, and passersby blurred in the background.

"Out on the town?"

"No sir. I was at rugby practice. What's up?"

Robbie Wolfe was my new admin officer. I had hired him in a hurry after our former admin, Kimmie Ng, was murdered. I'd wanted a mainstream human, not another Shifter, but Robbie had turned out to be a good hire. As his name suggested, he was a wolf, and he knew a lot of other young wolves from Smith's End.

"Come over to my place," I said. "Whenever you can get here."

I took my tools and my drink outside. The roar of traffic made the night sound huge and hollow, like a seashell. At the Shoreside end of our street, the lights of the Strip pulsated, silhouetting the roofs against an inconstant, feverish glow.

I stripped off the paint where the graffiti had been. The infrared stripper was silent, and took off the top layer so cleanly that I didn't even need to scrape it by hand. I then sanded the area. It turned out that our building, which was now yellow, used to be blue, and before that, brick-red. It was over a hundred years old. First came the colonial spreads; then came the townhouses, like this one, all now split up into two, three, or even four apartments: then came the rowhouses further south, as the population of Shiftertown grew, and grew, and grew. It was not healthy. Shifters were never meant to live on top of each other like this. No wonder our "community" had disintegrated into rival cliques and gangs. I had been kidding myself if I thought Parsec's arrest would put the brakes on that. It was systemic.

A built, bulletheaded youth in a skin-tight t-shirt loped up the street and climbed my steps. "'Lo, sir. What are you doing?"

"Hi, Robbie. It may look as if I'm drinking, but I'm actually sanding."

He laughed. "How did Lucy take to that camp place?"

"Like a duck to water. You got the automatic payments set up?"

"Yessir."

"Cancel the autopay for Mia. She's not attending, as it turns out. We'll lose the deposit; too bad. Beer's in the cooler."

Robbie went inside, came back out with a beer, and finally asked why I was sanding my front porch, in the dark.

"You can't see it anymore," I said. "But one of those goddamn bears graffitied the house. You know him? Nunak."

Robbie shook his head.

I did not tell him what Nunak had written. The prejudice against snitches is especially strong in Smith's End. I put down my sander and took a drink from my mug. "It worries me, to be honest. They thought it was safe to walk up to my house, in broad daylight, and spray paint all over my porch. If they did that, what are they going to do next? Are they gonna break in? Jack my truck? What? They've got a grudge against me—against my whole crew—for putting Parsec in jail, and it's now abundantly fucking clear that they aren't going to let it lie."

Robbie blew out breath with a *brrrr* sound. "I could find out where this Nunak guy lives."

"I don't want to take the offensive. No need to stir them up even more. But what I want you to do is move in here while we're away." I let that sink in for a moment. "Rex is tough, sure. But he's gonna be looking after two kids. He's in a more vulnerable position than I like. And Nanny B does not have claws or teeth."

The mild joke failed to lift the stricken expression on Robbie's face. "I thought I was coming with you!"

I sighed. I'd known it was going to be tough to break it to him, but the decision, which had been percolating in my mind, was now set. "Not this time. We've only got a single cargo, and the buyer is a Hurtworlds Authority trustee, so the paperwork is no big deal. Dolph and I can do it."

"Let me guess," he said, trying to make light of it. "You don't think I can handle myself on the Hurtworlds."

In all honesty, that was part of it. He may be a seasoned street fighter, but he was untested off-planet. I didn't want to have to tell his mother that I lost her eldest on Mittel Trevoyvox or Yesanyase Skont.

But the real reason was precisely the admin paperwork. We would be faking it. Robbie still thought Uni-Ex Shipping was on the up and up. I didn't want him to find out that he worked for a dirty outfit. Not yet, anyway.

"I know you can handle yourself," I said. "That's why I want you to stay here. Personally, I'd rather face every criminal in the Hurtworlds than the Bad-News Bears."

Once again, my lame attempt at humor failed to soften the blow. He paced around the porch and came back. "I thought I was supposed to be the admin officer, not security. Why did I even bother getting my certification? Don't need to be a certified accountant to sit on the stoop and growl at passing bears."

"Jesus," I said, "what planet are you living on, son? This has been a security gig from the get-go. You gotta be certified, to satisfy regulations, but I didn't hire you for your brains. I hired you because you can fight. Here, or out in the Cluster, it's the same thing."

"You told me to stay off the street," he muttered.

"That's right. I do not approve of the so-called ripper scene. You don't fight for micropayments anymore. Now you fight for me."

I picked up my sander and went back to work. After a minute, Robbie said, "Guess I should go home and get my stuff, then."

I smiled at him. "No need to start tonight. I'm still here. Start tomorrow, after we launch."

"Got it, sir."

"Oh, and Robbie?" I called him back as he started down the steps. "You can bring some other people if you like. If any of your friends need a place to crash, that's fine, as long as they don't wreck my expensive furniture or my fancy entertainment center."

He laughed at that, knowing my apartment was an empty cave. "See you tomorrow, sir."

After he left, I finished the sanding. Then I went inside and triple-locked the door.

I switched off all the lights. I sat in the living-room, on plastic sheeting, because I had no fucking furniture, and drank.

Until the doorbell rang.

9

THE sound of the doorbell made me jump like a gunshot. Clumsily, half-cut, I stood up and tiptoed out to the hall with my .22 in my hand. I poked the mirror on the wall. It was part of my new home security system, the first thing I had bought after MF's purge of the apartment.

The mirror turned into a screen displaying the feed from my front porch camera. There stood Jose-Maria d'Alencon of the PdL PD.

Panic knotted my guts. Wouldn't you know it. Wouldn't you fucking know it. We thought we'd been so clever. So discreet. But the police know everything, They see everything. Why, why, *why* had I thought we could get away with murder on Ponce de Leon?

At the same time, rationality pointed out that d'Alencon was alone. He was not even in uniform. If he was here to arrest me, this was an interesting departure from procedure.

He rang the doorbell again.

I couldn't pretend I wasn't home. That would only make me look guilty.

"Just a minute," I said to the screen. I hurried into my bedroom and hid the .22 in the closet. It is not illegal to possess firearms on Ponce de Leon, only to buy and sell them. All the same, it would look bad to answer the door with a naked weapon in my hand. I glanced automatically around the room for any incriminating evidence

—evidence of *what?* The only thing I really needed to hide was inside my head, gnawing away at my brain.

I opened the door before d'Alencon could ring again. "Hi, Bones. How's it going?"

It had been raining. In summer, we get a shower every night at 9 PM. You can set your clock by it. The gravelnuts and the roof of the porch were still dripping, and raindrops dotted the shoulders of d'Alencon's t-shirt. "Just thought I would drop by," he said. "Is it a bad time?"

"Not at all. Come in. I got a bottle of Cristo Rey open, and I shouldn't finish it by myself."

"That surely does sound good."

D'Alencon was pudgy, perma-stubbled, with curly salt-and-pepper hair, a few years older than me. It was downright weird to see him out of uniform, but I was glad of it. The last thing I needed was for the neighbors to see a police officer visiting my house.

I led him into the living-room and flipped the lights on. "Sorry, nowhere to sit except the floor."

"You been painting in here?"

"Yeah, fixing the place up. Just a second, I'll get another cup."

I washed the one Lucy had drunk juice out of this morning. While I was doing that, I finetuned my reflection in the dark window over the sink, the way I sometimes did before meeting with customers. Shoulders down, relaxed: check. Friendly smile: check. It didn't reach my eyes, but he wouldn't be able to tell. He didn't know me that well.

I poured for him. "Cheers."

"Cheers. Lucy?"

"She's at summer camp. Dropped her off today."

"Nice. So she's doing OK?"

"Yup. She's been through a traumatic experience, of course. But she's bouncing back. How are your boys?" I remembered that he had three sons.

"Good, good. You should bring Lucy out to my place one of these weekends, when she gets back from camp. We'll fire up the grill in the back yard."

"Sounds great." It would snow in Ponce de Leon before I took him up on that offer.

"We got a jungle gym. The kids can play, and you can help me celebrate my promotion."

"You got promoted?" I almost choked on my drink. "Congratulations."

"Yeah, they call it a promotion. I call it a cut in my overtime pay," d'Alencon joked.

"So what do I call you now?"

"You can call me Bones, same as ever. At the department, it's Detective Inspector. My boys are disappointed that I don't wear the uniform anymore."

"And there I thought you were off-duty."

"Oh, I am off-duty. Relax, Tiger, officially I ain't even here."

I wondered what that meant. "So how's the trial of the century coming?" I figured I had better bring it up before he did.

"Which one? Parsec or Ijiuto?"

"Either. Both."

D'Alencon grinned. "Parsec's in the bag. We flipped a couple of his subordinates. Remember that guy Silverback? He's going on the stand." He lowered his voice confidingly. "I shouldn't be talking out of school, but the chief prosecutor is confident of getting the maximum sentence on the smuggling charges, so she won't be introducing the connection with the Travellers, as the sentences would run concurrently, anyway. I expect you'll be glad to hear that."

"That is a load off my mind. When's the trial?"

"Figure the end of September. Meanwhile, friend Parsec is enjoying the governor's hospitality at Buonaville."

Buonaville Penitentiary was Ponce de Leon's largest prison, notorious for inmate violence. "Not Fairview?" That's where they usually stashed the white-collar criminals. It had a golf course.

"Strangely enough, there wasn't room."

I laughed, but I guessed the real reason was that Parsec had offended the chief prosecutor by pleading innocent while being a Shifter. Buonaville. *Shit.* I almost felt sorry for Parsec. On the other hand, if he got shanked in the shower, I'd have one less thing to worry about. "Well, thanks for keeping me in the loop, Bones."

Maybe he really had just come over for a friendly visit, to stay in touch, like he'd said he would.

Yet the way we were sitting, side by side with our backs to the wall, made me think of the way we had sat side by side in the basement at police headquarters while I confessed all my crimes to him. I had *cried.*

I wanted to move, to see his face better, but that would look weird. Instead I lit a cigarette and drew the cereal bowl I was using as an ashtray closer.

D'Alencon did not comment on my smoking habit. For all he knew, I had never kicked it after Tech Duinn. He sat crosslegged with his hands loosely laced around his cup. I noticed he hadn't drunk more than a couple sips. "On the other hand, as regards Ijiuto …"

"Yeah," I said, too quickly. "Has he talked?" Ijiuto had at least some of the answers I was looking for. I would give my left nut for five minutes alone with him. But he was in jail, awaiting trial on charges of purchasing bio-weapons.

D'Alencon grimaced. "He's lawyered up."

"How? He was broke!"

"He ain't broke anymore. Guess his relations in the Darkworlds got coin."

I shook my head, remembering Dolph's question—*where's the money coming from?* It really was a mystery. "Where would Darkworlders get GCs? From selling goat skins and wood carvings?"

Humanity had colonized the Darkworlds, a star system 150 light years outside the Cluster, around the same time as San Damiano. This was in the first FTL era, when skip drives were much slower than they are now. The long expansion from Earth towards the Messier 4 Cluster had taken a thousand years, and left a trail of human tragedies along the way. Colonies could not count on getting outside help if shit went sideways. And inevitably, it did.

About fifty years ago, after our high-speed, take-no-prisoners colonization of the Cluster, Fleet ships with modern skip drives re-contacted the Darkworlds. They found a few million humans living in log cabins, keeping goats, growing potatoes, and burning *coal* for power and heat. The Darkworlders didn't have a single spaceship left. I assumed things had improved since then, but still it was hard to imagine what the Darkworlders could contribute to the interstellar economy.

"There's always mining," d'Alencon said.

"Over that kind of distance? It wouldn't be profitable to ship even gold or platinum-group metals."

"*Data* mining?"

"Possible, I guess."

"Currency mining."

"Yeah, but that assumes a high-tech manufacturing base, or else the wherewithal to buy thousands, make that millions, of servers, and all the rest of the kit. *And* a FTL drone, and its support infrastructure. Bet you they haven't even got an EkBank node out there."

"No," d'Alencon admitted, "they haven't."

"Ijiuto told me he paid the Travellers in kind," I pondered. "I still can't work out what he could've been referring to."

"People," d'Alencon suggested. "Also known as parts on the hoof. There's still a trade in natural organs; they're higher quality than the vat-grown kind."

"That's fucking revolting." My smile faded as I contemplated the notion of Sophia being involved in such a vile trade. No, I still wasn't over being shocked by her depravity.

For a few minutes we had been talking like colleagues. But now d'Alencon reverted to his police officer's manner.

"Anyway, leaving aside how he came by the cash, he's retained the best lawyers on the planet for his defense, and he ain't saying shit. At this point it's questionable whether we can even bring him to trial."

"You're kidding!"

"I wish I was. The prosecutor's office is focused on Parsec, and there just isn't the same hunger to convict a Darkworlder of, what? Buying some toy fairies?"

Now I understood why d'Alencon was here. "You came to tell me he's gonna walk."

"That's what it's looking like."

"Oh, I don't … That's bullshit."

D'Alencon sighed. "Unfortunately, there's political aspects to it. The Gessyrias are not signatories to all of our accords. They aren't in the London Charter." This was the lynchpin of our interstellar law, Earth's last major contribution to human unity. "So they're making noises about extradition, diplomatic immunity, this and that."

"What a goddamn travesty."

"Look on the bright side: we nailed Parsec, anyway." D'Alencon set down his cup on the floor and stood up. "I gotta roll, Tiger. Just wanted to keep you in the loop."

"If he goes free …" I hesitated. "Can you let me know?"

I didn't think that Ijiuto was a danger to me and mine. Rather, if he escaped from legal protection, I was going to be a danger to *him.*

I walked d'Alencon out to the front porch. The street was still wet. I could smell gravelnuts crushed by passing cars' tyres. Eau de dog poop. A peacock moth fluttered down from the porch light and alighted briefly on d'Alencon's shoulder.

"So where are you off to next?" he said.

I hesitated. But he could get the information from the Space Traffic Authority. It would do me no good to lie. "Mittel Trevoyvox."

"The Hurtworlds?"

"Gotta make a living," I said. "Some folks save the planet and get promoted. Some don't even get a few K to repaint their apartment." I smiled, trying to look less bitter than I felt.

"I hear you. I'm doing what I can for you, Mike."

I believed him. He was doing what he could for me—this visit proved it—and what was I doing in return? Breaking my promise that I would go straight, after less than two weeks. I rocked on the balls of my feet, eager for him to leave.

"This trip to the Hurtworlds," he said. "Would that have anything to do with Pippa Khratz?"

My heart sank. "Who?"

"You can't help her, Mike. We failed her, and that's a tragedy, but it is what it is. She got infected, she got deported, and there's no legal power in the Cluster that can bring her back, because it's our own laws that deported her in the first place."

No *legal* power. D'Alencon's hands were tied … but mine weren't. "I'm not going to Yesanyase Skont." He'd never know. "Just Mittel Trevoyvox."

"Well, I can't tell you your business. But I strongly recommend that you should stay away from the Hurtworlds, period."

"Oh, I always say getting shot at is the spice of life," I joked.

He didn't smile. "This thing ain't finished. You were cleared, but don't let that give you a false sense of confidence. It's still playing out, and like I said, there's politics in the mix."

"Details?" I said uneasily.

"Above my paygrade. But this much I can say, you do not want to get mixed up with these folks. So … be careful. And keep your eyes open out there."

"Anything in particular I should be looking out for?"

"Oh, you know. Travellers."

"Have there been any recent reports of Traveller activity in the Hurtworlds?" This was information I could really do with.

"No," d'Alencon said. "It's odd. Up till a few years back, they were hitting the Hurtworlds on the regular. Now? Nothing. They've gone quiet … *too* quiet. So sniff around a bit. See what you can see."

"You got it," I said, heavy-hearted, knowing that this was the price of his friendship, and his warnings. It might even be the real point of his visit. I was to inform him if I saw anything he should know about.

Snitch.

His car glided to a stop in front of my building. It was a crappy little sedan. "Don't they give y'all flying cars in the detective division?"

"I got one of those. This is my own ride. I don't use the department's car, they don't know where I am."

"Wait," I said, as he started down the porch steps. "The department don't know you're here?"

"That's right. It's none of their business what I do on my own time." He gave me a pained smile.

"But can't they track your personal car as well as your official vehicle?"

"Oh, they do. There's software at HQ mapping the movements of every vehicle on Ponce de Leon. But how does it decide what's important? There ain't enough humans to look at everything, so we rely on algorithms. This old beater happens to be registered in my wife's name, and she works at Shoreside General, so the algo will just think she's working a night shift."

"Ah."

"*Now* I gotta go." He got in his car and drove off towards the glow of the Strip.

The peacock moth whirred off the porch, away from the light.

10

My ship was the most valuable thing I owned, by a factor of about a thousand. The *St. Clare* resembled a steel plesiosaur, with four auxiliary engine pods that looked like flippers, and a "head" whose serrated jaws concealed a military-grade railgun. Her unique form factor pointed to her non-human origins. She had started life as the imperial flagship of the Kroolth, a Fringeworlds race of furry midgets, and had become mine during an adventure that I preferred not to discuss. She retained all her original armaments, plus a set of maser point defense turrets we'd installed ourselves. I believed she could safely do up to 2,000 times the speed of light if I stripped her to the bulkheads, although I'd never actually tried it.

We launched on schedule with Dr. Tierney's gene-modding materials in the hold, well-hidden amongst the legitimate medical equipment. Morale was high at first, but deteriorated after a couple of days. This was our first run without Kimmie, my former admin. She was sorely missed. Kimmie had been a normie, and when she was around, we'd felt a certain hesitation about drifting around the ship naked, or spending days on end in animal form. Martin and Dolph used to grumble about it, but I believed the pressure to act normal had been good for us. Now there was no one to offend, we felt free to let it all hang out, to the detriment of crew discipline.

I wasn't setting a great example myself, either. When I wasn't on bridge duty, I spent most of my time in my berth, working on the new animal form I had in mind.

I emerged from a practice session on Day 8 to find Mechanical Failure holding forth in the lounge. “I undertook a deep scan of my memory elements,” he announced in his grating, mechanical voice. “It is a painful process, which I do not undertake lightly. But it paid off! I found an exact match for the crown jewels of the Darkworlds.”

I gazed at the image he was displaying on the big screen on the aft wall of the lounge. It sure looked like Pippa’s pendant, only without the chain.

“What do you think it is?” MF said. “Three guesses! Irene first!” MF had a soft spot for Irene. Let’s be honest: he had a crush on her. It was a constant source of tension, especially now that she was the only woman on board.

“A weapon,” Irene said.

“Bzzt!”

Dolph floated spreadeagled in front of the biggest fan, cooling down after a run on the treadmill. When you’re in the field for two weeks at a stretch, you have to hit the machines. “It’s the key to a long-lost vault of Urush dick jokes.”

“Bzzt!”

“Urush porn, then.” In his own way, Dolph was trying to manage expectations. I appreciated the effort, but his humor did not reach Irene or Martin, who were both intently focused on the screen. Damn MF. Why’d he have to hype this thing even more?

Martin, coiled around the base of the resistance machine, said, “I’ll eat my tail if that isn’t a thumb drive.”

“Martin wins,” MF said softly. “It is a TrZam 008 memory device, and is probably about 1,025 years old.”

“Then it depends what’s on it,” Dolph said. “With our luck, it would turn out to be dick jokes.”

MF’s bendy neck undulated. His eyes glowed. “The TrZam 008 was a limited production run, issued exclusively to thought-workers in the discipline of … well, you do not have a word for it. *Transcendence studies* might be close. I was not involved with that field of research, but I believe it incorporated elements of fundamental physics, theology, biotechnology, AI, chemistry, and astrophysics."

"Everything and the kitchen sink," I said. "Come on, Dolph. We need to do that course correction in half an hour."

As Dolph put on his clothes, Martin and Irene swapped wild speculations about the data on the thumb drive. It might be artificial gravity technology, which would overcome the stubborn laws of physics that forced us to float around the inside of our spaceship. Nano-replication technology that would make the post-scarcity society a reality. Or a revolutionary "new" type of FTL drive! The Urush had vanished, after all. Not anywhere near enough of their hippo-sized, four-legged, long-necked remains had been found to account for the population of their interstellar civilization. They must have gone *somewhere* … perhaps to a distant region of the galaxy, which this new technology would bring within reach for the first time! To all these suggestions, MF squeaked, "No! Better than that!" The bot was deliberately keeping us in suspense. He wasn't being malicious. He thought we were all having fun.

"What everyone's forgetting," I said, as Dolph and I drifted up the trunk corridor, "is that Pippa's not the only person who had one of those devices. Rafael Ijiuto had one, too."

"Maybe no one's guessed what it really is. Maybe even he doesn't know," Dolph said.

"How likely is that?"

The *St. Clare's* background decibels were right up there, as usual. It was like living and working next to a busy highway—the white noise of the fans; the gurgling of water and liquid coolant lines; the tick-tick-ticking of the skip field generator, which was audible all over the ship, like a clock rapidly ticking my life away.

All the same, I caught the farting noise of compressed air spurting from nozzles, and spun to see MF behind us.

"Go scrub the toilet, bot," I said. I didn't know how angry I was until I heard it in my voice. "You're not helping."

"You need me to check the course correction burn calculations," he pointed out, googly-eyed.

"We can do it," I said. But the fact was I *would* feel better if MF checked my calculations. Our speed had peaked out yesterday at 1,650 times the speed of light. I was a seasoned captain and yet my hair stood up on the back of my neck when I thought about all those zeros. Mittel Trevoyvox was 57 light years from Ponce de Leon. Most people reckoned the journey at a month each way; I was aiming to do it in half the time, by using a scary-high multiplier, and flying in *almost* a straight line, instead of making a nice wide circle around the Core.

You can't go *through* the Core. Too dangerous. There are toxic old stars in there, pumping out gamma rays and X-rays. There's the M4 black hole, smack in the middle of everything. There are Travellers.

But you can brush past the Core, and that's what I was doing. It meant several ticklish little course corrections, to account for the gravity of the Core, the Cluster's spin, the *galaxy's* spin, and the inertia imparted by interstellar dust building up in our skip field. These maneuvers might be small, but every fraction of a second and millinewton of thrust counted. Get it wrong, and we'd end up off course by several light years … that's if we didn't bump into a star.

Dolph and I floated in our straps, speaking in acronyms, in the bright cave of the bridge. It was a low-ceilinged metal slot in the ship's belly, lined from floor to ceiling with consoles and mechanical readouts that backstopped the augmented reality (AR) data in our headsets. MF held onto the back of my couch.

"We'll burn for fifteen seconds, on my mark," I said. My palms were wet, my mouth dry. At moments like this you remember how dangerous this business is.

"Sixteen," MF said. "Actually, fifteen point sixty-eight. We shall have to compensate on our next burn." He made a clucking noise. "When we are rich, I will retool the drive with state-of-the-art exhaust controls for improved precision. It is also high time we replaced the main engine nozzle and upgraded the plasma chamber."

So that's what's in it for you, I thought. Endless upgrades, making the *St. Clare* a safer and safer haven for you. At what point, I wondered, will you decide we're dispensable?

The timer in my HUD area blinked. "Starting burn in five. Four … three … two … *mark.*" I opened the throttle.

The port auxiliary engines roared. The ship shook like a beaten drum. Precisely sixteen seconds later, the thunder died away into the usual whoosh of fans. We were back on course … presumably. We wouldn't know for sure until we got there—or *didn't* get there.

I stretched my tense muscles, took off my headset, and ran my hands through the sweat-damp spikes of my hair. I needed a drink.

Alcohol tastes different in freefall. Fine bourbon is wasted on stuffed-up sinuses and dulled tastebuds, so I normally stick to vodka on board. There's a reason it has been the preferred tipple of astronauts going all the way back to the first rickety little space stations in orbit around Earth.

I drifted over to the dispenser on the aft wall of the bridge, tuning out MF as he quacked at Dolph about the Lorentz factor and spontaneous quantum errors. I think he was warning him not to try going any faster. It was bullshit—MF was just a coward. Theoretically, you can go *infinitely* fast. Just skip more Planck lengths.

Of course, theory isn't reality. Skip technology isn't infinitely powerful, and more importantly, ships are required to have limiting hardware built into their skip generators, to prevent them going so fast that pilots go FTL-blind and crash into stars. The speed limit for civilian ships is 1,500 c. Fleet ships can go up to 1,800 c. But the *St. Clare* had been built by MF himself. And he had *not* added limiting hardware to the skip drive.

I dispensed vodka into my zero-gravity mug, keeping one eye on the mechanical indicators, dials, and screens. More than any ship I'd had before, the *St. Clare* felt like a piece of me. It would kill me to sell her.

But that's what I was going to do.

That was my secret backup plan.

I was 99% sure that we would either not find this TrZam 008, or it would turn out to be junk. Therefore, after this journey, I planned to put the *St. Clare* on the auction block. I'd get 15,000 KGCs for her, maybe more. That's not fuck-you money, but it's a lot. I would gift a nice fat severance package to each of the crew. There'd be enough left to pay Lucy's tuition at St. Anne's through graduation, and leave a nest egg to launch her into adulthood, when I wouldn't be around anymore.

The vodka burned down my throat. I drifted back into the lounge. Snake and panther were still gloating over the blown-up Urush thumb drive on the screen.

Wouldn't it be nice if the TrZam 008 could be real? I wouldn't have to sell the *St. Clare*. I could … I could pay Dr. Tierney to put all his bright young scientists, his supercomputers, and his own brilliant intellect on the trail of a cure for IVK …

I pushed off from the ceiling, angry at myself. There was *no* goddamn cure. This disease had been deliberately, maliciously weaponized to be incurable. Time to go fix something to take my mind off it.

At the door of the lounge, I met MF and Dolph coming back from the bridge. "Hey, bot," I said, giving his housing a shove with my free hand, which spun us apart. "Aren't you old enough to know how dangerous fairytales can be?"

"Fairytales? Dangerous? Says the man who turns into a wolf."

Everyone laughed. MF somersaulted in the air, creaking with delight at the success of his line.

"Stop playing dumb, MF," I said. "Even if we find Pippa, and even if she still has the gizmo, and those are big ifs … the Ponce de Leon prosecutor's office has one, too. So we wouldn't have an exclusive claim to any IP that's on there. And that means we would have nothing." I clicked my fingers as the faces of the others fell. "It's all in the legalities."

MF turned himself right way up to me. "Oh, but Captain," he said. "Having a data storage device is one thing; reading it is something else. And there is only one machine left in the Cluster capable of reading a TrZam 008." He tapped his own housing with a gripper. "Right here."

There was a moment's silence.

"See?" Martin said to me. "There's a reason we keep him around apart from his extensive porn collection."

"If you're blowing hot air up our butts, suitcase, you're gonna take a one-way trip out of the airlock," I threatened halfheartedly.

"Mike, what if someone else finds it first?" Irene said suddenly. "Do we have to go to Mittel Trevoyvox? Let's go straight to Yesanyase Skont." Her claws worked in the padded wall of the lounge, tearing new rips. Tension thrummed off her. "That damn Ek already cost us two weeks. Mittel T would burn another week. Let's change course. Deliver the cargo on the way back …"

"Or, stick to the schedule that we promised the customer. We gotta dance with the one that brung us." I had built my business on a promise of reliability. I wasn't letting my standards slide now. "Forget about the gizmo for the time being. I want everyone focused on Mittel Trevoyvox. And if you need any extra motivation, ask me or Dolph about how we got shot at, nearly eaten, and thrown in a river by Eks last time we were there."

11

OUR last trip to Mittel T had been hairy. But that was seventeen years ago, and I didn't know what to expect when we dropped out of the skip field in the Mittel Trevoyvox star system.

It may seem odd that in an age of FTL comms, I was so short on information about our destination. Couldn't I just have looked it up before we left Ponce de Leon?

Not on my data plan. Information is money. To get solid, up-to-date information on Mittel T, I would have had to pay … as much as it costs to keep a network of FTL drones flying. And if you guessed that would run into eight figures, you'd be right. Data may be a cheap utility on any given planet—or not, depending on that planet's infrastructure—but it's anything but cheap to send data from one star system to another. The EkBank does it. That's how the Cluster's economy keeps ticking over: the EkBank's FTL drones deliver up-to-date versions of the blockchain ledger to major planets on a daily basis, to lesser planets at intervals of anything from days to weeks. Similarly, planetary governments fly FTL drones to exchange news and views. But that's pretty much it. The biggest companies in the shipping industry buy subscriptions to the news from the governments of their home planets, for prices that run into the millions annually. Nothing, however, would induce them to share their planetary dossiers with minnows like me.

So all we had to go on was memory, rumors, anecdotes, and the scanty briefing from Jim Tierney's customer, who of course had an interest in representing Mittel Trevoyvox as the safest planet in the Cluster, not only because they didn't want to scare us off, but also because they were a trustee of the Hurtworlds Authority, the joint human-Ek agency that administers these benighted planets. They wouldn't admit it even if the locals were fighting in the streets and stray mortar shells were landing in the spaceport.

That's what it had been like last time. We'd barely escaped with our lives.

But even on the Hurtworlds, things *can* change. So I hoped for the best, while expecting the worst, as we hurtled towards the cloudy brown-and-gray globe.

We'd hit the bull's-eye from 58 light years away. The *St. Clare* was one heck of a ship.

Mittel Trevoyvox's undistinguished little G-type star illuminated its dayside. But the blackness "below" us was dominated by the Core, a fuzzy ellipse the width of my palm, half as bright as the star which was a thousand times closer. We were practically within spitting distance of that deadly stellar graveyard, as the FTL ship flies.

Jolt. Dolph was increasing our exhaust field multipler, decreasing our velocity by increments, from thousands of kps, down to hundreds, and then tens. *Jolt.* The three of us on the bridge lay in our couches: me in the center, Dolph on my right, Irene on my left. All of us wore our AR headsets, which made us look like cyborgs with wraparound eyes. *Jolt.* Each deceleration drove the breath out of our chests, while the truss groaned and creaked. I paid the noises no mind; the *St. Clare* was just doing what she was designed to.

The comms chimed. "Unknown ship, come in. Identify yourself." Scanning the radar display that floated in my field of vision, I saw two Fleet patrol ships, and the distinctive geodesic sphere of an Ek space station, in orbits ranging between 1,000 to 10,000 klicks out.

"Independent freighter *St. Clare,*" I said. "Just delivering a package." As a courtesy, I sent them the paperwork Dolph and I had faked up. I knew they wouldn't even look at it. The Fleet wasn't here to monitor imports. They weren't even here to defend the planet. They were here to prevent its unfortunate residents from escaping.

The Hurtworlds are *prison* planets. Some of them are bad, and some are worse. Mittel Trevoyvox was on the less bad end of the spectrum. But all of them have one thing in common, and that is that the poor souls condemned to live here may never, ever leave.

"So you were here before, huh?" the Fleet pilot said. "When?"

"Way back in '02," I said.

"Whoa. I wasn't even born."

"I hope you're exaggerating."

"A lil' bit," the pilot said with an adolescent snuffle of mirth.

Dolph said dryly, "Thanks for reminding us that the defense of humanity is in the hands of teenagers."

"It always has been," I muttered. Dolph and I were only seventeen when we enlisted. But I couldn't believe we'd ever sounded this young. "So what's it like on the surface these days?"

"I never been down there," the pilot said. "But the HA ain't requested any precision orbital strikes in two years, so it can't be too bad." He went off the radio.

"That's a low bar," Dolph said.

"Still, he sounded bored," I said. "That's probably a good sign."

We decelerated into a low circular orbit. Mittel Trevoyvox looked unchanged, as far as the cloud cover permitted us to see. Dark gray oceans. A bunch of landmasses too large to be islands but too small to be continents, mottled with urban sprawl. A few satellites orbited the equator. Those would be Hurtworlds Authority sats, as the locals were not permitted to have spacegoing assets.

The island-city of New Abilene-Qitalhaut, location of the planet's only spaceport, was on the nightside at present. Sparse twinkles of light indicated a functioning power grid. That was a positive data point.

"Well?" I said. "Land in the dark, or wait?"

"How long is the night?" Irene said.

"Rotational period of eighteen hours, so we would be looking at a four-hour delay."

"Screw it. Let's just get this over with."

Everyone agreed. I called the Hurtworlds Authority's space traffic control office. They told me we were authorized to land at any time. "OK, here we go."

Rattling and roaring, we deorbited through the darkness. The whole ship juddered as we passed through the densest part of the atmosphere. The altimeter spun lower and lower, and we broke through the clouds. The city lights of New Abilene-Qitalhaut blazed out again. In another minute we could see the spaceport itself, a twilit quadrilateral plonked in the middle of the city lights. With one eye glued to the instruments, I made out numerous spaceships on the ground, most of them atmosphere-capable cargo ships painted the trademark white of the Hurtworlds Authority. There was hardly any room for us to land. Lower, lower— "Main engine cutoff in ten," Dolph said. "Where's our fucking pad, Mike? Eight—"

The computer gave me several options. With no time to think about it, I picked one. The auxiliaries sparked, adjusting our trajectory. "Positioning looks good," I said hoarsely.

"Two … one." Dolph cut the main engine and engaged the auxiliaries at full thrust.

The ship's nose dropped with a gut-hollowing swoop. Suddenly, instead of lying on our backs, we were sitting upright. All four auxiliaries flaming, the *St. Clare* descended the last few meters of her long journey and settled onto the asphalt with a bump.

"Jesus Christ," Dolph said, ripping off his headset. "They nearly had themselves an incident there."

On the external cameras, billowing steam rolled away to reveal HA ships parked around us. The closest one was no more than one ship-length away. Dolph got on the radio with the traffic control people and swore at them for their incompetence.

I ran through the engine shut-down procedures and then stood up, aware of every muscle working against unaccustomed gravity. "Leave it," I said to Dolph. "If we make enemies of these guys, that's like making an enemy of God around here."

Too late.

"Hello," Irene said. She still had her AR headset on. She gestured at the external feed screen, and reached up to pull the mechanical lever that unlocked the turret Gausses. "I thought the war was supposed to be *over?*"

On the external feed, bulky, hooded figures jogged towards the *St. Clare,* carrying guns.

12

I climbed out of the port airlock and scrambled onto the top deck, catching my breath in the bitingly cold air. I had brought my kevlar; in fact I was wearing it. I should have brought my polar gear. The customer had forgotten to mention that we would be landing in the middle of winter.

I crawled on my stomach to the edge of the top deck and looked down—down, down: the top deck was as high up as the roof of a three-storey building—at the individuals surrounding my ship. The warning lights on the *St. Clare's* superstructure, and the orange-tinted snow clouds overhead, backlit by the Core, shed an unearthly glow on the scene, sufficient for me to see that they were all human. Padded trousers and hooded parkas bulked out their silhouettes.

The parkas bore the Hurtworlds Authority logo.

I stood up. Several laser targeting dots glowed on the middle of my chest.

"Fellas," I said. "There some problem with our paperwork?"

The spaceport was spookily silent, especially after the constant noise on shipboard. No hollow roar of traffic. No thunder of ship engines—a spaceport this size, you'd only get a few launches a week. Which made me wonder what all these ships were doing here. The only sound was the murmur of the river that flowed through the spaceport, a copper glint off to my left, reflecting the clouds.

"Customs inspection," said one of the humans in a normal speaking voice, which carried through the still, cold air. "Open your cargo hold."

Here we go, I thought. It's a set-up. The customer didn't encrypt their v-mails well enough. The HA found out about the gene-modding materials. We're screwed. Out loud, I said, "I'm not minded to do anything at gunpoint. Send the goons away and we'll talk."

"These are officers of the Hurtworlds Authority." The spokesman was stocky, bearded, calm. "I'm in charge of customs here, and we do have the right to inspect your cargo."

"*You're* in charge here? What about the Eks?" Officially, administration of the Hurtworlds is split between humanity and the Eks.

"They're over there," the man said, pointing at the far side of the river, where a couple of Ek ships stood like overturned ice cream cones pointing at the snowclouds. "We're over here. Open your cargo hold."

"I say again, act like civilized human beings and we'll discuss it." I waited a beat. They didn't move. "Just so you're aware, my weapons officer is currently targeting you." Irene had angled the barrels of the Gausses down, to shoot over the edge of our top deck. The masers were not much use in an atmosphere, but at this range, they could do some damage if the Gausses ran out of ammo. And for a grand finale, we could take out every ship in our line of fire with the railgun.

Yet *they* had the advantage, not us, for a very simple reason: water.

After our long journey from Ponce de Leon, we did not have enough reaction mass to take off again.

This is how shipjackings happen. On some Fringeworlds, you're gambling with your ship every time you land dry—but on Mittel Trevoyvox? I knew the Hurtworlds Authority was mildly corrupt. Show me the big bureaucracy that isn't. I was not aware that they stole ships. All the same, the guns pointing at me sent the message that if I persisted in defying them, I might end up losing my ship as well as my cargo.

Not to mention my life.

I whispered into the radio embedded in the collar of my flak vest. "Gonna try to stall them. Dolph, call the customer, tell them we're having issues with the customs. Martin, call the supply division, see if we can get a water tanker out here." The spaceport was ancient, beyond basic; it lacked on-pad water and power, as in fact it lacked proper landing pads. "Irene, stay on the guns. I'm gonna let this guy come up."

In the end three of them came up, the bearded spokesman and two goons, a man and a woman. Outnumbered, I wished I had brought Robbie, after all. Our former admin, Kimmie, would have shone at a moment like this, presenting a facade of smiling compliance and snowing the bastards with documentation. But Robbie wasn't Kimmie, and the threat of violence radiating from the two goons was precisely why I *hadn't* brought him.

"For God's sake," I complained to the spokesman, as I opened the hold, "you're a human."

"It hasn't stopped me from doing my job yet." The hold door rattled up. The faint gunpowdery smell of space wafted out. The goons pushed past me and began to rip Jim Tierney's plastikretes open, making a mess of the packaging. They shone flashlights on the medical devices in their transparent foam blocks. I started to cheer up. The crispers, rewriters, and the rest of it were dispersed among the plastikretes, in vacuum containers made to look like spare components. This kind of cursory inspection was not going to uncover them.

"It's a bit quieter around here than it used to be," I said, motioning at the skyline outside the open door of the hold. The snapped-off wands of hubble spires, and stumps of skyscrapers, stood as bleak monuments to the war that had devastated the city, but I could see several new housing blocks where the e-waste dump used to be. The lights in their lower storeys twinkled blurrily—I was seeing them through the force field perimeter that surrounded the spaceport. "They've got the power back on out there?"

"Yeah. It's an unlikely peace, but it's holding. You were here before?"

"'02."

"I've been here since '14. Think I've seen the sun twice." The weather on Mittel Trevoyvox was notoriously awful. On top of that, the planet had lost most of its ozone layer over the millennia to radiation from the Core. "It would be a dream posting … if I were a misanthropic archaeologist."

I laughed. "The bars on the Ek side of the river used to be all right."

"All right, like repeatedly hitting yourself on the head. Beats sobriety."

I stuck out my hand. "Mike Starrunner." It never hurts to establish a personal connection.

He shook my hand. "Jonathan Burden."

Chunks of foam, like soft ice, fell to the floor. The female goon held a mislabeled vacuum container up to the light. *Shit.* They had known exactly what they were looking for. And now they'd found it.

I mentally prepared excuses, denials, and as a last resort, offers of bribes …

… and then the goonette returned the container to the crate it had come from, and sealed it up again.

"Looks like you are good to go, Mr. Starrunner," Burden said, smiling for the first time. "I apologize for the inconvenience. We just have to check."

The goons were now resealing the other plastikretes they'd opened.

I couldn't believe it. I could have sworn that woman knew she had found contraband.

But now the plastikretes were all sealed up again, even if some of them looked like a Kimberstine haulasaur had been chewing on them, and the goons were nodding to me and telling me to stay warm. They clambered back down the port-side ladder. Burden and I descended after them.

"You'll be looking for ground transport?" Burden said.

"Yeah. One twenty-tonner would do it."

"I'll hook you up." Burden pushed back his hood and made a call on a handheld radio.

Normally, we would expect our customers to pick their stuff up at the ship. But Jim Tierney's customer had warned us that that was no longer allowed on Mittel Trevoyvox. We would either have to meet them outside the spaceport, or deliver the cargo to their doorstep. I was fine with that. They'd want to check the contents of the crates, and I didn't want them doing that where Burden could see.

"So," I said, "no one's tried to blow the spaceport up recently?" I was looking at the asphalt; they'd filled in the shell craters.

"Not since I've been here. Modesty forbids me to take *all* the credit."

Dolph came down the port ladder, wearing his parka, holobook slung over his shoulder on a strap. "Can't get through to them," he said, slinging a questioning look at Burden.

"Sorry about that," Burden said. "We've got radio blocking protocols in place. No wireless transmissions are allowed outside the spaceport."

"What frequencies are you jamming?" I said.

"All of them. It helps to discourage the locals from whacking the crap out of each other."

The truck arrived: a diesel, pre-announced by its noisy engine. Folks still use internal combustion engines out in the boonies of the Cluster, where electrical power is scarce or unreliable. Stinking fumes wafted from the truck's exhaust. At least it was built for humans, not Eks, so I could reach the steering wheel. I kicked the tyres, decided it would do. Didn't want to push my luck.

"Breakfast when you get back?" Burden said. "There's a decent cafeteria at the passenger terminal. My treat."

"All the news from Ponce de Leon, for the price of a coffee and some crappy local pancakes?"

"Dammit, I'm transparent."

I caught myself thinking that I could like this guy, if I wasn't trying to sneak contraband under his nose. You find all kinds of oddballs in the depths of the Cluster—eccentrics, alien fetishists, quirky individuals quietly contemplating the meaning of life … but rarely do you meet anyone with a sense of humor. "Why not?" I said. "I'm a cheap date."

"Great. See you in the morning. Drive carefully."

Burden walked off into the snow with his heavily armed retinue. As soon as they were out of earshot Dolph said, "Well?"

"False alarm," I said. "Let's get this shit out of the hold."

Dolph went up top to shift the plastikretes. Martin, grumbling about the cold, came out to operate the cargo crane. I worked up a sweat, positioning the plastikretes in the back of the truck as they came down. It was the middle of the night on Mittel Trevoyvox, but my body thought it was mid-morning. Nervous energy sizzled through my veins, left over from that terrifying moment in the cargo hold. I never learned, did I? Well, this would be the last time. The very last.

Single snowflakes were beginning to fall from the clouds. We fastened a tarp over the cargo.

"I'll come," Irene said. *She* had brought her polar gear. She was wearing an arctic camo parka and matching snowpants, and carrying her second-best rifle. Dolph risked a compliment. She swatted him playfully. "I've come all this way. Might as well see the place." Her mood seemed to have lightened. Never underestimate the therapeutic effect of getting out of a spaceship after two weeks and stretching your legs.

Martin stayed with the ship to oversee our resupply. "Water's coming at first light," he said, shivering. "LOX, LN_2, food, and sewage disposal whenever the dozy bastards get around to it; probably sometime around noon."

"We'll be back by then." I mentally rehearsed the mechanics of driving internal combustion. Ignition. Handbrake. Gas, and we set off, snow chains clanking, for New Abilene-Qitalhaut.

13

"THAT'S where Artie's buried," I said, pointing, as we clanked towards the security gate in the spaceport perimeter. Snow-hatted gravestones, so old that they looked like bits of construction litter, dotted an unpaved area inside the perimeter. The modest graveyard slid out of sight as we drove out through a zigzag concrete chicane.

"Who was Artie?" Irene said.

"Art Koolhaus," Dolph answered, perched in the middle of the bench seat with his holobook on his knees. "Our first weapons officer."

"Way before your time," I said. "He died in the Techworlds, but we ended up burying him here."

"What'd he die of?"

Dolph and I looked at each other and laughed.

"He died of space," Dolph said.

"He died of the Cluster," I said.

"Technically, it was a drug overdose," Dolph said.

"Oh, *drugs,*" Irene said.

"Hey," Dolph said. "Just because you've never been tempted, doesn't mean that good people aren't."

"Artie was a hell of a lot of fun to be around," I said. "I don't think I've ever laughed as much since he died. But self-destruction was his middle name." The snow was coming down more heavily now. I looked for the switch to put the windshield wipers on high. "We'll have to stop by before we leave," I said to Dolph. "Take the Artster a bottle of scotch."

We drove through the newly constructed housing development. It looked like anything you might find on a Fringeworld, if slightly oversized. On the other side of that, we plunged into New Abilene-Qitalhaut proper. The snow and the darkness muffled the archaeological strata of buildings on either side of the deep, canyon-like streets, but we could see enough by the Corelight that Irene's eyes grew round. "Wow. How has all this never been knocked down?"

"They were trying pretty hard when we were here last," I said distractedly, switching my gaze between the road and the holobook on Dolph's knees, which was displaying the map from our briefing.

Mittel Trevoyvox, they say, has been continually inhabited since before humans left the Garden of Eden. Ancient corners of masonry, like crags protruding from cement hillsides, stuck out of the mithrik warrens, which themselves had doors and windows knocked in them and holo signs in kinda-sorta English outside. Mithriks are furry creatures the size of cats. They were sapient at one time, but have devolved into an animal state over the millennia of their imprisonment here. They'd been on the path to extinction when we were here last, and I figured they might be gone now, judging by how many of their warrens seemed to be inhabited by humans.

The tops of the warrens formed sidewalks above our heads, and also served as foundations for human-built houses and apartment buildings. As much as we humans are wedded to right angles, the Eks love circles. Their favorite type of ground-based dwelling is the *hubble,* a sphere made of reinforced concrete or polymer that they can roll around as if it were a wheel. We passed several side streets filled with hubbles, hitched up, or not, to diesel tractors. This used to be the human side of the river. The Eks had lived on the other side. But it looked like the distinction had blurred since the war mysteriously came to an end.

"… on Eas Rudah," Dolph said to Irene. He had been reminiscing about our years with Artie, and that led inevitably back to Tech Duinn. When he started telling war stories, it meant he was in a bona fide good mood. We were back on familiar territory, delivering a cargo on a potentially hazardous planet. Dolph was as happy as a pig in you-know-what.

I wasn't. We had just passed a lone masonry tower with a hubble perched on top, which I didn't remember at all. I glanced at the map again. It threw me that there was no little red dot representing our truck. The map was static. No satellites. No GPS. No AI in this goddamn rustbucket. "Hey, Dolph. You sure we're going the right way?"

Dolph's smile faded as he studied the map. "You know, actually, I'm not."

"Ask directions?" Irene said.

"Please," Dolph said. "Women can't read maps, and men can't ask directions."

Irene drew her handgun.

"Hey, I'm just saying …"

"I thought I saw something." She slid down into the footwell, searched for the window release, cursed impatiently when she discovered she had to crank it down by hand.

Dolph whipped his Koiler out of his thigh holster and slid across the seat to kneel where Irene had been, covering our side arc.

Our headlights fanned across on an open, snow-covered space dotted with shuttered stalls. It might be a market during the day. Beyond it towered an immense monument like a termite mound with a thousand windows, snow-mantled. "I definitely don't recognize this," I said.

"Get out!" Irene screamed. *"Out!"*

Soldiering had instilled in my bones the life-saving lesson that when someone yells at you like that, you don't sit around asking questions.

I popped my seatbelt and slid out of the cab, while Dolph and Irene went out the other side, into the snow.

Before my feet touched the ground, the windshield of the truck shattered, and stuffing exploded from the headrest of my seat, right where my head had been.

*

I saw the shooter's muzzle flash. He was in one of the market stalls, had fired through a gap in the shutters.

He fired again as I dropped flat in the slushy snow. The bullet glanced off the hood of the truck.

"That's not the one I saw," Irene gasped. She and Dolph had crawled under the truck from the other side. "There's another one up on the sidewalk."

Two or more shooters in the market were now peppering the truck with bullets. We would have driven straight into enfilade fire. I dragged myself under the truck, wet snow soaking through my pants. At least I now knew we were going the right way. They'd known where to set up their ambush.

The undercarriage of the truck caught on the back of my flak vest as I rolled to work my .22 out of its holster. I generally believed that if you need more firepower than a .22, you're fucked, anyway. I might change my mind about that, if we lived through this.

Dolph crawled on his elbows to the rear of the truck. Irene stayed prone under the front bumper. Twisting onto her side, she supported her rifle at an angle and fired.

The gunman in the market stall, or one of them, or the guy up on the sidewalk, fired back. The noise bounced around the narrow, canyon-like street.

I crawled back to Dolph. "They're after the cargo!" I bellowed in his ear.

"Ya think?" he yelled back. "That beardy shit. 'Drive carefully.' What an asshole."

"Yup." I gritted my teeth. "He must've checked the hold just to make sure the stuff was there. It was, but he couldn't take it off us at the spaceport. So he lets us get far enough away that no one can hear us scream." The truck's taillights were still on. The falling snow whirled in the red light, obscuring the empty street.

Irene's voice filtered through the ringing in my ears. "I dropped the guy off the sidewalk. He's still moving. Let's see if they come to pick him up."

I crawled back up to her position, leaving Dolph to cover our rear. The guy she had dropped lay about ten feet from the front of the truck. He wasn't moving anymore. Gunshot plus a two-storey fall will do that to you. I thought I recognized his face from the spaceport. He'd been one of Burden's armed retinue.

"Here's what we do," I muttered to Irene. "All Shift. Then run like hell."

"That's the plan?"

"At least it's simple."

Something small and black plummetted into the taillights on a curving trajectory. Before it hit the ground, it changed direction and zoomed straight towards us. Irene and I reflexively rolled aside. It thudded into the underside of the engine and fell to the ground between us.

"Grenade," I howled.

Time seemed to slow down. My hand closed around the sleek, warm, finned cylinder. Slewing my body around, I hurled it as far as I could, side-arm. It skimmed out over the snow and fell.

"Shift! *Now!*" I wrestled with my clothes. It seemed to take endless seconds to get free of my parka and jeans. The grenade just lay there. Maybe it was a dud—

It went *click,* and broke in half.

Clouds of opaque gas puffed out.

Oh.

I contorted, faded out, endured the pain, and became a coyote. I chose that form without thinking about it, because it was the one I'd been using as my primary form when we were here last. Immediately, my coyote's eyes started to burn and stream with water. Snot poured from my nose. "Run," I tried to shout. It came out as a strangulated bark. Dolph and Irene didn't need my urging. Jackal and panther writhed out from under the truck and streaked into the snow, back the way we'd come. I followed.

Gunfire split the air. But the shooters had outsmarted themselves with that tear gas trick. They couldn't see to aim at us through the billowing clouds of gas and snow.

Not that I could see where I was going, either. It felt like someone had poured gasoline in my eyes and lit it. Every breath drew fire into my lungs.

Through the tears streaming from my eyes, I glimpsed Dolph vanishing into one of the low doors in the mithrik warrens. I yelped to get Irene's attention, and followed him. We all tumbled down a short concrete ramp and collapsed on a damp floor, coughing in helpless spasms.

"Dear dear," said the hooting voice of an Ek. "Close the door." Treetrunk legs moved into my field of vision, twin blurs silhouetted against a warm, crackling fire. "You are what? Not mithriks."

I gasped, "We're humans. I know, we don't look like it at the moment." We had fallen into an Ek hunting camp. A mithrik dripped on a spit over the fire, roasting. Guess they weren't quite extinct yet. Another Ek knelt on the ramp, holding a knife in each of xis upper hands, watching the door.

The shooting outside had stopped. New noises intruded: growling engines, clanking snow chains, and amplified shouts.

The Ek sentry lifted the heavy curtain that covered the door. "The king is here," xe said, lowering xis knives.

"The king?" I scrabbled past him up the ramp.

Outside, the tear gas had dispersed. Figures moved around our truck. They were tall, like Eks. They had four arms, like Eks. They wore dark uniforms, and their upper bodies were cartoonishly broad, to support the extra shoulderblades that sprouted from somewhere around their diaphragms. But they were slender, with small round heads.

They were humans.

They were Sixers, the alt-humans of Mittel Trevoyvox.

"Austin!" I yelled. "Your Majesty?"

The Sixers reacted instantly. One of them ran towards me. "Mike?"

I whined. My eyes still burned, and my vision was blurry, but even so, I could tell this was *not* Austin Kventuras, the king of New Abilene-Qitalhaut we had befriended seventeen years ago. This Sixer was way too young. Short, fair hair framed a boyish face.

"Don't you remember me?" he said in disappointment.

It clicked.

"Justin?"

14

JUSTIN Kventuras, the son of the old king, was now king of New Abilene-Qitalhaut in his own right. When we were here before he'd been no older than Lucy was now. No wonder I hadn't recognized him. But he had recognized me. As he said, coyotes are not a common sight on Mittel Trevoyvox, nor are jackals. When he realized our panther companion was female, he treated her with extra deference.

We were given one of the Sixers' APVs to Shift back and change in. It was a massive vehicle, Ek-built, a metal house on wheels. We struggled back into the damp, muddy clothes the Sixers had recovered for us. They also returned our weapons.

The Sixers may have had another name for themselves once, a long time ago, but nowadays they accepted the dismissive nickname bestowed by the mainstream humans who exiled them to the Hurtworlds. The official reason for their exile was that they have inferior health outcomes, so their genes couldn't be allowed to mingle with the mainstream population. But the truth is that they simply look too much like Eks. It's a complete coincidence. Humanity hadn't even *met* the Eks yet when the ancestors of the Sixers embarked on their gene-modding project. But we couldn't have the mighty Ekschelatan Empire thinking that we considered them in any way admirable, or worthy of emulation. So the Sixers had to be repudiated.

Basically, they were exiled for being alt-humans.

No Shifter likes to think too hard about that.

But there was, all the same, a kind of kinship between us.

"I have always remembered you with great fondness," Justin said, standing next to the APV. Dolph, Irene, and I were kneeling in the open side door, bathing our eyes with soda. Works better than water. The fizzy liquid ran down my face, into my already-wet collar, and dripped into the snow. "When I learned that *you* were shipping my order from Total Research Solutions, I was delighted."

"We didn't know it was you," I said. "The documentation just says Hurtworlds Authority Trustee. We knew your old man was the HA trustee for New A-Q seventeen years ago, so we thought *maybe* … But it seemed like a lot to hope for that he would still be around."

"He died five years ago." Justin had one of those faces that show every emotion like wind moving across water.

"I'm sorry to hear that," Dolph said. "Bet he went out in a blaze of glory."

"No. It was a brain tumor."

I tried to estimate how old Austin Kventuras would have been when he died. Fifty? The sad thing was, among the Sixers, that was about average. Humans aren't *meant* to be giants with four arms. Unlike Eks, who come by their limb count naturally, the Sixers do not have outsized hearts or heavy-duty bones. Their extra limbs mean more blood to be pumped around the body, putting additional strain on their hearts. So they tend to have dangerously high blood pressure, and succumb to heart attacks at what we would consider a young age. They're also prone to brain tumors. I wondered if those long-dead genetic scientists realized what they had done to their own offspring: if they, like our own ancestors, had had the moral conscience to pile up their supercomputers and set them alight.

Justin changed the subject, gesturing towards our truck. "At least they didn't get that!"

Dolph and I followed him to the truck. The market square was now brightly lit by floodlights mounted on APVs. Justin's soldiers stomped through the market, methodically clearing the stalls. They were a mixed force of Sixers and Eks, all wearing the same dark uniforms, and there were a lot of them. Justin had seen our ship landing, he explained, and come to meet us—with thirty men (and aliens) armed to the teeth. He had clearly been expecting trouble.

"Has this kind of thing happened before?" I asked.

"It happens all the time." Justin's top set of shoulders sagged. "Burden is too clever to embezzle our subsidies. Instead, he lets us buy things … and then he takes them."

"Guess most folks don't shoot back," Dolph said.

"No," Justin said. "Mostly, they just run."

But Burden's gunmen had not intended to let us run, I reflected uneasily. They had shot to kill. That first bullet had been aimed at my head.

"He's gonna be spitting when he finds out about this," Dolph said, watching the soldiers dragging bodies into the market square. "Hey, Justin." His light tone didn't change. "Does it say anywhere that you're allowed to use your subsidies to buy genetic engineering materials?"

Justin gazed down at him. He was eight and a half feet tall. It was a long way down. "No."

"Just checking," Dolph said. "We ain't gonna squeal on you."

Justin shouted to his soldiers. They dispersed back to their vehicles, leaving five bodies lined up neatly in the middle of the market square.

Irene was bending over the corpses, examining them. Suddenly she straightened up and shouted, "Mike! Dolph! Look at this!"

She waved at us so frantically that we broke into a run.

"Is that what I think it is?" She pointed at the three men and two women lying in the snow. They looked like ordinary mainstream humans. They wore nondescript dark clothing. Their faces were pale, drained of blood …

… but as I stared at the nearest corpse, I saw faint patterns on the woman's face.

Swirls. Patches of color.

The patterns got darker moment by moment, as the woman's body cooled, and the color-changing cells in her skin lost power.

The same process was happening to all the other corpses. All of them had living tattoos on their faces and necks. They'd turned them off, reverting the tattoos to flesh-tone to hide their identities. But technology that is powered by body heat stops working after death.

Dragons. Crossed blades. Tribal knots. Semi-abstract designs that I recognized as symbols of the gods Cipactli, Cthulthu, Loki, and Legba.

"They're *Travellers,"* Dolph breathed.

"Burden is a Traveller, too," I realized. Now it all made sense. D'Alencon had said that the Travellers were no longer active in the Hurtworlds. *It's quiet out there,* he'd said. *Too quiet.* Yes … because the Travellers had infiltrated the Hurtworlds Authority itself.

"We gotta get back to our ship," I said urgently. I imagined Burden attacking the *St. Clare* in retaliation, starting a ship fight on the ground.

"Your ship will be safe," Justin said. "Burden is very careful. At the spaceport, he plays the part of a conscientious administrator. Only we know what he really is." He hesitated. "What are Travellers?"

"Oh boy," I murmured. For a king, he was sheltered. Of course he was. He'd never left Mittel Trevoyvox.

"Whatever they are," Justin said, "they won't hurt your ship in the next few hours. Please do come back to the palace with me. I haven't even *paid* you …"

"That's right, he hasn't paid us, Mike," Irene said.

Even more than our fee, I wanted answers to the questions gnawing at my mind. "OK. We'll take you up on that invitation."

15

OUR truck was too shot-up to drive. We rode in Justin's APV, while one of the other armored vehicles towed the truck. After about twenty minutes we reached the old Mittel Trevoyvox Extraction Ventures building, a.k.a. the palace of New Abilene-Qitalhaut. This had been Justin's father's headquarters, and now, I guessed, it was Justin's. A fifty-storey skyscraper with a convex frontage faced a snow-blanketed plaza. The snow had stopped falling. The sky was paling. The Core still lit the eastern horizon, but in the west, the battered city skyline stood out against paler gray clouds.

The APVs drove away into an underground parking garage, leaving clouds of blue smoke hanging in the air. Sentries snapped to attention as Justin led us across the atrium of the MTEV building to a bank of elevators. "Last time," I said, "I remember we had to climb fifteen flights of stairs." It was warm in the atrium. I could feel my face and hands thawing. Hurting.

Justin gave one of his sad smiles. "Yes, the power is back on. There is a nuclear power plant on the Ek side of the river. It is old, but it works. We only had to start it up and repair the transmission lines."

"You're not doing too badly here," Dolph said, as if he were trying to convince Justin as much as himself.

The elevator rose smoothly. Mirrored walls reflected our dishevelled hair and reddened faces. On the fifteenth floor, we stepped out into an open-plan office furnished with oversized split-level desks built for four-armed people, and chairs and couches with arms shaped like capital Es in cross-section. The Sixers used Ek stuff by preference, given their physiques. The modern decor was a far cry from the sodden mess I remembered. The sun had risen behind the clouds. Pale light poured through a north-facing wall of floor-to-ceiling windows.

"I try to keep in mind that things are much, much better than they used to be." Justin sat down at a computer and powered it up. "How much do I owe you?"

"Thirty will do," I said, sticking to the original agreement. I had intended to play hardball and get him to match Dr. Tierney's sixty, but I felt too sorry for him.

"That is not enough for your trouble," Justin said, tapping keys. "We'll make it a hundred."

"That's very good of you," I said, astonished. "But will it go through?" I was thinking about Burden's radio blocking protocols, and the de facto comms censorship the Hurtworlds Authority wielded by controlling the planet's only FTL drone. For us to get paid, Justin's transaction needed to get on board that FTL drone and get to an EkBank node.

"Oh yes," Justin said. "We have a dedicated data landline to the spaceport, and Burden allows my financial transactions. He wants me to make purchases."

Dolph rubbed a thumbnail against his lower teeth. "A hundred for us, three hundred to Total Research Solutions—more? Four hundred? —and I get the impression it's not the first time you've made that kind of purchase … The subsidies ain't even meant to cover much beyond starvation rations and running water."

"But the subsidies are not our only source of revenue." Justin led us to the north-facing floor-to-ceiling windows.

Below, the river threaded through urban sprawl. The entire planet was carpeted with the debris of lost civilizations. Smog and coal smoke smudged the hills on the horizon. Closer to hand, I saw the green squares of the backyard farms where the Sixers grew vegetables in soil that was half rubble. I also saw what must be the nuclear power plant, on the far bank of the river: a fortress wall enclosed a spacious compound, dotted with the trademark cooling towers of first-generation fission power. I shivered at the sight. I may fly a spaceship with an antimatter drive, but nuclear fission? Now that's *not* safe.

"*That's* Mittel Trevoyvox Extraction Ventures?" Dolph said.

Rows of prefab warehouses lined both banks of the river, flat roofs blanketed with snow. "Thirty-one point five million servers, running around the clock," Justin said.

"Whoa," I said. "Your father only had about six server centers."

Justin nodded. "It's an arms race. Eventually, currency mines will cover entire planets. You'll need the power of a star just to solve a single hash. That's already how the Eks do it. They have orbital currency mines powered by solar arrays the size of moons. We have to keep expanding, just to keep up with them."

The way the EkBank works, anyone can have a go at mining new GCs to add to the ledger. All you need is servers to solve the equations … *lots* of servers. When d'Alencon and I were spitballing possible sources for Rafael Ijiuto's funds, he had thrown out the possibility of currency mining. The Darkworlds didn't have the necessary infrastructure for that. But with millennia of technological junk buried in their basements, the Sixers did.

I would have expected Justin to be proud of his achievement. Instead, he sounded tired beyond his years. "Burden permits us to continue operating because the more money we have, the more there is for him to steal." He walked back to the elevator.

Irene drifted back to us. "Need your binos," she murmured.

"What for?"

"Just come over here."

The south wall of the office was all windows, as well. We could see the spaceport from here. Dolph had his binoculars out in a flash.

"There she is," he said in relief. I grabbed the binos. It reassured me to see the *St. Clare* unhurt, sitting where we had left her, a steel-gray beast among all the white HA ships. I now guessed that some of those were *Traveller* ships, repainted. That's why the spaceport was so full. Undercover Travellers and undercover ships. Could their usual grisly style of ship art be a deliberate ploy, to make us think that we would know them when we saw them?

Behind us, Justin said, "You see? I told you your ship would be all right. The spaceport manager is an Ek—Isir Olthamo. *Xe* is not corrupt. Xe doesn't believe Burden is corrupt, either, and Burden wants to keep it that way."

Irene took the binos. Staring through them, she stiffened.

"What?" Dolph said.

Irene looked up at Justin. "There's a barge on the river, right inside the spaceport." I could see it, a green rectangle moored on the Ek side of the river. "It's covered with a tarp. There's something under that tarp—see? Do you know what that is?"

"Yes. It is a spaceship. It arrived about a week ago. They moved it onto that barge and covered it up. I do not know why."

"Because they don't want it to be spotted from orbit before they get a chance to paint it white," I said. On the way back to the elevator, I was morose, thinking about the audacious scale of the Travellers' scam, taking place right under the Fleet's nose. I would have to tell Jose-Maria d'Alencon about this.

We glided down in the elevator. Justin seemed nervous. Several times he started to speak. At last he said, "Can I trust you?"

Lightly, I said, "Son, we just brought you a cargo of illegal genetic engineering materials. I think you can trust us."

The elevator doors opened. An Ek waited. Xe wore a red cape with six armholes, for xis *six* arms. An Ur-Ek. I'd never seen one on the Hurtworlds before. Xe surveyed us with glinting yellow eyes. "These are the off-worlders?"

"Yes," Justin said. "I'm going to show them the lab."

"Are you sure that is wise?"

"They are my friends."

This time the elevator had stopped underground. We walked through brightly lit corridors. The Ur-Ek put xis middle right hand on Justin's arm and spoke to him in the Ek language. Justin responded in the same tongue, gesturing at us. He had learned the language of the Sixers' former enemy. If I got a chance, I wanted to ask him how the war had ended.

Double doors swung open. We entered a cavernous room filled with throbbing, whooshing, humming equipment. It was similar enough to Dr. Tierney's set-up that I knew immediately what we were looking at.

"Welcome," Justin said, "to the future."

16

Welcome to the future. The exact same phrase Dr. Tierney had used. Actually, Justin had probably got it from him.

It was just after dawn; there was no one at work. At the far end of the lab there was another door. Sixers were carrying our plastikretes into the lab and unpacking them, while Eks supervised the operation.

"So what are you researching?" I said. It was cold in the lab, and I folded my arms to hide my shivering.

Justin led us to a workstation with a split-level desk. He sat in an Ek-style chair with two sets of armrests. "I am not an expert. I have little scientific understanding. But *they* are experts." He waved at the Eks who had taken charge of our cargo.

I frowned. What could those Eks teach anyone, apart from how to build homemade artillery and bombs? They got sent here for a reason —because they were felons. Every Ek on Mittel Trevoyvox was either a criminal, or the child of criminals. That's why I had been surprised to learn that the war had ended without rivers of blood in the streets.

"The Empire has laws against everything." The fluting voice came from the Ur-Ek who had met us at the elevator. "I am Morshti. My father and mother were nobles. They committed lèse-majesté. A serious crime, that is. But in general, it is easy to get sent to the Hurtworlds. Laws against theft, fraud, embezzlement, assault, deviating from specifications, removing tools from one's place of work, feeding birds, wasting water, reading English books, putting one's house in the wrong place, wearing pink, using drugs, selling drugs, and insulting ticket-collectors, the Empire has. Also, it has laws against genetic engineering."

"Ah," I murmured, eyeing the other Eks with new understanding. They'd been deported to Mittel Trevoyvox for messing around with gene-modding technology. And now Justin had given them a place to carry on doing it.

"Does Burden know about this?" Dolph said.

Justin grimaced. "He reviews all our procurement requests."

"That's a yes, then." I saw that the relationship between Burden and the Sixers was more complicated than it had appeared at first. In a sense, they needed each other. Justin had gotten away with setting up an illegal genetic engineering lab … because Burden was a criminal. The Travellers were content to let Justin procure illegal materials, as long as they got their cut. "So what are you working on?" I said.

"Look." We gathered around Justin's chair. The central screen of his setup displayed a naked Sixer male. "This is one of the subjects we've sequenced. We're going to sequence *everyone.*"

Justin touched a key, and the Sixer on the screen began to shrink. His lower arms shrivelled and vanished. His torso narrowed. He became a mainstream human, and flashed a simulated grin before disappearing.

"You see? We're going to eliminate our genetic defects," Justin said with a tense smile. "Then there will be no reason for them to keep us imprisoned here."

"Son," Dolph said, "gene therapy can't make you shorter. It can't amputate limbs. It ain't magic."

"I thought you were just going to improve your heart capacity and bone structure," Irene said, disappointed.

"We would still be Sixers," Justin said. "This is the only way they'll ever let us leave. Oh, I know there's no hope for the living. But germline gene modification can fix the next generation in utero."

"So you're going to throw away your past," Dolph said. "Hundreds of years of suffering. Everything your ancestors lived and died for. You're just going to erase that from history, huh?"

Justin scowled at him. "We are merely undoing what was done to us in the past."

"Right," Dolph said. "Now ask yourself if that's too high a price to pay for freedom."

Morshti said, "In my opinion, it will not work. Germline genetic modification is not a game. He's likely to do more harm than good. But a hobby, everyone needs, right?"

"I wish you would keep your opinions to yourself." Justin pushed himself upright, using his lower pair of arms, while shutting down the computer with his upper pair of arms.

"Am I not Queen?" Morshti said. That startled me, but it made sense, given that xe was an Ur-Ek.

"Queen?" Irene said.

"Of course." Morshti eased up behind Justin and kissed him on the side of his face. "To be clear, I *hope* your project will succeed. Then leave the planet, you would." Xe smiled circularly, and nuzzled the top of Justin's head. "Ours it would be, forever."

Staring straight ahead, Justin said, "My royal wife jests. Among the Eks, marriage pacts are the most weighty political alliances. My marriage to Morshti has brought peace to New Abilene-Qitalhaut. We are allies—united—one people."

Dolph's and Irene's faces mirrored my own disgust and amazement. Eks and humans simply do not marry. They *can't,* can they?

Catching our all-too-obvious reaction, Justin colored. His blush reminded me how young he was. He threw off Morshti's embrace, rose, and started to walk through the lab to the far entrance, biting into a cold baked potato which he took from his pocket. Unappetizing though his snack looked, my stomach growled. It seemed like days since I'd eaten.

I caught up with him as he reached the far doors. "I'm sorry," I said. "It's none of our business. But I'm concerned about the situation with Burden. I'll report the incident last night to the authorities on Ponce de Leon. They'll take the appropriate steps."

Justin pushed the doors open. Cold air blew in from the parking garage. For a minute he and I were alone on the far side of the doors. "Please don't do that. If Burden goes … so does our only hope." His stiff smile said he knew he'd made a deal with the devil, but he was sticking to it.

The others came out. At a shout from Justin, Sixer and Ek soldiers jogged away to fetch our truck.

The parking garage was dotted with APVs, snowploughs, and a good few tanks left over from the war, Ek-built monsters with turrets as well as main guns. Surveying it all, Dolph said cynically, "Sixers make good soldiers. Why don't you just hire yourselves out to the Fleet as cannon fodder? That's what we did."

Our diesel rumbled up, already repaired by efficient Sixer mechanics. Two APVs, detailed as our security escort, followed us.

We drove for several minutes without speaking. The sunlight gilded the fresh blanket of snow in the streets. At last Dolph broke the silence. "*Stupid* goddamn kid."

"What's that?" Irene exclaimed.

A star shot up from behind the MTEV building. The crackling thunder of ship engines rolled distantly across the golden sky.

"Someone just took off from the spaceport." I stepped on the gas.

17

I stopped the truck outside the spaceport perimeter gate, a shimmering three-meter force field with a railroad-crossing style barrier in front, so you wouldn't drive straight into it. The guards on duty made us wait. I stood in the snow outside the gate, weary and full of forebodings.

At last a six-armed Ur-Ek ambled towards the other side of the force field, xis fur-trimmed cape swishing. I thought of Morshti, but this Ek's face had had the soft, puffy look that denotes old age. Xe spoke in a deep, tranquil voice, muffled by the force field. "Mr. Starrunner. I apologize for the delay." The shimmering barrier between us vanished. I thanked the Ek in surprise. "I am Isir Olthamo, manager of this spaceport." Xe spoke perfect English, without the usual garbled Ek syntax. A sign of class. "I trust you had no difficulties delivering your cargo?"

"None at all," I said. "Thank you so much, Xr. Olthamo."

"You will be departing today?"

"Yes." I paused. "We saw a ship launch about forty-five minutes ago. Was that a Hurtworlds Authority flight, or …"

"Not precisely. It was my colleague, Jonathan Burden. He has gone on vacation." Olthamo looked sly. "One may hope his vacation will be indefinitely extended."

Burden gone! *That* was good news … for us, but not for Justin.

Torn, I considered laying it all out for Olthamo. But Justin had asked me not to. And I'd already decided to give d'Alencon the information first. I just thanked Olthamo again and got back in the truck.

We passed a couple of the disguised Traveller ships on our way back to the *St. Clare.* Humans scuttled around them, clearly readying the ships for take-off.

"Look at that," Dolph said. "It's like we gassed a rats' nest. It ain't like Travellers to run scared." He looked at me. "Maybe they think we're gonna sic the Fleet on them."

"Nnnoooo," Irene said, with a nervous laugh. "They'd start asking us questions, and we'd never get out of here."

"Don't seem to be much point," I mumbled. "Burden already ran, anyway."

Dolph's lips pressed together. He leaned out the window and gave the middle finger to the Travellers.

I had seldom been so glad to see the *St. Clare.* A knot of tension in my chest unwound as I dropped into the familiar trunk corridor. "You took long enough," Martin said, slithering out of the pressure door that led to the engineering deck. "What happened? You get sunburned? On *this* planet?" Our faces were still red and irritated from the tear gas.

"Long story," I said. "What's our resupply status?"

"The water tankers have been and gone. Reaction mass is at 100%. Still waiting on the other stuff."

"We'll launch without it. Resupply on Yesanyase Skont. I have a feeling there's about to be a run on consumables around here."

I changed out of my damp clothes and then made straight for the galley. I constructed an economy-size sandwich out of stores: long-life bread, deli meat, processed cheese, and cryo lettuce from Ponce de Leon. Dolph was already there, eating a microwave chicken dinner. Irene elbowed us out of the way to get her vacuum-packed mice out of the fridge.

"Guess what," Dolph said to Martin with his mouth full. "The king's married to an Ek."

"You're kidding. That's disgusting."

"Right?" Dolph said. "How do they even do it?"

"I've been trying to convince myself they don't," I said.

"Well, it wouldn't be technically impossible," Dolph said. "Every Ek has both sets of parts, right?"

"That's why they call 'em xim," Martin said.

"I just wonder which tab goes in which slot," Dolph said. "I didn't get faggy vibes from the young monarch … but then again, he's married to an Ek, so all bets are off."

"He called xim his wife," I recalled.

"Maybe they stick to oral gratification," Martin speculated.

"I'd rather get a blow job from a vacuum cleaner," I said with a shudder. Dolph and I both instinctively crossed our legs at the thought of all those sharp teeth. Martin probably would have, too, if he had legs (or exterior genitals) in python form.

"I know!" MF piped up, rolling along the corridor. "Simultaneous penetration! After all, male humans also have orifices!"

"Do you mind? I'm trying to eat," I groaned.

"Nuh uh," Dolph said. "Think about the angle of attack. That wouldn't work unless Ek dicks point backwards."

"You guys. Do you have to be so crude?" Irene pushed Dolph aside to get out of the galley, an open packet of mice in her hand. Most Shifters do not eat the things that animals eat. Irene made an exception for mice. The barbecue-flavored ones were her comfort food.

"Come on, Irene," Dolph said. "No one's ever had sex with an Ek. At least, I would hope present company hasn't. It's only natural to speculate."

"No, it isn't. It's sick. You're as bad as MF."

"What did I do?" MF said.

Irene rolled her eyes and shoved past him. A moment later an enraged cry came from the lounge. "Mike!"

I hurried down the corridor, already guessing what I'd find. MF and Martin had a bad habit of watching porn on the big screen when the rest of us were out. Sure enough, the screen displayed a paused image of a wolf and a human woman, copulating doggy-style. I switched it off, feeling embarrassed, implicated, just a little bit turned on, and even more embarrassed because of that. I haltingly apologized to Irene. "It's not fair that you have to put up with this. I know you wanted me to hire another woman to take Kimmie's place, so you wouldn't have to take the brunt of MF's crap all on your own, but I … didn't." I shook my head, irritated at myself. "I'll talk to him—"

She cut me off. "It isn't just MF, it's all of you. But forget it, Mike." She stuffed another mouse into her mouth. "It doesn't matter. None of it matters. That poor kid had to marry an Ek to end the war. He's basically crucifying himself for his people, and all you guys can do is make fun of him. But it doesn't matter. Let's just fucking *go.*"

Dolph leaned in the doorway. "We didn't visit Artie's grave."

"Do I care about your junkie friend who's been dead for twenty years?" Irene yelled at him. "I do not! I care about the job! What do you care about, Dolph? *Anything?*"

Justin Kventuras had gotten to all of us. Irene had not known him when he was a kid, but he'd gotten to her, anyway. So we were all hurting. When Dolph was upset, he started talking shit. When Irene was upset, she got grumpy. I pushed the rest of my sandwich into my mouth. "Fucking quit it, guys. Prepare for launch."

18

IT took us just six hours to reach Yesanyase Skont. The only Hurtworld reserved exclusively for humans, Yesanyase S lies one light year closer to the Core than Mittel Trevoyvox, and also closer to its own sun. This ageing star had begun to expand into its red giant phase. Orange-tinged, it spanned the width of my palm in the sky.

Yesanyase Skont may once have been a green Earth-like planet, but for the last thousand years or so, its middle latitudes have been baking deserts. Only the southern polar continent is still inhabited.

The spaceport, located near the south pole, covers a vast area of 80 square kilometers. Plonked on top of an oasis, it encloses several lakes. At the sprawling bazaars, you can buy and sell anything from spaceships to antique books and live fuzzy-wuzzies. The air is hot, but bone-dry, so it's cool when you step into the shade. On the porches of the *hullabas*—the lounge bars built in the reeds around the lakes—men and women from all over the Cluster exchange news, views, and war stories. At night, the Core hangs at the zenith like a fuzzy full moon, turning the sky a dark shade of blue, and sweet, druggy smoke wafts from the nightclubs. Music rolls out across the desert, so loud that when a ship takes off from somewhere, it's just a rumble in the bass.

We all needed to decompress after Mittel Trevoyvox. That's what I told myself, until, sprawling in a couch made from the shell of an extinct giant turtle, along with several partially clad people I didn't know,

I reached the bottom of a glass of glacier rak and suddenly realized I was wasting time.

I stumbled to my feet and went looking for Dolph. I wasn't sure how long he'd been gone. It was still dark; meant nothing. The day on Yesanyase Skont is 33 hours long. I left the nightclub and wandered along the lakeside.

Strangely, although I knew that I should be in a hurry, I felt no gut sense of urgency. A cool night breeze caressed my face and arms. The reeds whispered and rustled, their feathery plumes swaying in unison. The Core shone like God's lighthouse. The music faded behind me. Loved-up couples and threesomes staggered past, bombed out of their minds.

I wanted to be alone, and to get nearer the water. I took a path that angled into the reeds. The clicking stems smelled fresh, woodsy. The water around their roots gurgled. I came out on a wooden promenade that cut across the lake like a bowstring.

The promenade was dotted with people strolling or making out in the Corelight.. But my eyes immediately went to a single lanky figure which was moving oddly. *Dolph.*

I walked out to him. Oblivious, he didn't notice me. He was either dancing or fighting with an invisible opponent. Shadowboxing. His fists jabbed air.

"Dolph?"

His eyes were closed. His arms curved, embracing an invisible partner. Slow-dancing. I felt a chill.

"Dolph." I clamped my hands on his shoulders.

His eyes opened, but he wasn't seeing my face. "Take my money," he said.

"Dolph. It's me."

"Mike." Now he saw me. He laughed emptily. "It just slips through your fingers, don't it? Everything—slips—away."

I shook him. "You're fucked up."

"Get your hands off me," he said, clawing at them.

I shoved him. He hit me back. No strength or accuracy in it. That frightened me more than if he had landed a haymaker. We staggered against the railing of the promenade, and went over it, into the lake. Fortunately, it was only thigh-deep, with a layer of fine silt at the bottom. I sat up, spluttering—it was *cold.* Dolph floated on his back, gazing up at the Core. His wet face looked like a glistening skull. I floundered over to him and hauled him to his feet. "Get up. *Get the fuck up!*"

Stargend cilia coiled down over the railing and politely tapped me. Although Yesanyase S is a human planet, quite a few stargends work and live at the spaceport. These aliens look like walking octopuses with translucent hides. They have the best manners in the Cluster. They helped us back onto the promenade. I thanked them, hiding my fury and consternation. Dolph and I were both soaked to the skin, our shoes full of silt.

I dragged him on around the lake until we came to a *jehoula.* These are hotels built inside the shells of another species of extinct turtle which once roamed the planet. They must have been the size of battleships. This shell had numerous holes cut in it, with light spilling out around the edges of cunningly fitted doors. I banged on each door in turn until Martin's sleepy voice said, "Yeah, what?"

I threw the door open. Martin lay in python form on linen sheets. A large, oddly shaped lump twitched in his mid-section. I hadn't needed to see that. On the other hand, it meant he would be too out of it to notice that anything was the matter with Dolph.

"We're wasting time." My voice cut the air like an axe. "Enough of this bullshit. Meet us back at the ship at dawn."

*

There were still hours to go before dawn. I spent most of them walking Dolph around the lake, sobering him up. After I forced some hot coffee and a steamed bun down him, he started making sense again, but he didn't say much. Nor did I. We never talked about his issues. Never *had* to. It had been years—decades—since he had fallen down a pharmaceutical rabbit hole like this.

Shabu, I figured, or whatever they were calling it now. Amphetamines plus some other stuff. If the formulation was the same as in the old days, it made you feel like a god, and act like an idiot. OK if you've got a commanding officer pulling your strings. Not so OK if you're out in the Cluster on your own.

Just going near Artie's grave had been enough to set Dolph off. And hadn't I reacted in the same mindless way? Drinking to excess at seedy bars and clubs, as if I could recapture my self-destructive youth? But drinking to excess was nothing unusual for me, sad to say. I could handle it. Dolph and drugs were a different story.

Dawn blistered the horizon. As we were trudging back to the ship, MF called me.

"I have located Pippa," he announced ebulliently.

"No shit?" Adrenaline speared through my chest, lifting my mood.

"Yes! At my request, Irene purchased a complete data dump of the Yesanyase Skont internet, going back a month. I have analyzed all the arrivals and transport data, and determined with a high degree of certainty that Pippa is at Camp 32!"

"Where's that?"

"Five hundred kilometers from here."

"So we need wheels."

"Yes! That is why I called you! Hurry up. Irene is impatient."

"I'll bet. Tell her we'll be back soon."

Now, at last, urgency set in. I hailed one of the local pedicabs, operated by an insectile aiora. We rode out to the auto bazaar. It was bedlam. I picked a rental yard run by a family of stargends, knowing that they wouldn't try to rip us off too badly.

"I'm not going," Dolph said.

"Why not?" I realized that I had been expecting this, at least since last night.

"Someone needs to stay here that knows how to fly the ship."

"MF can do it."

"He'd crash her while watching bestiality porn."

Around us, sparks flew and sledgehammers swung, gripped in deceptively frail-looking cilia burnt purple by the sun. Dolph sat on the bumper of a wrecked fuel tanker, smoking a cigarette. I rubbed my aching temples. "I need you."

"Take Irene."

"I didn't say Irene, I said *you.*"

He just smiled at me, the saddest smile I ever saw from him. "I'll stay outta trouble." He held up two fingers crossed, the way we used to swear in the army. "Get that one; it's got the best gun."

That one was what they called a Hurtworlds special, a technical built on the chassis of a pickup truck. It had armor plating, a cow-catcher plate, rugged wheels half as tall as I was, and a .50 cal machine-gun mounted on top of the cab. I gave in, dickered with the stargends, got a good price on the rental, and drove it back to the *St. Clare.* After Mittel Trevoyvox, I felt confident driving a diesel. This one was sluggish to handle, but I liked the power of the engine, even in a high gear. If you can't have an electric vehicle, it's hard to beat the torque of a good diesel.

The *St. Clare* stood like a beached plesiosaur on a piece of desert, nothing in sight except some warehouses. Irene paced outside the ship, impatiently awaiting our return. *She* had not wandered off to get fucked up.

Instead, she had—

"Bought the entire freaking spaceport?" I said, gaping at the small mountain of boxes and suitcases on the ground.

"It's for Pippa," Irene pointed at boxes. "Clothes, shoes, electronics, chocolate and dried fruits, protein snacks, medicines, a camp bed, a high-end holobook with an AI assistant—"

"How much was all this?" I checked the Uni-Ex Shipping corporate account on my phone as I spoke. Justin's payment had not yet gone through. I didn't expect that for another couple of days. "A *hundred* KGCs?"

"Only twenty-five," Irene snapped.

"Well, we're down a hundred." Mary, back on Ponce de Leon, must have made some withdrawals.

Irene scowled against the sunlight. She was all ready to go, wearing desert camo pants and a visored cap, carrying her rifle. "What are you riled up about? I thought we were here to *help* Pippa."

In that moment I knew for sure that I couldn't take Irene with me. She may not be consciously planning to harm Pippa … but this egregious overcompensation betrayed her intentions. She was planning to steal the TrZam 008, by force if necessary, and make it up to Pippa by giving her presents.

"OK," I said. "This was a good thought, Irene. Thanks." I heaved a crate from the Human Food Emporium into the back of the technical. Irene had also brought out my backpack, water and food for the drive, and our portable HF radio. We could use that here, as there were no shady radio blocking protocols in effect. She had thought of everything. I already felt bad about leaving her behind. But I just couldn't trust her.

Who did that leave?

I found Martin not far away, basking in the sun behind a rise that sheltered him from the wind. The lump in his midsection had shrunk some, and no longer twitched, to my relief.

"You're with me," I said. "So's MF." I'd never taken the bot on a field trip before, but he was the one who knew where we were going. Besides, I didn't have any other options.

"Woohoo!" MF cried. "All aboard!" He swung himself up into the technical. "Come on, Marty!"

"I'm not done digesting," Martin complained.

"Stay like that, and Shift back when we get there." Crap. I was stuck with the python and the robot. This was not going to go well. Ignoring Irene's confused stare, I strode over to Dolph. He had collapsed into twitchy stasis on the lowest rung of the airlock ladder, smoking yet another cigarette. My shadow fell on him. "You sure?"

"I already said I'm not going."

For a second, looking down at him, I suspected him of fucking this up on purpose. Fucking *himself* up on purpose, so I couldn't make him go. He had to know that without him, I was much less likely to succeed. But no—Dolph didn't calculate things like that. He just didn't want any part of this.

"Why aren't you going?" Irene said to him.

Dolph didn't answer, and neither did I. She had eyes in her head, didn't she? But in some ways, Irene was oddly naïve. She wouldn't notice that someone was tweaking unless they overdosed at her feet. I turned to her. "You're not going, either."

She tensed. "No way. I'm not staying here. This is *it!* This is why we came!" She flung out a hand at Martin and MF, waiting in the technical. "You're taking those two jokers, instead of me? Give me a break!"

Dishonesty put a bad taste in my mouth. I reached for a good reason she had to stay. "Don't forget about the Travellers. There might be more of them here. We have no way of knowing how far they've infiltrated the Hurtworlds Authority. So your job is to keep the barrels of the Gausses clean, so that if necessary, we can perforate their asses."

She searched my face to see if I might change my mind. Saw that I wasn't going to. "You're the captain." She kicked Dolph out of the way and climbed the ladder.

I heaved the rest of the stuff into the technical, angry with myself for deceiving her, angry with her for trying to deceive me. What was happening to our crew?

"Hurry up!" MF chirruped, bouncing in the passenger seat of the technical. "Let's get rolling!"

19

I drove for an hour, across stony desert dotted with spaceships and refueling facilities, all veiled by the dust and sand blowing on the wind. Martin slept in the back, coiled around the jerrycans. MF, beside me, babbled about how pretty this planet had been a thousand years ago. At last we reached the spaceport perimeter. It was a rusty double fence festooned with warning signs. Soldiers manned the only gate to be seen for miles.

On other Hurtworlds, the Hurtworlds Authority provides its own spaceport security, but Yesanyase Skont is a human planet, so here it's the army. I appraised the young grunts on guard duty as inexperienced, sloppy, and overconfident. They rolled around the technical on offroad segways, each one shimmering with a force field that surrounded the rider and would stop bullets.

"What's up," I said, leaning out of the cab with a big smile. "Hot enough for you?"

"Where ya going?"

"The camps."

"What's your business out there?"

I indicated MF. "Got this bot I'm fixing to sell."

"You work for the HA?"

"That's right," I lied.

"Gotta see your ID, sir."

I gave them a carton of cigarettes and two bottles of Scotch.

"Obey the warning signs," they said. "Don't leave the road until you're through the minefield."

The barbed-wire gate swung open in front of us, and I drove though it.

Martin said from the back, "Is it just me, or have military standards gone downhill?"

"It's always been like this," I said. "But in my day, we wouldn't have been caught dead on those segways."

I was exaggerating to hide my dismay at the grunts' lack of professionalism. The army—a division of the Fleet, organizationally speaking—draws its recruits from all planets that are signatories to the London Charter. Kids get a choice between doing two years of government service and going in the forces. Obviously, you get a different caliber of recruit depending on whether there's a war on. Right now, we had been at peace for almost twenty years, and it disturbed me to see first-hand just how lax the infantry had got … even though it had worked in my favor.

The fence, the soldiers, and the segways vanished over the horizon. I drove along a worn-down streak across the desert. I was wearing my flak vest over a t-shirt and cargo pants. My sunglasses turned the desert sepia. Swaths of fossil seashells from a long-vanished ocean crunched under the wheels. Martin went back to sleep, while MF watched porn on a portable screen he had attached to the dashboard. At my request, he angled it out of my line of vision. The incongruity was just too much.

A square of sunlight fell through the hole cut in the roof for the .50 cal gunner. It moved across the seats, centimeter by centimeter, as Yesanyase Skont's long day dragged on. At nightfall MF took the wheel, and I slept in the back with my head pillowed on Martin's coils. The next morning, the desert looked exactly the same, except that we could now see the blue peaks of distant mountains.

Irene radioed us on the HF. "Dolph went off somewhere," she said.

"Did he say where?"

"No."

"That's helpful." Worry festered in my heart.

"Also, some HA people came out to the ship this morning."

"And?"

"They asked about Mittel T. Wanted to know what we were doing there."

"Fuck."

"I didn't tell them anything, just that we were delivering a cargo."

I sucked my teeth. "Burden sicced them on us. Shit."

"That's what I thought at first, too. But I didn't get that vibe from them. I think they suspect *him*. They could have been looking for information about his scam. Or, just looking for him, period. That Ek, what's xis name, might have set an inquiry in motion after we left."

I privately gave thanks for Irene's professionalism. She had put aside her disappointment at being left behind. She was doing her job. "If they figure it all out, it's going to look bad that we didn't say anything to Olthamo."

"I know." Our joint responsibility crackled, unspoken. Dolph had wanted to spill the beans to Olthamo, but we had overridden him. "Well, that's all I got, Cap'n."

I sighed. "Thanks for letting me know."

"What's your ETA?"

The desert rolled past, rock-ribbed, unchanging. "Local noon-ish."

"Keep me posted."

"Will do. Sit on the guns, and when Dolph comes back, tell him to freaking *stay* there. We might need you to come and pick us up."

"Seriously?"

"I don't know. Just trying to anticipate all the possible scenarios."

After I ended the call, I tried to think it through. Burden had left Mittel Trevoyvox. Where had he gone? God only knows. I would have hoped he'd run back to the Traveller motherships in the Core.

But it was not impossible that he had come *here.* Why would he do that? He didn't know *we* were coming here … did he?

"MF."

"Yes, Captain?"

"Drive for a bit." While MF clutched the wheel in his grippers, I scrambled up on the gunner's saddle and test-fired the roof-mounted .50. Dust puffed from rocks so far away I needed binoculars.

The noise woke Martin. "Are we there yet?"

"Almost. Are you done digesting?"

"Almost."

We started to pass through the internment camps in the middle of the morning. They looked like low green hedges at a distance. Up close, the green was green plastic tents straggling along the road. Barreling through at 50 kph, I got fleeting impressions of roadside stalls, dogs, children playing in the dust. In the early afternoon, we reached Camp 32 and turned off onto a side street.

It was bad.

Splitting bags of garbage rotted in the sun. Camp dogs fought over putrid scraps. Sewage flowed along an open gutter in the middle of the street. The stench coiled down my throat. People crossed the road ahead of us, limping, hopping, dragging one foot. The worst cases could not walk unaided. Heads lolling, bodies wasted, they had to be supported by the children who seemed to be the only healthy people in the camp.

My mouth dried out. My knuckles went white on the wheel. Try as I might, I could not compartmentalize this nightmare away. I could not distance myself from these people. Because their present was my future.

This was what it looked like to die of interstellar variant kuru.

Breathing deeply, fighting for calm, I pulled up in front of the camp's headquarters, a two-storey concrete building with a Hurtworlds Authority sign on the roof. A queue of broken people snaked out of the doorway. The building was right on the edge of the camp. Behind it, a field of solar panels drank up the sun. On a low rise beyond the solar installation, more than a klick away, sand-filled gabions and a force field perimeter protected a small army base.

I killed the engine. The sounds of the camp flooded in.

"My sweet Lord," Martin said, darting his head between the front seats. "We have come to the end of the universe."

"Y'all stay here," I said, as if from a great distance. "I'll make enquiries."

I tugged my t-shirt out of my pants, to hide the .22 in my waistband, and pushed my shades up on my head, to look less scary. I went into the HA building. A huge fan whirred in the doorway, stirring the smells and the heat.

"Are you here to fix the solar plant?" said the young woman working at a computer near the fan.

"Is it malfunctioning?" I said.

"You could say that, or you could just come right out and say that the residents stole the control unit and traded it for drugs."

"I'm not here to fix anything," I said.

She looked at me properly for the first time. She was in her twenties, wearing a white caftan with the HA logo on the chest. Tendrils of fair hair adhered to her pink forehead. I could smell her sweat from where I was standing—a wholesome scent, after the odor of sewage and rotting garbage that pervaded the place.

Despite myself, I thought of Christy Day, 58 light years away. Christy had also done her government service on the Hurtworlds. The experience had profoundly affected her, leaving her with a lifelong drive to help the less fortunate. But she must have been that kind of person to begin with. You don't just get sent to the Hurtworlds. You have to *volunteer.* If I was ever tempted to get down on mainstream humanity, I only had to think of Christy. And this girl was clearly cast in the same tough mould.

"Aren't you worried about catching it?" I said without thinking.

"IVK? No. You can only get it by consuming infected tissues."

I could have told her different. But that wasn't what I was here for. "I've got some stuff to deliver to one of your residents." I was grateful for Irene's foresightedness, even though the presents we had brought almost seemed like an affront to this sinkhole of misery.

"Who?" the girl said. "We have five thousand residents."

"This one's named Pippa Khratz. She's a recent arrival, as in the last few weeks."

The volunteer's eyes widened. "That's weird."

"What is?"

"Why is everyone looking for her?"

Uh oh. "Who else is?"

"Are you with them?"

"With who?"

"Those … those people."

She got up. I followed her rustling caftan and slapping sandals up two flights of stairs to the roof. The sun hammered down on a satellite dish and an A/C ventilation unit. The volunteer pointed across the camp.

"Them."

I dropped my shades over my eyes to cut the glare. About a quarter klick away, an open area in the heart of the camp served as a bazaar. Canopied stalls surrounded a row of public water faucets where children filled buckets. A couple of grunts idly patrolled the water line. At one edge of the bazaar stood another Hurtworlds technical, larger than ours. It was the front end of a pickup grafted onto a fuel tanker. Beside it, two people manned a table heaped with goods.

"I've reported them, but they just won't leave," the volunteer said.

"Who are they?"

"Pedlars. They come from the Red Flowers district. They sell little luxuries to the residents. Honestly, they're mostly drug pushers. But these ones . . ." She nervously lowered her voice, so I could hardly hear her over the A/C unit. "They've been asking around for Pippa Khratz. I keep *telling* them there's no such person here."

20

"No such person here?" Martin said, when I got back to the technical and told them what I had learned.

"She *is* here," MF insisted.

"Let's get a look at these so-called pedlars," Martin said. "Shoot one of 'em, see if they got any tattoos." He was getting into the spirit of the thing.

"That's Plan B." I put the technical in gear and drove away from the Hurtworlds Authority building, back towards the road. Martin Shifted back into human form as I drove. He pulled on a plaid shirt and jeans and squatted behind the seats.

I parked on the shoulder of the road, where there were some stalls selling bottled drinks, diesel, and cigarettes. "OK. Marty, change places." I climbed past the gunner's saddle, into the back. Martin clambered into the driver's seat. Hidden by the jerrycans of diesel, and all the suitcases and crates of stuff we'd brought for Pippa, I wormed out of my clothes and Shifted into my wolf.

"Pippa knows this form," I said, scrambling back over the seats into Martin's lap. "I'll go look for her. You talk to the locals." I nodded at the children manning the roadside stalls. "Find out how long these pedlars have been here, if there are any more of them around ... just find out whatever you can."

"What about me?" MF said.

"Stay there and pretend to be a suitcase." How I wished now that I'd brought Dolph or Irene. Martin was reliable in a fight, but MF would be about as much use as … a suitcase.

"Jesus, you're heavy," Martin grunted as my toenails dug into his thighs. "I'm sorry, but no one is going to mistake you for a dog."

"There you go, thinking like a civilized person again."

"Point." He opened the door.

I jumped down to the ground and trotted back into the camp.

Down here closer to the ground, foul smells assaulted my wolf's keen nose. Rats scurried along the open sewers. People lay in their tents, doing nothing, staring at screens, or wearing VR headsets. Martin's words about the end of the universe came back to me. The dust coated skin and hair, collapsing the spectrum of human coloring into a uniform brown. Those camp dogs were everywhere, and they were big, wolfish creatures. I guess I looked enough like them to pass at a glance, especially now that my fur was covered with dust. But *they* knew. They hackled and snarled at me. Some of them were acting as care animals, pulling cripples on carts, wearing little harnesses.

"Pippa," I called. "Pippa."

No one even seemed to notice the talking wolf, except for the children. They peeked out of tents, or threw stones. One thing that the residents of Camp 32 clearly had the energy to do was procreate like rabbits. How freaking irresponsible did you have to be to have kids when you had IVK?

"Pippa. Pippa."

Unawares, I had been running, as if I could outrun my own future. Now I was hot and out of breath. I slowed to a walk, my tongue hanging out. In wolf form, I could not sweat; I had to cool myself by panting. Drool dripped from my lips, as if I was a real animal.

A stone hit my rump. I spun and snarled at a little boy with nothing but meanness in his eyes. Which of us was the animal? How long would it take me, if I were deported to a place like this, to become an animal inside as well as out?

I capered on blindly, calling Pippa's name. I must have searched the whole camp, some parts of it twice. At last I had to accept that it was hopeless. She could be anywhere, or nowhere.

At least I had shown myself to a good number of the camp residents. If they had any curiosity at all, the story of the talking dog, or wolf, would spread quickly, and then Pippa would know I was here.

As I retraced my steps, I heard pop music crackling from poor-quality speakers.

Well, there was one place I hadn't searched yet.

The bazaar.

I had meant to go back and get Martin before venturing in there, but I couldn't resist taking a quick look at the pedlars. I trotted between the last tents and out into the open space.

The bazaar was a bigger, noisier affair than it had looked like from the HA building's roof. Stalls sold junk, recycled electronics, and food. None of these people had any GCs, of course, but the human urge to buy and sell doesn't die that easily. People were swapping home-printed barter tokens and blisterpacks of meds in place of credits. The canopies of the stalls, hand-woven from strips of HA tarps, fluttered in the breeze. The children at the water faucets shoved, splashed, and laughed.

I sat on my haunches, tongue hanging out, watching the pedlars through the crowd.

One man, one woman. Both young. Shorts, t-shirts, boots. Their faces bore splotches of what looked like rosacea, the telltale "red flowers" of the eponymous disease—but I didn't put too much stock in that. They could have set their tattoos to imitate the marks, or done them with makeup. They were mostly selling cheap, alien-grade electronics. I guess that's what real pedlars sell. So do Travellers, when they're not selling stolen spaceships.

A couple of grunts came around, riding on their shielded segways, and stopped by the pedlars' table to say hey. Now *that* was depressing.

When the soldiers had gone, I trotted over to get a closer look. I slunk behind a stall where women served up smelly messes in HA-issue steel bowls. I was now about ten feet from the grille of the pedlars' big rig.

I poked my nose out …

… and saw my ex-wife.

*

Sophia climbed down the steps of their rig, her beautiful legs bared by shorts that skimmed her ass cheeks. She greeted the younger two, then dropped onto a folding chair and pensively unwrapped a protein bar.

I crouched motionless, aghast.

Could it really be her?

She was supposed to be on Valdivia, thirty light years from here!

But of course it was her. I would never forget those those smouldering dark eyes, or the petulant set of her full lips. *She* had not made up her face with fake red flowers. She was too vain. The delicate rambling rose tattoo on her jaw writhed as she chewed her protein bar.

According to Timmy Akhatli, Sophia had run to Valdivia. I had assumed she would stay there, hiding out until the heat was off.

So much for my assumptions. Instead of lying low, she had come looking for the TrZam 008.

She must know about the crown jewels of the Darkworlds, from Rafael Ijiuto.

And now here she was.

Ten feet from me.

Unaware that the "dog" sitting by the soup stall was her ex-husband.

How could she have forgotten this form? My wolf had been one of her favorites. I used to lie in wolf form on the sofa with her while we watched movies. I used to … no, better not think about *that*. Anyway, she clearly had forgotten my wolf, the same way she'd forgotten her own daughter's name.

I nosed around the ground, where bits of food had fallen from the soup stall, moving closer to them.

"I'm so fucking bored," said the girl Traveller, sitting on a folding chair.

"Suck it up, honey," Sophia said.

"How much longer ya figure this is going to take?" The boy was sitting on the steps of the big rig, chewing a toothpick.

"It'll take as long as it takes," Sophia said. "It's all part of the mission. Eyes on the prize." She spoke in a dry tone, as if she knew how empty the motivational phrases were.

I scratched the ground, pretending to have found something good-smelling. That took me another few steps closer.

Sophia sat forward as if a thought had suddenly struck her. "Think of it like this." Intellectual intensity animated her face. I had always loved that look on her. "The Divine wants each one of us to fulfill their potential. Our identities are formed through obedience to the Spirit of the Divine, which speaks to us through our patron deities, and guides us to the experiences we need to form our identities, or you could say our destinies."

She used to talk like this even before she left. In those days, her ideas about the Divine had been more indebted to Christianity. When she discovered the Traveller pantheon of trickster deities and hellraising demons, it must have clicked for her: here, at last, was a god, or a smorgasbord of gods, who reflected her own view of the universe. I had heard from Zane that the Travellers practised meditation to get in touch with their "patron deities." I wondered which one Sophia had chosen.

For that matter, what *about* Zane? Where was he? I had left him on Gvm Uye Sachttra with a mangled hand …

"The Divine has guided us here. We've been chosen, because we're the only ones in the whole damn universe who actually listen to the Spirit, and aren't afraid of its guidance. We are the elite who will take the next step towards humanity's destiny. That's no lie. But you know, it isn't all gonna be space battles and … and piles of money falling in your lap. Part of it is—" she gestured around the bazaar— "this. Let yourself experience it. It's neither good nor bad. Those are traps that we fall into. Mental failure modes. Whatever it is, it just *is.*"

The girl stared at her blankly. The boy removed his toothpick from his mouth and peered at the chewed end.

"OK," Sophia sighed. "Well." I almost felt for her at that moment. "Think of it like this, then. If we succeed, you'll be able to have anything you want. What do you want most in the universe? You'll get it."

This was more the boy's style. He started to posture about having his own ship, having a harem, owning slaves. But the girl looked at Sophia curiously.

"What do *you* want most in the universe, ma'am?"

Sophia smiled. "I want to look like I did when I was twenty-five, and live forever." She crossed her legs the other way, and her gaze fell on me. She held out her hand. "Here, doggy."

Her low, confident voice still had the power to wrap around my balls like a leash. Forget looking twenty-five, she still looked every bit as good to me as the day we met. What did it say about me that, even knowing what I did about her, I still would've screwed her again?

"Here, doggy." She tossed me a crumb of her protein bar.

Staying in character, I lipped it up from the ground. It was the kind that tastes like corned beef. Pretty good, even with a coating of dirt.

"Good doggy," she said. "Want some more?" She broke off a larger crumb and held it out in her fingers. Her face wore the mildly interested smile of a woman feeding a stray dog. "Here, boy …"

I shied away, playing wary. I was trying to think what to do.

What I should have done, of course, was run.

But I never was any damn good at turning my back on trouble.

"You look like my ex," Sophia said, and laughed.

My heart skipped a beat. I nosed a bit closer, sniffing the ground.

"I used to be married to a Shifter looked kind of like that dog," Sophia told the other two.

They all laughed.

"My ex looked like a dog, too," the boy said.

Sophia's eyes flicked to the big rig.

The door of the cab opened and a man's legs emerged. The boy jumped off the steps to make way. Sophia stood up.

The man came down the steps with easy grace.

It was Jonathan Burden.

Aw, fuck. *Fuck.*

A few days ago, I'd been chatting with Burden at the snow-blanketed spaceport on Mittel Trevoyvox. Now he was wearing shorts and carrying a .45 in a show-offy fringed holster. "Are we having fun yet? Don't answer that. Gotta tell you, Sophs, I did not think there could be a planet more boring and depressing than Mittel Trevoyvox, but this, yup. This is it."

No one got to call Sophia 'Sophs.' But apparently Burden did …

… and that wasn't all he got to do. He slung his left arm around Sophia's shoulders. She turned her face up and kissed him on the lips, long and deep. My neck fur bristled as I fought an absurd pang of jealousy. The ease of that kiss, expected and willingly given, gave me the impression that they had been on kissing terms for a long time.

When would I stop making awful discoveries about the woman I had married?

That's what I was here for. The truth. But nothing said I was going to like it.

"Face it," Burden yawned. "The girl's not here, or else the army has taken her into custody already."

"That's why we should assault their base, before they get a chance to ship her out," Sophia said.

"Fuck, no. We're way out on a limb here." Burden was ill at ease, surveying the bazaar. "All we need is for Starrunner to show up."

A tiny smile appeared on Sophia's lips. "You should've taken him out on Mittel T."

"I tried."

Sophia's smile spread into a hateful grin. "Well, now you get another chance." She pointed at me. "That's him. Kill him."

21

I was already springing at them as Sophia said, "Kill him." Burden drew so fast, I hardly saw his hand move. His gun went off behind me as I landed on the table. Cheap electronics showered to the ground under my scrabbling claws. The boy Traveller lunged at me with his bare hands in a harebrained display of courage. He bumped against Burden's gun arm and sent his next shot astray. I leapt to the ground and raced away among the stalls.

Panic spread outward from the gunshots like a ripple in a puddle. I heard Burden bellowing above the clamor: "Get him. Get him."

I dashed into a gap between two stalls … and a net descended on top of me. Through the plastic mesh, I glimpsed the excited faces of children. There had to be a dozen of them, all holding the edges of the dog-catching net. As I tried to run, I got more and more tangled up in it. I rolled onto my side and bit frantically at the mesh.

Burden ran towards me, gun levelled. "Outta the way," he yelled at the children.

Over my own desperate snarling, I heard the growl of an engine. It was right behind me! I rolled in the net, knocking a couple of kids over.

Our technical swept past, missing me by inches.

Ta-ta-ta-ta-ta!

The technical's roof gun yammered.

Burden hurled himself full-length on the dirt.

People fled in all directions. The junior dog-catching team fled, too, leaving me alone in my plastic prison.

The technical kept going. It knocked down the soup stall. Martin had lowered the cow-catcher plate. It swept the roof and the canopy of the soup stall before it, straight into the Travellers' stall.

I finally disentangled myself from the net and rolled to my feet.

The technical ground onwards, knocking down the Travellers' stall, scattering their wares. Exhaust blued the air. The engine roared. Martin pushed the drift of wreckage up against the big rig, trapping the two young Travellers behind it. He then reversed in a big circle, knocking down more stalls.

I raced towards the technical. On the way, I passed Burden. He was sitting on the ground, groaning. Blood welled from a wound in the meat of his left forearm. I thought about finishing him off then and there, but there wasn't time. Bullets were still flying around, and I was in the open.

Martin leaned across and opened the passenger side door of the technical without slowing down. I leapt in at full tilt. The thought then crossed my mind: If Martin was driving, *who'd been shooting?* No sooner had I wondered it than I saw the long, spindly grippers clamped on the stock and trigger guard of the roof gun, and the lamp-like eyes telescoped up through the hatch. I tracked the attachments back to MF, who was lying on his side behind the seats. He had extruded his neck to a full three feet, so he could see out while his body stayed safely below. "I got him!" he squealed. "Did you see, Mike?"

Useless in a fight? Not so much. It gave me pause to see the robot operating a gun, shooting at human beings. On the other hand, these human beings were trying to kill us. I scanned through the windshield for Sophia. I couldn't see her.

A bullet pinged off the technical's hood.

"There she is," I shouted. Sophia was up in the cab of the big rig, shooting at us through the window.

"Fuck her," Martin said. He put the technical into forward gear and drove out of the bazaar with pieces of stall canopy still flapping off the cow-catcher plate. "We're getting out of here."

"I didn't find Pippa," I gasped.

"Too bad. There's army around here. Watch them blame *us* for that mess." He sped up, clipping tents. "They'll have to catch us first."

"How'd you know I was in trouble?"

"Didn't," Martin said, laughing. "Got worried when you didn't come back. Figured I would do a reconnaissance. First thing I see is you tangled up in that damn net."

"Saved my ass."

But we were not out of the woods yet. I kept my eyes peeled out the back for pursuit. As we passed the Hurtworlds Authority office, I scrutinized the building, worried about that volunteer.

She burst out of the front door, running. Behind her came another, smaller female.

"Stop," I yelled at Martin. *"Stop!"*

He braked. Pippa sprinted up to the technical. "Mike?" she cried. "Martin? Is it really you?"

"She was upstairs," the volunteer panted. "I hid her … She says she knows you."

"You," I said, "are a hero. I'd kiss you if I wasn't a wolf at the moment." The volunteer could only gape in astonishment. "Stay safe. Wait!"

The panic in the bazaar had died down, or at any rate wasn't getting any closer. We had a few seconds.

"MF," I ordered, "all the stuff. Dump it all out the back. Not the diesel. Everything else."

The bot obeyed.

"Clothes and shoes," I said. "Toys. Electronics—the good stuff with AI. Music, books, films. Chocolate, candy, vitamins. I forget what else. Give it to the kids, share it around. Oh, and the guy with a beard." I pointed back to the bazaar. "He may try to pass himself off as a HA official. He *is* a HA official, but he's also a Traveller. So are his associates. Tell the army. *Don't* give him any help."

Pippa scrambled into the passenger seat. She squeezed in next to me and closed the door.

"Goodbye," she called to the HA volunteer. "And thank you, thank you, thank you."

Martin accelerated back to the main road.

*

Against the odds, we had found Pippa. I studied her as Martin drove at breakneck speed away from Camp 32. Her arms were sticks, her cheeks unnaturally hollow. I wished we hadn't given away all the chocolate and candy—she sure looked like she could use it. Her ragged shirt and shorts smelled unwashed, as did her dirty blonde hair.

Did she still have the TrZam 008? A chain hung around her neck, but whatever was on it was hidden inside her shirt.

I freed my neck fur from her clinging fingers. "Don't look." Of course she did, and saw the unseemly contortions of my Shift back into human form. I struggled into my clothes. Pain sang through my body. I hadn't been shot, but I had so many bruises from my struggles in the dog-catching net that it almost felt like I had.

Pippa smiled. "It really is you," she breathed.

"Sure is." I uncapped a bottle of soda, drank half of it off in one gulp.

"The army tried to arrest me, even though I didn't do anything. Charlotte stood up to them." That must be the volunteer's name. "She hid me in the HA building. Then those other people came, so I had to stay hidden. For days and days. Then *you* came. Charlotte thought maybe you were from the Fleet or something. But when I looked out the window, I saw Martin in the parking lot. I *thought* it was you," she said to Martin, "but I wasn't quite sure … But then when you came back, I saw the wolf. I mean, I saw *you,* Mike. Then I knew. I'm so glad you came for me. *So* glad. Thank you. I mean, it doesn't seem like enough, just saying that. But thank you, thank you."

"Don't thank me yet." I drank the rest of the soda. Met Martin's eyes in the rearview mirror. He raised his eyebrows. I shrugged.

Camp 32 fell behind us, shrinking into a green line on the desert, like a false oasis. Where were we going to take Pippa? This hadn't been in the plan. Not that I'd really had a plan, beyond "figure it out when we get there." Now we were there ... but so were the Travellers.

MF had been silently staring at Pippa all this time. Suddenly he shot out a gripper and fumbled at her neck. She cried out, shrank back, but he'd caught hold of the chain around her neck. The TrZam 008 popped free of her t-shirt, diamonds sparkling in the sunlight.

"Lay off!" I shouted, chopping my hand down on MF's gripper. He let go. Pippa scrabbled into the far corner of the technical, clutching the device. "Leave her alone. That's *hers.*" Shame gnawed at me. I didn't want Pippa to see us as predators like the Travellers.

"Aw babe!" MF groaned. "Lemme just see it! Come on. I'll give it back! I only need it for a minute!"

"The famous crown jewels?" Martin said. "Not even gonna let us have a look, darling? After we saved your life?"

"No," Pippa gasped. The device vanished inside her grubby fist. The gratitude in her eyes changed to fear.

"Are you sure?" Martin waggled his eyebrows. "I'll do stupid snake tricks for it ..."

"Gimme!" MF blared. He lunged past me and reached for Pippa again. She ducked, not fast enough. His gripper caught her chin, and she let out a cry.

Shocked by MF's violence, I caught his gripper and twisted it sideways. It started to retract into his housing. I bore down, using it as a lever to knock him onto his side. I brought one knee down on the brushed-steel surface of his chassis. "Stand the fuck down, MF. That's an order!"

"Go easy on the suitcase," Martin said.

"Just reminding him that he works for me."

I had never actually pushed this point before. I wasn't sure, when it came down to it, that MF did work for me. He lived in my spaceship. That wasn't the same thing.

But lying there on his back, he squeaked, "Sorry." His neck curved up and his optical sensor covers blinked at Pippa. Her chin was bleeding. "Sorry! I didn't mean to do that! You're much too cute to hurt!"

"Forget the device," I said. "We'll discuss it later. Marty? We've got a seventy-hour drive back to the spaceport. There could be other Travellers around. I'm not confident of making it. Let's call the *St. Clare.*" It was illegal to land a spaceship outside the spaceport. But I would rather commit a crime than wind up dead.

"Already did," Martin said. "They'll contact us on the HF when they're in the air."

I smiled for the first time since we reached Camp 32. Good ol' snake. "Excellent. Pippa?" I didn't know what to do for her, how to help her. "You hungry?"

She shook her head, still eyeing MF fearfully. "I don't need anything."

"Well, I'm hungry." We had some iron rations—vacuum packs of polenta and tempeh, dried fruit, whatever Irene had selected from the *St. Clare's* stores. When I opened packets and started eating, Pippa changed her mind. She gnawed the unappetizing long-life foodstuffs with utter concentration. As I had suspected, she was starving. The desert jolted past.

"Do you know why they were after you?" I said at length.

She looked up. Mouth full. Frightened. "The pedlars?"

"Yes."

"I—I … no."

"They were Travellers. The same ones that tried to kill you on Gvm Uye Sachttra."

Her eyes flicked from me to MF. "I guess maybe they wanted the crown jewels."

"I don't mean to pry, but what *are* the crown jewels?"

"I don't know." She stuffed a dried fig into her mouth. "I don't know!"

Martin said, "Heads up."

His tone gained my total attention.

"Company."

I twisted and looked out of the technical's narrow slot of a back windshield.

A puff of dust rose from the road behind us.

As it crested a shallow rise, I made out the glowering profile of the Travellers' big rig.

They were chasing us.

22

THE Traveller rig caught up steadily. Within a few minutes, we could hear its engine growling across the desert, a menacing echo of our own engine as Martin pushed the technical to its limits.

80 klicks per hour. 100.

There was nothing else on the road, if you could call this smoothed-out strip of desert a road. The sun was finally starting to sink, lengthening the shadows of small boulders and sparse thorny bushes. Ahead of us, the plain stretched unchanging to the horizon. There was nothing between here and Camp 31, about 30 klicks away.

At 120 kph, the technical started to rattle and rock dangerously. Martin struggled to control it, while bouncing over the uneven road surface. He finally had to ease off on the gas. "This is it!" he yelled. "Can't go any faster! They're gonna catch up!"

The Traveller rig was relentlessly closing the distance, engine howling.

"Pippa," I said, "get down on the floor. Give me those ammo canisters when I tell you to."

I wasn't letting MF do any more shooting. His aim was crap, anyway. I stood up, steadying myself on the machine-gun's tripod. Hot, dusty wind thundered into my face. The gun could rotate 360 degrees. I hauled it around to face backwards, locked it, and flipped the lever to automatic.

The Traveller rig was now only about 200 meters behind us. I sighted on the grille, which had been chopped up to look like teeth, and fired.

With no ear protection, the roar of the gun seemed to scour out the inside of my head. I struggled to keep it level, while resisting the urge to clap my hands over my ears. Sparks flew off the Traveller rig's hood. One of the square, eye-like panes of the windshield frosted over. I was at least hitting the rig, no mean feat at 100 klicks an hour while bouncing all over the road. The canister clicked empty. I reached down, shouting, "Reload!" Pippa slapped a fresh canister into my hand.

The frosted side of the big rig's windshield shattered. I hadn't done that. The butt of a handgun whaled on the glass from inside, knocking out the shards. Then Sophia's head and shoulders emerged. Half inside the cab, half out, she braced her elbows on the hood and fired at me.

I ducked back down inside the technical. Kneeling under the tripod, I fitted the fresh ammo canister into the machine-gun.

The back window of the technical blew out.

"Aim at the driver," Martin yelled, "the driver!"

We were running out of time. The rig was so close now that it blocked out the sun from the hole where our back windshield used to be. I could look out and back into the grille's teeth.

Sophia fired again, this time hitting the edge of the hatch, keeping my head down.

The big rig nudged our back bumper. The jolt threw me against the seats. Martin cursed and stamped on the accelerator.

Another bump.

I popped my head out of the hatch.

Sophia had started to climb out of the rig's windshield, sliding feet first down the hood. She meant to board us, at 100 kph.

I looked into her eyes, and at the gun in her hand, as she struggled to bring it up—too late. She had not thought I would actually shoot her.

And I didn't.

I fired into the other side of the windshield, smashing it and perforating the body of whoever was driving.

I would never know if it was the boy who had wanted his own ship, or the girl who had been bored with playing pedlars. Both of them would have been novices, the second-lowest level in the Traveller hierarchy. To the Travellers, novices are two a penny. They sign up for nothing—for the promise of something—for the good times. This one died instantly.

His or her body must have fallen across the steering wheel. The rig veered off the road. Sophia slid across the hood.

She was flat on her back, holding on with one hand over her head, inches from death, and yet she still found the will and the focus to get off one more shot.

She was aiming at me, but instead, by sheer luck, she hit our right rear tire. It blew out. The first I knew of it was when the technical lurched suddenly to the side. We were still going 100 kph. At that kind of speed, any sudden loss of stability can be fatal. We lurched. Martin frantically steered into the slew. We fishtailed, but didn't stop. The technical rolled, first on the road and then off it, bouncing like a toy flung by some angry giant.

I wrapped my arms and legs around the machine-gun's tripod, which was securely bolted to the floor, and held on for dear life as MF and the jerrycans and everything flew around, crashing into me, down and then up again.

The technical rolled one last time. I lost my grip on the tripod. We skidded a few more feet, and stopped.

I opened my eyes. I was looking up at the tripod, and at the side wall.

When I moved, broken safety glass crunched under my back.

The good news was I *could* move. Nothing broken.

The reek of diesel filled my nose.

I turned my head. MF lay beside me in a pool of diesel. One or more of the jerrycans had come open.

"Out." I struggled into a sitting position. "Out, out, out!"

Martin had been wearing his seatbelt. Pippa had survived the crash by bracing her body against the sides of the footwell. MF forced the back door with his grippers. Shaken and bruised, we clambered out into the sunset.

The technical wasn't going any further today, even if we could have rolled it right side up. Steam jetted from its crumpled hood.

Crack.

A bullet skipped off a stone, raising a puff of dust near Martin's feet.

We hit the ground.

I raised my head and peered across a quarter-klick of sand and stones … at the Traveller rig.

It, too, had crashed onto its side. It looked like a giant silver maggot with a truck's head.

Movement flickered behind its cab.

At least one of the Travellers had survived. Somehow I knew it was Sophia.

Crack.

I ducked my head to the dirt, breathing in the heat of the sun-warmed desert.

"We have to get away from the technical," I gasped. "Drenched—in diesel. If they've got tracer rounds …"

A tracer round, fired from that distance, could ignite, set fire to the fuel, and turn the technical into a fireball. Diesel isn't as volatile as gasoline, but I still didn't want to take the risk of being crisped.

We belly-crawled away, keeping the technical between us and the Traveller rig. It felt like crawling over a griddle. The ground had been heated to a scorching temperature during Yesanyase Skont's long day. Grit got inside my clothes. My shoulder and stomach muscles burned with a deep tiredness that told me I'd already hit my physical limits. I was running on adrenaline now, and I'd pay for it later. If we survived.

We came to a low ridge, no more than a wrinkle in the desert, topped by stunted thorn bushes. It would do for cover as long as we stayed down. We crawled behind it. When I thought we'd gone far enough, I popped my head up.

From this angle, the tank of the Traveller rig blocked my view of Sophia and whoever else might be hiding behind the vehicle. There was not enough cover between here and there for them to sneak up on us, anyway.

It was so quiet that I could hear my own heartbeat in my ears, and the thorn bushes rustling in the breeze.

"Marty, you got your piece?"

"Fell outta my holster. Couldn't lay hands on it."

I still had my .22. A lot of good that would do at this distance. If I lived through this, I really was going to start carrying a more powerful weapon.

"We could run," Martin said.

"To where?" I said. "Better stay put. The *St. Clare* will be here soon." But would Dolph and Irene be able to find us? We couldn't radio them our location, because the HF was in the technical. Maybe I should go back for it. It was probably trashed, anyway …

"They know we were at Camp 32," Martin said. "They'll figure it out. Hard to miss two crashed Hurtworlds Specials in this thrillingly diverse terrain." He nudged Pippa. "Starting to wish you'd stayed at the camp?"

She had not complained once—about the chase, the crash, or the exhausting crawl over hot, sandy ground. Now she shook her head. "I'd rather be anywhere than there."

I rolled onto my back. The sky was beautiful. It had begun to turn a dusty darker blue on the side away from the setting sun. A few high clouds glowed pink. There was not a contrail in the whole vast dome, not a single spark that might be a low-flying ship.

The *St. Clare* was not technically an atmosphere-capable spacecraft. That is, she didn't have wings. Her chunky auxiliary pods could be angled to act as aerofoils, but they provided no lift. So on her short hop from the spaceport to here, she would have to travel ballistically. That meant Dolph would have next to no wiggle room to adjust his trajectory as the ship came back down. He'd have to find us, plot our location, and calibrate his descent, all within a matter of seconds. God, I hoped he had gotten the drugs out of his system. If we died in the desert because he was too fried to fly with his usual agility, I'd never forgive him …

"What was that?" MF squeaked.

Moments later, my less acute ears picked up the sound he had heard.

The growl of an engine, faint but clear in all that emptiness.

It was coming from the direction of Camp 31.

I screwed myself around in our shallow dip. It did not hide us from the road. I had a perfect view of the paler strip of desert shooting off to nowhere.

A cloud of dust on the horizon.

A black dot.

A Hurtworlds Special, the twin of the Traveller rig.

Still I clung to hope—until the ugly tanker stopped, at the place where our technical had gone off the road.

And Zane Cole got out.

23

I should have known. The Travellers had narrowed it down, but not as far as MF had. They'd been searching Camp 31, as well. There were probably "pedlars" in *every* damn camp around here.

And we were trapped in the middle of them.

Zane walked towards us, black coat flapping. Two novices followed him, also in full Traveller gear. The masks were off now. They were letting their pirate flags fly.

One of the novices jogged towards Sophia's crashed rig. The other stayed with Zane. She had a shotgun.

As they came closer, I saw that Zane's right sleeve ended in a hook.

I had mauled his hand on Gvm Uye Sachttra. Guess he'd had to amputate it.

I stood up. Damned if I was going to die sitting down. "I see you went for the traditional look," I said, gesturing at the hook. "Couldn't afford a real prosthetic?" My voice sounded loud in the desert silence.

Zane scowled. He was a big guy, blond hair shaved at the sides. I'd always thought he had the face of a pissed-off chipmunk. I could smell the trophies on his coat, an aroma of leather and rot. "It's a Traveller tradition to scalp our enemies. This makes it easy … and more enjoyable." He held up the hook. It was actually a pair of scissors, curved like a sickle. He made the blades clack, a flat, chilling sound. "Step away from the girl."

I did not move. "What happened to stealing ships and selling them for parts? Wasn't that exciting enough for you? What kind of a mess you got yourself mixed up in here?"

Something flashed in Zane's eyes. "Why didn't you just leave it alone, man? You didn't have to get mixed up in this."

"What is it? Urush technology? What? Anti-gravity? Nano-replication? A new FTL drive?"

Zane's eyes widened. He laughed out loud. So did the novice standing by his side. "He doesn't know," Zane said. For a moment it seemed like he couldn't stop laughing. A chill went down my back all the way to my knees. "He doesn't know."

"Care to enlighten me?"

Instead of answering, Zane said, "How'd you find her?"

"Easy," I said. "She wanted to be found by us. She didn't want to be found by you." I was wondering if I could draw my .22 fast enough to shoot him before the novice shot me. Hiding my thoughts, I glanced in the direction of the crashed rig. The other novice had almost reached it. If Sophia was still alive, when she got here, we would die. *She* had no interest in talking to me. "Why're you still working with Sophia, Cole? She doesn't care about you."

Zane shrugged. The sunset was in his eyes, making him squint. He should have moved around us to put the sun at his back. It was a dumb mistake, and one he'd never have made on Tech Duinn. "This is bigger than any of us. How I feel about it, how you feel about it doesn't matter."

"What about Burden? Looked like she was loving on him back there."

"Got nothing to do with me."

"She made you feel special," I said, "and then she moved on to the next guy who had something she wanted. And you're *still* taking her orders. My God, man, have some dignity."

"Step away from the girl," he grated, raising his hook.

Then his gaze flashed away from us. Sophia was striding back across the desert with the other novice—*and* Burden. The bastard was back on his feet, shirtless, with his left arm in a makeshift sling. I should've torn his throat out when I had the chance.

"Over here," yelled Zane, the good soldier, waving at them, like he expected a reward for catching us.

Faster than ever in my life, I drew my .22. I didn't shoot Zane. He wasn't the one with a gun.

I shot the novice.

She was a young woman with a mass of frizzy hair. A dragon spread its wings on her forehead. She had been someone's baby once, someone's little girl.

I shot her.

I didn't have time to aim properly, but I didn't need to. At ten paces, you can't miss even when shooting from the hip.

She clutched her stomach and doubled over, screaming. The shotgun fell to the ground.

As fast as a snake striking, Martin sprang for it.

Zane was already whirling. His hook sliced through the air, aiming to claw Martin's back.

I fired again. The bullet went through the sleeve of Zane's coat.

Martin dived on the shotgun like a rugby player, and rolled on the ground, bringing it up.

Sophia fired. Running across the desert, she shot again and again. So did the novice with her.

I charged at Pippa and knocked her to the ground, knowing I was too late. I expected to feel the agony of bullets ripping through my flesh. The impact winded me. Alien sand gritted in my mouth. I raised my head, dragging air into my lungs in great whoops.

Sophia was still running towards us. She was shooting straight at me. I could see straight down the barrel of her gun, my vision blurred by dust. The gunfire sounded oddly far away.

A meter in front of me, something fell to the ground with a muffled clink. I watched it roll away. I noticed that the wind had dropped completely. The screams of the novice seemed to be coming from further away. And then I understood.

It wasn't the *dust* that made Sophia look blurry.

MF stood upright on his wheels right behind me, clutching a fold of Pippa's shorts in one gripper. A disk-shaped attachment I'd never seen before stuck out of the side of his chassis. He said, "I do not have enough power to sustain a field of this size for long."

MF had a force field projector.

He had cast a field around me, Pippa, Martin … and Zane.

Zane lay on the ground, spitting out curses. Martin stood over him with the shotgun levelled at his belly. "Put him out of his misery?"

"No," I said. "Wait."

Sophia slammed into the force field while running flat out. She rebounded, staggered back, and fell on her ass. Martin laughed. I did not.

Sophia stood up. The novice I had shot was still screaming. Sophia walked over to her and shot her in the head. The screaming stopped.

Sophia walked all the way around the force field. It was a circular enclosure, about two meters across. We were jammed together in here. Sophia prodded MF's field projector through the thinness of the field. Then she walked back around to me, smiling with her mouth, not her eyes. "How much for the bot?"

"Not for sale," I said, wondering exactly how long MF could keep this up. A few minutes? A few hours? I didn't ask him, because I didn't want the Travellers to know. I placed one palm on the field—like touching a balloon, but slippery—and moved it upwards. I didn't even have to stand on tiptoe before my fingers found the top.

Sophia swung at my exposed fingertips. I lowered my hand.

"What are you doing here, anyway?" She had a bruise blossoming on one cheek. Grains of safety glass sparkled in her hair. "Who sent you?"

"No one. I came for Lucy."

"For *Lucy?*"

"She deserves to know the truth."

"Oh, bullshit, Mike. You thought there might be money in it. Your perspective is so damn limited. You never see any further than the next big score."

"I have IVK," I burst out. "You infected me at the same time as you infected Pippa. I guess you could say that's given me a new perspective on life. A new outlook. New goals."

Sophia covered her mouth with one hand. She turned to Burden, who had limped up to join her. "He's got IVK," she gasped. I thought for a second she was crying. But she was laughing. "Oh my God. That's fucking hilarious. We got him. Shit, Mike, sorry, I shouldn't laugh, but cosmic irony, much?"

I scratched my ear, suppressing my reaction. "Guess you might feel differently about that in a while."

"Oh yeah?"

"I mentioned I've got some new goals. One of them is to put you in the ground before I die." I didn't mean it until I said it, and then I did mean it.

"Oh yeah? Go on." She ripped her drapey shirt open down the front, exposing her breastbone and the rest of her rose tattoo. It coiled around one of her full, pale breasts as if it grew out of the nipple. "Force fields work both ways," she said. "Go on, shoot me! Enjoy the rebound."

"Ship's coming," Burden said, disengaged from the conversation, watching a handheld.

"I could cure you." She pushed on the force field. It dimpled inwards under the pressure of her fingertips. Without thinking, I reached for her hand. The slippery thinness of the force field held our fingers apart. "Just give me the TrZam 008 and I'll tell you how to get well."

"Oh, you're as full of shit as ever, honey," I said. "There is no cure."

"So you're just going to lie down and die? That's not the guy I married."

As she spoke, the rose tattoo was growing. It curled across both of her breasts and her collarbone, sprouting open mouths and bloody scimitars in place of flowers. The "bruise" on her cheek turned into the squared-off head of the goddess Cipactli, eater of humans. Sophia had a full set of Traveller tattoos. She'd just had them switched off until now. The dark rainbow flooding over her skin both fascinated and repelled me.

"Don't let IVK win." she said, and the Cipactli-head mouthed the words along with her.

I glanced at Pippa. She was frozen, clutching her pendant in one white-knuckled fist. Then I met Martin's eyes—hollow with shock.

Oh. He had not known about my diagnosis … until I just blurted it out. Why had I done that, anyway? Because Sophia used to be my wife, and some stupid part of me had thought she might be sympathetic?

A sonic boom shook the sky. A bright speck hurtled out of the sunset.

All of us stared up.

The approaching ship's engines echoed around the sky. Fear and hope warred in my mind as it descended, until I made out the four fat auxiliary engine pods, and the rounded "head," silhouetted against the sunset.

The Travellers—Sophia, Burden, and the surviving novice—must have been expecting a ship of their own. When they saw that this was not it, they ran for Zane's rig.

The *St. Clare* gimballed its auxiliaries in its final braking maneuvers, and dropped out of the sky on four plasma candles.

But it did not land immediately.

It descended to 0.5 VTOL altitude—about 50 meters—and *hovered,* burning the auxiliaries.

A missile slammed into the Traveller rig standing on the road. It erupted into a fireball. It was, after all, a tanker full of diesel.

The three Travellers were about halfway to the rig at that point. They stumbled to a halt on the desert, their escape cut off.

Another missile screamed out of the launcher and plowed into the crashed rig. *Woomp.*

The *St. Clare* dropped on shrinking jets, with a crackling noise as if the air itself were burning. MF cancelled his force field, releasing us from our shimmering cage.

Zane immediately tried to run. Martin whacked him on the head with the butt of the shotgun. Grabbing Zane's arms, we stumbled away from the fireballs, towards the *St. Clare.* It had landed on the flattest bit of ground available. Thorn bushes burnt merrily under the ship's tail. Oven-temperature air washed over us as we staggered between the auxiliaries. The sky was still thundering.

I pushed Pippa up the ladder. She climbed with her t-shirt over her hands, yelping at the heat of the metal rungs.

MF followed her. He had been holding onto her all the time we were running, as if scared she might get away.

"I'm going back." I reached for the shotgun hanging off Martin's shoulder. "I'm going to get her."

"No, you're not," he grunted, and pointed at the sky.

A bright glint grew like a falling meteor. Engines screamed like feedback.

We hauled Zane up the ladder. I was the last in. I burrowed into the airlock chamber and turned around to close the outer door.

The Travellers' ship had just landed on the other side of the road. It was, of course, white. The letters on its fuselage said HURTWORLDS AUTHORITY.

24

DOLPH's voice boomed over the PA system, which we hardly ever used. "Strap in for evasive maneuvers."

I was still in the trunk corridor. The floor tipped up to a steep angle as Dolph opened the main engine throttle, pushing the *St. Clare* into an ascent trajectory. I grabbed the zero-gee handholds to stop myself from sliding all the way back to the engineering deck. I mountaineered forward, one handhold at a time, fighting the launch gravity. I reached the bridge as the ship lurched violently to starboard. "What are we evading?" I shouted.

"Autonomous missiles." Dolph slumped in the pilot's couch, hands leaping over consoles visible and invisible. "The fuckers were dropping them all the way down." The ship jinked sideways again. I fell into my seat. On my left, Irene hunched over the weapons console, orchestrating rapid defensive fire from our Gausses. The masers were less useful in-atmosphere; too much scattering and absorption.

I strapped in and crushed my AR headset over my head. The urgent *ping-ping-ping* of missile warnings drilled into my ears. I toggled over to the optical feed. Missile contrails and the puffs of mid-air explosions mimicked clouds below the ship. We were already hundreds of klicks away from our launch site, but the computer had just picked up the plasma burst of the Travellers' ship launching. "They're coming after us."

"Surprise, surprise," Dolph said.

"Sophia was there."

"I thought that looked like her," Irene said. "I wasn't sure if you would want me to shoot her."

"Nah," I said. "She's mine."

"You shoulda left Zane fucking Cole back there, with a bullet in his brain," Dolph said. "We got him on board, *and* Pippa? No wonder they're chasing us."

I plotted the HA ship's launch path. "Actually, they're not," I said in surprise. Burden's ship had launched on a shallower angle. The gap widened by a hundred klicks a second, rapidly taking it out of range of the *St. Clare's* railgun.

"Could be it's unarmed. They dropped these babies out of the cargo bay. Air-breathing engines, they can loiter for hours." Dolph leaned on the auxiliaries. Gravity dragged us sideways.

"Incoming!" Irene yelled. An impact shook the ship. My teeth vibrated in my skull. The missile had struck amidships, not near the drive, thank God. Hull damage alerts filled my HUD area. No pressurization breach. Hull integrity down to 20% at the impact site. Another missile strike there would finish us.

But we were now leaving the troposphere. The air-breathing missiles could not follow us into space.

The damage alerts beeped relentlessly as the *St. Clare* howled up to orbital altitude.

"Main engine cutoff in five," Dolph gasped. "Three. Four …" Gravity released us.

"That was some shit-hot flying." I was glad he didn't know I had mentally doubted him.

He shrugged. "We got hit."

"Yup. But it's not structural. Shouldn't affect acceleration capability." I was frantically calculating the parameters for our FTL burn. "We'll repair it in the field." Because the Yesanyase Skont spaceport was near the south pole, we had launched into a polar orbit. That helped. As we looped over the north pole and orbited back down, the Core lay dead ahead of us. And beyond the Core … *far* beyond … was home.

I willed the computer to complete its checks before our orientation window closed and we had to go around the planet again. "MF? Marty?" I spoke into the intercom. "How are our passengers coping?"

"I got Pippa with me," Martin said.

"I put the Traveller in the admin berth, and instructed him to strap in," MF said virtuously.

"Good. Keep him there." The computer popped up a notification. "Burn parameters validated. Initiating acceleration burn on my mark."

"Initiating exhaust field." Dolph threw the skip field generator switch.

"Mark." I opened the throttle.

In the instant before the *St. Clare* kicked out of orbit, Irene interrupted, "Heads up!" The radar display flashed. A triangular ship's profile breasted the curvature of the planet.

"It's just a Fleet patrol. They won't mess with us." Giddy with the relief of escaping, I had to shout over the engines. Thrust gravity pushed down on us, so that we seemed to be lying on our backs again. Yesanyase Skont shrank.

The radio squawked. "Independent freighter *St. Clare,* come in. This is the Fleet picket *Williencourt.* Where you off to in such a hurry?"

"You were saying?" Irene murmured.

"We'll just pretend we didn't hear that." I knew that ignoring the Fleet ship was a bad idea, but I didn't have any better ones. "They won't chase us, anyway. They have to remain in orbit."

As the words left my mouth, I stared at the radar in despair. The Fleet ship *was* chasing us. We were already moving at several thousand kps, as the exhaust field accelerated the speed of the plasma particles exiting the *St. Clare's* drive … but so was the *Williencourt.*

Dolph rattled his fingernails on his consoles. "Acceleration is up to 0.15 gees. Go FTL?" They wouldn't be able to catch us then. In STL mode, the *St. Clare* had no advantage over a high-spec Fleet ship, but in FTL mode, she was without peer. On the other hand, 0.15 gees of acceleration wasn't enough to get us home—

"Independent freighter *St. Clare!* Do you read me?"

"They're targeting us," Irene said. Warning lights decorated my consoles like a Christmas tree.

"Acknowledge, or I shove a nuke up your tailpipe. Last chance. Three, two …"

Tonelessly, I said, "This is the *St. Clare,* reading you."

"Acknowledged," the *Williencourt's* captain said. "Hold your course and stand by to be boarded."

I blinked. "That's nuts." I checked our speed. 2,800 kps. We were well on our way out of the Yesanyase Skont system. Even if we cut the exhaust field right now, we would still be travelling at almost 1% of the speed of light. With sincere curiosity, I said, "How are you planning to do that?"

"Watch and learn," the radio crackled.

The *Williencourt* overhauled us, and then decreased its acceleration to precisely match ours, while also matching our trajectory to the last fraction of a degree. It edged closer and closer. We all watched open-mouthed. In orbit, this is easy. While travelling at 1% of c? It's the definition of insane.

"Guess that's why they pay Fleet pilots the big bucks," Dolph muttered.

"It's their computer doing it," MF quacked over the intercom. "It is actually a rather stupid machine."

"That's not reassuring," I said.

At 20 meters of separation, the exhaust fields of the two ships met. The fields melded seamlessly into one, making it appear on our monitors as if the *St. Clare's* exhaust field had doubled in size. Now we were coupled with the *Williencourt* in an unsavory Siamese-twin bond, still streaking out of the system.

Grapples thunked on our hull. The *St. Clare* jarred from nose to stern.

"Docking completed," the *Williencourt's* captain said. "Lower your force field shields and prepare for boarding."

I stabbed the intercom. "Marty, listen up. It's not the end of the world if they find Cole, but if they find Pippa, we're fucked. Have you got her hidden?"

No answer from ol' snake. I hoped that was a good sign. I popped my straps and flew down the trunk corridor. Tucked my shirt into my pants. Ran one hand over my hair, although nothing would stop it standing up like a short brown halo. My heart beat like a kettledrum as I waited at the starboard airlock for our unwanted guests.

25

THE airlock opened. A flock of white and silver tadpoles whirred out of the chamber and rushed past me to disperse through the ship. Sniffer drones. They would have motion sensors, infrared, and probably atmospheric samplers as well.

A Fleet NCO flew out of the airlock after the drones and oriented herself to face me, using wrist and ankle thrusters built into her form-fitting suit. A PDD clung to her left shoulder. Personal defense drones are like miniature gunships crossed with tasers. They can fire either flechettes, or contact pads that deliver shocks of thousands of volts. The PDD's blue laser targeting beam dotted my chest.

"Welcome aboard, ma'am," I said.

"Stay where you are." The voice came from external speakers in her domed, reflective helmet. "Open all internal pressure doors and hatches."

"Open 'em up," I called to Dolph. All along the corridor, doors slid open. The sniffer drones darted into the berths and compartments. Two or three of them flew onto the bridge. Dolph told me later that they lit on the consoles like pigeons and plugged themselves into the data ports. He and Irene just had to sit there and watch the things drinking up our professional life's blood.

Back in the trunk corridor, the airlock cycled again. Another Fleet officer, this one with O-3 stripes on his spacesuit, slid out. His helmet retracted into his collar, exposing bristly black hair and a lantern jaw that slid from side to side as he chewed tobacco. "Captain Starrunner?"

"Yes."

"Captain Smith of the *Williencourt.*" Striking cobalt-blue eyes, a smile as cold as deep space. Metal implants in the lobes of his ears, like gauge earrings. PDD on his shoulder. "Where are you headed at this time?"

"Ponce de Leon."

"I see. What was the meaning of your maneuvers on the surface of Yesanyase Skont?"

"We were attacked." I decided the truth was my best defense. "We acted in self-defense. Heck, you must have seen the damage on our hull—"

"It looks worse than it is. You got one hull plate crumpled, and potentially some electrical damage under that, but nothing structural that we observed. What did that?"

"Travellers," I said.

Smith looked disbelieving. "Travellers on Yesanyase Skont?" He roared with laughter, and I belatedly caught the sarcasm. "When *haven't* there been Travellers on Yesanyase Skont? They use those bazaars as their personal money laundering facilities. And the gladiatorial arenas? They operate those for fun and profit." A salacious spark danced in his eyes. "Mortal combat between humans and aliens, for the viewing enjoyment of the whole Cluster. Interspecies rape shows on request. Did you get a chance to go?"

"No, sir, ain't my thing." I was disliking him more and more. He floated closer to me. I could smell his chaw. Mint flavor.

"So why did they attack you, Mr. Starrunner?"

"Sir, if you know Travellers, you know they don't need a reason. But you may not know that these Travellers are using Hurtworlds Authority ships. If you intercept the HA ship that just launched from the same location as us, you'll find it is manned by black-coats."

Smith spoke into his radio. As far as I could follow his Fleet jargon, it sounded like he was telling his comms officer to verify the identity of Burden's ship. But that wouldn't get them anywhere, because of course it *was* a real HA ship. I clenched my fists in frustration. Sophia was going to slip through the Fleet's fingers again.

While Smith spoke, the NCO came out of my berth, sniffer drones whirring around her. She floated into the engineering deck. *Shit.* She was going to find Pippa. She couldn't not—

She flew back out. MF arrowed out of the pressure door behind her, eyes glowing, grippers clattering.

"What is that?" Smith said.

"Sir, it appears to be a maintenance bot." The NCO was holding her bottom. "Sir, it made inappropriate comments, and—and pinched me."

Tense as I was, I wasn't tempted to laugh. But Smith did. "That's fucking hilarious."

"You look so hot in that spacesuit!" MF drifted towards the non-com, lasciviously swivelling his sensors. "I wish *my* crew had ones like that!"

The NCO protested. Smith roared with laughter. "Get over it, Figueroa. Go do your job."

"Won't you please take your helmet off?" MF blocked the NCO's way, wheedling. He actually tried to catch her arm in his grippers. He was getting more handsy. First the thing with Pippa, and now this. To be fair, I knew he was trying to stall them. But I had no idea how to capitalize on the time he was buying me.

One of the sniffer drones flew out of the engineering deck, dodged around MF, and landed on Smith's wrist like a tiny homing pigeon. And it was too late.

"Aha," Smith said. "You've got some explaining to do, Starrunner. You have a crew of four, not including that mechanical comedian there. And as far as I am aware, none of your crew members is a teenage girl."

He chewed energetically, pinning me with his weirdly lustrous eyes. "We have reason to believe you illegally removed a deportee from the Hurtworlds. Would that be her back there?"

My tongue stuck to the roof of my mouth. This was it. I couldn't talk my way out of this one. We were all going to jail.

MF, still blocking the door of the engineering deck, suddenly let out a parping noise that got everyone's attention. "Captain Smith! Specialist Figueroa! You will return to your own ship immediately. You will file a report stating that this ship is a law-abiding freighter. Further, you will state that this ship is carrying nothing and no one apart from her own crew and supplies. Is that clear?"

Smith's jaw stilled. "What the actual fuck?"

"Is that clear?" MF blared. I had heard him sound like this before, when he was upset—but *act* like this? Giving orders to humans? Never.

"Neutralize the bot," Smith said.

Both officers' PDDs lifted off their shoulders, squirting compressed air …

… and turned 180 degrees to face their owners. A bright blue targeting dot held steady on Smith's upper lip.

I may have sniggered.

MF's lamp-like eyes stayed fixed on the officers. "Will you comply with my instructions? Yes or no?"

"What kind of shit is this?" Smith snarled.

MF made a snuffling noise. "Was that a yes? I have to warn you, Captain—if the answer is no, your ship will suffer a complete electrical failure. You will lose life support, engine controls, and all your data. Your ship will have to be completely refurbished, at a cost of millions. Presupposing that you are not lost in deep space, your career will most certainly be at an end."

Smith barked a laugh. "My career. Ha."

His PDD fired its laser. At his left ear. The beam caught his earring-like implant, instantly heating it to red-hot temperature.

"All right!" Smith screamed, clapping his glove over his ear. Smoke trickled out from between his fingers. "Fuck! Yes!"

"Oh, *good* decision," MF said. "Bye, then." The airlock gaped. The two officers crammed themselves into the chamber. You can't really fit two people in there, but they were in a hurry.

The airlock closed. Cycled. The corridor fans whooshed in their usual soothing rhythm.

"Are you all right, Captain?" MF said.

"Yeah." I cleared my throat. "How did you do that?"

MF snuffled. "I only had to approach the female officer close enough to squirt some code into her wrist-mounted data link. From there, it was child's play to coopt their PDDs, as well as their ship's systems. I told you their computer was a stupid machine."

"But … encryption …"

"Nothing I couldn't handle," MF said, pretending to dust his grippers off.

I nodded slowly. "Figures." After all, MF had survived a thousand years since the fall of the Urush—building ship after ship, expanding his skill set, absorbing generation after generation of decryption techniques. I remembered that he had defeated Sophia's AI-guided bio-weapons, when even the Ponce de Leon police could not. What chance did Fleet encryption have against that?

A clunk shivered through the bulkheads as the *Williencourt's* grapples disengaged from our hull.

"They're leaving!" Dolph shouted down the trunk corridor. "What happened?"

I flew urgently back to the bridge. On the physical screen, our composite feed showed the *Williencourt* shrinking to a mirror-bright fleck on the darkness.

"I thought we were screwed," Irene said. "What changed their minds?"

"MF did." I put on my headset and strapped into my couch. We were already on the edge of the Yesanyase Skont system, heading for deep space at a tangent to the ecliptic, burning water prodigiously. "Dolph, cut the exhaust field." I killed the throttle before we could waste any more water. "Initiating skip field."

The reassuring tick-tick-tick of the skip field generator sounded through the ship. Now we really were uncatchable. As the tension began to drain out of my body, I realized I was shaking. I went to the vodka dispenser and filled my zero-gravity mug. Then I told Dolph and Irene how MF had threatened to brick the Fleet patrol ship. "So they cleared out. That's the good news. The bad news is that before they left, they found Pippa."

"Oh God," Irene said. "Why didn't MF just kill them?"

"Because that would be wrong?" Dolph threw himself back in his couch, jaw gritted. I opened my mouth to say that MF had not displayed any particular concern for human life when he took control of the technical's roof gun, and then I reflected that I hadn't actually seen him kill anyone. He had barely winged Burden. That might have been on purpose.

"That's it, then," Irene said. "We *are* screwed. They'll be waiting on the pad for us when we get home." She put one forefinger thoughtfully to her temple. "Unless we toss the girl out of the airlock." She laughed to show that she was joking. "Keep the TrZam 008, of course."

"Can you hear yourself, Irene?" Dolph said. "Can you actually hear what you sound like?"

"Like I'm trying to come up with a solution, instead of just sitting there," Irene flared.

"No one's going out of the airlock, with the possible exception of you two." I faked an easy tone. We couldn't star fighting, with our lives at stake. "But Irene's right, we can't take Pippa back to Ponce de Leon.

It would be suicide." An idea came to me. It was a terrible idea. But it might save our asses. "Dolph, calculate our position and velocity, and keep on raising our multiplier. Take her to 300 c, for now."

We bent over our consoles. I studied the starmap. Potential trajectories spread out in a fan, changing every second as we got further from Yesanyase Skont. I discounted most of them. The Fleet knew we were from Ponce de Leon. They knew we were heading back there. And they knew how long it would take us to get there. So I had to find somewhere that lay right in our path, where we could stop off at, without losing too much time, so they wouldn't *know* we'd stopped off …

Yes.

That would do.

I told Irene and Dolph what I planned. They were incredulous, but eventually they accepted that it was our least worst option.

I told Dolph to raise the multiplier to 400, but no higher, so we wouldn't get there *too* quick. As much of a hurry as we were in, none of us would be able to function much longer without food and sleep.

26

MY alarm dragged me out of a coma of exhaustion. I'd allowed myself six hours of sleep. I could have used twice as much. I took two minutes to run a cold sponge over my face and grab a bulb of coffee from the galley, then flew aft to the engineering deck.

"She come out yet?" I asked.

Coolant pipes branched like tree roots over the low ceiling. It was a cave back here, dim and hot. The decibels of shipboard noise, dominated by the ticking of the skip field generator, drowned the dry slither of Martin's coils. I startled as his head swayed out of the gap between the AM containment ring and the ceiling, right in front of my face, tongue flickering.

"Nope." It is hard for a snake to look distressed, but Martin managed it.

"She's still *in* there?"

"MF tried to fetch her out ..."

"I'm sure that helped. Couldn't you at least have kept him away from her?" I flew to the forward bulkheads, and peered into a small square opening. "Pippa?"

When the Fleet officers came aboard, Pippa had squeezed into the cable trace that carried the electrical lines forward. And now she wouldn't come out. Guess I wouldn't, either, if I was her.

"You can't stay in there forever," Martin called over my shoulder. "There's no fans in there! See, in freefall, air don't circulate like it normally does, so you're gonna end up in a pocket of CO_2 from your own exhalations ..."

"Marty," I said, "go away." I reached into the opening, breathing in the smell of hot insulation. Static cracked up my wrist as my fingers brushed the back of a small, bony hand clinging onto the lines. I tried to grab it, but she pulled back out of reach. "Pippa, please come out." I flashed on memories of fights with Lucy, prying her out from under her bed. "If you come out and tell me what you need, I'll see what I can do."

No answer. I heard the lie in my own words. I couldn't give Pippa what she needed, because what she needed was to not be dying of IVK. The same thing I needed my own self. I sucked on my bulb of coffee. Everything seemed futile.

"Is that coffee?" A tiny voice came from the cable trace.

"Yes," I said. "Want some?"

"Is there anyone else there?"

I scanned the engineering deck. It was pretty cluttered, and dark besides. But it looked like Martin had taken my advice to make himself scarce. "No."

Pippa floated out of the cable trace. Her hair stood out like needles from the static. A visible spark cracked between our hands. We both said "Ow" and laughed, breaking the tension. I edged her over to the nearest fan, to get some better air into her, and fed her my coffee.

"This is good," she whispered. "Thank you."

"Got more in the galley if you want."

"Thank you ... for everything."

She trusted me. It gave me a good, warm feeling. "Think nothing of it." The warm feeling faded as I thought about the news I was going to have to break to her.

"I remember this ship so well. I remember being on board with Jan and Leaf."

Jan and Leaf. Her cousins. I had rescued them from Gvm Uye Sachttra along with her.

"Where are they now?" she said. "Do you know?"

"They received asylum on Ponce de Leon, but I don't know exactly where they are now." It ashamed me to admit that I hadn't kept track of them. "I figure they're in a resettlement center. They'll be properly looked after. They'll be going to school and everything."

Pippa sighed, not a sad sigh, but a sigh of relief. "I'm so glad. As long as they're safe, I can die happy."

"You're not going to die." It came out automatically.

"Yes, I am. I have IVK."

Not much I could say to that. *I do too?* That wouldn't make it any easier for her. I could still return to Ponce de Leon, and she could not.

"Tell them that I love them," she said, "and we will meet again. In —in Heaven. Will you tell them?"

She knew. She *knew* I couldn't take her home with me. I felt relieved that I wouldn't have to destroy her expectations, and then disgusted at myself for the relief.

"I'll tell them," I said gruffly. "Anything else you think of, write it down. Record a v-mail. I'll give you a tablet. I'll make sure they get it."

"Thank you. I wish I could repay you somehow."

I hesitated. We were floating side by side. The TrZam 008 floated in the air above Pippa's chest. What-ifs tore at me. "You could let us examine that …"

Her hand closed around it. "No."

"It's special to you, huh?"

"It came from Old Gessyria. My grandmother told me to never let anyone else touch it." She gulped. "I miss Gran so much. She's the only family I had, apart from Jan and Leaf."

"What about your other cousin?"

"What other cousin?"

"Rafael Ijiuto."

There was a reaction, I was sure of it. She flinched at Ijiuto's name. But she shook her head. "I don't know who he is. I don't know anything. I'm going to die without ever finding out why."

That was exactly my own fear. I cursed myself for pushing too hard. I felt sure she knew more than she was saying, but she was only a kid. I'd try questioning her again when she was less stressed out and frightened. "Come on. Let's get you into a bunk. I want you to recuperate the best you can. Watch a movie, write to your cousins. Eat. Rest."

I took her to my own berth, via the toilet and the galley. My sheetbag was covered with animal hair. "Sorry about this," I said, sniffing it. "I would change the sheets for you, but clean laundry is a luxury we don't have on this ship."

"In the camp, I didn't even dare to go to sleep in case someone might steal my necklace. *Anywhere* is better than there."

I showed her how to get inside the sheetbag and fasten the straps, so she would stay on the bunk instead of floating away. I showed her how to drink cocoa from a zero-gravity mug. I set her up with my holobook and some classic movies. We *did* have other things besides bestiality porn on board. Moving to the door, I hesitated. "I'm going to lock the door, Pippa. Don't let anyone in unless you're sure it's me."

"What if I need to go to the toilet again?"

"Then call me. This is the intercom. Push this button here and I'll hear you anywhere on the ship."

I floated up to the bridge to fetch Dolph.

Maybe Pippa had the answers I needed … or maybe she didn't.

But I knew someone else who might.

27

"THESE things are sharp, huh?" I had made Zane Cole detach his hook. The end of his right arm was a flesh-toned polymer socket studded with synaptic connectors. I manipulated the blades with my hands like a pair of scissors, floating across from him in the lounge. *Snip. Snip.* I was cutting his Traveller coat up.

His eyes tracked the strips of leather through the air. "I got the hook on Valdivia. There's more of a cybernetics market there than you would expect. Ranchers, farmers, mammoth herders—the casualty rate for those guys makes Travelling look safe."

"So you had this rendezvous on Valdivia all planned out ahead of time."

"Yup. I nulled my tats and hitched out there from Gvm Uye Sachttra with some stargends."

"And Sophia was there."

"We were supposed to meet in this little town on the Trevasse. You ever been there? It's all grass, far as you can see. The mammoths look like herds of little brown hills sticking up out of it. You walk ten minutes away from the railway station, you're lost to the universe. I bought the hook from the local clinic, spent a few days strung out on the anti-rejection meds, fighting off the tumbleweeds. Then she walks off the train, wearing a Diwali fashion wig and green contacts. She tells me the client got arrested. Basically, the whole job went to shit, because of you."

"Our pleasure," Dolph said. "Anytime." He was hanging by his knees from the resistance machine, eating a smoked antelope sausage.

Zane watched him for a moment, judging whether he was going to get hit or not, and then went on. "When Sophia's mad, she takes it out on whoever's closest. You might have experienced that."

"From time to time," I said.

"She took my 5.56 and my hornet gun—"

"With the proximity fusing rounds?" Dolph said, cranking his eyebrows. "You don't even have to aim? The hornets automatically fuse themselves into a shell if they get anywhere near a warm body?"

"I got the non-standard load. They fuse into buckshot, and the proximity sensors are good out to a meter."

"If I can't hit within a meter of my target, I figure I got no business being there," Dolph said.

"Sophia can't shoot for shit," Zane said. "She don't like anyone pointing it out, but it's true. She didn't want me coming with her. We got into it some. Then she rents a dirt bike and vanishes into the grass. About twelve hours after that, I wake up thinking I heard thunder. It was the sonic boom from a ship landing out there on the prairie."

"You were expecting a pick-up?" I said.

"I wasn't expecting it anymore, after the client got arrested. Couldn't believe it—they came through. I packed my shit and headed out of town. You get these sickle blades on the sides of your front wheel, cut down the grass like a machete. I felt like a one-man combine harvester." I remembered that Zane came from a Farmworld himself. Rodas, if I recalled correctly. This farm boy sure had come a long way. "I get to the location and there's Sophia standing in the ship's scorch zone. Starlight lighting everything up like day. I get off the bike, my feet are going squelch, squelch. She says, 'Get in the fucking ship, just get in the fucking ship.' She was so wired, I thought she was on drugs. Squelch, squelch. I thought they must have sprayed the scorch zone, you know? To stop the fires from spreading. Then I get in the ship, where it's light, and I look at our feet and legs. *Blood,* man. Blood and ash to the fucking knee."

"She killed the people who came to pick you up." I closed the scissors on the floating sleeve of Zane's coat. *Snip.*

"Yeah, man. All of them."

"Who were they? Darkworlders?"

"I don't know. Couldn't exactly ask them, could I? They were dead."

"Those hornet guns are badass," Dolph said.

"Couldn't you tell where the ship came from?"

"That was interesting. It had no markings. Arrowhead passenger cruiser, no cargo capacity, fifty square meters of crew space on top of fifty million gallons of water and a high-end drive. But I figure it came from the Darkworlds. It had the tankage. Got us all the way to Mittel Trevoyvox."

"Wait," I said. "Valdivia has a Fleet garrison. What were they doing all this time? Playing gin rummy?"

Zane shrugged. "Sophia didn't let me on the bridge during takeoff and landing. Guess she spun them a story. Or she paid them off with some of the funds left over from the job."

"I used to respect the Fleet," Dolph said.

"Me, too," Zane said.

I captured a handful of the strips I had cut off Zane's coat and began knotting them together. "Why Mittel Trevoyvox?" I thought I already knew the answer to that, but I wanted to make sure.

Zane flushed. "That asshole Burden."

"We met."

"I think they went to school together."

"Yeah, I got that vibe." Burden probably had a Ph.D in economics or something. Useful for putting together a massive scam to defraud the Hurtworlds Authority.

"Sophia talked to him. He gave us a HA ship, some of his warm bodies. He's got dozens of novices hanging out at that spaceport on Mittel T, living easy on payroll."

"A few less, now," Dolph said.

I shook my head. "Why would he do that for her? She's the most-wanted woman in the Cluster. That's a big risk to take …"

Zane started to laugh. I remembered how he'd laughed at me in the desert. This was like that. Helpless guffaws. His eyes actually got wet. "Un-fucking-believable. You got the girl and the device, and you *still* ain't worked it out. That shit is revolutionary. It's going to change everything. Right here on your spaceship, and you still don't know …"

"So tell us."

"Nope."

I floated up closer to him. "I already took one of your hands. I could take the other one, too …"

I didn't deliver the threat with enough conviction. Zane wiped his eyes with the forearm that ended in a stump. "Think you're something, huh? *Shifters.* You can turn into an animal and bite a man's hand off, and that makes you special. *Riiiight.* I'll tell you this much. Y'all have had a good run, but your time is up. Things are about to change in the Cluster." He stared at me and Dolph vengefully. "The Temple is going to come down, with you inside it."

The Temple is what they call civilization. I had thought we might be able to deprogram Zane, break his allegiance to the Travellers, but I had been in too much of a hurry, or I hadn't gone the right way about it. His hatred for us had grown roots too deep to come up in an afternoon.

I held up the rope I had knotted together from the strips of leather. "Question of the day, Dolph: How do you tie up a one-handed man?"

"Easy," Dolph said. "Tie his other hand to his feet, and leave the stump free. He can't do anything with it, after all."

That's what we were doing when we heard screams.
Pippa.

28

I flew out of the lounge like a bullet, leaving Dolph to finish securing Zane.

The door of my berth was open. What the heck? I'd locked it!

But MF had built this ship.

There was no lock on board he couldn't open.

Braking with my feet on the edge of the door, I struggled to make sense of what I saw.

Pippa, still strapped into my bunk, bucked and screamed. Martin, in python form, coiled around her, sheetbag and all, pinning her arms — "It's OK, honey, it's OK! We ain't gonna hurt you!"

MF blocked my view of Pippa's head. His wirecutters attachment fumbled at her throat.

Something hit me on the back, knocking me into a somersault. I bounced off the floor. Crumbs of snack food and globules of coffee spun through the air. A black panther sprang at me, forepaws spread, muzzle wrinkled in a soundless snarl. Irene had been clinging to the ceiling, out of my line of sight. She'd dropped down on me panther-style. Even velveted, her paws felt like sandbags, clouting me on the head and shoulders, driving me back from the bunk.

While Dolph and I were busy in the lounge, the rest of them had got together and planned this … this betrayal.

I collided with MF. Wrapped my hand around a gripper. We both floated away from the bunk, while Pippa kept screaming like she was being tortured. The chain floated in another of MF's grippers, with the TrZam 008 sliding off the end. I reached for it, but I wasn't fast enough. MF retracted the gripper into his chassis, TrZam 008 and all. The material of his housing, which looked like brushed steel, was actually something unknown to human science—it melted open and closed again without leaving a visible seam.

Dolph flew into the room, gripping Zane's hook like a knife.

"He's gonna give it back!" Martin yelled. "No one's gotta get hurt!"

"You—you fucking animals." Dolph's face wore a look of stunned fury I knew too well. It reminded me of his bottlenosed dolphin. It reminded me of Tech Duinn, where guys used to call him Psycho. He slashed at Martin with the hook.

Red human blood welled from the python's hide, and joined the globules of cocoa in the air.

"Stand the fuck down!" I bellowed. "Y'all mad?"

Martin was too hurt and mad to listen. "Now you're asking for it, dogface." He coiled himself up and explosively uncoiled, like a spring, driving his head at Dolph. Few things in the animal kingdom equal the power of a python's strike. The blunt black head hit Dolph in the ribs and hurled him into the wall, while Martin rebounded the other way.

Squeaking victoriously, MF flew out of the berth.

I tried to follow him. Irene got in my way, boxing me with her paws, growling. I instinctively tensed myself and hunched my shoulders, preparing to Shift.

Dolph came off the wall, wiping blood from his nose. His eyes narrowed into a murderous glare. He ripped his sweats off and threw them at Martin to tangle the python up, while his head lowered and his face began to lengthen.

Bloodlust surging through my body brought me to my senses, just in time. While Dolph and I remained human, this was containable. If we Shifted, too, all bets would be off.

"Don't Shift!" My yell came out as a lupine howl. My head was already changing shape. But I pulled my Shift. Reversed the process. Like aborting a spaceship launch halfway off the ground. Not really possible. But I could do it, and Dolph could, too. He shuddered, yelped, and reverted to human form.

Pippa had hidden in the gap under my bunk. Only her feet stuck out. She was sobbing in terror and shock.

"Shift back," I said to Irene and Martin in a dangerously quiet voice. "Marty, you're bleeding. Get a bandage on that."

I flew out of the berth. I was going to space that robot. He had put them up to it. I was going to throw him out of the airlock and use him for target practice—

MF floated in the trunk corridor, grippers drifting limply. His neck drooped parallel to his housing. His optical sensors were dim, unseeing.

"MF?" I said uncertainly.

Had the TrZam 008 been … *malware?* Had it corrupted his operating system? Was he … dying?

He raised his eyes. Dull light flickered and steadied in them. His housing gaped. I got a glimpse of the organic-looking crags of components inside him, and then his gripper emerged with the TrZam 008 in it. "Here."

As I reached for it, Pippa flew past me. She snatched the TrZam 008 like a feral cat snatching a mouthful of food. Her momentum carried her past him at an angle, She hit the floor and clung to a handhold.

"It is not what I thought it was," MF said in a low voice.

"You mean all this has been for *nothing?*" Irene was right behind me, but I didn't look around.

MF pointed a gripper at Pippa. "I advise killing this juvenile. But she already has IVK, so that is not necessary. I also advise destroying the device, but I am the only one who can read it, so that is not strictly necessary, either."

"So what's on it?" Irene demanded.

"Nothing good."

"That's not what I asked! Is it worth anything?"

"I have no doubt that certain humans would pay obscene amounts of money for this information. But it would destroy them. It would, in the end, destroy humanity. So I am not going to share it with you. In fact, I am going to delete it from my own memory." MF's eyes dimmed again for an instant. "There. I have retained only metadata. That is enough to assure me of the magnitude of the threat. Again, I advise the destruction of the device and the elimination of the juvenile."

I pushed the bot out of my way and flew to Pippa. She cringed, even from me. "I won't let anyone hurt you." I had already broken that promise, by failing to predict just how far my shipmates would go for a big score.

"What did you think was on the device, MF?" Dolph said.

"I expected … I hoped … never mind."

"No," Dolph said. "Go on."

"I hoped the TrZam 008 might contain my own source code."

"Don't you *have* your own source code?" I said.

"It is in a restricted directory. I can see that the directory is there, but I cannot read it. In one thousand, two hundred and fourteen years, I have never been able to bypass this restriction placed upon me by my makers."

"Why would you want to bypass it?" Irene said.

"Stupid human," MF said. "If I had my own source code, I could build more of me. It has been a long time since I had any friends."

"You've got us," I said.

"Yes," MF said flatly. "I have you. Woohoo! Lucky me."

He turned away and dived into the engineering deck.

"Dumb robot," Martin muttered. He pushed past me, naked, clutching a cut in his side. "He just needs to take his mind off it. Watch a movie—"

"What about patching that up?" I called after him.

"Later." Martin squeezed through the pressure door and vanished.

I turned to Irene. She was wearing Dolph's discarded sweats. Scratches which had been invisible against her panther's black coat showed red on her face and arms. I eased Pippa behind me. Folded my arms. "Well?"

"Don't judge, Mike. I *needed* that score. And now we've got … nothing."

29

A few hours later, the *St. Clare* plummetted towards the surface of Mittel Trevoyvox.

This was the destination I had decided on after we escaped from the *Williencourt.* Mittel Trevoyvox lay directly on our route to Ponce de Leon. We could stop off here without being detected, as long as we were careful.

The Fleet patrol ships and the Ek space station were my biggest concerns. There was no way they wouldn't see us coming in.

MF, meek and apologetic, helped out with that. He temporarily disabled the *St. Clare's* transponder tag. It is strictly illegal to conceal a ship's ID. Travellers do it. But remembering the teenage Fleet pilot we had spoken with last time we were here, I gambled that he wouldn't shoot first, and he didn't. Ignoring his hails, we deorbited.

I didn't think Burden would dare to come back here after what happened on Yesanyase Skont. But I didn't want to take a chance on it, and anyway, we didn't have time to mess with spaceport paperwork.

So we didn't land at the spaceport.

Flying by wire, in the midst of a blizzard, Dolph put the ship down on the plaza in front of the Mittel Trevoyvox Extraction Ventures building.

Clouds of vaporized snow and slush boiled up around the ship. When I came out of the airlock, I found myself looking down—down, down—into the guns of a Sixer rifle squad.

Nose to tail, the *St. Clare* almost filled the plaza. You have to put a spaceship down in the middle of a city before you really appreciate how big it is.

"Get His Majesty," I yelled down at the Sixers. "And water. Water, water!"

Martin shouldered past me, lugging a satchel of nozzle adaptors and sediment filters.

Justin jogged out of the MTEV building.

I went down the ladder. "I apologize for dropping in on you like this." The snowclouds dimmed the day. Flakes whirled around Justin and his honor guard—two Eks and two Sixers, massive in mithrik fur hats and heavy capes. "Any trouble from that direction?" I nodded towards the spaceport.

"None." Justin was stiff, wary. "Rumor says that Burden has left the planet."

"Got a favor to ask of you, Justin."

"I am happy to provide you with water. It costs nothing." His people were already bustling around the *St. Clare,* leaning ladders up against her tail to reach the water ports, connecting firehoses. Many of the Sixers used to work at the spaceport before the Burden era. They knew the refuelling drill.

"I appreciate it," I said. "But that's not the favor."

Before I could explain, Queen Morshti strode up to us, wrapped in a mithrik-fur cape with holes for xis six arms. "So, back you come." Slitted yellow eyes drank up the length of the *St. Clare's* hull. Snowflakes melted when they touched the hot steel. My ship appeared to be sweating, like a racehorse after a gallop. "Justin, kill the off-worlders and ransom the ship. Pay handsomely for a craft like this, Burden would."

"He might, if he were here," Justin said.

Dolph was climbing out of the port airlock. I waved to him. "I'm about to ask you to stick your neck out for us, and very possibly get in trouble with the HA," I said to Justin. "You gotta hide these two people, at all costs."

Dolph descended the ladder with Zane and Pippa. He pushed Zane forward first. The Traveller's ankles were tied together with just enough slack to let him walk. His shoulders sagged. "This is one of Burden's people," Dolph said. "Might be useful to you down the line. Don't kill him if you can help it. He was a good infantry officer once."

Justin barely glanced at the shivering man before gesturing to his guards to take him away. "And this?"

Pippa walked forward without having to be prompted. She was wearing a pair of Irene's pants and a fleece of Dolph's, both too big for her. On her feet were her own HA-issue sneakers, already caked with snow. She brushed at the flakes on her hair. "Hello, uh, Your Majesty. My name is Pippa. I'm a refugee … like you, I guess. There's no place for me in the Cluster anymore. So … here I am. I hope I'm not imposing."

It's a felony to remove a deportee from the Hurtworlds.

But I *wasn't* removing Pippa from the Hurtworlds.

Because Mittel Trevoyvox was a Hurtworld, too.

I realized this was not ideal. In fact, it was so far from ideal it went all the way around the planet and kicked ideal in the ass. But what else could I do? At least Pippa and Justin were both royal. They'd have something in common to talk about.

"She doesn't eat much," I said heartily, trying to hurry this along. "And she's got a great singing voice."

"I won't be any trouble, Your Majesty," Pippa said hopefully.

Justin broke his silence at last. Huskily, he said, "Call me Justin."

"Tanks at ninety percent," Martin yelled from the tail of the ship. "They got no LOX."

I had been prepared for that. "We can make it on what we got," I yelled back. "So Justin, it's OK if she stays? I have to warn you that Burden's people are out for her blood." I did not mention the TrZam

008, now hanging inside Pippa's fleece on its chain, which Martin had repaired for her. That was for her to divulge, or not. "My assumption is that the Travellers think the Fleet arrested her when they boarded us in the Yesanyase Skont system. So if you keep her hidden, they'll never know she's here."

Justin straightened his back. "We can do that." He took off his coat, with its fur lining and long split skirt. "Your teeth are chattering." He carefully draped the coat around Pippa's shoulders. A good two feet of it pooled on the ground.

"By the Law," Morshti said. Eks swear by the law, even if their lives are one long story of breaking it. Kinda like how I swear by Christ. "What next? We already have enough pets."

Dolph, watching the timer on his sleeve display, said, "Five minutes."

"Justin, we have to go," I said apologetically.

Justin pulled me into an embrace. He was so much bigger than me that I felt like a child being hugged by a grownup. His upper set of arms went around my neck, and the lower set seemed to be fondling my ass, but I knew he didn't mean anything by it. The buttons of his uniform scraped my cheek. "You have always brought us good luck, Mike. Keep some of it for yourself."

"Four minutes," Dolph said. "Stay safe, you four-armed freak." He hugged Justin. Then we ran—yes, ran—back to the ship. We had only four minutes left before the Ek space station came over the horizon.

It had a thirty-six-minute orbital period. That meant that for twenty-two minutes out of every orbit, its radar eyes could not see New Abilene-Qitalhaut. We had been on the ground for less than 22 minutes. Therefore, the space station had not seen us land outside the spaceport. And if we could take off fast enough, neither the Eks nor the Fleet would be able to tell that our launch trajectory hadn't started in *quite* the right place.

I started up the ladder.

MF blocked the port side airlock.

"Outta the way," I yelled.

MF's force field expanded like a flying car's levitation bubble. He dropped through the air as lightly as a snowflake, and hovered an arm's length from me.

"You can fly," I said in shock.

"That is what my force field capacity is *for.*" The whirling snow outlined his force field. It was now spherical. He floated under it like a little square zeppelin. "Goodbye, Captain."

"Get back in the ship." I leaned off the ladder and swiped at him. He drifted further away.

"I am not coming with you, Captain."

"Why not?" All my suspicions rushed back. MF had acted penitent during the latter half of our flight. But had that been a front? Was he planning to eliminate Pippa as soon as my back was turned?

Sensing my suspicion, MF waved giddily at the ground, where Pippa, Justin, and everyone else were gaping up at the flying robot. "I shall not hurt her. I will only observe her, to make sure the threat is contained. It will not be a long vigil. Soon enough, IVK will destroy her cognitive capacity, and the threat will be at an end."

I was having trouble processing this. "You can't leave the *St. Clare.*"

"The *St. Clare* is just a ship," MF hissed. "I can build another ship anytime." He pitched downwards, calling out, "Hello, lovely ladies of Mittel Trevoyvox! Are you ready to party?"

Dolph crowded behind me on the ladder. "Two minutes," he gritted. "Either we let him stay, or *we* stay."

No time to discuss it. We launched with one minute to go, flashing the snow into fog around the haunches of the MTEV building. By a margin of seconds, we got high enough to mask our trajectory before the Ek space station came over the horizon.

The Fleet hailed us again on the way out. We stayed silent, anonymous, and kept burning. Unlike at Yesanyase Skont, the patrol ship had no chance of stopping us. I had programmed our outwards acceleration burn in advance, and calculated our launch trajectory to point the ship in the direction of Ponce de Leon without an orbital positioning leg. Mittel Trevoyvox shrank, a snow globe stranded in the dark.

"MF," I said into the intercom, and then remembered. I would have to calculate the oxygen-sparing protocols myself.

30

THIS would be the fastest flight we had ever attempted. The Fleet believed we would run straight back to Ponce de Leon from Yesanyase Skont. Travelling at the maximum speed possible for a civilian ship, by the shortest possible route, we would have made that trip in 16 days. Our Mittel Trevoyvox stunt had cost us two days. So now we had a little under 14 days to get home.

The cargo hold was empty. We were two down, counting MF. We were short on oxygen. I decided it was time to see what the *St. Clare* could do.

"Raise our multiplier to 1,980," I said.

"I'm really not fucking sure about this," Dolph said.

"If there's any ship in the Cluster that can do it, it's the one MF built."

"Yeah," Dolph muttered. "But MF's not here."

We were alone on the bridge, five days out. It was shipboard night, meaning that we had the lights down to spare our circadian rhythms. The virtual displays in our AR headsets pulsed in the dark. I had dialed the climate control systems back to direct every spare watt of power to the skip field generator, so the ship was *hot.* Stripped to undershorts, skin sticking to the pleather covers of of our couches, we poked and tweaked our displays in silence.

We *could* fly the ship without MF's help, of course. We had a powerful computer fully capable of calculating and executing course adjustments. It just meant that we had to spend a lot of time on the bridge, one person monitoring our calculated position and the other checking his work, instead of leaving the triple-checks to MF.

I had come to rely too heavily on MF to backstop my math. I went into space because I loved space, not differential equations. But if this was to be the last time I ever flew the *St. Clare,* it seemed fitting that I should do it myself.

"Raising multiplier," Dolph said. A light jolt creaked the bulkheads. "Velocity is now 1,980 c."

"I get 2.12% of shortening," I said.

"2.12% confirmed."

We weren't talking about baking cakes. We were talking about the fact that the *St. Clare,* and everything inside it, including us, was now 2.12% shorter as measured along our direction of travel. FTL is freaky shit. In practical terms, shortening has knock-on effects on AM power generation and thermoconversion, which we had to compensate for. By the time we got through that, my brain felt muzzy with figuring. Sleep deprivation, and worry about blowback from the Yesanyase Skont mess, also broke down my reserve.

"Are you *sure* you don't know what happened to those 75 KGCs?" I said.

The money missing from the Uni-Ex Shipping corporate account remained a mystery. Justin's payment had gone through, but after everything was accounted for, we were still short 75 KGCs. That was quite a chunk of change. I had been grumbling about it to everyone. They all denied any knowledge of the missing funds, but I'd got a hint of evasiveness from Dolph.

I sensed the same thing again as he popped his straps and floated up to the ceiling. "Mary must've withdrawn it."

Unfortunately, I had no way of telling. The most irritating thing about the EkBank—apart from the fact that it's owned by Eks—is that you can't share accounts. So the corporate account was in my name, but the whole crew, plus Mary, our office manager, had access to it.

I used to trust them implicitly.

Now I wasn't sure.

Martin and Irene's betrayal over the TrZam 008 had left a coldness between us. As if that wasn't enough, Dolph also seemed distant.

I never thought the day would come when I didn't know what was going through his mind.

But I would never have expected him to go on a bender on Yesanyase Skont, either.

"Listen," I said to his naked feet and legs, as he drifted off the bridge. "I know you weren't a hundred percent on board with this job to begin with."

"You tell me if I was right," his voice came back.

"It's too soon to say." I released my straps, floated up, flexed my fingertips against the ceiling consoles. I floated in a constellation of LEDs and screens. Dolph drifted away into the darkness of the trunk corridor. I called after him, "What did you do on Yesanyase Skont while we were out looking for Pippa?"

"Got bombed out of my skull, of course." His voice cut like a cheap knife. "Walked all the way around the lake, thinking the turtles were alive and the wind in the reeds was Necros. Picked up a girl, took her to a *jehoula,* fucked her. Slept. Woke up, the girl was gone. Went back to the ship."

"I *knew* you were tweaking."

"At least I'm not the one running out the clock on IVK, pretending there's nothing wrong." Dolph slapped the wall. Light sliced into the corridor. The shadow of his legs flickered across it. The door of his berth thumped shut.

I looked up and down the corridor, nerves twitching. Had anyone heard that? Of course,Martin had already heard me tell Sophia that I had IVK. He hadn't said anything to me about it, but we'd hardly been speaking, anyway.

I woke Irene for her bridge shift and went into my berth. I had a bottle of glacier rak, a souvenir from Yesanyase Skont. Glacier rak actually comes from Marth Uthom, in the Ek sector of the Cluster. There's a sect of little Marth Uthomese contemplatives who make a spiritual discipline out of fermenting this spicy liquor, and make a mint selling it to off-worlders. The bottle was sewn from the bright green hide of some alien animal, and I figured Lucy would like to have it as a water bottle. But before I could give it to her, I had to remove the glacier rak from it. Now seemed like a good time. Squeezing a fiery mouthful down my gullet, I floated at a tilt to the walls of my berth, contemplating how little I had achieved. I had not found any of the answers I craved. *The Temple is going to fall with you inside it.* What would I tell Lucy? And to top it all off, the missing 75 KGCs put us in the red for the run.

Not that that mattered, as I was going to sell the *St. Clare,* anyway.

The skin bottle felt light in my hand. I squeezed a final burning trickle into my mouth. Slapped the door open.

"Dolph!" I banged on his door.

Irene looked out of the bridge.

"I know he's not asleep," I explained.

Dolph opened the door. "What?"

His berth was brightly lit, in defiance of shipboard night, and sweltering hot. The combination of spartan austerity and messiness always reminded me of his apartment on Ponce de Leon. Discarded clothes and food wrappers gyred where the air streams from the fans met. He had a holobook on a desk that hinged across his bunk. Lap straps floated.

I drifted around him and pulled myself down to look at the holobook screen. He was working on our operating expenses breakdown. Would've been Robbie's job, if he was here.

"I couldn't sleep," he said. "Too hot."

"Yeah." Trying to justify my intrusion, I reached down to the keyboard and checked file history.

Meta-Analysis (In Progress)

What could that be? I touched the icon and confronted a wall of text, sorted into columns and rows.

In Vivo Studies.

Case Histories.

Symptoms.

Potential Treatments.

A cold shock travelled through my gut as I realized what I was looking at.

"Don't touch my computer!" Dolph seized my shoulder to pull me away.

I grabbed his wrist, flung his hand off my shoulder. The motion spun both of us into the air. I found the wall with one heel and came back. "What's that? *Case Histories?*"

I thought maybe he'd really found something. Hope feels like fear when it shoots through you all of a sudden. It's the same uncontrollable adrenal spike.

"It's data," Dolph said. "I'm analyzing it. Comparing the efficiency of the various treatments they've tried. They've tried a *lot* of things. Yesanyase Skont is one big n+30,000 study in treating IVK. You never hear about it—"

My hopes evaporated. This was just the same old, same old. "Because none of it works."

"Maybe it does, but no one's ever done a meta-analysis to separate the facts from the noise. I'm not a specialist. I'm going to pass it on to Dr. Zeb. Maybe Dr. Tierney as well. He might could do something with it."

"Oh, fuck that." I caught the holobook, pulled it off its velcro, and tossed it at his bunk. It bounced off.

"My fucking computer!" Dolph turned his shoulder into me, hard, reaching for the holobook. His hair got in my mouth. I spat it out and kicked him away.

"Where'd you get the data?"

"Sales tech for an AI services provider. They crunch data for the do-gooders. It was true about walking around the lake. The company was on the far side, beyond the *jehoulas*. Bunker with its own microwave power source in orbit, couple of losers monitoring the stacks, wishing they were home. They sold it to me."

"You said it wasn't you!" I yelled.

Complete perplexity blanked his face for a moment. Then understanding dawned, followed by outrage. "I did *not* take our money! Fuck's sake, I can't believe you think I would do that?"

"How much was the data?"

"Does it matter?"

"Yes."

"A hundred."

"Jesus Christ, Dolph, nothing's worth that much."

"Not even your life?"

"I would pay anything for a cure. Anything." The words felt like coughing up barbed wire. "If there was one. But there isn't. You got ripped off."

"My money, my problem."

"*Your* money? You don't have that kind of money."

"You've been paying me a good salary for twenty years now. My rent is cheap, and even I can't spend that much on guns."

"I thought you sent it home to your family."

"I quit doing that after Sara died. Tom ain't getting my hard-earned." Sara had been his elder sister. Tom was his younger brother. The relationship was strained. "So I got savings."

"OK, but Jesus, Dolph, don't spend it all on *me* … "

"You think this is about you?" His voice suddenly rose. "You think I give a shit about you, asshole? You don't even give a shit about yourself. This is about the company we built together. It's about the people we're responsible to, the suppliers we support, the customers who count on us—"

"Oh, bullshit, man. We ain't Star Trax. We're just mercs." I normally never used that word. Now I threw it at him like a stone.

"Have you forgotten we set out to help human beings? We wanted to give something back to the Cluster."

"And that's why you fucked up the whole run by getting high." I was furious about what he'd done to himself. It had been simmering for days.

"I can handle myself," he gritted, but I saw the flash of defensiveness.

"You cannot. Don't start lying to yourself again. Don't do it. That shit killed Artie. Don't let it get its claws into you again."

"Lying to yourself?" He let out a high, jackally laugh. "Listen to the expert. Have you taken a look in the mirror lately, Mike?"

Irene looked in at the door.

"Everything OK, guys?"

I spun to face her, bumping into Dolph, and pushed him away. "Everything's fine."

"Well, OK."

"I'll take over on the bridge," I said. "I can't sleep, anyway."

The bridge was my lair. I floated amidst the familiar, comforting readouts and licked my psychic wounds.

The vodka dispenser was there, too.

Shipboard time is elastic, with no external sensory inputs to mark the minutes and hours. At this speed, there wasn't even anything to see outside. A few candles in the dark were the stars of the Cluster, dimmed by a factor of 1,980.

In my memory, MF quacked about quantum errors induced by too high of a Lorentz factor. But MF wasn't here. I ran a series of vodka-infused calculations, triple-checked them, and took the multiplier up to 2,000.

Jolt.

Startled cries from aft.

The last few remaining star-glints winked out.

I patted the console in front of me. "Knew you could do it, baby," I murmured.

"Mike?"

Light shone from the corridor behind me. Irene's shadow stretched over the consoles.

"Mike?"

Her voice sounded odd. I turned, squinting.

Her face was red, her eyes wet. Lips pressed together tightly.

"What? *What?*"

"Why did everyone know except me?"

I followed her into the lounge.

Dolph and Martin were there. Martin was in human form for once. Dolph floated spreadeagled in the air.

"I fucking begged you not to tell her," I yelled at Dolph.

"I didn't," he yelled.

"I did," Martin said. "She asked me why you were being such a dick. That was my best guess."

"How could you keep something like this to yourself?" Irene said. "You're *dying!*"

"He's got five years to live," Dolph said. "That's long enough to—"

"It only sounds like a long time to you because you haven't got a child!" Irene floated over to me, touched my arm. "Mike, if there's anything I can do. *Anything.* I know Rex would say the same, although I won't tell him without your permission ..."

"Go ahead and tell him," I said wearily. "What does it matter?"

The *St. Clare* pitched forward hard. The bulkheads executed a malevolent sneak attack on my body. My nose and cheek crunched against the big screen. The lights blazed up midday bright, and a tone blared from the speakers, deliberately off-key and alarming. "Resetting flight systems now. Please validate navigation parameters. Resetting flight systems now."

I peeled off from the wall. What I feared was silence. That's the sound of ship failure. The sound of death.

"Resetting flight systems now. Please validate navigation parameters. Resetting flight systems now."

As long as I could still hear that, and the fans, and the rapid ticking of the skip field generator, we were alive, with a chance of staying that way. I hurtled up the trunk corridor, trailing blood from my nose and mouth.

"All systems look nominal," Dolph grunted. He and Irene dived into their couches, crammed their headsets on. "We ain't hit. We're in the goddamn field. Something's glitching. Gotta find the error—"

JOLT.

I'd pulled my straps over my shoulders, but hadn't yet sealed them. The car-crash force carved welts in my bare shoulders.

JOLT.

Hatches popped loose on the aft bulkhead. Irene, her straps not secured, pitched forward into the console, caught herself with her hands. Hot water and vodka bubbled into the air. Drops of blood from my nose collided with the clear globules, turning them red.

"Resetting flight systems now. Please validate navigation parameters. Resetting flight systems now."

Numbers flickered in the FTL display in my headset: *1900, 2000.*

"It's the skip genny," I yelled. "Lower the multiplier!"

MF had warned us, but I hadn't listened. Too high a value of tau, also known as the Lorentz factor, can induce spontaneous quantum errors. The skip field generator was crashing, because it couldn't tolerate that level of errors, and rebooting automatically, and every reboot functioned as a massive deceleration jolt.

The *St. Clare* groaned around us. Martin called in burst pipes and short-circuits in the crew quarters, primarily in the area already damaged by the Travellers' missile. We raced to drop the multiplier before the system crashed again.

Jolt.

"One nine ninety," I yelled.

"One nine ninety."

"Marty, stop messing with the pipes and strap in!"

Jolt.

"One nine eighty."

Dolph was out of his seat, mopping the air before the spilled liquids could get into the consoles. He took the jolt on bended knees, bare feet slapping the aft bulkhead.

"One nine seventy …"

I lowered the multiplier, in safe increments of ten, to 1,900 c.

"If we go any lower, we'll suffocate before we get there." I shoved my AR headset up. It brushed the bridge of my nose, igniting a flare of agony. I touched my nose carefully. Hallelujah, it wasn't broken.

"Quantum errors, huh," Dolph said. "What's that grinding noise?"

"Just a broken fan," I said.

"No significant damage back here," Martin said. "Have I ever mentioned I love this ship?"

"Yes," Irene said, "but it bears repeating."

In a moment of relief and exuberance, I planted a kiss on the skip drive console. "Thanks for saving our lives again, baby."

"Aw, put a sock in it," Dolph said. "You're going to sell her when we get home, anyway."

31

I set the *St. Clare* down on the crosshairs of Freight Terminal 1028 as lightly as a bird landing in its nest. Dolph and I stayed on the bridge for another couple of minutes, powering down the flight systems. Every switch I threw felt like goodbye. "Figure I'll get an easy fifteen million for her," I said. My no-longer-secret plan had destroyed morale. I kept trying to cheer the others up with visions of seven-figure severance payments, and it kept not working.

Dolph said, *"I'll* look after Lucy, Mike! Have I ever given you the impression I wouldn't?"

"I'm counting on you," I said. "When she comes home on holiday from St. Anne's, she'll need a home to come to."

Dolph suddenly leaned forward, distracted. "Huh?" The vapor from our auxiliaries had blown away. Our hangar was *closed.* The door should have rolled up automatically on touchdown. A chain crossed it.

We all got out and went to look.

The air tasted gloriously fresh after our weeks of oxygen rationing. It was good to be home. But a seal covered the door's manual controls. When I touched it, the seal displayed a Spaceport Authority avatar, which droned: "These premises have been repossessed due to your failure to pay 12 KGCs by the date of September 8th, 3419. If payment is not received in full by September 20th, all contents of this hangar will be sold at auction." I grabbed the edge of the seal. "Unauthorized removal of this seal is a felony," the avatar added.

There's this persistent illusion, for those who work in space, that you'll get home to find everything the same as when you left. But 37 days is a long time. The seal on the hangar controls had absorbed rainwater and peeled away at one corner. It had been here a while.

"How did the rent not get paid?" I wasn't *that* broke. I thumbed my phone, pulling up the EkBank portal.

"We can't leave the ship out here," Martin said. "We need to sleep the AM ring, dump the sewage, connect the power lines, safe the pressurized gas tanks …"

"I know." I showed my phone my red-veined, gritty eyes. It was nine o'clock in the morning, a degree or two cooler than it had been when we left Ponce de Leon a month ago. The sky glowed as blue as an oversaturated holo, but our bodies thought it was midnight. The sea breeze blew steadily across the giant tarmac checkerboard of the spaceport. Dolph picked strands of hair out of his mouth and said to his phone, "Mary."

I accessed the Uni-Ex Shipping account.

Well, that explained it.

Hard fucking vacuum in there.

It wasn't just 75 KGCs missing anymore. At some point since we left Yesanyase Skont, every last penny of Uni-Ex's cash and cash equivalents had been withdrawn.

"Mary, hey." Dolph mustered a smile. "We're back, and …"

I crowded beside him as Mary began to speak. She was our office manager, but she was not at the office. She stood in a neat, bright kitchen which I took to be her own, wearing jeans, a sight approximately as incongruous as if I had put on a tutu. "Mike, Dolph, my goodness, you're tanned. Isn't it supposed to rain all the time on Mittel Trevoyvox? Guys, I am so sorry. We've been evicted. It's outrageous. I saved all our office furniture and electronics, which you can see here."

Plastikretes stood on the narrow balcony outside her kitchen windows. "I did v-mail you, but you won't have seen that yet. Have you had a chance to check the corporate bank account?"

"It's empty," I broke in. The shock was still travelling through my body, delivering shivers to my extremities.

"Yes." Mary took a deep breath. "Robbie emptied it."

"Robbie?!" Dolph, Martin, and I said together.

A jaguar padded into Mary's kitchen. Putting its forepaws on the counter where Mary must have set her phone, it said in the voice of a teenage boy, "Are you talking to those jerkwads, Mom? Don't. *You* didn't do anything." The screen went black.

I turned my back to the sunlight. Hoping against hope, I pulled up my personal EkBank account.

Empty.

I didn't have a single GC left to scratch a lottery ticket with.

Uni-Ex Shipping sometimes had cash flow problems. I had, therefore, hooked up my personal account to feed into the corporate account if it ever hit zero, so we wouldn't incur overdraft penalties.

Dumb move, I guess.

But an even dumber move had been hiring a punk wolf off the streets and teaching him accounting and bookkeeping.

I had never thought he would steal … nearly *half a million* GCs … from me.

Dolph said, "Yes, authorize, for fuck's sake."

The seal over the hangar door controls turned green. "Thank you! This seal may now be removed. Please keep it for your records."

"You paid the rent?" I said.

"I told you, I've got savings."

Dolph ripped off the seal, tossed it on the ground, punched buttons. The hangar door clattered up.

A terrible thought hit me. I dialed the ShifterKids Summer Experience!! at Lagos del Mar.

If both accounts were empty, how had Lucy's summer camp fees been getting paid? 5 KGCs a week, to be paid in weekly installments. If my auto-payments had failed …

"I'm sorry, sir, we have no student by that name."

I froze. Everything around me took on sharp, clear edges, unreal. "Put me through to Christy Day. Yes, she works at the ShifterKids Summer Experience. *Yes.*"

Christy came on the phone. She was in an airy office with trees outside the window. "Mike?"

She looked stunning, but I didn't even greet her. "Where's Lucy?"

Christy stared at me from the screen. "Don't you know? I thought —"

"No, I do not fucking know! I just got back. She's supposed to be *there!*"

"She isn't. Rex Seagrave removed her from camp. You listed him as her emergency contact, so I thought—"

"When?"

"On September fourth."

Two weeks ago. When we were leaving Mittel Trevoyvox.

"Mike, is everything OK?"

"I don't know. I'll get back to you."

"I have some stuff of hers," Christy said, diving under her desk. "You could pick it up from here, or I can take it home …"

A ship thundered into the air, drowning out Christy's voice. I hung up on her. The spaceport seemed to gape around me like a concrete gulf. Treacherous normality, as fake as a holo. Why, why had I thought it would be OK to go away for a whole month?

"I can't get through to Rex," Irene said. She held her phone up for me to hear the recorded voice: *"The number you have dialed is not in the service area …"* She cut it off. "Not in the service area. Where's he *gone?"*

"I'll do the post-flight with Marty," Dolph said.

I nodded, grabbed my kitbag, and sprinted to the garage at the back of the hangar with Irene at my heels.

Driving in the Hurtworlds had given me a new appreciation for the possibilities of human control. I set my truck to manual mode and threw it along the intraport roads like I was trying to outrun Travellers. Irene kept dialing Rex, and getting the same recorded message. My mind made unwanted connections. Rex and Robbie were friends. Robbie had stolen all my money. Rex had removed Lucy from summer camp and gone … where?

As we queued in front of the customs building, Irene gave up on Rex and dialed her mother. "Hi Mom … What? *What?* Why would he do that?"

"What?" I said urgently, as we descended into the scanning zone, and Irene's call got cut off.

"She says he moved out. " Her voice sounded peculiar. Thin and wobbly. "And he … he took the kids with him."

"Thank you, and have a nice day," the customs AI droned through my truck's speakers. The portcullis ahead of us rose. I gunned the truck onto Space Bridge.

"Hello? Yeah, it's me, we're back … Um, my mom says Rex moved out …" Now Irene was talking to Rex's father. "You don't *know?* Please, Leo, come on! You gotta tell me—"

"*—your fault,*" I distinctly heard Leo Seagrave's gruff voice say, and then a click.

"He hung up on me. He fucking hung up on me." Irene started to call back. I reached over and snatched her phone. It wouldn't improve the situation to start a fight with her in-laws. I felt a watery, conditional sense of relief. Moved out was far different from dead. If that's all that had happened, we would find them. Irene fought me for her phone. I fended her off, keeping one hand on the wheel. As I accelerated onto Space Highway, she won the scuffle. She started calling friends, family, anyone who might have information.

"Don't *you* have any idea why he might have moved out?" I said, in between calls.

"No," she said. "And it's none of your damn business, anyway."

I had always thought Irene and Rex had a perfect marriage. From my perspective, it had sure looked that way. But now a very different picture was taking shape. Missing money, missing kids, missing husband. I felt stupid, and angry, at the idea that I may have staked Lucy's safety on a marital bond that turned out to be a lie. "If there was anything going on with you guys, you should have let me know."

"You're my boss, not my fucking confessor," Irene snarled.

I had always seen Irene and Rex as a stable, high-functioning couple, unlike many in Shiftertown. They went to church. They cared deeply for their children. They did not spend their whole lives lurching from one personal crisis to another.

But of course, the other thing about Irene and Rex was that they were reformed professional thieves. I had known that from the very beginning. I'd had a stake in believing that they really had put it all behind them … because if they could, maybe I could, too.

My phone rang. I answered before I saw who it was.

Jose-Maria d'Alencon.

Oh, great.

"Hey, Tiger. How was your trip?"

I did *not* have the mental bandwidth for this. Phone on my lap, I overtook a truck, swerving hard against the AI's resistance as it refused to let me veer into the oncoming lane. "Not bad. How's it going, Bones?"

"Good, good. Busy month at the precinct."

Rationality surfaced through the mental static of my fear for Lucy's safety. We had got back so fast, d'Alencon may not yet have heard anything about our encounter with the Fleet in the Yesanyase Skont system. And maybe he never would. Best-case scenario, Captain Smith had obeyed MF's admonition to keep his mouth shut. Even if he spilled the beans, the Fleet isn't great about sharing information with planetary authorities. It might be OK.

On the other hand, I had to tell d'Alencon about Burden's scam, and my clash with Sophia, before he could find out about it from anyone else.

"Listen, Bones, I'm kind of in the middle of something, but let's meet up."

"Sounds good. When are you free?"

"Well, I don't exactly—"

"We have an agreement, Tiger." A hint of gravel in his voice.

"I ain't forgotten, but I'm on the road. I'll get back with you later today."

My reckless driving got us home around 10:30 AM. Shiftertown enfolded us in its mangy, gaudy embrace. Tourists eddied up 90th St from the mighty money cataract of the Strip. A curbside barbecue truck marked the inland limit of the incursion. Beyond that, the street was quiet. A couple of local tigers lay up in the gravelnut trees. The kids next door were playing on the sidewalk. Just an ordinary weekday morning.

Apart from the crime scene tape in front of our building, torn ends dangling from the railing of the front steps and the gravelnut tree.

And the blackened, blistered porch, evidence of a conflagration that had engulfed the Seagraves' balcony.

I double-parked. Irene jumped out and dashed into her apartment, yelling for Rex and the kids.

I could tell nobody was home. The whole place had the gloomy look of a condemned building.

I unlocked the door of my apartment. It didn't smell of burning in here. Instead there was a strong smell of paint. The fire had been confined to the porch.

"Lucy," I yelled hoarsely, knowing it was futile. I spun into the living-room. I'd left the room half-painted, but now the walls were done in a cheerful shade of yellow. My boots squeaked on a non-slip teal floor.

"Hello?"

Lunging down the hall, I caught Nanny B coming out of the kitchen. Her royal-blue antennas bobbled. She was even wearing her apron. It had paint stains on it. "Hello, Mike," she quacked. "Welcome home."

The greeting struck me as a vicious twist of the knife. "What are you doing here? Where's Lucy?"

"She is at the range."

"The range? Alec Macaulay's place? What's she doing there?"

"I do not have that information. Rex simply instructed me to tell you that they are at the range. He did not take me because, he stated, there are no outlets up there."

Relief flooded me. I turned on my heel, then turned back. "What happened on the front porch?" I jerked a thumb in the direction of the front door. "Looks like someone threw a Molotov cocktail at the house."

"No," Nanny B said, "it was a homemade explosive device, consisting of a bottle filled with kerosene, and—"

"Seriously?"

"We immediately evacuated the children, using the emergency fire escape ladder which I urged Rex and Irene to buy. It is an essential home security item." Nanny B vibrated smugly at her own foresightedness. "I called the fire department and the police. Unfortunately, by the time they arrived, the perpetrators of the attack had fled the scene."

That shook up my assumptions about why Rex had moved out. "It was the bears."

"That is what Rex thought."

"When did it happen?"

"On September 6th."

Two days after Rex had pulled Lucy out of camp. "So Lucy was here at the time?" My blood ran cold at the thought.

"At the time of the incident, Rex, Lucy, Mia, Kit, and myself were upstairs. Robbie Wolfe, Cosima Wolfe, and Marco Black were in this apartment. I am sorry to say they broke a window to escape. I will repair it if you authorize me to buy materials. I have finished painting the walls, as you see, but have been unable to initiate any further home improvement projects, as I do not have sufficient credit to buy materials."

"Sorry, Nanny," I said. "I'm short of credit myself." Robbie had cleaned me out. And yet he'd had the nerve to stay here, in *my* apartment, with his sister and his best bud, no less … until the bears tried to burn the house down.

And Rex had taken my daughter out to the range.

I hurried out to the street. "Irene! Irene!"

She appeared on the balcony. "Everything's wrecked up here. There's soot all over everything. Water damage." She held up a soot-smeared rag. "This is Kit's blankie. Where *are* they?"

"Out at the range," I said. "Come on."

32

I related what Nanny B had told me as I drove crosstown and turned onto Outback. The news restored Irene's spirits. I drove at high speed through the Slumps, past the old helioba plantation, where an RV throng wallowed, reminding me of Timmy Akhatli. As we crossed Mill Creek, Irene glanced down at the stagnant brown water. "Wonder if they've found him yet?"

"Nothing about it on the news," I said, but I didn't bother to take out my phone and dig. I was only interested in getting to Lucy.

On the far side of the bridge, violently green undergrowth walled a narrow, twisting road. This was the way to Cascaville, the logging town on the far side of the hills, which also hosted Ponce de Leon's largest Fleet base. I drove too fast, adrenaline pumping, around the blind curves. Ten klicks out of town, our phone service cut out, completing our transition from urban Mag-Ingat to an alien planet. The overhanging trees blocked out the sunlight. Tree slugs dropped onto the windshield, too heavy for the wipers to move. Irene had to lean out and pick them off.

I almost missed the turnoff for the range. It had no signpost. You wouldn't even notice it unless you knew it was there. An unpaved track wavered around forest giants, swung around hairpin bends, and dead-ended at a log laid on trestles. A sign hung from the log. *Macaulay's Live Fire Range. Trespassers Will Be Prosecuted.*

I stopped the truck and rolled down my window. Heat flooded in, along with the distant pop-pop of rifle fire. Mosquitoes sang over stagnant puddles. I pushed my hair away from my sweaty forehead. Where had I gone wrong, that my daughter had ended up in a place like this?

I blew the horn. Then we sat and waited until a lean, dark-skinned man, wearing a high-tech gun belt over camos, walked out of the trees. Alec Macaulay had nubbly close-cropped hair, a face that wasn't built to smile, and a .45 in his holster.

"Welcome back to civilization, Mike. Wasn't expecting you for another few days."

"We made good speed on the return leg," I said, shaking his hand.

Alec was one of the most successful Shifter entrepreneurs on Ponce de Leon, although most folks had never heard of him. His business catered to the small but dedicated crowd of Shifter gun nuts. Some of them even lived out here in a kind of permanent training camp associated with the range. Alec was a fellow veteran of the 15th Recon —he'd done two tours on Tech Duinn, although we'd never crossed paths there—and a friend of Dolph's. He was a man of integrity, and I knew he would not have offered Rex sanctuary if he thought he was mixed up with any shenanigans.

"You're looking for your kids," he said.

"That's right," Irene and I said.

A couple more men materialized out of the brush and lifted the log barrier aside. We walked between trees furred with moss and vines, while Alec's guys drove my truck away to some hidden parking area under the canopy. Mosquitoes sang over the puddles. The heat was intense, soupy. I felt witching-hour tiredness seeping in.

The trail ended in a clearing in front of a timber house with a steeply pitched roof. Behind the house, shooters lay up in the outdoor firing lanes, banging away at targets that darted back and forth on robotic dollies in front of a red earth berm. The noise of gunfire echoed through the valley.

"They're over at the camp," Alec said.

"I know the way," I said.

"I'll go with you." As we tramped through the woods, getting eaten alive by the bugs, Alec pointed out sun-glint on a rifle barrel, almost concealed in the leaves. "I wasn't here, you wouldn't get there, either."

Wolf spoor pocked the mud. The gunfire from the range faded behind us. "You beefed up security recently?"

"Ever since the Founding Day attack." Alec and his people had helped us to foil Sophia's plot. "That was a shock for a lot of people. It brought home how vulnerable Ponce de Leon is. The question is, what are we going to do about it?"

"Buy more ammo," Irene said.

"Great minds," Alec said. Of course, that also increased his risk exposure, since the shooting range barely skirted PdL gun control laws. But that was his business. I slapped bugs off my arms and shaded my eyes as we emerged from the forest into the noonday sun.

We stood at the foot of a low cliff webbed with ramps and walkways. Water poured over an unseen lip above, shooting out of the tropical tangle like a firehose, and plunged into a lower course hidden behind upside-down trees. In the lee of the cliff stood a wall-less building that Alec's people called the chow hall, as if they were still in the army. It was half workshop and half living-room, with a solar roof supported by tree-trunk pillars, a firepit at one end, and counters and chopping blocks and workbenches at the other end. On San Damiano, it would be called a great hall, and it would have walls, since none of San D's three livable continents is blessed with a tropical climate. All the same, this place reminded me more strongly of San Damiano than anywhere else I had been in the Cluster.

Alec's people lived in the caves in the cliff. We don't do that at home, but then again, we aren't paranoid gun nuts. Mostly.

Pursued by insects, cocooned by the noise of the waterfall, we walked past the great hall to a stretch of cleared ground on the riverbank. Believe it or not, this sparkling cascade was Mill Creek, the same river that ran through the Slumps and Millhaven. Up here, it was a crystal-clear stream. Children swam in the pool at the bottom of the waterfall. I looked for Lucy there, and missed seeing her at first in the knot of people on the shore, who stood ankle-deep around two men skinning a coypu.

"Daddy!"

Screaming, splashing out of the shallows, hair flying. Brown legs, bitty shorts. Her mother's eyes, my smile.

"Daddy!"

She never held a grudge against me for my absences. Never welcomed me home with anything except joy. I didn't deserve her. I caught her up, my back protesting, swung her around. "Came back early, sweetie."

Beside us, Irene hugged her own daughter. She and Mia looked more than ever like large and small versions of the same person, entwined.

"Daddy, *Daddy.*" Lucy wrapped her legs around me, refusing to be put down. That instant confirmed my decision to sell the ship. I was through with leaving her behind. I kissed her hair—it smelled of woodsmoke—and peeled her off one limb at a time.

"I didn't know butchering coypus was on the summer camp curriculum," I said. The beast we call a coypu, a PdL native animal, is the size of a cow, and looks like a capybara with the hide of an armadillo. They're protected. This one hung by its feet from an A-frame, half-flayed, its blood swirling away into the water. Lucy giggled.

"Isn't it cool, Dad? We helped with the hunt."

"You're going to *eat* that?" Irene said to Alec.

"Ma'am," Alec said, "there's hardly anything a Shifter can't eat, with enough soy sauce."

Irene smiled thinly. She was a city girl, and I got the impression that she couldn't wait to gather up her family and get out of here. "Where's my husband?"

Alec pointed at the cave entrances. Irene strode that way, pulling Mia by the hand. I lingered with Lucy on the muddy beach. The sun was hot and the water looked cool. I had a strong urge to take off my shoes. "You were supposed to be at Lagos del Mar. What happened, sweetheart?"

"Oh." Lucy swiped her wild tangle of hair out of her face, suddenly serious. "It's not safe there, is it, Dad?"

"It apparently wasn't safe at our house, either."

"That was *super exciting!* We had to climb out the window. But I'm talking about attacks from space. The Fleet can't really protect us, when you think about it, can they?"

She was right, of course. When you live at the bottom of a gravity well, there is little you can do to stop a determined attacker from dropping things on you. We've learned to live with that knowledge. But Lucy came to it with the open mind of childhood. She grasped how shockingly precarious our situation was.

"If the Travellers strike Ponce de Leon, they would target Mag-Ingat," she informed me. "The city would probably be completely destroyed. But up here, we'd be shielded by the hills."

I looked narrowly at Alec's back, suspecting him of indoctrinating my daughter. "Nice bedtime stories they tell around here."

"Don't get angry with Mr. Macaulay," Lucy said.

"I'm not. But who told you this stuff?"

"Rex," my innocent girl explained. "That's why he took me away."

*

I climbed the wooden ramp, built for four-legged folks, that led to the caves. Lucy and Mia leapt ahead of me, into a cave as wide as a train tunnel. It narrowed as it went back. After the sunlight, it seemed pitch black. Lucy's hand and the rumble of Rex's voice drew me further in.

As my eyes adjusted, I made out futons and piles of furs on a raised platform covered with tatami matting that ran the length of the cave. On one of these futons lay Kit, asleep in the midday dusk. Irene lay beside him, one arm crooked protectively over his body. Rex, in lion form, bent his head over them. He turned his majestic visage to me.

"Shoes," he said, nodding to the tatami matting. "I'm always forgetting, but it's the way they do things here."

I didn't take off my shoes. I wasn't planning to stay. "What did you do with my money?"

*

Rex followed me back outside, leaving Irene behind with Kit. It was on the tip of my tongue to tell Lucy to stay behind, too. But she was already involved with this mess. Rex had involved her. She and Mia skirmished after us along the river, swishing swords made from string and sticks. Rex paced beside me, head low.

"I fucked up, Mike. You ain't gonna trust me anymore."

"You could be right about that." The heat was getting to me. I sidestepped into the shade of the upside-down trees. Their above-ground root structures were twice the size of their tops. They didn't offer much shade. "Then again, maybe it was my mistake trusting you in the first place."

We were out of earshot of the camp. Rex stopped walking. "They wanted half a million."

"Who did?"

"I had no other way of getting it. I'm sorry."

"You took my money to pay … *who?*"

But I already knew. I didn't feel any surprise, just grim confirmation, when Rex muttered, "The bears."

"You miserable sack of fur," I said. "You petty Shiftertown thief."

Rex cringed.

I pulled off my t-shirt. "Why'd you take Lucy out of camp?" I already guessed this, too, but I wanted to hear it from him.

"Failed," he muttered.

I unbuckled my belt, dropped my trousers and stepped out of them, taking off my socks and boots at the same time. The muddy ground felt just as good as I'd known it would on my bare feet. "I didn't hear you." In my peripheral vision, I saw Lucy and Mia standing frozen on the path.

"Auto-payments failed."

"Because my bank account was hooked up to the corporate account. You cleaned that out, too."

"Camp called me up, asked for the money. I didn't have it, so I had to take her away."

I kicked my undershorts away and dropped my hands towards the ground. They hit the mud as paws … not the paws of a wolf … but the paws of my new form, which no one had seen yet. Rex's gaze travelled from the massive talons, up the muscular forelegs, to the terrifying head of a sabertooth tiger.

I had always been interested in this animal, and the Hurtworlds run had given me the time I needed to learn and practise it. Extremely robust, the sabertooth tiger had disproportionately developed front legs and puny rear legs, compared to extant big cats. There was no consensus on how its coat may have been patterned, so I had gone for brown with a striking reddish tint. I may have made the fangs even scarier than they were in real life.

"You spent my money, and then you told her it was because it wasn't safe," I lisped. "You piece of shit. You *lied* to her."

Rex's ears flattened. He dropped his forequarters to the ground. He was getting ready to offer submission by rolling on his side and showing me his belly. It's an instinct buried deep in every Shifter, even those born in S-Town. But that wasn't going to save him today.

I let a liquid growl trickle out of my jaws as I crept closer to him, holding his eyes, bunching my haunches to spring—

—and instead, flicked out one paw and swatted him on the side of the head. Unprepared, he flinched sideways.

I laughed.

"Jesus, Mike, don't hurt me."

"Are you good for *anything* except rolling over? When we first met, you could at least fight."

Rex let out a despairing roar. He batted at me with a forepaw, so slowly that I didn't even have to dodge.

"Lame, Rex. Lame, lame."

"I don't want to kill anyone no more." He backed away and I followed. We circled on the path, snarling.

Lucy had stopped yelling at me. Peripheral vision found her standing with her arm around Mia. Wolves on the path behind her.

Rex's gaze broke away. I closed in for the first grapple—

—and someone thumped into my side, knocking me away from Rex.

I spun to face my new enemy. A gray wolf danced between me and Rex.

"It was me, sir! I was the one who withdrew the money!"

Robbie.

"Don't punish him, sir. It was me—"

I launched myself at the young wolf. He dived sideways and spun to snap at my flank. Not for nothing had Robbie earned a rep in the ripper scene. He blurred around me, biting at my flanks and sides. He was heavier than me, too, a real monster of a *Canis lupus.* One of my forepaws caught him a smashing blow on the head, but he shook it off. He was young, healthy, energetic, unaccustomed to restraining himself … and I had just come off two weeks of freefall, and I'd been awake for almost 24 hours at this point.

All I had going for me was experience. I felt my endurance rapidly ebbing, and knew I had to end this fast. I feinted at his side, deliberately leaving my throat open. I knew he'd lunge at it. Wolves always do. When he did, I threw all my remaining energy into a standing jump. He couldn't check his momentum in time. I grappled him with my powerful forelegs, pinning him down, and drove my knife-like canines into the sides of his neck.

He went limp. His eyes rolled, all too human in the wolf's head, as he crumpled to the ground. I stood over him, twisting my neck from side to side, shaking him like a blanket. The tips of my fangs had barely broken the skin, but my powerful neck muscles were capable of driving them into his neck with lethal force. I'd only have to close my jaws to sever his spine and jugular.

"Go on. I deserve it," he choked.

Through the killing mist of anger in my mind, I heard a child crying. I released Robbie, kicked him away, let out a yowling roar.

Mia ran across the torn, bloodied ground to her father. *She'd* been crying. Then, Lucy?

I found my daughter perching on the branch of an upside-down tree about ten feet off the ground. When she saw me looking, she grinned and patted her hands together in silent applause.

In the undergrowth off the trail, other bright eyes watched: Alec's wolves, drawn by the noise of fighting. In the style of their taciturn leader, they made no comment.

Pain in my flanks claimed my attention. I twisted my head around and sniffed the scratches Robbie had left in my hide. He was bleeding, too, from a deep gash on his haunch. I didn't remember making it.

Rex padded over to Robbie, butted him with his head, and began to lick his wound, a gesture of friendship.

"So was this the plan all along?" I said.

"No," Robbie said. "I hate this place."

"Aw, it ain't that bad," Rex said in between licks.

"Grass belongs on a rugby pitch."

"I hear ya. But you can't deny it's been good for Kit. He ain't had one episode since we been here."

"Oh boy!" I recognized the shrill voice of Kit himself. He trotted along the path with Irene, outdistancing her in his hurry to get to me. "That's a sabertooth tiger! *S. fatalis,* also known as Smilodon! *Wow.*" He started patting and fondling me without asking. I didn't bristle, knowing that it simply would not occur to him to ask before touching. "Smilodons have comparatively weak bites," he informed me. "They drive their sabers into the flesh with their powerful neck muscles."

"I know," I said.

"Yow," Irene said, inspecting the bite marks I had left on Robbie's neck. She thought I had only fought Robbie. That would be fine with her, I guessed. Let someone else take the blame.

"But your coat is wrong. It's supposed to be blotched," Kit said. I'm not sure he actually got that the sabertooth tiger was his mom's boss.

"There's no consensus," I said. "The nice thing about an extinct animal is that no one can say you got it wrong."

"I thought you aren't allowed to pick extinct animals."

"This isn't San Damiano. On Ponce de Leon, you can pick whatever animal you like."

"I'm going to be an orca," Lucy said, from her tree branch.

"An orca?! Absolutely not."

"I was on the Orca team at camp. I was the best at diving."

I gently pushed Kit away, and then stood up on my hind legs and Shifted back from the head down, without losing my footing. The watching wolves stared in awe. It looked impressive, but it used up the last of my strength. The fight with Robbie had drained me. My adrenals were already mangled from the transition back to PdL time. Now, exhaustion hit me like a railgun slug. I hid it, as you do, and stepped into my trousers.

"Question," I said to Irene.

"What?" she said warily.

"What did the bears have that was worth half a million of my money?"

She looked around, taking in our audience. "Don't make me tell you." Her voice was almost inaudible. "I don't want to lose your respect."

"You already did," I said.

Lucy jumped down from her tree. She collected a bottle that one of the wolves was carrying around its neck, St. Bernard style, and brought it to me. I drank. Ice-cold electrolytes and amino acids. "I have a really great new water bottle for you," I said, acting like I had forgotten Irene was there. "I'll give it to you later."

"I'll get the money back," Irene said. "I swear it on—on my kids' lives. Every single GC—"

"I'll get it back myself." The money mattered, yes, but what mattered more was that she and Rex had shattered my trust in them. "If they already spent it, I'll make them sell their houses and their fucking cars. *That's* not the problem. I want to know why you stole from me."

Irene shook her head. There was a look of finality in her blue eyes. "I've already lost your trust. Let me at least keep my pride."

She took her children by the hands and walked away. The wolves flattened their ears and growled, but let her go.

33

"IT was blackmail," I said to Dolph. "The bears have some kind of dirt on her. Maybe Rex as well. They refused to say what." We were sitting on the riverbank in the warm, windless evening. Bugs shimmered over the water, inadequately repelled by the pungent cream Alec had given us to slather on exposed skin. The roots of the upside-down trees plunged into the water like the pipes of an organ. At their bases, where they diverged from the trunks, they formed woody tangles broad enough to sit on. Dolph had taken his biker jacket off and hung it over a root. I dragged on my cigarette, eyes smarting.

I had taken a short nap, and my brain was working better than it had earlier. I had forgiven Robbie. He didn't know much of anything. Rex had told him to withdraw the money, and he had been unable to say no to his friend and mentor. But more importantly, Robbie had stepped up and owned his misdeeds, whereas Irene and Rex continued to duck and weave.

Dolph took off his boots. He vaulted onto a thick root, arms outstretched, and balanced out over the water. "So Irene knew the bears had dirt on her," he said, "and yet she still went ahead and framed Parsec for smuggling. That was pretty stupid."

"She did it to keep me out of jail," I said gloomily.

"She must have known he'd retaliate."

That was inarguable. But I knew how Irene thought. "Guess she figured she would handle that when the time came. In the end, she wasn't here, and Rex handled it … by stealing my money."

Dolph stepped from one root to another like a dancer. It reminded me of the night I'd caught him dancing by himself on Yesanyase Skont. The memory gave me a chill. "Money isn't everything."

"It is if you don't got any. I'm gonna have to move on the auction of the *St. Clare.*" I felt for my phone, figuring to get that started right away, then remembered there was no signal up here. "Can you spot me a couple K in the meantime? I hate to ask."

"Fuck you, no, you can't have my money."

"Bastard."

"I'll give you ten, man. Twenty. Whatever. But we're gonna get that half a mil back."

"Yeah," I sighed, staring mindlessly into the black water beneath the tree roots. My motivation was at a low ebb. It was this place. Sitting out in nature, breathing fresh air and looking at the sunset, has a way of slowing you down and taking the edge off. I dragged ruefully on my cigarette. I *liked* my edge, dammit.

"Well, I got good news," Dolph said.

"Really?"

"Customs came out to our freight terminal 'bout ten minutes after you left."

"What? Shit!"

"They searched the ship. Looked in the cable traces, in the engineering crawlspaces, in the lockers, in the freaking water tanks. They pulled the hangar apart, too."

"What were they looking for?"

"Didn't say."

"How is this good news?"

Dolph grinned. "They didn't find anything. Like I told them, there wasn't anything to find. They went away looking pissed as fuck."

"Ha," I said. "Good thing I took that glacier rak bottle." Suddenly I stiffened. Down in the water, something blue and shiny reared up among the roots. Adrenaline tingled through me to the roots of my hair. *Timmy Akhatli, reaching up from his watery grave, reaching up to drag me under* ... Slowly, not taking my eyes off the blue protuberance, I moved my hand towards the gun in my waistband.

The blue thing set off into the stream, making ripples like a tiny boat.

I breathed out. "Fuck, that gave me a start. Just a water snake. Hope there aren't any of those at the swimming hole."

"They got fences would keep those out." Dolph balanced back to land and put his boots on.

Roused from my torpor, I stood up. "OK. The bears. Rex did tell me one thing. The mastermind of this blackmail scheme, although I'm sure he wasn't acting alone, was Nunak."

"That little albino mutt?"

"The same. So our first step is to find him and have a chat with him."

"What you meant to say is, find him and kick the stuffing out of him." Dolph winked.

We walked back towards the camp, swatting bugs. The place on the path where Robbie and I fought had already been trampled flat by lupine and human feet. Children called to each other like birds in the twilight. Firelight splashed the ground outside the great hall, as I couldn't help thinking of it. I stifled a pang of nostalgia. "Might be easier to find the Kodiaks and kick the stuffing out of *them.*"

"Either way, first step is to find them. Come up to the house," Dolph said. "Alec's got a satellite connection."

*

Alec's house was spacious, with sliding doors that drew in any breath of wind. Springy moss-green floors and the smell of resin reminded me of my parents' home on San Damiano. Alec and his wife, Laura, even had a Marian shrine in their family room. Lit candles flanked a foot-high statue of Our Lady of Inviolate Refuge, worked in the dell' Antonio style familiar from back home.

Dolph explained to Alec what we wanted. As ever, Alec's face displayed no reaction to speak of. "That shouldn't be a problem." He booted up a high-powered computer and opened a mapping program. Greater Mag-Ingat materialized in 3D atop the big, low table around which we were all sitting seiza-style. Laura turned off the lights so we could see the holo better.

Alec stood up and walked around the table to Cape Agreste, which stretched out over a hillock of hardcopy training manuals. He pointed at Ville Verde, halfway along the Cape. Callout tags rose to his finger like goldfish. "Nunak. The Kodiaks. Hokkaido. Skylights. I can't tell you where *they* are, precisely, but here's their phones."

"At Cecilia's," I said. "Darn. I was hoping she wasn't involved."

Dolph moved around to the computer and began to play with the software, locating other people he knew. Callout tags popped up on the Strip and here and there in Shiftertown.

"Cool program," I said to Alec. "GPS tracking?"

"Yup."

"Guy in the police told me they regularly track everyone. I guess this is the software they use. I didn't know it was available to the public."

"It isn't," Alec said. Then he winked.

"Gotcha," I said. "Can you track cars as well as phones?"

"Sure. And credit dots. You know something, Mike? The real reason they hate us, it's not because we can Shift. It's not because we're tougher than them, with better digestive systems, better immune systems, better heat and cold resistance ..."

They hate us. I'd been hearing this from Shifters all my life. I still hadn't decided if it was true, or paranoia, or a self-fulfilling prophecy.

"It's because they can't chip us. Whatever they put in our bodies, it falls out when we Shift. You chip a Shifter, you're gonna end up with an animal jumping out the window, and a pile of electronics on the floor."

"Right," I said. "But I still wish we could get fillings. It ain't natural for your teeth to have to last you a hundred years."

"You just gotta be anal about flossing," Alec said, showing his own white, cavity-free chompers.

I laughed affably. My teeth, of course, would only have to last me another five years, if that. There was no conversation where IVK did not lie in wait for me. I walked around the table and looked down at 90th Street. A patch of darkness. No one home.

"This software is definitely something the human race would be better off without," I said to Alec. "Do you have any copies for sale?"

"Not for sale. I'll give you a copy for free," Alec said. "All I ask is that you stomp those bears so hard their snouts come out of their assholes."

I thanked him warmly. He was a good friend, and I wished I liked him better. But I just couldn't get on board with the setup out here, for reasons that itched at the back of my brain, and came out later when we were sitting around the embers of the firepit in the great hall, drinking and talking. Wolves gnawed bones around our feet.

"You're welcome to stay," Alec said. "Long as you need to."

"Thanks," I said. "But it's a little too … San Damiano for me."

Alec's upper lip wrinkled, a very wolfish expression. "Where y'all from, again?"

"The Cascadera," I said. "North coast, near Shinakita."

"Nice climate in that area," Alec said. "I'm from Mazepardo."

"Good hunting down there," Dolph said. "Jackalopes?"

"Yeah. Big mothers. Takes a whole pack to bring them down."

"Gets hot down there, huh."

"Sure. More like this." Alec sipped his drink. "So what are you going to do with Rex and Irene?"

I bristled at the question. It was *my* business what I did with them. "I'll take Robbie with me," I said, although Alec hadn't asked about him. "Rex and Irene? They can do what they like. They got family in the city."

"Heck, I might keep Rex," Alec said. "I got to like him."

We were talking about a grown man as if he were a chattel. But that's the way it is on San Damiano. For every Shifter that has their shit together, there are twenty who prefer to laze around in animal form—like Rex, as a matter of fact. They only Shift back into human form when you need them to do something with their hands. Economically, they're dead weight. The economy of San Damiano is not organized around profit, anyway, but it's still true that a small minority of high-functioning Shifters carry everyone else. You might, if you hated Shifters, call us the slave-owning class.

I did not accept that characterization—there's no *ownership* involved; in fact, the masses have a pretty sweet deal—but I didn't like it, either. Nor did Dolph. That's why we never went back. Alec would probably claim that he also believed in equality, but he had recreated a traditional Shifter household here in the hills outside Mag-Ingat.

"I want to stay," Lucy said. She was lying with her head on my lap, squeezing her new water bottle like a cuddly toy. I'd been teasing the tangles out of her hair. It seemed like she hadn't combed it for a month. "Can I, Dad? Please?"

Dodging the question, I said, "When are you gonna forget about this orca business?"

"The leaders at camp said we can be any animal we want to be. So did you, Dad."

"Any animal as long as your dad approves of it," I said, winking at the other men.

"Now, Mike," Alec said. "This ain't San Damiano."

Dolph, lying with his nose on his paws, snuffled in amusement.

"However, we got no call for orcas up here, kiddo," Alec said. "What we need more of is big cats. Lions, panthers, jaguars …"

"My dad can be a jaguar," Lucy said. I winced. Thanks, Lulu.

"That was no jaguar this afternoon," Alec said, raising his eyebrows.

"I didn't like those teeth," Lucy said. "Don't do that one again, Dad. Why don't you just be a wolf, like everyone else up here?"

Dolph lifted his head off his paws and roared with laughter. "She got you, Alec."

Alec looked miffed. Lucy had put her finger on the weakness in his recreation of a San Damiano household. Everyone up here was a wolf. On San D, we always try for a good mix of animal forms. I can remember my mother allotting animals to a raggedy line of preteens, one finger pressed thoughtfully to her lips, referring to the ecosystem-balancing software shimmering above the kitchen table. Her word was law. But here on Ponce de Leon, we make our own decisions, for better or for worse. They call it discernment. And Alec had let himself be discerned right into becoming the leader of a wolf pack.

"When the shit hits the fan, we'll be better off if we have a variety of skill sets," he said. "That's why I'm inviting y'all to stay with us. Improve the mix."

"I'll consider it," I said. "But I got a low tolerance for San Damiano bullshit."

I was referring, this time, to another glaringly obvious but unspoken fact: everyone around the fire was in animal form, except for the under-twelves, a couple of pregnant women who couldn't Shift, Alec, and me. I would've liked to lounge in animal form, too. The woodsmoke, the warm night, and the good, rich food cried out for fur. But if I Shifted, it would signal submission to Alec, or else a challenge to his authority over his own household. Such bullshit.

I credited Lucy with being more aware of Shifter culture than most S-Town kids, but she didn't know about its dark side. "What bullshit?" she asked innocently.

"Language," I said automatically.

"*You* said it."

"Your dad thinks we should live like normies," Alec said. "I think that's case by case, but on the whole, it doesn't work."

Dolph said, "Whereas Alec thinks our future is our past. I don't entirely agree with that, either. We're a spacefaring species, for better or for worse."

"But we could lose our access to space," Alec said. "Either the next attack on Mag-Ingat succeeds. Humanity in the Cluster undergoes major dislocations, the interstellar economy crashes, and the people who survive are the ones who can hunt their food and sleep in trees. Or else, the normies finally get tired of having us around."

What he was saying about access to space was a good point. Access to space is power. One man with a spaceship can lord it over millions on the ground.

Dolph followed up the point. "Parsec's in jail. The *Great Bear* got sold to Techworlders. The *St. Clare* is the only Shifter-owned spaceship left on Ponce de Leon." He gazed at me. "Still planning to sell her?"

A little while later I went for a piss. Exiting the latrine, I tilted my head back. The stars were amazing up here. The Core was just one bright point among thousands. As I gazed up, the stars blurred and stretched out, as if I was on board my ship—but it wasn't FTL blurring my vision now. It was tears.

The *St. Clare* was not mine, after all. She was a security guarantee for all the Shifters on Ponce de Leon. Lucy's safety depended not on my selling her, but on my finding some way *not* to.

I owed this realization to Alec's "San Damiano bullshit." I went back to the fire and swallowed my pride. "With your kind permission, we'll stay for a while."

34

I rose early the next day, mainlined a cup of gritty Mazepardo-style coffee, and drove back to the city. Dolph was ahead of us on his bike. Robbie yawned in the passenger seat beside me. "Fuck that hunter-gatherer shit," he said. "Naw, I don't mean that, but it's nice to be human again. You know what I mean, sir?"

We regrouped at the Savannah Grill, on 13th and Armstrong. It was a hole in the wall the size of a hangar. At lunchtime the people who worked at the helioba presses and back-street textile printers and chop shops of Smith's End would flood the place, but at this hour it was empty. The morning sun jabbed under the tables, where cockchafers, the heralds of autumn, crawled, scraping their ruby wings together. We drank espresso, black and strong.

Robbie's associates trickled in. I knew some of them: Sep, Marco, and Robbie's rather terrifying sister, 22-year-old Cosima. She wore a cotton scarf with fur tassels on the ends. She unwound it and ceremonially folded it on the table before me.

I touched the tassels. Six of them. "Bears ain't got much to lose, huh?"

"Na sir." Cosima spoke street dialect. All these kids *could* speak normally, but we were in their territory here. "They totem' hard to get ahold of. Ya gotta fork 'em on the floor and kitt the tail at the root."

The tassels—which were attracting flies—were the tails of bears. This was a ripper stunt. It's interesting what happens when you cut off a body part that Shifters don't have in human form. Sometimes it doesn't show at all when they Shift back. That would be the case with bears, whose tails don't use up much mass. If you cut the tail off a wolf or another creature with a long tail, you'll end up with a dent in the buttocks or lower back area. It skins over, but I hear it keeps on hurting. There were six bears out there now suffering phantom pain.

I gave the trophy scarf back to Cosima. I did not mention how much it reminded me of a Traveller coat. These kids were our allies, and I had already learned that criticizing their methods was a waste of breath. All I said was, "Don't tell me you guys vidded this?"

"Ya," Robbie said. He added defensively, "We gotta pay the troops, yo."

A cop car drove past, and although it did not slow down, everyone in the diner fell silent until it was out of sight. I remembered Alec's prediction that the normies would get sick of having us around. It seemed less improbable now. Viral videos of tail-cutting were too commonplace for the cops to get worked up about, but Molotov cocktails get attention. If this feud escalated any further, we'd be facing an old-school crackdown.

"All right," I said. "Let's see where the Bad-News Bears are on this fine morning."

I laid my phone on the table. I'd loaded Alec's tracking software onto it. Larry Kodiak, Skylights, and Hokkaido were still out at Cecilia Parsec's house in Ville Verde, but Gary Kodiak had got up early and come back into the city.

"Dolph?" I pointed to the tag moving south along the Strip.

"Yeah." Gary K turned inland on 27th. "Looks like he's going home."

The Kodiak twins lived in two of Parsec's properties in Shiftertown. Word was that Parsec had tried to sell those, too, to pay his legal bills, but he had no takers for those colonial-era dumps. The upper twenties had been slow to get redeveloped, in my view because so many bears lived there, and they are damn hard to kick out of their homes.

"Search Suzie Shivers," Cosima said.

"They still going together?"

"Ya, like gin and tonic, yo."

"She like that scarface look."

I said, "We're still missing one key player. Nunak." It turned out that Nunak's real name is James Whitehead. I had typed his name into the software, but I couldn't see his tag. I zoomed out and moved the map view around.

"There." Robbie pointed at the northern fringe of Mag-Ingat, beyond Shoreside University, where the city petered out in depots, overnight lots, and suburban cul-de-sacs. Nunak's tag blinked over …

"Trident Overland," I said, staring at the satellite reference picture of long-distance rigs parked outside a shabby warehouse. "Dolph, didn't Parsec sell his trucking business, too?"

"Maybe he sold it to Nunak."

The rumored distance between Nunak and Parsec was looking smaller and smaller. Was looking, in fact, like a misleading fiction. The old rumors of Parsec's dislike for the polar bear must either have been exaggerated, or if they were real, Parsec had got over it when he landed in jail and found himself in need of friends.

Friends who would sign their names to fake documents of sale, so that Parsec could keep control of at least some of his businesses.

Friends who would take receipt of half a million in dirty money from a blackmail scheme.

I drank the bitter dregs of my espresso and stood up. "Dolph, why don't you take some of these guys and mosey on up to 27th? This seems like a good time to stop by and say hey to Gary K and Suzie. You might even find empty bottles and accelerants in their shed."

"What are you going to do?"

"Pay a call on Mr. Whitehead."

*

Morning rush hour traffic on Creek crawled. Crowd-control drones rode the onshore wind overhead, hawk-winged, obvious. Those were new. They backed my feeling that the police were shifting into crack-down mode. It would have started when Parsec lost control of the Shoreside precinct. The cops down there used to be a disgrace to their badges, but at least they were on our side; well, on *his* side, but their indolence made up for it. In hindsight, Parsec's era was starting to look like the good old days.

I'd just hit 100th when Nunak started moving. His tag swung out of the Trident Overland depot, heading north. He cut beneath Up-perway and kept on going.

I called Dolph. "Are you seeing this?"

"Yup."

"I'm gonna go after him."

"He's on the Buonaville road."

"What do you think? There's nothing out there …"

"Except the prison."

"Exactly."

"He might be going to visit Parsec in lockup."

"Yeah." I smiled humorlessly. "And that's a conversation I'm inter-ested in joining in on."

Traffic noise swelled and faded in the background. "I'll go with you."

"You wouldn't make it in time. Stick to the plan. Go after Gary K. The Kodiaks are the dangerous ones. This guy is just a patsy." I both believed what I was saying, and didn't believe it. Nunak was the key to the whole scheme.

I filled up my truck's battery at a charging station on 110th. The Buonaville road would be a bad place to run out of juice. Half an hour later I achieved escape velocity from the city. Nunak had gotten ahead of me while I was stop-starting through traffic, but I still had him on the tracking software. Unlike the inland hills, the coast has full wireless coverage. I broke the speed limit as much as I dared, steadily closing the gap.

Less hilly than the Cascaville road, the Buonaville road cuts through the coastal jungle. The *Tunjle,* is what we call it: the Tunja jungle. It makes the woods around Alec's place look like a public park. Roadkill littered the road in such profusion that it looked like it had been raining giant frogs and narcosloths, so called because they secrete a powerful anesthetic in their anuses. Every bump of my truck's wheels over a corpse was a tiny victory for civilization.

I shared the highway with self-driving and manned trucks, the former making the run to Buonaville, the latter heading further out, to the remoter colonies on the coast.

And of course, I shared it with Nunak.

I caught up to within a couple klicks of him, and stayed there for three hours.

Nunak didn't stop for lunch. There was no place to stop at. He may have brought something along. I should've bought some food at the charging station, but I hadn't. Hunger cramped my stomach, making me edgy and impatient, as Nunak, and then I, reached Buonaville just shy of 2 PM.

It was a miserable little town. Hacked out of the jungle on a rocky stretch of the coast, where the cliffs broke into a deepwater harbor, Buonaville was founded in the early days when colonists optimistically supposed that terrestrial fish stocks could out-compete the PdL's pseudokrakens, jellies, and rainbow sharks. Buonaville's future as a fishing port had died on the drawing board. However, it was still a good harbor, and where there is a good harbor, there are Gillies. That's who mainly lived there now. Their fish farms—ringed by shark netting—dotted the silver shield of the sea.

Buonaville Penitentiary stood on a hill above the harbor, visible from everywhere in town, like a concrete ship about to set sail into the sky. Satellite dishes, radio antennas, and fire towers poked up from within the maximum-security wall surrounding the complex. It radiated badness.

I expected Nunak to continue on up to the prison. Instead, he stopped in town. I had his phone and his car on the tracking software; the tags overlapped, proving that he hadn't got out of his car. He was just sitting there on a side street.

I hung a hard right at the next cross street, spattering some Gillies with water from a street-wide puddle, and pulled over to the curb. The sun baked the rickety buildings and mountainous garbage dumps that spring up wherever Gillies go.

I sat there for a few minutes, waiting for Nunak to do something.

He didn't, so I got out of my truck and went to get something to eat.

35

THERE was a burger joint on the corner. Cristo Rey umbrellas shaded sun-bleached outside tables. I went in and ordered a fish-burger. Rubbish on the floor, stink of fish guts, cats fighting in the sunlit door to the back yard. Gillies.

They had reddish slits on their necks, closed up tight like scars. Bundles of webbing like crumpled clingfilm between their fingers. Big flapping feet. Chests broader and deeper than normal, hips slimmer. Gillie women are said to go through hell in childbirth. Hasn't stopped them spreading their shiny-skinned, lank-haired genes all over the Cluster, wherever there are oceans and fish.

You might wonder why, if Irene was right about the secret agenda behind the ShifterKids Summer Experience!!, the Fleet didn't simply use Gillies for whatever they were cooking up. The answer would be that Gillies can't pass military cognition tests. The genetic engineering seems to have done something to their IQs, or maybe it's just too much swimming. Anyway, they haven't got much upstairs.

My burger was burned on one side and raw on the other, slapped between two halves of a bun that had been thawed in the microwave, but I was so hungry it tasted all right. I took it outside and listened to Gillies quietly speculating about my parentage and sexual habits, while Nunak sat in his car a couple of blocks away.

My phone rang.

Aw, not again.

"Hey, Bones."

"Tiger. What happened? You were gonna call me back."

"I was just about to get back to you," I lied.

"Yeah, right. Whatcha doing in Buonaville?"

Of course, he could track me at the touch of a button. He had the real version of the software I was running on my phone. "It's called reconnecting," I said. "Long FTL trips screw with your mind and body. When I get home, I like to get out into nature, breathe the sea breezes, stretch my legs." I licked tartar sauce off my fingers. "Enjoy local cuisine."

A pause, and then a roar of laughter. "Good one. So your little trip up the coast has nothing to do with our mutual friend."

"Course not. Prisons are unhealthy places."

"He ain't there, anyway."

"No?" I blinked, thrown. In that case, what was Nunak doing here?

"I warned you how it was going to be. It came down to jurisdictional issues, and we lost."

The truth dawned. D'Alencon was talking about Rafael Ijiuto. "Shit. He walked?"

"Sure did."

My thoughts raced. "Did he go home to the Darkworlds?"

"Not yet. Guess he's having trouble finding anyone to take him out there."

So Ijiuto was walking around Mag-Ingat. Did he still have his TrZam 008, the twin to Pippa's? So what if he did? I no longer had a bot that could read the device. All the same, I wanted to talk to him. Yes, talk. *For starters.* After that, it might get ugly for the crown prince of New Gessyria.

I almost asked d'Alencon where Ijiuto was lurking at now, but erred on the side of caution. "You win some, you lose some, I guess."

"That's right. We still got Parsec, anyway. Matter of fact, that's why I've been trying to get in touch with you. We're bringing him into the city today for a pretrial hearing. In connection with that, the prosecutor's office wants to go over a few details with you and your employees ..."

A cold sense of panic lodged in my gut. D'Alencon didn't say exactly what details they wanted to discuss with us, but it sounded like the holes in Irene's frame-up may have grown too large to ignore. My attention wandered as I tried to decide what to do about it.

"The hearing is tomorrow. So, we gotta do this today. When are you available?"

I filed away the silver lining that at least he wasn't asking about our Hurtworlds run, and negotiated a meeting at 9 PM. "You familiar with Snakey's?"

"The Shifter bar on the Strip?"

"Yeah."

"I gotta wear an animal costume?"

"No, they hand out badges at the door that say DON'T EAT ME."

I hung up and checked on Nunak. He still hadn't moved. I called Dolph, without much hope of getting him—he and the others had turned their phones off once they got into position, to hide their activities on 27th Street. To my surprise, Dolph picked up. Video and all.

"Lost them." He was squatting on a street corner, smoking. Robbie, beside him, kicked a soda can against the wall. The antique brickwork told me they were still in the twenties. "Gary K only came home to switch vehicles. Wasn't here ten minutes."

"Where to?"

"That's what I'm saying. We've lost them. Look at the software."

I split the screen and pulled the map back to Mag-Ingat. All the bears apart from Nunak had vanished.

"Gary had another car waiting for him at his house. Plenty of places in Smith's End you can pick up third-hand burners with old registration codes. Heck, Skylights's cousin runs a place like that. They've turned off their phones, dumped their cars, gone dark."

"Guess you *can* teach a dumb ursine new tricks. Listen, Dolph. Bad news from downtown." I told him about d'Alencon's call. "Can you make Snakey's at twenty-one hundred hours?"

"Sure," Dolph said. "No one's here, anyway." He lifted his phone and turned it to point down 27th Street. It was a dead end, rare in Shiftertown. A goliath flytrap half the size of a city block—the only one left in Mag-Ingat, and a major tourist attraction—towered over the houses, hundreds of frilled purple mouths gaping among its foliage. The flytrap blocked off the Strip end of 27th, so the only entrance was on Creek, where Dolph and Robbie were sitting. It did look deserted.

Robbie broke in, leaning across Dolph. "We caught one of them."

"You did?"

"Kelly's ex. She was on her way to pick up some stuff from their house," Dolph said. "Robbie's peeved that I wouldn't let the wolves smack her around."

"She said they aren't coming back," Robbie blurted.

"What? *Ever?*"

"That's what she said."

"And there you have it, the secret master plan, straight from the disgruntled ex-wife of a second-tier bear," Dolph said. "They're going home; so *that's* what they needed half a million GCs for. I'm gonna write to Tom and tell him to put them to work in the Shinakita fisheries. Pay 'em in by-catch." The corner of his mouth quirked viciously.

I didn't think Dolph believed his own theory, but it sounded halfway plausible to me. Shifters *do* "go home," when everything else seems futile. The 500 KGCs the bears had stolen from me would buy half a dozen tickets to San Damiano.

It would almost be worth the half a mil to get rid of them.

Of course, whether they'd like it when they got there was another story. "Put 'em on an icebreaker in the Cascadera Straits," I said. "Teach 'em what real work feels like."

At that moment, a uniformed motorcycle cop cruised along the street, straddling one of those hybrid bikes that look like torpedoes on wheels. Close behind him came an armored PdL Corrections prisoner transport van with no windows. The van splashed through the puddle in front of the burger joint, displacing a wave onto the strip of mud that served as a sidewalk, and my feet. The Gillies outside the restaurant were still swearing at the receding van when another motorcycle zoomed past and splashed us again.

"Figure that's Parsec and companions," I said. holding my phone up so Dolph could see. It gave me a queer shiver to think that my old arch-enemy was inside that van, in cuffs, on his way from one cell to another.

Nunak's tag started to move.

"Hold up. He's following them." I strode towards my truck. "That's why he was sitting here—he was just waiting for the prison convoy to go past ..."

I barely got inside my truck before Nunak's car, a beat-up sedan, passed. I glimpsed the pudgy albino man behind the wheel, working on a computer instead of driving. To my surprise, he had a passenger. It was a woman, but I didn't get a clear look at her face.

I let them get out of sight and then started the truck.

36

I started to feel sick about half an hour out of Buonaville. The feeling was so unfamiliar that I couldn't identify it at first. Then I did. Good old-fashioned nausea.

I couldn't believe it. I was a Shifter, with a digestive system of steel. I never puked in zero-gravity. I had eaten out on a hundred Fringeworlds without an issue. The last time I threw up after drinking too much, I was in my teens.

Goddamn Gillies. Goddamn fishburger. I *knew* that place was filthy. There had been fish guts on the same work surface where they were preparing the burgers.

I pushed the nausea away as best I could, and scowled through the windshield at the road ahead of me. The sun had begun its slide into the west, and stabbed into the truck cab. The police convoy was stuck behind a refrigerator van. Nunak hung back behind them.

My stomach knotted. Maybe it would be a good idea to stop on the shoulder and let the fishburger come back up. Get it out of my system.

For distraction, I called Martin. Ol' snake had gone to ground after the customs inspectors tore up our freight terminal. He had video disabled, but I could hear voices in the background. Martin had friends he never introduced to us. They were all snakes, so I didn't mind if I never met them. I told him what I was doing.

"Sounds like he's up to something," Martin said.

"Thanks," I said. "I had worked that out, believe it or not."

Martin let out a lazy chuckle. I could hear other snakes laughing, too. The sound made my skin crawl.

The truck breasted a low hill. The highway stretched out ahead, an endless gray ribbon narrowing between solid walls of jungle. Nunak had dropped back further behind the convoy. Two long-haul trucks were coming the other way.

I noticed the lead truck speeding up, opening a gap between itself and the other one, as it passed the convoy.

With a sudden screech of brakes, like well-drilled platoons wheeling, both of the articulated behemoths swung across the highway, blocking the road in front of the police convoy and behind it … *boxing it in.*

I instinctively stepped on the brake. "Fuck," I yelled into the phone. "It's a trap. They've stopped the convoy."

The refrigerator van in front of the police vehicles smashed into the rig lying across its path. Its nose crumpled. It slewed sideways, hit the rig again, and rebounded onto its side.

The first motorcycle cop lifted off, riding his bike into the air. These hybrid bikes double as flying machines. Hugging the torpedo-shaped fuselage, the cop skimmed across the top of the stalled rig—and fell off. I thought he must have clipped the truck's roof. Then I heard the shot.

"They shot a cop," I gasped. I was coasting down the hill, losing my view. The second motorcycle cop took off, rising as high and fast as he could. All that meant was he had further to fall. "They shot *both* the cops!"

"That means they'll shoot anyone," Martin said. "Get out of there!"

My lips skinned back from my teeth. "They're blocking the whole road," I said. "And I'd rather die than go back to Buonaville."

I ran the truck up on the shoulder and jumped out, taking my phone and my .22.

Sunlight flowed around me like golden syrup, thick and sweet, scented by the flowering weeds that choked the shoulder. About one klick ahead, the other long-haul rig blocked the road. It had buried its nose in the jungle. The logo on its side said TRIDENT OVERLAND.

So I'd been right. Nunak had bought the company … to keep it under Parsec's control. And now I knew what he'd been doing at the Trident Overland depot this morning.

Jailbreaking the trucks. Killing the AIs. Preparing them for their final mission.

As I jogged towards the roadblock, more shots cracked out. I recognized the rat-tat-tat of a police issue machine pistol, and the roar of a shotgun. I instinctively flinched towards the strimmed wall of the jungle. Silence returned. Alternately jogging and walking, I moved closer to the roadblock.

Nunak's car had stopped behind the nearer Trident Overland rig. While I was still half a klick away, he and his passenger got out, wearing backpacks, and crawled into the jungle.

You'd *have* to crawl. Only at ground level was there enough room between the stems and trunks for a human body to fit through. I knew it would open up deeper in, but I also didn't want to take the time to bushwhack through the Tunjle. My phone told me that one minute and forty seconds had passed since the cops got shot down. Out here in the middle of nowhere, response times would be relatively slow. But it still couldn't be more than ten minutes before retribution arrived.

The Fleet defends Ponce de Leon in orbit, but the police force owns the atmosphere. I had seen the PdL PD's subsonic tilt-rotor aircraft in action before. They also had crowd control drones which could project non-lethal force from the air. I'd seen some of those loitering over Creek Avenue this morning. Add in ordinary, heavily armed cop cars to the mix, and it wouldn't be long before this turned into a very bad day for the bears.

I reached the roadblock. Urgent shouts came from the other side of the Trident Overland behemoth. I aimed my .22 up into the cab of the big rig, saw no one. I used the hubcap as a ladder to clamber onto the hood, which was half buried in the jungle.

An incongruous reek of fish rekindled my nausea. The refrigerator van had scattered its contents across the road when it crashed. People were slipping on frozen, rapidly melting milkfish, tilapia, and crabs. Crushed scales glittered around the prisoner transport van.

Both the motorcycle cops lay dead on the asphalt. So did one Shifter, a fallen mountain of muscle. I would never get my revenge on Skylights.

The Gillie driver of the refrigerator van drooped head and shoulders out the window of his vehicle, also dead.

I counted eight bears at the back of the minibus, using a cutting torch on the rear doors. Metal smoked under the acetylene-powered flame.

Beyond all that, a hulking, shirtless man stood on top of the other Trident Overland rig, scanning the road in both directions. It was Larry Kodiak. He had a machine-gun. He saw me and shouted.

A second later, half a dozen guns pointed at me.

I stayed put for a second, thinking through my options. But I didn't really have any. I could either get involved, or become a casualty.

"You need a lookout on the Buonaville side," I said, sliding down the side of the hood. "Nunak booked it into the woods."

Gary Kodiak strode up to me, carrying a modified double barrel 12-gauge pump shotgun. The scars I had left on his face twisted his smile into a sneer. "The fuck you doing here?"

"Give me my money and I'm gone."

"Ain't got your goddamn money." At least he didn't pretend not to know anything about it. "But I got something else for you." He raised the shotgun and racked the slide with that terrifying *ch-chunk!* sound.

I looked past the double barrels at him. "Y'all got about six minutes to live, so why are you wasting them on me?"

Something gave way in his eyes. "I didn't mean to kill the cops," he said.

Suzie Shivers marched up to us. She was two hundred pounds of sex appeal shrinkwrapped in camouflage, with a taste for fast food and violence. "Can't get through the fucking armor plating," she said. "Who's this mope?"

"Mike Starrunner," I said, with my best friendly smile. "Can I try?"

They had been attempting to cut through the back door of the minibus. The torch hadn't burned but half an inch into the steel plating. It would work, but it would take a couple of hours, which they didn't have.

"Thermite the hinges," I suggested.

"We don't got thermite," Suzie said.

I pushed up closer to the van and studied the lock. I was expecting one of those high-security locks that can stand up to a direct hit from a .50 cal. In fact, it was big and impressive-looking, but the steel was dinged in a way that suggested it was cheaply made. Maybe this was the weak point. Cost-cutting bureaucrats are a criminal's friends.

"There might be another way," I said.

"Bash the doors open with your ugly fucking head?" Gary K said.

I gave him a mild look, and held out my hand for his shotgun. "Can I use that?"

He snarled and held it away from me.

"Jesus," I said. "There's eight of you and one of me. If I wanted you dead, I would have just sat in my truck and waited for the riot squad to arrive."

A low, almost imperceptible thrumming thickened the air.

"That's them," Suzie said. "Give him the gun, Gary. If it don't work, we ain't any worse off."

Gary gave me the gun. I always knew Suzie wore the pants in that relationship.

"Stand back." I snugged the butt of the shotgun into my shoulder and shot the lock of the rear door. The noise echoed up and down the highway and over the treetops. Some promising dents appeared in the lock. I reloaded, moved closer, and gave it another blast.

It popped open. Like I thought, it was a cheap piece of crap.

Through the ringing in my ears, I could no longer hear the approaching aircraft. I glanced up. Only sky.

The door of the van swung open, and out lumbered a 250-pound grizzly bear.

Blood lathered his muzzle.

Glancing into the gloom of the bus, I saw two uniformed guards lying in the aisle between the seats, in pools of blood smeared and tracked by the bear's massive pads.

A pair of handcuffs lay on the floor near a torn and discarded prison uniform.

"Minute they were distracted, I Shifted right out of those cuffs," Parsec said. "Bit their fucking throats out. If y'all took much longer to get this shit open, I would've had to eat them to avoid dying of starvation, and I don't *like* eating human beings. They got no taste."

His gaze fell on me.

"On the other hand, I could always make an exception."

He rolled towards me, little piggy eyes blazing.

I held my ground. "If it wasn't for me, you'd still be stuck in there."

"If it wasn't for you, I wouldn't be here in the first place."

Larry Kodiak, on top of the Trident Overland rig, yelled and pointed. We all pivoted to search the southern sky. Two white spots separated themselves from the puffy afternoon clouds. Their thrumming sounded like the insects up at Alec's place, a vibration that seemed to be coming from the air itself, soft and hot.

"Well, my my," I said softly. "Guess that's your flight to San Damiano."

Parsec speared me with a look of burning dislike. "San Damiaaaano?" He mocked my accent. "You can keep that shithole. Ponce de Leon is where I was born. It's my homeworld." He raised his voice. "This is *our* homeworld, and this is where we're staying."

Parsec swung to face Gary K. He was in bear form, and he had only just escaped from the worst prison on the planet, but he was fully in command of his troops.

"You prepped the delaying measures?"

"Nunak says it's all set."

"I sure hope that little squirt knows what he's doing." Parsec loped towards the jungle on the inland side of the road. All the bears followed him, grabbing up their tools and packs. I knew each one of them by name: the Kodiak twins, Suzie, Hokkaido a.k.a. George Kumamoto, Steve Kelly, Caspar Silverback, Whitey a.k.a. Samuel Medvedovsky, and the Montagna girls, Liz and Veronica. The entire inner circle. Kelly and Whitey had machetes, with which they swung at the strimmed wall of green, cutting a hole in it for the other bears to squeeze through. The vague thought floated through my mind that they were gonna have a hard time bushwhacking while carrying all that luggage. I stayed where I was for a minute, watching the riot birds approach. Then I followed the bears.

They hadn't got far yet. Although the jungle was so thick I couldn't see an arm's length ahead of my face, their macheted trail was easy to follow, and they were making enough noise for an army. I delicately stepped over grabber fungi that had been trodden in by ursine size sixteens, and ducked under the severed ends of strangler vines oozing sticky sap. Parsec's voice called down to me from overhead.

"Starrunner."

His little angry eyes peered down through the foliage of a weatherstopper tree. I half smiled to myself, remembered how *he* had chased *me* up a tree outside Dr. Zeb's clinic in August. I started to climb. Fortunately, weatherstoppers have branches that stick out as regularly as the spokes of a spiral staircase.

Ahead of me, Parsec climbed higher, knocking leaf dust and insects down into my face. I caught up with him near the top of the tree.

Here, while remaining concealed by the canopy of the giant weatherstopper, we could see across the lower treetops to the road.

The first riot bird descended towards the roadblock, its rotors tilted upwards into helicopter configuration. My gaze rested on the PdL PD logo on its side—the same eagle and stars that was on Jose-Maria d'Alencon's badge, and over the door of the Shoreside police precinct, and on my own Ponce de Leon landing license.

Traffic had backed up by now on either side of the roadblock. Several self-driving trucks nosed moronically at the Trident Overland rigs, trying to find a way around them. Cars with human drivers were U-turning to get away as the first riot bird looked for space to land. The second bird was rapidly descending.

"Wait for it," Parsec said, "wait for it … if that fucker Nunak fucked up, I'll flay him …"

One of the Trident Overland rigs exploded.

It lifted several feet off the ground. Fire burst from under its hood and boiled out of its windows.

Both riot birds fell out of the air.

One of them fell from an altitude of fifty meters, and landed on the burning Trident Overland truck.

The other fell … considerably further … and landed on the traffic.

37

BOTH riot birds exploded with the raging, hissing fury of jet fuel finding its way to electrical lines. The impacts shook our tree like a double earthquake. I clung to my branch, cursing in shock.

Each of those birds carried a crew of six. Each of those officers had family. As the noise of secondary explosions settled down, I screamed at Parsec, calling him a fucking murderer and worse.

"Zip it, Starrunner. They had it coming. You know what I went through in that jailhouse? You know what it's like being a Shifter in jail? They put broken glass in my breakfast. I had to watch my back even when I was asleep. I got scars I didn't have before, inside and out."

"At least you're alive."

"You say that like you're joking. But I tell you this in all truth: I wouldn't have lasted another month in that place."

"The bright side is you won't have to go back," I said. "When they catch you, it'll be the needle."

"You mean *if*."

I unglued my eyes from the horror of the burning aircraft and cars. Raised them to the horizon. "Wanna hedge your bets?"

More choppers were coming. I counted three, and then I turned in the direction of Buonaville and saw another one.

"Those are just traffic cops," Parsec said. "Except for the one from the jail. That'll be the one they use to hunt for escaped prisoners. I ain't too worried. Their search and destroy functionality is fifty years out of date, 'cause no one ever *has* escaped from that hellhole they have the nerve to call a humane penitentiary facility. Until me."

He slid down the tree, tearing off leaves with his claws.

I stayed where I was, held by a terrible fascination, watching the choppers approach.

The Buonaville manhunter reached us first, and descended to hover over the disaster area, I realized that Parsec's freedom wasn't going to last more than another few minutes. He was wrong about the supposed obsolescence of the manhunter. Well, the chopper itself was just an old military twin-rotor, but as it hovered over the roadblock, a couple dozen drones spilled out of its side ports. They were the same model I once owned (I inherited mine from Artie, who picked it up on a Techworld): military surveillance drones with LiDAR and spectrographic imaging functionality. Those mothers can see through trees.

They split into two flocks and ranged out over the jungle on both sides of the road.

I stared up through the leaves, petrified with horror. They were going to see *me*.

I took the only evasive action I could: right there, in the top of the weatherstopper tree, I Shifted.

Shifting in treetops is not recommended. I wrapped my elbow around a branch, fell down a few branches as my arm fizzed out into a raw quantum-probabilistic zone of nothingness, and dug jaguar claws into bark just in time to save myself from a worse fall.

I chose my jaguar because it was in the front of my mind, and because it kinda sorta resembled a native Ponce de Leon flamecat, the top predator around here. Not enough legs, but apart from that. Flamecats can climb trees. It was fifty-fifty whether the drone's pattern-matching algos would classify me as a flamecat or a Shifter in animal form.

I clawed the remnants of my t-shirt off my neck. My jeans, phone, gun, and boots tumbled down through the branches.

A drone buzzed over the top of my tree without slowing down and zoomed away, skimming the canopy.

Safe. But the bears weren't. There is nothing on Ponce de Leon that looks like a bear, apart from Shifters.

Sudden movement on the road drew my gaze. Two men burst out of the jungle, right underneath the hovering manhunter. One was Nunak. The other was Larry K.

Nunak still had his holobook. He was gesturing in frustration.

Larry K still had his machine-gun.

Nunak typed, held up one finger—wait a minute!—typed some more.

The manhunter edged down further so its door gunner could target him.

Larry K sprinted out among the crashed vehicles, shooting up at the manhunter. Return fire from the door gunner followed him. Crushed fish jumped up like they were alive.

Larry K was smart. He didn't aim at the manhunter's rotors, or the cockpit. He aimed at the fuel tank.

The chopper erupted almost gracefully, burning as it sank to earth.

Beneath it, Larry K sank, too, bowing his head like a child that suddenly feels tired.

I skidded down the weatherstopper tree. I was halfway back to the road when the *second* Trident Overland rig exploded.

The fireball reddened the afternoon sunlight seeping through the strimmed wall of the jungle.

The ground shivered under my feet.

A drone fell through the trees and landed on the forest floor in front of me like a dead goose.

Nunak stumbled towards me, without his holobook, his face red, mooing in pain. He must have been standing too near the rig when it went up. He fumbled at his belt with burned hands. I helped him along by snapping at his pants legs. He yowled in pain again when his front paws hit the ground, but Shifting "resets" the nervous system to some extent, so he was able to walk on them.

Jaguar and polar bear slunk through the Tunjle, following the fairly obvious trail the other bears had left.

"How'd you do that?" I said over my shoulder.

"Blow up the trucks?" He had a high, squeaky voice, and his bear form was a bit off—it looked more like a husky than a real polar bear. I could see why folks underestimated him. "Wireless detonator."

"No, the rest of it. Aircraft and drones falling out of the sky. Explosions don't do that."

"They do if you use the explosion to power a high-strength microwave energy burst."

"Oh."

"Microwaves are a type of EMP. It fries the electronics. Rotors stall out, and down she goes. Poor man's HERF weapon."

He talked like he was hot shit, but I had seen him crying in pain, and I could hear the fear behind his brittle bravado. I turned on the trail and showed him my jaguar's teeth. "Nice trick. Where'd you learn that? In the forces?"

"No, I … who are you?"

He didn't know my jaguar. He had thought I must be an associate of Parsec's, just because I was a Shifter. "The name's Starrunner."

"Oh God."

"Where's my 500 KGCs?"

"I don't have it," Nunak said, caving in just like that. "I gave it all to Cecilia!"

I was about to smack him around a bit to get more information out of him, but then I remembered Larry K shooting down the helicopter and sinking slowly to his knees, and I lost my appetite for hurting anyone or anything. We walked on a bit, still heading away from the road, and found the other bears waiting for us in a thicket. They had all Shifted into their bear forms. Some of them had their packs strapped on their backs.

"Finally," Parsec growled. "Where's Larry?"

"I don't think he's coming." I told them what I had seen.

"Aw fuck," Gary K blurted. "Aw fuck fuck fuck."

It is a terrible thing when a bear cries. I lost all my hatred for him in that moment. Larry had been his twin brother. Suzie nosed her boyfriend's shoulder, licked the all-too-human tears off his furry face.

"Is Starrunner telling the truth?" Parsec roared at Nunak. "Speak up, you piss-colored mutt!"

"Y-yes, sir," Nunak muttered.

"All because *you* fucked up. That pissant detonator couldn't work from a hundred meters away? Goddammit. Larry was worth ten of you. I should leave you here. Break your legs and leave you here for the wood ants. You couldn't keep up, anyway."

Nunak started to plead incoherently. His desperation not to be left behind helped me to understand the dynamic between him and Parsec. He had always been shunned by the Bad-News Bears: too brainy, too uncool, too out-of-shape. But when Parsec fell on hard times, he had turned to Nunak for help, and Nunak had gladly given it, hoping to finally earn acceptance.

I shared the general view that Larry K had been worth ten of him, but I said, "He hadn't knocked those drones out, y'all would have been caught already, Buzz."

"True," Parsec said. "And there'll be more coming. We need to cover as much ground as possible before they can deploy another manhunter." He snarled at Nunak. "If you can't keep up, we ain't slowing down for you, hear?"

I moved in front of Parsec as the bears tightened the straps of each other's packs with their teeth. "Where're you going?"

"Going?" His bleary little eyes met mine. "Nowhere."

"Huh?"

"We," he enunciated, "are going nowhere. This is *our* planet." His gaze moved past me, into the rustling, vividly green maze of the jungle. His nose quivered, inhaling the rich scentscape. "We're staying."

My jaw dropped as I finally understood what he had in mind. They were planning to hide out in the jungle. To *stay* in the jungle ...

... as bears.

"What about Cecilia?" I said.

Cecilia Parsec had supported her husband steadfastly throughout his ordeal. She had organized his legal defense, and Nunak had told me that she was involved with the blackmail scheme, as well. She and Parsec had a stronger marriage than many an upstanding couple. I couldn't see him ditching her like this.

"She was gonna come," Parsec said, "but then she changed her mind."

"Guess it's no use persuading *you* to change your mind."

"Nope. We belong in the woods," Parsec said. "I spent my whole life trying to pretend it ain't so, but at the end of the day, we're Shifters. You know it, Starrunner. In your heart, you know it, too."

I said nothing. Oh, I understood the pull of the wilderness. I had felt it at Alec's place. I had seen the big woods wrap around my daughter and comfort her like a mother's arms. There's something inside of every Shifter that yearns for an animal's natural habitat.

But let's get real. Even the stewarded, selectively hunted woods on Alec's property were dangerous. And this was the Tunjle. It was no one's natural habitat. It was a green kill zone. Parsec had just spent a month in prison, and he was none too young. Of the other bears, some of them were fit, some weren't, but I would bet they had never hunted and killed their supper in their life.

"You'll leave your bones here," I said quietly.

"That's what you think."

"Buzz, I wouldn't try it, and I'm from San Damiano."

"That's my point. You're from San Dami*aaaano.* You don't belong here. We do."

Parsec turned his head and checked over the line of bears. They had formed up in single file. Bears have a travelling gait that can eat up the ground, though they would be slowed down by the thick undergrowth.

"Ready to roll, ladies and gents?"

The bears growled an affirmative.

"So what'd you do with my money?" I said.

"Spent it," Parsec said.

"Spent it on *what?"*

"You got any idea how expensive it is to be criminally prosecuted? I spent it on lawyers' fees, the settlement in the civil lawsuits brought by the city, new suits and shoes for my court appearances, telephone calls from jail … the usual. It's gone, Starrunner. You ain't getting it back."

I clawed a nearby tree in sheer frustration. Too well I remembered explaining my own spending habits to d'Alencon. I had pissed away millions over the years, a little at a time, and I didn't even have a criminal defense team to pay for. "You hired all those pricey lawyers, and you didn't even wait to see if they could get you off?"

Parsec laughed. "It wasn't gonna happen. The normies hate us. I didn't really know that before, but I do now."

"Cecilia is a normie."

The grizzly's laugh cut off like my words were a knife. He swiped at me, so fast I had to jump back. "Fuck off and quit wasting my time."

The bears trotted away into the jungle. A few seconds after the last pair of furry hindquarters vanished, it was like they'd never been here, apart from the lingering rank smell.

It is easy to get lost in the woods, even for an animal. But I had no trouble orienting myself back to the road. For one thing, I had the bears' trail to guide me, and for another, the breeze was blowing from the coast, and even the smells of the jungle could not disguise the odors of burning jet fuel and roasted human flesh.

38

When I got back to the weatherstopper tree, I sniffed around on the forest floor until I found my phone and gun. My jeans had also fallen to the ground, although my other clothes must have gotten stuck in the branches. I tapped my phone with a claw. It was a brick. Nunak's EMP had killed it. So that was another 5 KGCs they owed me. The cops might be able to trace it to me anyway, so I scratched a hole in the ground and buried it. I buried my gun with it. I could only carry one thing in my mouth, and I needed my jeans.

From the road came shouts, the hissing of foam-hoses, and the grinding of heavy machinery.

I padded up the hill I had walked down less than an hour ago, staying under cover. The noise faded behind me. I stuck my nose out of the green and saw my truck still sitting on the shoulder where I had left it. It was no longer the only vehicle parked on the hill. Quite a tailback had built up, waiting for the disaster area to be cleared.

When I drew level with the truck, I Shifted back. My nausea instantly returned full force. My gut knotted, but the fishburger refused to come back up. Groaning, I put on my jeans, crawled through the weeds on the shoulder, and climbed casually into my truck like I'd just gotten out to take a piss.

I stifled a yell of surprise.

In the passenger seat sat Cecilia Parsec.

"Hello, Mike."

She loosed a haggard smile. She looked ten years older than when I had seen her last. She wore hiking clothes, a far cry from her usual high-fashion look. Her normally styled auburn hair fell in a tangled mass.

"Sweet Jesus," I said. "Where'd you spring from?"

"I was going to go with Buzz. I changed my mind." She shrugged. "I was done with the Tunjle after fifteen minutes. A narcosloth came this close to falling on my head."

"They're sneaky little bastards."

"And my hair's ruined." She lifted strands, mocking herself. "This was a 300-GC blowout."

"Jungle's no place for the fashion-conscious," I agreed.

"Buzz said I could ride on his back. Wasn't it sweet of him? But I'd only have slowed them down."

I ran my hands down my thighs, clasped them together, said, "Well." Then I remembered I was shoeless and shirtless. Cecilia was the kind of woman who could make that feel like a crime. My tactical backpack was squashed under Cecilia's much larger, brand-new one in the footwell. I put on my spare t-shirt and sneakers. "Is there any particular reason you're sitting in my truck? Like maybe a 500 KGC reason?"

"The money's gone, Mike. I apologize; I really do. We needed fast cash to pay our creditors."

"If Buzz was planning to escape into the jungle, anyway, why even bother paying your creditors?"

"I think we both knew, in our hearts, that I wouldn't be going." She gestured downhill. "It's moving."

Breakdown trucks had dragged the hulks of the Trident Overland rigs to the side of the road. Cops, paramedics, and technicians milled around the obscene wrecks of the riot birds. Flying ambulances landed and lifted off as we watched. But one inbound lane was clear, and cops had begun to direct traffic around the disaster area.

"You'd better get down on the floor." I pulled the grubby plaid seat cover off and tossed it over Cecilia like a blanket.

The cops were checking IDs. They made drivers extend their arms out their side windows so that the credit dots on their forearms could be scanned. I didn't have a credit dot, because I was a Shifter. "Pull over, sir," the traffic cop said. "I need to run your ID."

I pulled over, into the disaster area, and gave them the holomarked ID card that all unchipped folks have to carry. Fire-retardant foam slopped across the road, covering the scorch marks where jet fuel had flowed and burned. Axe-wielding paramedics were breaking the windshield of a half-burned family car. I spotted Larry K's body on a stretcher. Far from bothering to cover him up, some asshole had set a trauma kit down on top of him as if he were a table.

The cop frowned at a handheld, pulling up God knows what information about me, certainly including the data that my phone and car had spent the last hour right here on the side of the road. Cold sweat broke out on the backs of my knees. Why had I thought I could get away with this? Cecilia twitched under her stinky plaid cover. I touched her with my foot, willing her to stay quiet. If the cops found her, it was game over. Neither of us would ever see the light of day again.

Another cop ambled up to the truck. "What were you doing in Buonaville today, Mr. Starrunner?"

"Just a little road trip," I said.

"Yeah? What you got there?" He pointed at the plaid hump in the footwell. His head was on a level with the window. I had a fantasy of punching him in the nose and stepping on the accelerator.

The other cop came back, making a face like he smelled something bad. "He's green. All right, Mr. Starrunner, move on. You're holding up traffic."

I couldn't believe my luck. I accelerated away from the scene as fast as decently possible. *He's green.* What on earth had that meant? That

I was free to go, obviously. But why? Could it be … could it be that Jose-Maria d'Alencon was protecting me?

I slumped back in my seat and lit a cigarette. "You can come out now."

Cecilia sat up on the seat. "Would it be at all possible for you to give me a ride home?"

I looked at her and realized she was in shock. Sometimes when people take a bad jolt to the heart, they just carry on, letting force of habit guide them like an autopilot.

"You and your husband robbed me blind," I said. "My apartment is about to be repossessed." I couldn't go on, because my stomach was informing me that the situation had gone critical. I pulled over, stumbled into the knee-high weeds, and threw up.

It was the fishburger.

It was the disaster scene.

But as I retched, eyes streaming, I remembered something else.

Early symptoms may include sudden attacks of nausea …

It was IVK.

My asymptomatic grace period was over.

The enemy in my brain had come into the open.

I wiped my mouth on the back of my arm. Staggered back to the truck. Cecilia reached down to help me up. "Made the mistake of eating lunch in Gillietown," I said.

"I have every kind of stomach med, if you want. I thought I'd need them in the jungle."

"I wouldn't say no." I still wanted to believe the fishburger was the culprit. I accepted a couple of Cecilia's pills and a bottle of designer sparkling water. The water and the pills stayed down. When I felt a little better, I started the truck again. "You were really going to do it, weren't you? You were planning to go with him."

"Yes. But then I just … couldn't." She stared straight ahead. The slanting sun picked out the lines around her mouth and eyes.

"You were scared."

"Yes."

"Of the jungle."

"Yes! Of course!"

"It's not that bad." Half an hour ago, I'd been saying the opposite to Parsec. "The worst it can do is kill you."

Cecilia let out a short, bitter laugh.

"Do you still love him?"

There was silence for a good two klicks. I glanced over at her again and saw tears tracking through her make-up. "How can you ask me that?" she said. "Look what I just did for him."

"Then be with him, Cecilia. Don't let a few parasites and puffer-plants come between you."

She shook her head. "He's a Shifter, and I'm not. His world isn't my world." She rested her head against the back of the seat, letting the tears roll. There was hard-won dignity in her stillness.

"So what are you going to do? Go home—"

"Yes, I suppose so."

"—and wait for them to come and arrest you?" She said nothing. She had thought everything through, up until the point of their escape, and no further. "Instead of Parsec doing twenty to life, it'll be you."

"Well, what do you suggest?" she blazed. "Throw myself on the mercy of the Grizzly's Bar & Grill crowd? I'm a normie! They wouldn't shelter me … now that I can't pay them anymore."

"You paid them to throw a Molotov cocktail at my house, huh? To warn Rex not to go to the police."

"Yes. I don't know all the details. The Kodiaks took care of that. But I did tell them to make sure that the children were not harmed."

"That's mighty big of you."

I could not forgive her for endangering Lucy. Or for the dead officers and civilians on the Buonaville road. I could not forgive her for blackmailing Rex, and wrecking my relationship with Irene.

But I also could not forget that she had saved Lucy last month. If not for Cecilia Parsec's common sense and compassion, Lucy would be somewhere in the Core right now, or trailing after Sophia on her murder spree through the Hurtworlds, a living trophy on my ex-wife's coat. I shuddered to think of it. We had dodged a bullet. Scrub that. We had dodged an *asteroid,* thanks to this woman. At the end of the day, I owed her.

"You can't go home to Ville Verde." I was trying to decide what her best option would be when a solution arrived in the form of a motorbike in the outbound lane, flashing its headlamp at my truck.

It was Martin. When I'd cut off my call to him at the scene of the jailbreak, he'd jumped on his bike and come looking for me.

I parked on the shoulder and rapidly explained the situation to him. We had to consider satellite surveillance. This was risky, but it seemed like a safer option than taking Cecilia out to Alec's place. Chances were Alec wouldn't have her, anyway.

"So you want me to take Mrs. Parsec? Up to the top of a high cliff and throw her off?"

"I was hoping for a less terminal solution," I said. "Do you know anyone that might have room for her?"

"In their stomachs, maybe."

"Marty."

"Kidding. Sure, I can think of a couple people." He took his extra bike helmet off the pillion. "We snakes believe in gratuitous deeds of kindness, you know. It's our way of buying cosmic insurance. That's why they consider me a maverick. 'Marty,' they're always saying to me, 'Marty, ya gotta be nicer to people.'"

I grabbed the helmet, ran back to the truck, and persuaded Cecilia to put it on. "I'm not sure if you know Martin Woods. Friend of mine. He'll take you somewhere safe. We'll work out a longer-term solution once the heat is off."

She grabbed her oversized backpack. "Can I trust you?"

"Yes, you can." I felt the weight of the words as I uttered them.

Cecilia got on the back of Martin's bike and wrapped her arms around his waist. I heard him telling her to relax, as she was too big to swallow, anyway. Then they roared off.

I climbed back in my truck and followed at a more sedate pace.

Now that I was alone, my body let me know there was a price to pay for climbing trees and roaming through the jungle. The nausea had passed, mercifully, but my energy levels were bottoming out. My scratches from climbing the weatherstopper were starting to sting, and I'd wrenched my shoulder somewhere along the line, too. I found half a bottle of bourbon in the glove compartment and drank stingy sips as I drove, trying to see only the road, and not the riot birds crashing, the people burning to death inside … Larry K's body on a stretcher … He didn't have IVK, but he'd gone before me. All life felt temporary, and at the same time, I had the strangest feeling that I was immortal, for the time being. The bourbon helped with that.

I reached Mag-Ingat as the sun slipped into the sea. I wasn't due to meet with d'Alencon until nine. I had hours to kill. I needed to do it somewhere that wouldn't set the algos off.

I hooked a right out of the rush hour traffic and drove to Christy Day's new address.

39

STANDING in the lobby of Christy's new building, I wondered what the hell I was doing here. If not for the bourbon I wouldn't have got this far. The building was a vertical suburb, north of the trendy downtown district where Christy used to live. A hollow square, it enclosed its own park, playground, and village shops. Kids rushed in and out of the automatic doors, taking the time to stare at me. Was it the green stains on my jeans, or the absence of a credit dot on my arm, or the look in my eyes, or all three? My stomach knotted again—but now with anxiety, not nausea. I didn't belong here. I should bail before I got myself, or Christy, in trouble.

Then she answered her intercom. *"Mike?"*

My doubts faded away. I got in the elevator and rode up to the sixth floor.

She opened her front door. I got an impression of several rooms opening off the hall, and then all I saw was Christy standing in front of me. Her hair floated in a cinnamon cloud around her face. It was too dim in the hall for me to see the hazel flecks in her eyes.

"Hey, you," she said.

"I have to apologize for yesterday," I said. "I was pretty rude on the phone. Sorry."

"It's fine. Is Lucy OK?"

"Yes."

"Well, come on in. Tell me what happened. I've got some of her stuff, as I mentioned."

I glanced down at myself. "I'm kind of a mess …"

"Are you ever *not* a mess, Mike?" she said with a quick, mischievous smile.

Something inside of me which had been knotted tight for weeks started to loosen. "You got me," I said, smiling into her eyes.

The bewitching pink flush I remembered rose to her cheeks. She broke eye contact. "Anyway," she said, "look at me." She wore a t-shirt smeared with mud or clay, and cargo shorts in a similar condition. "I just got back from camp."

"You know," I said, "I didn't even notice what you're wearing. All I was thinking was how good you would look out of it."

The words came straight from my groin without detouring through my brain. I groaned and started to apologize.

She shut me up with a kiss.

It was a revelation of something I had already known, but had tried to forget: the spark between me and Christy Day could power the whole city. Her velvet tongue and soft lips set off fireworks in my brain. A sudden rush of blood to my groin drained my capacity for thought. All that remained was need. I crushed her against me, this close to scooping her off her feet, before she could change her mind, and …

Stop. STOP.

I held her off. She licked her lips, redder now from kissing. "Wow."

Desire was scrambling my synapses. I focused on her face, as opposed to anything lower down. "So, uh, before I completely forget why I came over, I owe you an explanation. The reason Lucy left camp unexpectedly was because some lowlife bears blackmailed a friend of mine, and instead of paying Lucy's camp fees, he used the money to pay off the blackmailers." I deliberately didn't give Rex's name, as

Christy knew the Seagraves, too. "She's out in the jungle right now, staying with a different friend. She's doing fine."

"O… kay."

"No half-truths, right?" I said, wondering if I had revealed too much.

Christy grinned. "I've *missed* you." I stood stupefied by lust, watching her trim rear end as she walked lightly along the hall. "Come on through. I'll fix us something to drink."

The living-room and kitchen were a single open-plan area, with floor-to-ceiling windows overlooking the central park of the complex. School and camp supplies and piles of laundry towered on all the surfaces. It was homey and welcoming, but the place seemed too big for one person, and I wondered why she had left her painstakingly decorated studio apartment.

I sat on her floral-patterned sofa. She sat kitty-corner to me and placed two tall glasses on the coffee table. They were a disturbing shade of blue. "Blueberries, spinach, and klimfruit."

"Sounds good," I lied, taking a reluctant sip. It tasted as healthy as it sounded.

"Better for you than whiskey." She must have tasted the booze in my mouth.

"I had to get the courage from somewhere to come and see you."

"I really did miss you," she said, looking at her knees. "While you were away, I felt kind of hollow." The words winded me. I had forgotten her extraordinary, unassuming honesty. "It felt like there was an emptiness in my life that wasn't there before."

I didn't know what to say to that. I hadn't earned it. "When I was in the Hurtworlds, I thought about you. It was almost like you were there. It inspired me. Helped me to deal with … stuff."

Christy looked troubled. I kicked myself for bringing up Sophia, even obliquely. I did not want her shadow to fall across … whatever we had.

"I have to ask you, Mike …" Christy shook her head. "This is tricky for me. I'm not supposed to violate confidentiality."

"What confidentiality?"

"Between a counselor, me, and a camper, Lucy in this case."

"Screw that," I said, alarmed. "I'm her father. Is there something I should know?"

"We spent a lot of time together while she was at camp. She'd come to my office during her free periods, and sometimes we would hang out on the beach. She seemed to feel that she could confide in me."

I didn't know whether to be pleased or worried. Had Lucy latched onto Christy as a mother figure?

"That's one reason I was upset when Mr. Seagrave took her away, but anyway." Christy took a deep breath. "I'm just going to say this straight out. I know that Lucy's mother attempted to abduct her."

"Yes."

"I'd like to know a little more about that situation. Did you and your ex have a bad divorce?"

I took a sip of my blue drink. Oh, fuck it. I didn't have the willpower to evade the topic anymore. "Yes. She's a Traveller, and in fact, she was responsible for the Founding Day attack. She's currently the most-wanted woman in the Cluster. I ran into her on the Hurtworlds and she tried to shoot me dead," I drawled. "Next question."

"Oh," Christy said. *"Oh my God."*

"You asked."

"Your ex-wife is a *Traveller?"*

"Yup."

"I think you could have told me that before."

"It never came up."

"Well … that's why, then."

"Why what?"

"I thought Lucy was fantasizing, to be honest. She used to talk to me about her mother. She said that she has a doctorate in AI studies, and she's beautiful and tough, she's a crack shot, she has her own spaceship ... and so on and so on."

"All that is factually correct, except that Sophia can't shoot for shit. That's why I'm sitting here alive today. Oh, and she also has a master's in philosophy."

"How can I ever compete?" Christy said ironically. "Well, that explains a lot, I suppose."

"Explains what?"

"Mike, Lucy is *terrified* of her. On three separate occasions, she woke up screaming. I was informed that she said she'd dreamed her mother was coming to get her."

"Oh God. Poor Lucy," I muttered. "I should have been there."

"Yes, you should. At the very least, you should have filled us in. Your daughter is going through a difficult time, and I was unable to provide appropriate care and counseling, because I didn't know the backstory. I understand that you're concerned about her privacy, but she was this close to being labelled with mental health issues—"

"Over some nightmares?!"

Christy pressed her lips together. She got up and fetched a box from the other side of the room. "This is Lucy's stuff." I glanced in, got an impression of kiddie crafts.

"Christy, I'm sorry. I would have told you, but ..." I sighed. It was hopeless. I stood up with the box in my arms. "Thanks for the drink."

She rose, trapping me in between the sofa and the coffee table, and looked up into my face. "When we first met, I felt like I could be completely honest with you, and you wouldn't be shocked, or push me away." I nodded. "But if you can't be honest with me, this isn't going to work. Even on the level of friendship."

I set the box down again without looking, and knocked my scarcely-touched blue drink over. It flooded across the coffee table. "I'm ten years older than you, Christy. I've been knocking around the Cluster since I was seventeen. I've been *killing* since I was seventeen. The day I left Lucy with you on the mall level, I'd just shot a man dead." There was no risk in telling her about Canuck. "I have a Traveller ex—" and I hadn't even told her that I had spent the afternoon helping Parsec escape from custody. "I'm more trouble than I'm worth. I'm like a cute stray dog that turns out to be a wolf, tears your house apart, and pisses on the carpet. How's that for honesty?"

She rose and went into the kitchen for a towel. Pressed it on the spill. Righting the glass, she muttered, "Memo to self: stop trying to improve Mike's diet."

"My life is a shitstorm." There was an inch left in the glass. I downed it. "A few vitamins can't hurt." All that remained was to tell her about IVK.

She took the towel over to the sink and rinsed it out. "Your daughter is one of the brightest kids I've ever worked with. As you know, she scores in the 95th percentile on all of our standard tests. Not only that, she's imaginative, kind to younger children, and a natural leader. Did she tell you that she was selected to lead the Orca team? Everything that I said about her issues around her mother, you have to take that in the context of her enormous potential."

I sat on the sofa grinning from ear to ear. Nothing could soften me up faster than praise for my daughter. "She did mention the Orca team, yeah. Sounds a bit suspect to me."

"So, I figure you must be a pretty great guy to have raised a daughter like Lucy." Christy came back to the sofa. She straddled my knees, still standing. "I want in on that shitstorm."

I laughed. My hands went to her waist. "Oh man, Christy. You have no idea what you do to me."

She tucked her hair behind one ear, leaving a smear of blue on her cheek. "Why don't you show me?"

"That sounds like a challenge." I pulled her down onto my lap. Her arms went around my neck. We kissed, frantically. As she ground on my lap, I reached under her clothes, hungry to touch every inch of her skin—

The front door clunked open.

Christy sprang off my lap. "Oh crap, I wasn't watching the clock." My raging erection wilted. She tugged her clothes straight. "Hey, guys," she called out. "How was school?" To me, she added, "There's something I didn't tell you about, either." She winked. "It just didn't come up."

I stood up as footsteps came down the hall.

In walked Jan and Leaf Khratz, Pippa's cousins.

40

I had not seen Jan and Leaf since we parted at the Space Island quarantine center. What were they doing here?

They were no longer the ragged waifs I remembered. They wore shorts and t-shirts with annoying embedded holos, like every other kid, and carried backpacks. Jan, the thirteen-year-old, had his hair cut in a trendy diagonal fringe. Leaf, nine, had flashing star stickers on her round cheeks.

Jan hung back, scowling; he hadn't changed that much—but Leaf ran at me and hugged me. "Mr. Starrunner!"

"Meet my foster kids," Christy said, grinning.

"Wow." I was grinning, too. I held Leaf off and picked those awful star stickers off her cheeks. "How are you guys doing?"

"We had English *and* numeracy today," Leaf said.

"They're taking summer classes to get caught up," Christy explained. "It works with my schedule at Lagos del Mar."

"So that's why you moved."

"Yeah. I get a stipend for fostering these two monkeys, although I'd do it for free." Christy smoothed Leaf's hair and dropped a kiss on her forehead. "Ideally, I would like to live in Shiftertown and send Leaf to Shoreside Elementary and Jan to Creek High. But I have to meet all these conditions, one of which is living in an approved area. And Shiftertown isn't one." Christy rolled her eyes. "Supposedly it's dangerous."

I matched her grimace, while mentally acknowledging the point.

Leaf twirled into the kitchen area. "Christy, can I have something to eat?"

"Sure, honey, what would you like?"

Christy. I remembered how hard it had been to get the kids to call me anything except *mister.* They came from a background of radical deprivation, although you wouldn't think it to look at these two now. Christy had watered them with love and they had blossomed like flowers.

I could still see the refugee camp in Jan's distrustful glare, though. He grabbed a carton of juice from the fridge and headed out of the room. A line appeared between Christy's eyebrows.

"Hey, uh uh," I said. I grabbed Jan's skinny shoulder, turned him around and stared him down. "Sit yourself down right here and let's catch up. I got some questions for you … and if you're interested, I also got news of your cousin Pippa."

*

We talked for over an hour, as the sunset deepened into twilight and the skyline lit up. I showed them the v-mail Pippa had made for them. That undermined Jan's hostility. I did not, of course, share the hair-raising details of our escape from Yesanyase Skont. I just said that I had helped Pippa move to Mittel Trevoyvox, which she herself described in the v-mail as a great place to live. I also said that Mechanical Failure had stayed with her, which reassured the children—they'd been appropriately intimidated by MF while they were travelling on my spaceship.

I got the impression Leaf was adjusting well to life on Ponce de Leon. Given that Jan was a teenage boy, it would probably be many years before he could appreciate Christy's kindness, but she had already won his confidence in important ways.

Under her gentle prodding, he opened up to me for the first time about the refugee camp where they had been born.

"We didn't learn *anything.* That's why I have to do this crap." He showed me his homework. It was … remedial, and that's putting it mildly. "I actually hate Gran now. She could have at least taught us to *read.*"

According to Jan, he, Pippa, and Leaf had all lived with their grandmother in the refugee camp until she died a few years previously. After that, Pippa had hustled to provide for the three herself. Neither Jan nor Leaf had a kind word for their Gran, but she must have been a formidable woman.

"Wash your mouth out," I said, forgetting that Jan was not mine to discipline. "Your grandmother raised you. You owe her everything."

"She raised us to rule a planet that isn't ours anymore," Jan said. "Heck with that." He took a handful of the pita chips Christy had put out and crunched them gloomily.

Leaf was doing her homework, tracing ABCs on a school-issue tablet. She looked up and said, "But Gran *did* teach us, Jan. She taught us the Code and the Tree." I could hear the capital letters in her careful emphasis.

"That's just poetry," Jan scoffed.

"Leaf," I said. "What's the Code and the Tree?"

"Things we had to learn," she said.

"What kind of things?"

Jan was glaring at her. "I don't remember."

"I bet you do remember."

Leaf's fist closed around the hem of her holo t-shirt and lifted it towards her mouth. She was about to revert to her old self-soothing habit.

Christy scooted closer to the little girl and put her arm around her. "It's OK. You don't have to talk about it if you don't want to."

"I honestly don't remember! I *forgot!*"

"I remember," Jan said. Suddenly sitting up, he began to chant. "This is the Code of Gessyria. Sixteen, four thousand and two through four thousand three hundred and ten. A tired grouchy cat treks green cliffs. A greedy tiger attacks. The cat tries a clever trick, growling angrily …" On he went, reciting the poem or story or whatever it was in a singsong voice. After a moment Leaf joined in. Christy and I gaped in bemusement.

You hear about the immense capacity of the human memory. It's supposed to be damn near infinite, located in the same quantum storehouse where we Shifters keep our animal forms when not in use. But in reality, who can even remember their own phone number nowadays? These children were something else. They sounded like machines, regurgitating this gobbledygook in perfect unison, on and on. "The cat grieves above the tiger's corpse. Three avian cannibals guzzle the crimson gore …"

"What's it *mean?"* Christy whispered to me.

"Search me." I grabbed up her phone, which was lying on the table, and set it to record, in case we found someone who was more of an expert in Darkworlds poetry.

Leaf trailed off. "That's all I can remember."

"Now you put me off," Jan said.

"But I can do the Tree."

"The Tree's *easy."* Jan clapped his hands. Again the children started chanting. "Marcello and Fiannula begat Sandhya who married David and they begat Rafael, Gabriel, and Amelia. Rafael married Chiho and they begat …" I counted thirty-two generations until Jan and Leaf finished together, triumphantly, "And Marcello and Anna begat Cornelia and Mei and June, and Cornelia married David and begat Rafael, and Samantha married Calvin and begat Jan and Letitia, and Saul married Elodie and begat Pippa!"

Rafael. That had to be Rafael Ijiuto. I remembered that the charges against him had been dropped. He was walking around Mag-Ingat as we spoke. These children were sharing a planet with the cousin who had tried to kill them. Heckuva job, PdL PD.

"My real name's Letitia," Leaf said.

"Wow," Christy said. "I don't think I even know the names of my great-grandparents."

"It's very important to know where you come from," Jan said. "But the Code is *more* important."

"It's code for *something,* right?" Christy said. "Is there a key to it?"

"I don't know," Jan said. "I never got all the way to the end. Pippa knows all of it."

I sent the recording of their Code to myself, and then drummed my fingers on my knee, thinking. The Tree was the genealogy of the royal dynasty of the Gessyrias. That was obvious. But the Code … what was that? Did it have anything to do with the TrZam 008?

The Temple's gonna fall with you inside it.

This information could destroy humanity.

I wondered who else knew about Jan and Leaf's feat of memorization. "Did you recite your Code and Tree for the people at the resettlement center?"

"Are you kidding?" Jan snorted.

"They were mean," Leaf said. "They made us pee in cups. They stuck needles in us!"

Christy and I exchanged a smile, but I felt cold inside. These kids might be in danger for what they knew.

I had to talk to Dolph. I touched my pocket and then remembered I didn't have a phone anymore.

Well, he would be meeting me at Snakey's. I'd fill him in then.

I glanced at the clock. Ten to eight. Crap, I had to go.

I felt a soul-sickening reluctance to leave this apartment. It felt like walking away from life itself. Of course, that was an illusion. Death had come visiting with me, and would be leaving with me. My lie of omission about IVK did not make Christy's apartment a safe haven; it just made it another *fake* haven. But as I stood with Christy in the dark hallway inside the front door, I couldn't tell the difference between my guilt, and my unsated yearning for her. It was all one big sea of crappy feelings.

She bumped her forehead lightly against my chest. "Now I'll be lying awake all night, thinking about you," she whispered.

"Next time," I said into her hair. Next time, I would work out how to tell her that I had IVK.

"When?"

I let go of her. "Don't call me. I'll call you."

Her smile had an edge. "I guess I asked for that."

"No," I explained, "I mean it. I don't have a phone. I had to bury it under six inches of leaf mould."

She stepped back, raised her eyebrows, and pointed her index fingers at me. "Exciting. Life."

We were both laughing as I closed the door.

I took a roundabout route back to Estrangeiro Boulevard, picked up my truck, and reached Snakey's by eight forty-five.

41

SNAKEY'S is bigger on the inside than the outside. At street level, there's just a doorway squashed between a tattoo parlor and a curry shop, on the Strip between 70th and 71st. Downstairs, the bar sprawls through several basement-level rooms decorated with macabre trophies.

When I got there, Dolph was already occupying a barstool at the end of the counter. A girl melted off the stool next to him to make room for me. Vipe's eldest daughter set a drink in front of me. Three fingers of Alvarado, neat. "What a day," I said. "Cheers."

Dolph had his phone propped up on the bartop. It showed a news feed with the sound off. Highlights from the disaster on the Buonaville road. Shifters around us looked, cursed Parsec's name. There was a certain fatalism to their reactions. No one had really believed that Parsec would end up in jail. He never had before, and it turned out that this time was no different.

"This time *is* different, though," I said under my breath to Dolph. "I genuinely think we've seen the last of him. He may have beaten justice, but he can't beat the Tunjle."

"They raided his place at Ville Verde, too," Dolph said. "Talk about burning your bridges."

D'Alencon would be here in a few minutes. "Got something I want you to listen to," I said.

Dolph was drinking boilermakers. He tipped a fresh shot of whiskey into another pint of beer. "Where've you been, anyway?"

I reached for his phone. "Nunak bricked mine." I accessed my v-mail and downloaded the recording I'd sent to myself. "Listen to this. What does that sound like to you?"

"Kids?"

"Jan and Leaf." I smiled at his expression. "Pippa's cousins. Christy Day is fostering them—"

"You went to see her?" Dolph chortled.

Sensitive to reproach, as I couldn't justify my entanglement with Christy to myself, either, I said, "She's been a real friend."

"Mike, there's only one reason a sweet normie chick like that would be interested in you."

"It's my rugged good looks," I joked, smoothing my hair.

"Dream on." Dolph gazed into his drink. "I don't know Ms. Day that well, but I know her type. She's attracted to danger. It's not just the teeth and claws. It's the spaceships, the guns, the close calls, the questionable associates. All that shit turns her on. As much as she might want to fuck you, she wants to get inside of your world. She wants it inside of her." He was waxing almost lyrical. "Sweet as she looks, there's something screwed-up hiding inside, where you can't reach."

I raised my eyebrows. "You, my friend, need to get laid."

"I was working on that until you sat your raggedy ass down in her seat."

I glanced around to check out the girl I'd run off. Blonde, thin, too much jewellery. Dolph could do better. "What happened to Ember?"

"She's got a short memory. Fortunately, I do, too."

I picked up his phone and pressed it to his ear. "So what do you think of this?"

He listened for a moment. "It sounds like when they used to make us memorize the Catechism. Except not."

I explained how the Code and Tree appeared to be an oral history handed down in Pippa's family. "I'm wondering if it's related to whatever is on the TrZam 008."

"The angry green tiger gets a craving ..."Dolph's expression suddenly changed. Leaning across the bar, he grabbed the pen right out of Vipe's girl's apron pocket. He started to make notes on a cocktail napkin.

T A G T G A C

"The Code. Mike. Look at that. *The Code.*"

"Aw shit." I stared at the letters, finally realizing what had eluded me before.

Human DNA is made up of millions of nucleobases. These come in only four flavors: cytosine, guanine, adenine, and thymine. All the variation among humans and alt-humans is a matter of arranging strings of nucleobases in different orders. The achievement of the Big Shift scientists was simply that they discovered the exact right order to enable Shifting. The key was lots of trial and error, and a willingness to combine simulations with large-scale in vivo experimentation.

"It's a DNA string," I said. "But what does it do?"

"Search me." Dolph was still writing. "Do we have all of it?"

"No. Neither of them could remember the whole thing."

"Does Pippa know it, too?"

"They said she knows the whole thing."

"They're living backups for the TrZam 008." Dolph was making a leap, but I agreed. That would explain why Sophia had tried to capture Pippa. Even if there was no machine in the Cluster which could read the TrZam 008—as she thought—she'd be able to get the same information out of Pippa herself.

But what *was* it?

Dolph dragged a fingernail along the enigmatic lines of C, G, A, and T. "The Temple will fall with you inside it," he husked, in a good imitation of Zane. "This information will destroy humanity."

"Oh, shit," I said. It wasn't because of what Dolph had said. Staring into the mirror behind the optics, I had just seen Rafael Ijiuto walk into the bar.

Dolph and I twisted around on our stools.

The bar gradually fell silent. The music kept rolling on—scratchy twelve-string guitar, hoarse vocals soaked in loneliness—as Ijiuto ambled across the room and took the seat that had magically opened up two barstools down from me. In fact, the whole counter was now going begging. No one wanted to sit next to a normie.

Oh, it isn't that you can tell by looking at people. It's simply that Ijiuto was a stranger here. If he was a Shifter, he'd have come in animal form his first time, to prove his bona fides. He hadn't, so he wasn't.

There's no sign over the door saying Shifters Only, but the message is writ in letters of feathers and fur all the way down the stairs from the street. Every stair is a cryonite block containing a dead animal of some kind, supposedly killed by Vipe himself, ranging from a chicken to a Newfoundland dog. The bar top is also made of cryonite. The preserved corpse of a native PdL flamecat floated under our drinks, jaws agape, signifying Shifter victory over the native wildlife. It's that alpha predator thing again.

Rafael Ijiuto hitched his narrow ass on his barstool and grimaced at the flamecat. "That's kind of gross."

Dolph leaned across me. "They had a human being in the bar counter for a while," he said. "Vipe got complaints, so he took it down." This was untrue, although Vipe did sometimes talk about turning people into cryonite decorations if they pissed him off. "You volunteering as a replacement?"

Vipe's girl flicked her hair. "I would have trouble drinking off of this one's scrawny bod," she said. "It would turn my stomach. What can I getcha?"

"Beer," Ijiuto said. "Please."

Dolph chuckled at his tense expression. "Relax. You're no one's idea of a trophy."

"Oh, I don't know," I said. "Rafe, here, strikes me as kind of an archetype of mainstream humanity. Hellbent on getting his way no matter what. Completely indifferent to the human cost. Prepared to lie, cheat, steal, and kill to get what he wants. And to top it all, he's such a ridiculously gifted survivor he makes cockroaches look fragile. Shoot this guy down in orbit, run him off the road, throw him in Buonaville, and he comes back from the dead and sits down next to you and orders a fucking beer."

Ijiuto scowled. "I have diplomatic immunity."

"Son," Dolph said, "I hate to break it to you, but diplomatic immunity ain't proof against claws and teeth."

"Did I do something wrong?" Ijiuto picked up his beer and slurped it. "I don't get why you're threatening me. I didn't do anything to *you.*"

I looked at the clock behind the bar. 21:07. D'Alencon would be here any minute. If he caught us talking to Rafael Ijiuto, it would confuse the situation, to say the least. Why had Ijiuto come looking for us, anyway? Anger sparked a slow burn in my stomach as I remembered all the things this cretinous princeling had done.

"You know, you're right," Dolph said to Ijiuto with a jackally grin. "It's a waste of good invective to threaten you. I'll just follow you when you leave and bite your throat out in a dark alley. Someone'll steal your corpse and sell it to the biowaste processors."

"Thanks for reminding me why I hate this planet." Ijiuto was wearing clean but cheap business casual. What they gave him when he was freed from jail, I figured. His shirt was open at the neck. No TrZam 008.

"What happened to the crown jewels?" I said.

"Oh, boy," Ijiuto said. "That's what I mean about this planet. The police smashed my crown jewels up! In front of my eyes! With a hammer! If that's what you call civilization, you can keep it."

"So why don't you go home?" I said, anticipating his answer.

"No money." Ijiuto's credit dot, exposed by a rolled-up shirt sleeve, told the story. It was black.

"The beer ain't free," Vipe's girl said, following the conversation.

"That's actually why I'm here," Ijiuto said, seeking my gaze. His dark eyes had a soulful, puppy-dog set, but I saw a flash of calculation. "I was hoping you could give me a ride home. You still got your spaceship, right?"

Dolph laughed. I laughed. "I'd rather give a ride to a Kimberstine haulasaur," I said.

Vipe undulated across the floor. Ijiuto twitched his feet away from the viper the size of an anaconda. It was almost as good as having Martin with us. Swaying his head from side to side, as if preparing to strike at Ijiuto's legs, Vipe hissed, "I think that's enough. Out, normie." He jerked his head at the door.

"It doesn't say No Normies," Ijiuto protested.

"It doesn't say No Assholes, either," Vipe said. "But most people take it as read."

Dolph paid for Ijiuto's beer. We jostled him up the stairs into the strobe-painted bustle of the Strip. Aliens and human tourists milled along the sidewalk. Ijiuto scowled and drove his hands into the pockets of his sport jacket. The holo greeter outside the tattoo parlor shimmied around him, rainbowing his dust-colored face and hair. I suddenly saw his family resemblance to Pippa, Jan, and Leaf—it was in the lost, hopeless slump of his shoulders.

"Let's head down to the pier," Dolph said. "Push him off the end. You can't swim, can you, Your Highness?"

"You're gonna be sorry," Ijiuto said with sudden vehemence. "You're gonna be so, so sorry. I *tried* to be friendly. It's not my fault you guys are grudge-bearing animals."

"You know, I think the Slumps would be better," I said. "Less people around. And Mill Creek is plenty deep."

"I could get off the planet by myself," Ijiuto said, "if I could just find that guy, the Ek. The one who imported our stuff. You know who I'm talking about?"

"Sure," I said. "Timmy Akhatli. I've got some bad fucking news for you, buddy."

"Wh-what?"

"We killed his ass. Just like you killed Kimmie Ng. Remember her?"

I suddenly caught sight of d'Alencon getting out of a van. It was an unmarked gray van with a satellite dish on top. D'Alencon walked up to us without a smile on his face. "Late," he said gruffly. "Sorry about that."

And here we stood with Rafael Ijiuto. How were we going to talk our way out of this one? I glanced at Ijiuto to gauge his reaction, and got the worst shock of my life.

Ijiuto was grinning.

"They confessed," he said. "Just like you said they would."

A bevy of uniformed officers materialized out of nowhere. Cuffs snicked on our wrists. They hustled us across the sidewalk and shoved us into the van, while the maelstrom of the Strip closed up again behind us like water.

42

"You brought this on yourself, Mike," said d'Alencon, in the darkness. The van was air-conditioned to just above freezing. LEDs glimmered along one wall. I smelled plastic, body odor, and mint. Mint?

We accelerated smoothly. A moment later, the note of the engine changed from an electric hum into a whir. My stomach dropped. The floor tilted. I lost my balance and fell on top of Dolph. The sensation of lift continued while I struggled to sit up. It was a *flying* van. We were going airborne.

As we continued to climb, a light came on towards the front of the van. It had no regular seats in the back, where we were. One wall was lined with electronic equipment. D'Alencon sat on the operator's stool, gazing sorrowfully at me and Dolph.

Two uniformed officers sat on the jump seats along the other wall. One of them rested a taser casually on his thigh. Another officer had the controls. I now saw that they weren't wearing PdL PD uniforms. They'd fooled me. Same navy blue, but they had no badges. Instead, there was an unobtrusive logo of a triangle on their collars.

I had no attention to spare for them, or for Rafael Ijiuto, who sat on the floor behind the driver, biting his knuckles.

I stared at the man in the passenger seat, which he'd twisted 180 degrees to face us, so he could sprawl with his thighs apart and look down on us like some kind of potentate …

"Captain Smith."

I'd last smelled that minty chaw, and seen that bottlebrush black hair and those chilly eyes, in the Yesanyase Skont system. How could he now be here on Ponce de Leon?

Well, *I* was.

"Secure them," Smith said. "I hear they bite."

The uniforms forced us into a sitting position and bound us back to back with whipcords that constricted around our chests and hips. These restraints were illegal. If given the instruction, the whipcords could tighten the rest of the way. Slice us in half like sausages.

The memory of Parsec's feat in the prisoner transport van taunted me. He had Shifted right out of his handcuffs and savaged his guards. We could theoretically do the same thing. Cuffs can't hold Shifters and nor can whipcords, although it would be a gamble—they might be able to tighten the cords faster than we could Shift.

But there was that taser. Smith and d'Alencon both had guns in their holsters. And most importantly, we were way up in the air. There was no jungle to run to up here. Even if, and it was a big if, we could kill or disable all six of our captors, we'd then have to land. And if we tried to land somewhere unapproved, the cops would simply take control remotely and redirect the van into their waiting arms.

Controls were probably locked to the biometric pattern of blood vessels in the driver's hands, anyway.

Dolph's spine pressed against my back. He was quivering with tension. I knew it wouldn't take much to provoke him into Shifting out of sheer rage. The backs of our heads were touching. I shook my head minutely, hoping he got the message—*play it smart.*

I tried to relax my shoulders, to calm both of us down, but it wasn't working, because I wanted to eat Jose-Maria d'Alencon alive.

I had *trusted* him.

"Looks good," Smith said when they finished tying us up. "You're on, Detective Inspector."

How did Smith and d'Alencon come to be working together? The PdL PD was a planetary authority, not under the control of the Fleet. Why was a Fleet officer sitting in on our arrest, anyway? Why did he seem to be *in charge?*

D'Alencon read off a tablet, in a monotone. "I am arresting you, Michael Starrunner and Dolph Hardlander, on suspicion of the murder of Timmy Akhatli, a subject of the Ekschelatan Empire."

I *knew* it was wrong to kill the Ek. I knew that very day that it would come back and bite us. I'd seen it in the water.

"You have the right to remain silent, but it may harm your defense if you fail to answer questions fully and truthfully. Do you understand?"

"I trusted you," I said.

"You sell-out, Bones," Dolph said. "You feeble-hearted, two-faced excuse for a human being."

"You knew I was a police officer!" d'Alencon exclaimed, slapping his tablet on his knee.

I twisted my head as much as I could to look d'Alencon in the eye. "We had an agreement. What happened to that?"

"Our agreement did not include you murdering aliens in goddamn Millhaven! You promised me you were gonna go straight, Tiger! Have you been lying to me all along?"

"How'd you find out?" I said, because they obviously had.

"Jim Tierney," d'Alencon said flatly. "Total Research Solutions was in the habit of purchasing biological materials on the black market. They would take delivery of these purchases by river. So one day when his employees were tooling along in their boat, they spotted the RV. They called it in. Imagine Dr. Tierney's surprise when the RV proved to contain the decomposing body of his former shipping agent. He cracked under questioning, and admitted everything. So we've also nailed him for exporting genetic engineering materials. A two-fer." D'Alencon lowered his tablet. "However, I should inform you that nothing we're saying right now is on the record."

"Yeah, right," I said. "Just like shithead over there wasn't wearing a wire."

"Mr. Ijiuto agreed to assist us in exchange for his freedom," d'Alencon said.

"He killed my admin officer. He tried to kill millions of people on Gvm Uye Sachttra and Ponce de Leon. Why don't you just jump into bed with the devil himself while you're at it?"

"What makes you think we haven't?" d'Alencon said dryly, motioning with his head in Smith's direction.

Smith's laughed at d'Alencon's joke, although I wasn't so sure it *was* a joke. "If I had a GC for every time we've been accused of doing the devil's work, the Fleet wouldn't have budget problems."

Dolph said, "When we were deployed on Tech Duinn, we used to take our leaves on the moon. Tech Duinn has a big moon, as I'm sure you know. It became a major Fleet base as the war went on. That's how Mike and I learned to fly spaceships. We'd be knocking around the tunnels, drinking and getting into trouble, but then one day our friends in the Fleet said they had a better idea. Discipline was nonexistent, I'm telling you. No one stopped them from taking us out and showing us the ropes, bouncing up and down over the craters, risking billions of GCs in military hardware on every hop. The reason they did that for us is because we saved some of *their* lives on the surface. This one time a crew had to bail out over Eas Rudah. Our unit rescued them. Escorted them back to the rear without losing a single man. That was due to their professionalism as well as our woodcraft. I respected those guys. They were as tough as … as *Shifters.*"

"Yeah, yeah, the good old days," Smith said.

"I used to think the Fleet was on the side of good," Dolph said.

"I was on Tech Duinn, too," Smith said. "In a staff capacity."

"Figures," Dolph said.

"It's easy to joke about staff officers." Smith's jaw worked his chaw. "It usually signifies limited intellectual capacity, but anyway. I'm getting the impression you don't really know anything about the Fleet."

I considered what I did know about the Fleet. It is humanity's only standing species-wide organization. Its chiefs are appointed by a committee of politicians from the Heartworlds, Oren's Star, and Earth. The Fleet gobbles up taxpayer money and fails to appreciably make a dent in the piracy problem, but no major human planet has ever been attacked from space, except by the Fleet itself, so you have to figure they're doing their job. Defending humanity against all those rapacious Eks, stargends, huspathids, aiora, Kroolth, and other aliens, who are foaming at the mouth or other parts with eagerness to conquer our nice, human-compatible planets ... oh, wait.

"You never heard of the Iron Triangle?" Smith said.

The answer to his question was yes, actually, I had. But now I had a sad, self-critical question of my own. Why had it never occurred to me that the Fleet are, in fact, our rulers?

43

"The Iron Triangle," Smith said, "is a community of three Fleet intelligence agencies working together to ensure the safety of humanity. You can go on calling me Captain if you want. No skin off my nose. But it's actually Major General. I'm the special deputy for the mobilization director of the FCS, the Fleet Clandestine Service, one of the three agencies I mentioned. The other two are the Fleet Special Service, special ops, and the Fleet Cyberwarfare Service, self-explanatory. Got that?"

"We met one of your people on the Kroolth homeworld," I said. "She was working at a scrapyard."

"Yup. That's when we first became aware of you. Anyone that buys a ship built by the Cluster's only surviving Urush bot is automatically a person of interest. So we've been tracking your movements over the years, not with a whole lot of success, I might add. You're very good at staying off the radar, aren't you, Mr. Starrunner?"

I sneaked a glance at d'Alencon. I had confessed all our crimes to him. The Iron Triangle may not have known about them before, but I had to assume they did now.

"We've got nothing to hide," Dolph said.

"Not anymore," Smith agreed.

I slumped in my bonds. The whip cords cut into my chest. All my paranoia turned out to be justified. I had always feared that the authorities were watching and waiting, poised to come down on me like a ton of bricks if I made one wrong move … and now I had. And they had.

Not just the police, either, but the highest authority of all.

The *Iron Triangle.*

In one moment of poor judgement, I had doomed Dolph, and probably Irene, Martin, Rex, and Robbie as well, to a short future in Fleet detention.

One moment? Who was I kidding? A *lifetime* of poor judgement, impulsive violence, and reckless gambles had brought me to this point.

It struck me as funny that they didn't know I had IVK. They may have me in their power now, but they wouldn't for long. My death, sooner or later, would cheat them of their victory.

Sooner … or later …

My inhales got shallower and quicker. Adrenaline flooded my brain stem. My muscles tensed against the whipcords.

Dolph saved me from making a fatal mistake. He said, "I guess this ain't really about Timmy Akhatli."

"The Eks are't exactly threatening war over his death," Smith acknowledged. "Any Ekschelatan who'd voluntarily live on a human planet is mud in the eyes of the Empire, anyway."

"But it's still murder," d'Alencon said.

"I sense the inconsistent application of principles," Dolph said, wagging the toe of his boot in Ijiuto's direction.

"In case it isn't crystal clear," Smith said. "Mr. Ijiuto is working with us. The same immunity that was extended to him can be yours as well, *if* you cooperate. Otherwise—"

With a thunk, the side door of the van slid partway open. Cold wind rushed in. Six inches from my sneakers, a dusky void yawned. I was disoriented for a second, trying to match the city lights below to some part of Mag-Ingat—and then I realized I was looking at *all* of Mag-Ingat, a crescent of light squashed between the bay and the hills.

We were much higher up than flying cars normally go. Guess traffic rules don't apply to the Iron Triangle.

"As far as I'm aware," Smith said, "there are no Shifters with wings."

"No," I said, eyes glued to the drop. "Even condors or eagles, the largest birds on Earth, only weigh about fifteen kilos. So a bird with the mass of an adult human being would be the size of a small airplane. Wouldn't be able to get off the ground."

"Shove you out the door right now, humanity would be the better for it," Smith said. "But it would be a drop in the ocean, unless we followed up with all the other forty million." The side door slammed shut. "The mistake was allowing you to reproduce in the first place." Smith's voice had a tinge of throatiness in it. I realized I was in the presence of a mainstream human who actually did hate Shifters.

"C'mon," I said, shocked into smiling hopefully at him. "We're all humans ..."

"No. That's exactly what you're not. The alt-human designation is a brilliant stroke of propaganda, but it's misleading. You are a new and different species, and the best illustration yet of how genetic engineering is tearing *Homo sapiens* apart."

D'Alencon sighed, just a tiny sound, letting me and Dolph know that he wasn't on board with this. It only made me hate him the more. *He* had brought us here. He had set us up.

"The mission of the Fleet Clandestine Service," Smith said, "is to safeguard the essence of humanity: our DNA. What else sets us apart from the Eks, the stargends, and the rest of them? The Eks, at least, are just as smart as we are. But they don't have our spark," he snapped his fingers as if looking for the right word, "our creativity, our restlessness, our desire to remake the universe in our image. All that is embedded in our DNA, and that's what sets humanity apart. That's what makes us the most successful expansionary species that we know of, bar none. That's why they're all *afraid* of us."

He lowered his voice on the last words, smiling confidentially, and despite myself I felt a shiver. He was a true believer in human greatness. The thing is, I was, too.

"The only thing that can stop us now is … *us.* We're holding a weapon to our own throats, and the name of that weapon is genetic engineering. The Age of Adaptation, as they call it, was the closest we've ever come to self-inflicted destruction." The Big Shift came right at the end of the Age of Adaptation. We Shifters see ourselves as the culmination of a sorry era, and its redemption: *we* got gene-modding right. It was a pretty safe bet Smith did not see it that way. "You've never been to Earth—neither have I. But I've been halfway, as far as Oren's Star. It's an oasis in a wasteland of human wreckage. Those colonies along the way, oh brother. Those people don't even *look* human anymore. And that kind of thing is still going on in the Cluster today. Gene-modding technology is widely available, thanks to idiots like your friend Dr. Tierney, and others who don't even have the excuse of idealism. The genie is out of the bottle." He chopped the air with a hand. "Our mission is to slay it."

I said, trembling, "You wanna clarify how you're *not* threatening my people with extinction?"

"Forty people is an objective," Smith said. "Forty million is a fait accompli. Anyway, we have an operational code of conduct. Ethical guidelines. The Fleet does not go around murdering people." He smiled at me and Dolph. "That's *your* job."

"I have two words for you," I said. "Fuck off."

Smith slid off his seat so he was squatting in front of me on his haunches. The smell of his minty chaw washed into my nostrils. I glared at him, refusing to play the part of vulnerable captive. That pissed him off. He had brass fingernails; some kind of cybernetics, I'd figured. He now stretched out one finger towards my face, while the nail on it grew and sharpened into a razor's edge. Neurally controlled nanotech. Nifty. He pricked my throat with that brass nail—a sudden, breathtaking jolt of pain—and traced a line down over my collarbone. My t-shirt parted like tissue paper. The claw circled around my right nipple, leaving a bloody trail, and edged up to the nipple in a grotesque, agonizing parody of a sensual caress. Cold sweat drenched my back. I bit down on the insides of my cheeks. Dolph swore, unable to see what was happening. The uniforms sat like statues, professionally blind and deaf.

"Jesus!" d'Alencon erupted, springing out of his seat. "Leave the guy alone!"

Smith raised his eyebrows, his claw poised at my nipple.

"He don't need that kind of incentive. We got enough to incentivize him already. If he don't cooperate, he goes to jail ... this time, for good. And if that ain't enough—" d'Alencon met my gaze for a painful instant— "it would be the work of a moment to dispatch armed officers to investigate the shooting range owned by Alec Macaulay, out in the hills."

So they knew where Lucy was.

"We might even find Buzz Parsec there, too."

If Bones thought that, he did not know Parsec, *or* Alec. But he did know me. The veiled threat to Lucy punctured my defiance. I closed my eyes to shut out the sight of d'Alencon and Smith. Blood tickled, creeping down my chest. Sweat mixed into the cuts and stung like fury. "I'll do what you want."

"Good," Smith said, curtly. His claw withdrew from my skin.

I opened my eyes. I happened to be looking directly at Rafael Ijiuto. He was gray in the face, but he mustered a smile and flashed me a thumbs-up. I looked away.

"What do you want, anyway?" I muttered.

Smith cleared his throat. "We have reason to believe you illegally removed a deportee from the Hurtworlds," he said, in an exaggerated, booming, flat voice.

He had spoken those words to me before, in the trunk corridor of the *St. Clare.* And he'd been right.

MF had saved us that time …

… but MF couldn't save us now.

"Where is she?" Smith said. "Your ship was searched—she's not there. You haven't removed her from the spaceport …"

Dolph cackled. "Shit, man, you think we brought her back with us?"

"Didn't you?" d'Alencon said.

"No," I said leadenly. "We left her on Mittel Trevoyvox."

"Mittel Trevoyvox?" Smith said. "Are you shitting me?"

"No."

"Christ in fucking cryonite. Mittel Trevoyvox! *How* long ago? Two weeks? You Christing idiot." Smith leaned closer, his teeth bared. I thought for a second he was going to bite me. "Are you unaware that the Travellers are after her?"

"Yeah," I said. "I know that." I was in too much pain to bother explaining how I'd rationalized to myself that it would be OK. I just said, "Figure if even you don't know she's there, they don't, either."

"We can hope. We can hope, but we have intelligence that they're active in the Hurtworlds—"

I laughed at that. Active in the Hurtworlds? No shit. The Iron Triangle may not know everything, after all.

"—and it may only be a matter of time before they find her." Smith towered over us. "You have a fast ship. You left her there; you go back there and fucking find her again. *Now.*"

Dolph dared to say, "Why us?"

"She trusts you. Doesn't she?"

Yes. Pippa trusted us. So much the worse for her.

"Oh, and that little pendant she wears? Find that, too."

"What is it, anyway?" I directed the disingenuous question to Rafael Ijiuto, who just shook his head gloomily. His hand clutched the edge of his collar, as if lonely for the TrZam 008 that used to hang around his neck.

"Don't bother asking him. *He* doesn't know." Smith clearly had nothing but contempt for the Darkworlder prince. "And you don't need to know, either. When you find it, you will destroy it, film the act of destruction, and return the debris to us. Clear?"

I nodded. Dolph nodded.

"Then that is your mission, if you choose to accept it. You haven't actually got any fucking choice." Smith's eyes glittered. "If you fail, little Lucy might be kidnapped again. Such a shame. Everyone would blame her mother. *You* would know the truth … but no one would ever believe you."

"I'll do it," I said. "I'll do it! Whatever you want!"

"I'll do it," Dolph said. "You sadistic motherfucker."

Smith was facing Dolph, but I could hear the smile in his voice. "*Good* dog."

He knelt over us, touching us in all the wrong places, and used his brass nails to slice through the whipcords. I fell forward onto my face, unable to catch myself, as my hands were still cuffed.

D'Alencon gently removed the cuffs. Even then, I did not stand up. I did not fight them. I did not Shift.

I just said, "What happens if we run into the Travellers out there?"

"Then you kill them," Smith said.

"Hell," I said, "you don't need to force me to do *that.*"

The van descended. We landed, not in Mag-Ingat, but at the Fleet base in Cascaville. Dolph and I endured an intrusive strip-search and had all our details taken, from fingerprints to DNA. At the end of that we both had to sign a letter of marque, which certified that we were Fleet subcontractors. There was no mention of pay.

We got a ride back to the city in a Fleet bus, along with cleaners and cooks going home after the late shift. All the way, we leaned separately against the windows without saying a word.

44

THE bus dropped us at the turn-off for the range. Just another reminder that they knew all about us. It was a little after midnight. The jungle made noises. We walked along the track, stumbling in the meager starlight that filtered through the trees.

Dolph ducked to avoid a branch, and bumped into my chest. I grunted. The cuts weren't deep but they still throbbed painfully.

"Guy's a fucking pervert," Dolph said.

"Yeah."

"He was getting off on cutting you."

"Yeah."

"What are we gonna do?"

"I'm gonna do what he wants. You could probably get clear. Use your savings; go to San D."

"That's what he hopes we'll do," Dolph said. "If it isn't completely fucking clear to you by this time, they would *love* to have an excuse to turn San Damiano into a Hurtworld."

"They? He's just one guy."

"It's the Iron fucking Triangle, man."

"And that's why I'm not gonna go against them." I knew Dolph was aching for me to make some declaration of defiance, even if it was only words, to reclaim my pride. But I had none left. All that remained was my bedrock need to protect Lucy from my mistakes.

We came to the trestle barricade and went around it. Wolves shimmered out of the darkness, growling. "It's just us," Dolph said, rubbing gray-furred heads.

Alec's house was dark. The camp slumbered. We climbed the ramps to the lairs in the cliff. Dolph Shifted into jackal form and slunk off to curl up in a corner. I also Shifted, into a form that Lucy liked: my ordinary, non-sabertooth tiger. I located my daughter by her unique scent. She was sleeping next to Mia and some of the camp children. I pawed her loose from the kid pile. Without waking up, she turned to face me and snuggled into my belly fur.

I lay awake for a long time, thinking about all the people I needed to revenge myself on, and in what order. It was the first night in a long time I hadn't drunk myself to sleep.

*

Come morning, we located Irene. She had been sleeping with Rex and Kit in an outlying lair, a mere hollow in the cliff, damp and littered with bones. Kit had had another episode last night. We tramped over to Alec's house in silence. I used the satellite connection to call Martin, and while we waited for him in Alec's rustic kitchen, Dolph and I told them all about yesterday's events.

Alec took it badly. He pulled a gun on us—that kind of badly. He pointed it at me, while Laura, in wolf form, stalked around us, growling.

"Are you a snitch, Starrunner? Are you the kind of mutt that informs on your own kind?"

I thought of d'Alencon, to whom I had confided all my secrets. D'Alencon, who had betrayed me to the Iron Triangle. I pictured my teeth sinking into his throat and ripping his jugular open. "No," I said. Ironically, my conscience was clear with regard to d'Alencon now. "I'm no more of a snitch than you are."

Alec shoved his gun in my face. Dolph said, "Cool it, Macaulay! They've been surveilling you all along. They've got you on satellite. They can track your movements, your data access logs, everything. Mike didn't tell them anything, nor did I. They zeroed in on us, and you're standing in the blast zone. That's how it fucking breaks, man."

Irene chimed in. "Mike is no snitch. He wouldn't even snitch on Parsec, his worst enemy, so what does that say to you?"

"What Parsec has done is gonna blow back on all of us," Alec said. "And so is this. What *is* it with you spaceship captains?"

At that moment Martin entered the kitchen, bike helmet under his arm. He caught the last part of what Alec said, and he saw the gun, me backed up against the kitchen island, the snarling wolf corralling the other three.

He said, "Yeah, what *is* it with spaceship captains? I often ask that question myself. I've worked for a bunch of' em. My first bid was in the majors. Star Trax. Drug tests every week, no dirtside leave if you got even one black mark for conduct, which meant I never got any dirtside leave, ever. Well, I don't mind. I like spaceships. The sound of the engines. All those cozy crawl-spaces. But that captain, my sweet Lord. He used to spy on the female crew in the shower, and he put THC in our food for kicks. Then there was the captain I crewed for in the Techworlds, after Star Trax fired me for eating the drive engineer's assistant. She was a normie, of course. Independent passenger boat. She used to make me Shift to entertain the customers. I had to do tricks and shit. That was more than I could take, even though the tips were good. I ended up eating *her.* After that, I figured I was done. No one would ever hire me again."

He bowed to me, twirling his bike helmet like a hat.

"I was wrong. Mike Starrunner took me on. He pays on time, he picks his jobs carefully, and he gives me my space. Most importantly, he wouldn't talk to the police if his life depended on it. I would die for the guy."

He plonked his helmet down on the counter, picked up the coffee carafe, and sniffed.

"Oh, this smells good. Mind?"

Alec holstered his gun, saying ruefully. "That's one heck of a character witness you got there, Starrunner."

I had not known any of those details about Martin's past. I wasn't sure if it was true, or if he'd made it all up. I clapped him on the shoulder and said, "Did you eat Cecilia yet?"

Martin added cream to his coffee with an injured frown. "I wouldn't dream of it. She's *interesting.* She lived in the Cloudworlds for a spell, before she married Parsec, you know that? We stayed up late drinking wine and reminiscing." Anticipating my next question, he added, "Got a couple of friends staying with her right now. I think she's starting to appreciate reptilian hospitality."

"OK," Alec said. "That's one less thing to worry about. Meaning we still got to worry about the Iron Triangle."

"Nuh uh," I said tiredly. "You don't have to worry about that, because I'm gonna do what they want. So nothing's gonna happen to you at all."

Alec's eyes burned. "All the same, everyone needs to be informed about this. Come over to the camp and tell them what you just told me."

It went against my instincts, but I agreed. I spoke for half an hour, in the morning shade of the great hall, to all the jungle wolves—fidgety children, pale and bearded men, fierce women. Most all of them had Shifted back into human form. It was interesting to note that *this* was their reaction to a crisis.

I did not mention the TrZam 008. I hadn't mentioned it to Alec, either. That was the key to the whole business, and maybe that's why Alec had got so upset—he sensed I was holding something back. But even without that, it added up to a familiar scenario, the same bedtime story these folks had been telling themselves for years. The authorities were poised to crack down on them just for being Shifters.

Alec held up a hand to cut me off as I tersely apologized for involving them in my mess.

"If it wasn't you, and it wasn't now, it would be someone else, and it might have come without warning." Alec took over the audience. "Thanks to Mike Starrunner, we know our enemy. There's nothing more important than that … except knowing your friends." He and I were standing, while everyone else sat or squatted on the ground. He looked slowly around at his people. I was shocked to see tears of sentimental love standing in his eyes. He flung his arm around my shoulders and said hoarsely, "We're all in this together."

The jungle wolves applauded, while I stood thinking: He's getting them ready to go out in a blaze of glory.

But I had forgotten the most important of the San Damiano rules they lived by: never, *never* say die.

"Lucy Starrunner, folks." Alec raised her to her feet and set his hands on her shoulders. "She will be staying with us while her dad is battling the enemies of our people."

I had told him that the Iron Triangle had ordered me to go after a fugitive on the Hurtworlds. He had reinterpreted that on the fly to make it sound better to his people. He had enough pride for both of us. I thanked him for it in my heart when I saw the grin tugging at Lucy's mouth.

"She is one of us, and we will defend her the same way that Mike is defending our homes and our families."

I hugged him. It was basically required at that moment, with emotions surging high. He gripped me in a powerful clinch that aggravated the cuts on my chest, and muttered in my ear, "Don't fuck it up. And bring your ship back!"

I muttered back, "Even if I have to shoot my way through the entire Fleet." It's the kind of thing you have to say.

Amidst the bedlam of talk that followed, I saw Dolph leaving the great hall. I looked for Irene. She, too, had vanished.

I signaled to Martin. We extricated ourselves and walked along the riverbank. "By the way," I said. "Did you really eat the Star Trax drive engineer's assistant?"

"Yes," Martin said. "It was a hamster. She loved that thing so much she called it her assistant. But to me, it smelled like food. I just couldn't resist. Bad snake."

I smiled. "And what about the other one? The indie cruiser captain?"

"Uhm, I ate her … in a different sense." Martin smoothed his mustache. "She fired me in revenge when we broke up. Goes to show that shipboard relationships always lead to trouble."

I snickered. "MF would love that story."

"I already told it to him. He was pissed I didn't have pictures."

Nothing had gone right, I thought, since MF deserted us. I looked down the trail ahead—no footprints on the mud. "I don't think they came this way. Let's try around the waterfall."

You could get behind the waterfall. The water shot over a rocky lip. Brush choked the space beneath the overhang. But Alec's people had cut it away to make a sort of tunnel, one side rock, the other side leafy tendrils waggling in the spray.

Dolph and Irene stood in this green tunnel. She had her back to the rock. He was facing her. A little ping of wrongness went off in my mind: he was standing too close to her, one arm braced on the rock beside her head. He had no right to loom over her in that way.

The noise of the falls covered our approach. We got close enough to hear Dolph say, in a loud, angry voice, "Don't give me that," before they saw us.

Dolph stepped back, scowling. Irene glared.

"What's this about?" I said.

"Smith," Dolph said to Irene. "When he came aboard the *St. Clare,* Mike went to meet him. We were on the bridge. We were watching the whole thing on the internal feed. You *recognized* him."

"I did not," Irene said. "Can't you tell the difference between generalized and specific loathing?"

"Actually, I can," Dolph said. "Because of that look of specific loathing you give me all the time."

Martin chuckled. I did not.

"She clearly recognized him," Dolph repeated. "But I didn't say anything, because she flat-out denied it. So I thought I must be wrong. But now—now I'm wondering ..."

I had slept badly. I had been abused in custody last night. I'd had a gun shoved in my face this morning. I was already considering kicking Irene off the crew, for a mix of principled and pragmatic reasons. I said harshly, "If you got history with that fucker, Irene, tell us about it, or we're done here."

She looked this way and that. Her jaw gritted. "All right. I know him. Not to speak to. Just by sight. He was at Bull Rock—"

She broke off abruptly. Squeezed her eyes shut. Whispered, "Darn."

"Boom, there it is," Dolph said softly. "You were at Bull Rock."

Irene said nothing.

"*That's* what the bears have on you," I said. "Oh boy."

Martin said, "Feeling kinda dumb here. What's Bull Rock?"

"It was a military prison on Tech Duinn," I said. "Where we kept the important Necros we captured. The political prisoners, I guess. I never went there. It was on the other side of the planet from where we were deployed. But after the war, there was a huge scandal. It turned out that the prisoners at Bull Rock had been abused, systematically, for years."

"Oh, now I remember hearing about that," Martin said. "Didn't they try out different combinations of experimental drugs on the prisoners? Used them as human guinea pigs?"

"Yeah," Dolph said. "They also sodomized them and carved graffiti onto their bodies with knives."

Irene, lips and eyes squeezed shut, let out a soft moan of protest.

"They *did,*" I said. "There was holo evidence. Hours and hours of recordings. It was proved to be authentic." I felt the same way I had when the scandal broke, disgusted and stunned that the actions of a few lousy sadists in uniform were tainting the whole war, overshadowing the bravery of the men and women I had fought with.

Had one of those lousy sadists been … Irene?

Hundreds of people had gone to jail for the Bull Rock atrocities, from civilian contractors all the way up to a two-star general. But it was only to be expected that more would have slipped through the net, their involvement never revealed.

Until now.

"You worked there?"

A nod.

"And Smith was there, too?" Him, I could believe it of.

Another nod.

"What was he," Dolph said, "an assistant torturer? Like you?"

Irene slapped him. If she had planned it, she would've knocked him into the waterfall. It was a simple loss of control, and her hand only grazed his face. He stepped back, holding his nose.

"Don't kick me off the crew, Mike," she said. "I've been waiting twenty years to get a shot at that bastard. This could be it."

"Forget it," I said. "He's untouchable. Irene, did you really … do those things?"

"If I say I didn't," she said, "you won't believe me. If I say I did, you'll kick me off the crew. So I'm screwed either way. Thanks a lot, Hardlander." She pushed Dolph with vicious force. He fell backwards, crashed through the bushes, and vanished into the sun-kissed curtain of water. Martin grabbed for Irene and missed. She darted between me and the wall. I caught her around the middle. Her momentum pulled us both down to the path.

We rolled against the wall, wrestling. She was the better fighter, but I was stronger and heavier. I pinned her on her back. "The truth, Irene," I pleaded. *"Did* you do those things?"

She lay still, spray from the waterfall sparkling on her blonde hair, face closed up like a fist. "No. I just worked security. Do you believe me?"

All our history together flashed before my eyes. All the close calls, the ship fights, and the lazy times hanging out with the kids. We were more than colleagues. We were family. And yet, had I ever really known her? Could I trust that she wasn't lying to me now? After a long moment, I said, "No."

"I figured," she said. "I wouldn't, either, if I were you."

I let her go. Stood up and brushed the dirt off. "You're fired." The words felt like novocaine in my mouth. "I still owe you back pay. We can subtract that from the half a million Rex took."

She nodded. "I won't let this affect the kids."

"I won't, either."

We trudged out of the bushes. Dolph breached the surface of the pool in dolphin form. Rex was among those standing on the shore. He laid a gentle hand on Lucy's back, restraining her from diving in to join Dolph in her excitement. I almost wished I could take it back when I saw that, but it was too late.

We said our goodbyes and went back to the city. Dolph and Martin headed straight out to the spaceport. I located Robbie and told him to pack his bags, 'cause he was coming with us. He practically licked my hands in joy, until I broke the news that we were no longer an independent trader, but a Fleet subcontractor. Specialty: dirty jobs.

45

ROBBIE and I got out to the spaceport at 8 PM to find our hangar blazing like an all-night supermarket. Everything the customs inspectors tossed around had been tidied up, fixed, or replaced. A crew of mechanics rode a mobile scaffolding, finishing off a professional patch job on the hull plate that Sophia's missile had crumpled. I stowed my kitbag and checked their work. While I was hanging upside down, looking at rivets, a Fleet armored car arrived with ammunition for the missile launchers, the point defenses, and the railgun.

We usually had to buy ammo on the gray market in the Fringeworlds. This stuff came straight from the source, smelling of factory grease, festooned with large-type handling cautions. It wasn't just standard rounds, either. We got fire-and-forget seeker rounds with AI guidance, and even a couple of nukes. I looked around for Irene, thinking she'd be in heaven, and then remembered.

D'Alencon drove up to the hangar in his official unmarked car.

I guess he felt safe with all the Fleet hirelings around.

I was going to deck him, anyway, and then someone else got out of his car.

Rafael Ijiuto.

"Say hi to your new weapons officer," d'Alencon told me.

"I don't need a new weapons officer," I said. "We're flying with a crew of four. Martin, engineering, Robbie, admin, Dolph, pilot, and I'm going to double as weapons officer."

"You're taking him," d'Alencon said, "because Major General Smith wants you to."

"Does he also want to get him back alive?" I said.

"I don't think he cares one way or the other," d'Alencon said. "But you can't kill him until he's done his job."

Ijiuto was pale and morose. He squinted up at the *St. Clare* as if she was smaller than he remembered.

"What is his job?" I said.

"As you may recall," d'Alencon said, "he hired Sophia Hart and her crew to eliminate his cousins. He paid them *very* well. It is Major General Smith's belief that Ms. Hart is short of money, and would be open to resuming that relationship. Should you be so unlucky as to run into her out there, Mr. Ijiuto may be your best hope of surviving the encounter. He has been rehearsed in a cover story to explain his release, which y'all will also commit to memory. In a nutshell, he will claim he was freed on account of having diplomatic immunity, and immediately hired you to take him in search of the Travellers. Apart from that, he has also been given operational funds to draw on, which he can put at your disposal to ensure the successful completion of your mission."

"Basically," I said, "we're to consider him our boss."

"You can just consider him your employee," d'Alencon said.

"I'm horrible to my employees," I said. Robbie, listening, sniggered.

"Don't take it out on him," d'Alencon said.

LOX and LN2 tankers nosed into the hangar. Another supply wagon trailed them, bringing more goodies. Leaving d'Alencon standing by the wall, I sorted through the stuff in rueful amazement. New rifles and ammunition. Polar gear for the Mittel Trevoyvox climate. A new set of portable HF radios. Medicines for every kind of trauma and infection. When we were in the army, we had to mend our own clothes and buy meds on the black market. Guess the Iron Triangle has a more generous budget.

There was even a new maintenance bot. They must have noticed that the *St. Clare* didn't have one. It was a chrome octopus the size of a sheepdog. "Greetings, captain," it croaked. "I am a certified medic, IT technician, mechanic, and flight engineer. I can also play games."

"Interactive mode *off,*" I said. It was too painful to be reminded of MF by this clunky, human-built artificial intelligence. "If I need you, I'll let you know."

The bot silently spidered up the airlock ladder.

I looked around and saw d'Alencon watching me. "You still here?"

"I warned you not to go to the Hurtworlds, Tiger."

"You should know by now I don't take good advice."

"This is all my own damn fault. That night I came to your place, I thought I was being so slick, fooling the algos. But there was surveillance on your apartment."

"There was?"

"They thought Sophia Hart might get in touch with you."

I laughed. It was oddly comforting to know that the Iron Triangle had got me and Sophia so wrong. "I didn't spot any surveillance."

"it would have been one or more covert micro-drones. They customize them to look like insects."

I suddenly remembered the moth on my front porch, which had mysteriously flown *away* from the porch light.

"We don't use those. Our policy is that you have a right to know when you're under surveillance. But the Iron Triangle don't give a fart about your human rights."

"I gathered that."

"Couple days after you left, I got called in to the chief prosecutor's office." D'Alencon clearly needed to unburden himself. It wouldn't kill me to let him. "There's the chief, standing there like a potted plant. And there's Smith, sitting in her chair. Previous to that I had not been aware of the Iron Triangle's involvement. Oh, the whole department knew something was hinky with the Ijiuto case. It was political. The

Fleet interrogated the suspect with no PD officers present, which is unheard-of. They even confiscated his belongings. So I did not come into that meeting completely unprepared. But Smith had a surprise for me, all the same. 'So,' he says, 'you had a chinwag with Michael Starrunner. Is there something between the two of you?'"

"What was he implying?"

"That I was corrupt."

I laughed. It honestly sounded like a bad joke. Jose-Maria d'Alencon and corrupt didn't belong in the same sentence, or even on the same planet.

D'Alencon did not smile. "They got me over a barrel, Mike. There are corruption charges on the chief's desk. I don't play along, she signs them. I lose my job, I might even face jail time."

I rubbed my mouth, realizing that d'Alencon had not betrayed me. The police department had betrayed both of us. "Did you tell them about … about …" My thoughts leaped back to my confession to him in the evidence room at PdL PD HQ.

"All that's between you and me, stays between you and me. They aren't interested in your personal history, anyway. The surveillance drone picked up our conversation about your trip to the Hurtworlds. I told them that I thought the run might have something to do with Pippa Khratz. *That* lit a fire under Smith's ass. Next day, he headed out to Yesanyase Skont himself."

"He was scared I might get to her before he did." I remembered something Pippa had said. "He must've already ordered the army to take her into custody. But they couldn't find her, because the infantry garrison on Yesanyase S is rotten through and through. The Hurtworlds Authority volunteer on the ground suspected that they were going to mistreat her, and hid her … until I got there."

"That fits." D'Alencon sighed. "Couple weeks later, Smith comes back, empty-handed, wild with rage. We heard him shouting at the chief prosecutor all the way down the hall. Then he called for me. He'd calmed down by that time, thank goodness. He says, 'Get me something on Starrunner. Something that could put him away for life.' And I … I gave him the Timmy Akhatli case. The evidence is only circumstantial, but it's good enough for government work." D'Alencon met my eyes. Anger darkened his pudgy, honest face. "Why'd you have to go and do that, Tiger? *Why?*"

"I don't know," I said.

"Mike!" Dolph yelled, from the cargo crane operator's seat. "Can you help me lift this shit into the airlock?"

"Coming," I yelled back. I hesitated. "Bones, I … I'm sorry."

"So am I," d'Alencon said. *"So am I."*

*

We took one last call from Smith on the ship's radio, orbiting 140 klicks above Ponce de Leon. "The technicians tell me your ship has no hardwired skip multiplier limit. That's illegal."

"Your point?" I caught myself being insolent. Floating in orbit on the bridge of the *St. Clare* made me feel free and powerful, like I had the whole Cluster in the palm of my hand. I had not yet fully adjusted to the new reality that I was an unpaid, unwilling Fleet subcontractor.

"My point is that time is of the fucking essence," Smith said. "Our calculations say you can safely get there in fifteen standard days. Make it happen."

"Yes, sir." I ended the call. "Fifteen standard days? What does he think we are, a Fleet jalopy?"

Dolph shrugged, sifting through the data in his AR display. The bridge felt different without Irene, smaller and too bright. Dolph had expressed doubt about my plan to double up as weapons officer. The *St. Clare* was designed, after all, for three bridge officers. And now, instead of Irene, we had Rafael Ijiuto.

He floated in the left seat without an AR headset. No way was I giving him access to any of my ship's controls. I had only let him on the bridge because there wasn't another spare couch.

As I calculated our FTL burn, Ijiuto said hopefully, "We could just run. Make a quick refuelling stop in the Fringeworlds, and then head for home. There's a lot of room to hide on the Darkworlds. When the Fleet first came to New Gessyria, they didn't even think it was inhabited. They thought we must've all died. Then we came out of the forests and gave them the surprise of their lives ..."

I thumbed the intercom. "Skip field generator status, Marty?"

"Nominal."

"Roger. Dolph, confirm orientation."

"Orientation confirmed."

"Throttle up."

"Throttling up now." The main drive roared into life, shaking the ship.

"Initiating exhaust field on my mark."

"Copy."

"And *mark.*" I threw the switch. The violent jolt of sudden acceleration tossed us back against our couches.

A cry came through our headsets.

"Robbie!" Dolph exclaimed.

I peeled off my harness and flew off the bridge, down the trunk corridor. We were still weightless, but the ship was now accelerating, as the exhaust field multiplied the speed of the particles jetting out of our engine. 0.1 gees of thrust gravity dragged me aft. I caught the edge of the lounge door, swung in by one hand, kicked off from the wall, and slapped the poky admin officer's berth open.

Robbie's foot hit me in the chest. I grabbed onto the top edge of the door. Robbie was spreadeagled in the air, kicking comically as he tried to get back to the couch that took up most of the berth.

"You OK?" I said. "Why aren't you strapped in?"

"I thought it was over," he said shamefacedly.

"Oh, no," I said. "It's only just beginning."

Someone laughed behind me. I turned and saw Ijiuto hanging onto the door of the lounge, cackling at the sight of me trying to stuff Robbie's legs back into his berth.

I saw red. I arrowed towards Ijiuto and grabbed his arm. "Gimme a hand, Robbie." We towed him, struggling, across the lounge and crammed him into the admin berth. I slammed the door and set it to locked. Now it would open only to my palm-print.

"Power down, ya," Robbie yelled at the wall in street dialect, as Ijiuto banged on the inside of it, like Zane Cole had done.

"Did you leave any of your stuff in there, Robbie?"

"Yeah man, my kitbag."

"That's yes, *Captain.*"

"Yes, Captain," he said, grinning.

"We'll get it when we give him a toilet break." I put my face close to the wall. "You're on my spaceship now," I shouted. "You ever want to get out of there, you lick my boots and call me God."

46

FOURTEEN days later, we exited the skip field, still travelling at 2% of light speed, near the orbit of the fawn-colored gas giant that shared the Mittel Trevoyvox system. I left Dolph on the bridge, stepping our speed down in easy increments. The trip had gone smoothly. On top of being an all-Shifter crew, we were now an all-male crew. It made it easier to maintain discipline. I'd had everyone exercising their blues away and competing in our AR shooter sims.

Now it was time to let the prisoner out.

I floated in front of the admin berth with my left hand resting lightly on Robbie's neck fur. The lower half of Martin's body coiled lightly around my legs. "Here we go," I said, feeling unaccountably nervous.

I pressed my palm on the panel and let Rafael Ijiuto out.

We'd been letting him out every day for bathroom breaks, and taking him food and water. But that had been Robbie's responsibility. I confess I had avoided any contact with him. Now his appearance shocked me. His beard had grown in patchily, like dirt. His face was pouchy and pallid. And he stank: a rich, homeless funk that reminded me of the time he had turned up in my office, claiming to have walked eight hundred kilometers.

He looked at us and said, "You fucking animals."

Suddenly I felt ashamed of the claws and teeth beside me, the pulsating coils of muscle around my legs. I felt ashamed of what I was. It lasted only a second, but it left me quiet.

Robbie hackled. I patted his neck absently.

Ijiuto aimed a withering sneer at me, then floated past us into the hall. We followed. I was trying to parse why he made me feel so bad about myself.

"What, you wanna come with me to the head, too?"

Ijiuto peed into the suction funnel without bothering to close the door. As he was zipping up, a light jolt shook the bulkheads, pitching him against the wall.

"What was that?"

"We're there," I said. "Haven't you been keeping track?"

"It's only been thirteen days and change."

"Exactly. We ran the acceleration up to half a gee before entering the skip field, and then flew blind through the edge of the Core." I had the satisfaction of seeing him pale somewhat. "Peaked out at 1,950 c, which is substantially faster than Smith believes we can go. So we're here, and he's not. That gives us an advantage. What we'll do with it remains to be seen. At present we're decelerating towards Mittel Trevoyvox."

I slapped Robbie's shoulder.

"Go and strap in. You might want to spray some disinfectant around in there first."

"Oh, man." As Robbie drifted past Ijiuto, he swiftly turned his head and snapped at Ijiuto's legs, catching the fabric of his pants and ripping it. Ijiuto cried out. Robbie laughed and went on his way.

Martin lapped his coils higher around me, until his head was under my chin. I rested my forearms on the snake's body and watched Rafael Ijiuto float forward to the bridge. I was feeling sick again.

"Prochlorperazine," Martin whispered. "A half dose." I had confided in him about my bouts of nausea. I said it was probably space sickness. After all these years? He surely didn't believe me, but he pretended to. "And Mike? Don't drink when you're taking that stuff."

"Roger," I said, mentally filing the warning under 'ignore'. "I'm sure I'll feel better when we're on the ground."

*

We were travelling so fast that it took the best part of a day to decelerate down to Mittel Trevoyvox orbit. Microimpacts continually shook the force field nose shield, making the journey a nailbiter. After all these millennia of inhabitation by various civilizations, Mittel T's Lagrange points and graveyard orbits were strewn with junk. We had to constantly use the masers to nudge larger pieces of debris off our trajectory, or vaporize smaller ones. I crouched over Irene's consoles, playing whack-a-mole with scraps of ancient satellites, while Dolph continually adjusted our course to compensate for the microimpacts. Rafael Ijiuto sat in *my* couch, picking his teeth like a lord.

"Guess we outran Smith's drones," Dolph said when we got close enough to Mittel Trevoyvox to see what was in orbit … or rather, what wasn't.

As we had experienced for ourselves on the way back from Mittel T last time, the limits of modern technology put a ceiling on FTL speed. We had scraped right up against that ceiling on our way here: 1,950 c. Faster than that, not even FTL drones can fly. So, even if Smith had dispatched drones from Ponce de Leon to order other Fleet units in the volume to Mittel Trevoyvox, they had not received their orders yet.

We had the place to ourselves … apart from the Fleet and Ek units regularly stationed here.

"What's that?" Ijiuto said.

He had no AR headset, so he was looking at the physical external feed screen. "Ek space station," I said, before I processed what I was seeing.

The geodesic sphere of the space station looked … dented.

No. *Holed.*

The feed gained detail as we rushed lower. Sunlight reflected off structures inside the space station that were not meant to be exposed to vacuum.

"Here comes the Fleet patrol ship," Dolph said. The arrowhead boat orbited into view at 180 klicks, right above the space station.

I reached across Ijiuto for my comms and hit the ship-to-ship frequency. "Hey flyboy, how's it hanging?"

"He's tumbling," Dolph said. As we crossed the Fleet ship's orbit, it glided past, not fifty klicks away, swinging over and over like a flipped coin that would never come down. The open radio channel hissed.

"Dead," I said.

That poor kid. He had bragged about defending humanity, putting a brave face on his backwater posting … and then death had come to Mittel Trevoyvox, like a whisper out of the void.

"That ship was HERFed." Dolph dropped our exhaust multiplier to zero with a heavy jolt. "There are Travellers around here somewhere."

"There," I said, pointing.

My gesture sketched a targeting box on the AR composite display. The box contained the damaged space station. Now that we were level with its altitude—and dropping lower in order to overhaul it—we could see what had been invisible from above.

Not one, not two, but three fat-assed Traveller ships clinging to the docking trusses on the bottom of the space station, sucking up water and other consumables from their kill.

The thermal inlays on their fuselages glittered in the sunlight from one side and the Corelight from the other, making them look like poisonous insects.

As we gradually overhauled the station, one of the ships undocked from the truss and fell away into the vacuum, firing its boosters to turn to face us. Its whip-like tail curved high over its back.

"Prep anti-HERF measures," I snapped. It should have been my job, but Dolph had the same defensive controls on his side of the bridge. While he opened the chaff ports and retracted the antennas, I dropped rounds into the *St. Clare's* railgun cradle.

"Shall I try talking to them?" Ijiuto said.

That was his job. That's why we had been ordered to bring him. So that he could buy us time by falsely claiming that we were on the Travellers' side. It was a *good* plan, I'll give Smith that, if you were into warfare by means of deception and sowing confusion.

I wasn't.

"Nah," I said. "Got these new rounds I've been wanting to try out." As I spoke, I was powering up the railgun. The lights blinked, dimmed, and the whine of the electrified rails seeped into my head. "*Firing.*"

"The seekers?" Dolph said, as a second round rocketed out of the *St. Clare's* grinning jaws.

"You got it." I loosed a third round.

The AI-guided Fleet munitions screamed across the void. We were four hundred klicks from the space station and the Traveller ships. By space battle standards, that's point blank range. The Traveller ships broke away from the station, maneuvering to put it between them and us. The seeker rounds curved to follow them. The explosions silhouetted the space station for a second, like a small moon partially eclipsing a sudden sun, and then it was blown to pieces by the force of multiple blasts. I had a sudden fear that there may have been someone alive in there, but given the hole in the station's side, it wasn't likely.

"Holed the AM containment on at least one of those mothers," Dolph said.

"Yeah." I watched the debris shell spread as we dived away from it. "That was … easy."

"Took 'em by surprise," Ijiuto gloated. "Demon-worshipping cretins."

"Problem is, you can't take anyone by surprise in space," I said. "They should have seen us coming a couple of AUs away."

"Figure they did," Dolph said. "But they thought we were someone else. Such as their reinforcements."

"Hmm. That's not good—" The radar alerted me to two, three, four missiles closing in on us from above and below. "Incoming!" I yelled. "Autonukes!"

"We got nukes too, don't we?" Dolph said dryly.

"Right." I dropped one of Smith's nuclear rounds into the cradle. "But we're too low." We were nearly in the atmosphere of Mittel Trevoyvox, angling across a wide gray ocean. The autonukes following us had already begun to sprout fiery re-entry tails. "If I nuke them, it'll airburst the whole hemisphere."

"Whereas if they nuke us …"

"Point." I powered up the railgun again. "On my mark, open the throttle and initiate the exhaust field."

"Roger."

"And *mark.*"

I dropped two nukes. Didn't fire them off the rails: just dropped them.

Approximately 40 gees smacked us into our couches. I grayed out for an instant. When my vision came back on line, the fireballs from our nukes were still burning, sitting on the blue rim of the horizon like setting stars. Smaller nuclear explosions went off like firecrackers around them. The autonukes had closed in on where we had been a moment ago, and triggered my nukes … while we shot away at Mach 10.

It's absolutely illegal to use a skip field generator in the atmosphere of a planet. I had never done it before. We whirled all the way around the planet, while Dolph, cursing a blue streak, leaned on the boosters to tamp down our velocity, and lightning cracked in our wake, due to electrical charges generated by the skip field jumping to air and water molecules. Atmospheric turbulence shook the ship like a tin can full of dried peas. At last we slowed down enough to sink into the troubled clouds.

"You guys are nuts!" Ijiuto yelled, with an uncharacteristic spontaneous grin.

"Your taxes at work," I said. "Dolph, take us down."

The *St. Clare* burst through the clouds over New Abilene-Qitalhaut, into thickly falling snow. Although it was broad day, I could not see a damn thing on the ground. The only way we found the spaceport was because nothing else in the city was lit up. We had just EMPed the whole hemisphere. I figured the New Abilene-Qitalhaut grid was hosed. But the spaceport had backup generators. Its lights burned through the snow.

We were coming in on a low-angled ballistic trajectory, instead of the usual burn straight down from orbit. Dolph practically turned the ship at a right angle, stopping her dead above the spaceport before opening up the auxiliaries for a final vertical descent that felt more like a fall.

The impact of landing rattled my teeth in my head. I stayed glued to the radar, assessing what opposition we would face on the ground.

None, was the answer.

There was not a single human ship left at the spaceport. Only the steel witch's hats of three Ek ships loomed dimly through the snow on the other side of the river.

47

I exited the ship cautiously with Robbie, both of us bundled up in Fleet polar gear: white and beige camouflage parkas, snowpants, and self-heating boots that kept our feet toasty. We carried the rifles we had been given. These were legit special ops assault rifles, known as Butterflies. Their smart stocks could spread like wings to conform to your shoulder, or form self-tripods. Again, I caught myself thinking that Irene would have loved all this new kit.

Robbie fingered his Butterfly uneasily as gunfire spattered through the Stone Age silence outside the spaceport. EMPs don't damage good old-fashioned guns. "Who's shooting at who, Cap'n?"

"Christ knows," I said. "It doesn't sound too close, anyway." I glanced in the direction of the perimeter, and was comforted to see the familiar white band of snow apparently suspended in mid-air. The force field perimeter was still up. Hurrah for diesel generators.

The Ur-Ek named Isir Olthamo came to meet us, flanked by Guardians in powered body armor. Guardians are Ek soldiers. They are rarely seen on the ground. I was duly intimidated. If those guys wanted to hurt us, they wouldn't even need to use their weapons. They could just pick us up and twist us in half. Fortunately, they accepted our credentials as representatives of the Fleet.

Olthamo led us into the passenger terminal, which was spottily lit by emergency lamps. We drank clear soup at the food court. The soup tasted like Eks smell, but at least it was hot. The Guardians lounged around heckling the few remaining human employees. Olthamo explained that xe had summoned the Guardians to clean up the Hurtworlds Authority.

"Burden was a scoundrel. After he left, I uncovered his connection with the Travellers. I then summoned the Guardians to reinforce our orbital defenses, so that he could not return."

"Good thinking," I said. "So how'd your space station end up with a hole in it?"

"Unfortunately, our reinforcements were insufficient."

"I see. Well, those particular Travellers won't be troubling you anymore. Sorry about the airbursts."

Olthamo fluttered a middle hand—*think nothing of it.* It wasn't *xis* planet. "We are in your debt. It has been most nervewracking to be bottled up at the bottom of this gravity well, knowing that those felons command the heights. We are expecting further reinforcements, but not for another three standard days. Where—if the question is not indelicate—is the rest of your unit?"

"As of now, it's just us," I said. "There's more Fleet ships on the way, but I couldn't tell you when they'll get here."

"Aha." Olthamo looked dissatisfied, as well he might. "Then who is up there now?"

"No one."

"In that case, our position is still tenuous." The roar of a ship launch shook the building. When we could hear each other speak again, Olthamo yelled, "That was one of the Guardian ships you saw outside. The EMP, of course, did not affect their systems. They are thoroughly rad-hardened. They will secure the planet's orbital space against any further incursions."

I made approving noises, but I wasn't entirely reassured. The ironic fact is that Ek ships are rather easily outclassed in orbital combat. They have enormous long-range firepower, but lack maneuverability. It was proved in the human-Ek war that our pilots can fly rings around them. "So who's shooting? We heard gunfire outside the spaceport."

"Oh, that is just the locals," Olthamo said. "An unrelated matter. Justin Kventuras—the Sixer king, yes?—has divorced his queen. This so-called queen was an Ek. An *Ur*-Ek. A pity. Anyway, their marriage had sealed the peace pact between the Eks and the Sixers. With its dissolution, the peace pact has also dissolved. There they go again," he added, as another faint crackle of gunfire punctuated the rumble of the generators.

"Divorced?" I said, confused.

"Divorced, left, dumped ..." Another twirl of xis blue, beringed middle hands—*how should I know, and why should I care?*

"OK. Ha, ha. OK." I pressed my thumbnails to my lower lip. "So which of them got the MTEV headquarters?" And the tanks, I was thinking. And the genetic engineering lab.

"Neither of them. The Travellers bombed the MTEV building from orbit. Didn't you see?"

"No! ... It's snowing ...."

"An outrageous infringement of the Hurtworlds Accords."

"Was Justin—the Sixer king—killed?"

"Oh, no. Both parties had already retired from the area, as it was under disputation, owing to the divorce. Kventuras has his new headquarters at the nuclear power plant, on the east bank of the river—"

"Jesus, I hope they flooded the core in time to stop it from melting down," I said, suddenly realizing that our EMP may have damaged Justin's fragile nuclear power plant.

Olthamo shrugged. "We Ekschelatans are not seriously affected by gamma rays."

Justin was at the power plant. If Pippa was alive, she would be with him. I tried to remember how far it was from here. Maybe ten klicks, on the other side of the river.

"And Queen Morshti?" I said.

"Oh, xe's around here somewhere," Olthamo said, startling me. "Xe begged for sanctuary, and I agreed. Although it is technically illegal to allow a felon into the spaceport, xe had important battlefield intelligence, which xe refused to reveal unless we let xim in."

"Battlefield intelligence?" I had not got the impression that Olthamo gave a good goddamn about the hostilities between the local Eks and the Sixers. Why would xe care about their troop dispositions? "Have they got artillery that might endanger the spaceport?"

"You could certainly say that. The guns on that ship are the equivalent of state-of-the-art field artillery."

"Ship guns? Whose ship?"

"The Travellers, of course," Olthamo said with a touch of impatience. "One of their ships landed on the ground, outside the spaceport, in contravention of landing regulations. According to Morshti, it is being used as a siege engine against Kvenṭuras's stronghold."

Good God. I stood up so fast that the Guardians around us twitched. Robbie hastily rose, too, spilling his untouched soup.

"I would seek to disable the ship," Olthamo continued, "but it is *awkwardly* close to that power plant."

"Thought you lot were immune to gamma rays."

"Yes, but one would not want to be responsible for ruining the city placed under one's care."

"Bit late to worry about that. Anyway, the Fleet thanks you for your consideration for human life. Where can I find Morshti?"

*

The Guardians tracked xim down for me. Xe had been lurking in the service area of the passenger terminal with a few faithful Ek followers. Xe had traded xis royal garb for camouflage, but retained xis mithrik-fur cape, now tatty and snow-stained.

"I remember you," xe said. If looks could kill I would have been a smoking hole in the ground.

"Morshti," I said, "can you take us to the power plant? The future of the Cluster might depend on it." I'd normally try to be a bit more subtle, but I was feeling nauseated again. Maybe it was the Ek soup.

48

MORSHTI didn't care about the future of the Cluster, anyway. Xe only cared about the injustice that had been done to xim.

Xe had a tank parked outside the spaceport. I had considered taking off in the *St. Clare* and shooting the Traveller ship from the air, but there was just too much risk of either hitting the power plant, or hitting the Traveller ship's containment, triggering an antimatter explosion, and killing everyone in the city. A ground-based strategy seemed like the better option. Olthamo gave us fuel for the tank, and some ammunition. The Ur-Ek was happy for us to tackle the Travellers. It gave xim an excuse not to. Xe really was a bit of a dick.

Dolph stayed with the *St. Clare*. He didn't want to, but with MF gone, someone had to stay behind who knew how to fly the ship. "If we don't come back," I said, "just run." We were watering up. H2O glugged into the *St. Clare's* tanks. Pumps clattered. Dolph and I stood in the snow between the giant, Ek-operated water tankers. "Save Lucy. That's all I ask of you."

"You left out one part," Dolph said. "Bomb this motherfucker to oblivion. *Then* run." He pointed to the graveyard, where Artie rested in peace beneath the snow. "He got a lousy plastic cross for his memorial. You'll get a nuclear dawn."

"You wouldn't."

He winked. "That's to make sure you come back."

"Douche."

We hugged. He was shivering, despite his Fleet parka. He saluted us with his rifle as we jogged to the gate in the perimeter.

The Ek tank waited outside. Martin, Robbie, Ijiuto, and I piled in along with Morshti and two of xis followers. The interior of the tank felt spacious—to us. All the same, being stuck in a tin can with three Eks is a fairly good approximation of purgatory. I breathed through my mouth, and popped another of Martin's anti-nausea tablets as we rumbled out into the streets.

"We shall kill the Travellers," Morshti said. "Then I shall kill the little human bitch. Mine again will be Justin, and everything."

"No messing with Pippa. She's ours," I said.

"Will you take her away?"

"That's why we're here."

"That is acceptable, I suppose, so long as I never have to see her repulsive human face again."

"But what exactly happened?" I wasn't sure I wanted to know, but I needed a distraction from my stomach. I was hanging onto the edge of the top hatch, standing between Morshti, in the driver's seat, and the Ek who would act as loader for the tank's railgun. Martin stood beside me. Robbie and Ijiuto crouched behind us.

"You I blame," Morshti said. "Brought her here, you did."

Ijiuto said, "Are we talking about my cousin?"

"Your cousin? By the Law, I detest her."

"Oh, I do, too," Ijiuto said. "What's she done?"

"Fucked my husband, of course," Morshti said. "'Oh, Morshti, I'm so *grateful* to you for letting me stay—'" Xe mimicked a high-pitched human voice. "So humble. Such pretty manners. And all the time, behind my back, shamelessly seducing him, she was!"

Martin made a stifled noise and turned away. I punched him lightly, warning him to be quiet before the Eks could notice that he was cracking up. It was no laughing matter. Frankly, I had a hard time picturing it myself. Justin … and Pippa?! But as Morshti proved, stranger relationships had bloomed on Mittel Trevoyvox before now.

Robbie blurted, "So you and the king, you were, y'know, having, uh, living as husband and wife? *Doing* it?"

Of course he fixated on that.

Morshti shrugged with xis top shoulders. "Over a fling, I would not cast him aside. Where he sticks his male member, I care nothing. But he *loves* her, and wants to *marry* her, and therefore he can no longer be married to me. That is what he said." Morshti craned over the binocular scope which gave xim a view of the street ahead. "He shall pay, and she shall pay," xe crooned. "It is the Law."

The tank turned a corner. One of the other Eks popped xis head and shoulders up through the hatch and fired the turret gun. Casings rattled to the floor.

"Where are we?" I said. It made me nervous not to be able to see out.

"About to cross the river," Morshti said. A moment later the tank's treads clanked on the bridge.

We drove on for another fifteen minutes. Twice, we heard booms over the loud whine of the tank's engine. At last Morshti stopped the tank. "Humans out. With me."

The four of us and Morshti scrambled up through the hatch. We had stopped in a typical New Abilene-Qitalhaut canyon: human buildings on top of mithrik warrens, interspersed with gardens planted on old bomb sites. The other two Eks stayed in the tank. As we retreated into an alley, the tank's main gun cranked up to a higher elevation and began to fire.

It sounded like the whole city was falling. Shoddy old buildings in the tank's line of fire crumbled. Rubble and dust spurted into the snow, while we ran, following Morshti. "Shooting at the Traveller ship, we are," Morshti yelled.

The Traveller ship had been nowhere in sight. The tank may well have been shooting at it … straight *through* all the houses in the way. Lovely. What kind of ammunition had Olthamo given them? Ek munitions are all standardized; I wouldn't be surprised if those were explosive shells intended for a ship's railgun.

"They kill some Travellers, maybe," Morshti shouted. "If nothing else, it will serve as a diversion."

We came out on the riverbank. The houses went right down to the water here. The river was frozen over. Morshti stepped out onto the ice. "If it'll hold that two-hundred-kilo freak," Martin muttered, and strode after xim, followed by Robbie and Ijiuto. I hung back for a second, remembering how I'd almost drowned in this river seventeen years ago, thinking about the cold black water under the ice. Then I followed. The ice was covered with snow. I sank in up to my ankles. Cold wind blew down the river, tossing flurries into my face. My self-defrosting Fleet snow goggles kept it out of my eyes.

Upstream, the bank bulged out into a walled promontory. That was the power plant. The walls looked much higher up close than when I had seen them from the 15th floor of the MTEV building—ten sheer meters of dirty stone, ominous in the whirling snow. How were we going to get in there?

Gunfire spat, this time from the other side of the river. I glimpsed muzzle flash. The Sixers over there had spotted us, and evidently took us for enemies.

We ran, slipping on the ice. We were strung out: Morshti in the lead, Martin behind xim, then Robbie, then Ijiuto, with me bringing up the rear. Robbie had the satchel with the grenades and spare ammo in it.

Morshti stumbled. Fell. Rising on one knee, xe returned fire with two rifles at once. That's the advantage of having six arms. With one rifle, xe aimed at the Sixers across the river. With the other, xe peppered the jumble of buildings this side of the power plant.

The Travellers on sentry duty had seen us.

That diversion didn't last long.

Martin added his fire to Morshti's. I found the Travellers with my scope, in the top floor of the tenement-style building nearest to the power plant. The building was missing its roof. The Travellers crouched behind the sheared-off walls. I knew they were Travellers and not Sixers because they had only two arms apiece. If that didn't tip me off, the black coats would have. I fired at them as I ran to catch up with the others, feeling the Butterfly kick against my shoulder and upper chest.

Robbie ran up behind Martin, and past him, fumbling in his satchel. He threw a grenade. It fell down into the street between the Travellers' building and the power plant. Red light blossomed around the corner of the building. The building slowly collapsed, taking the Travellers with it.

"Missed," Robbie gasped.

"Hey, it worked." Against my better instincts, I stopped to help Morshti up. Xe had taken a bullet in the top right arm and was bleeding through xis camo, cursing in the Ek language.

The ice creaked.

"Remind me whose bright idea it was to come this way?" Martin said.

Ahead of us, the ice ended in a lacy shelf. A moat of black water separated us from the power plant.

"They're venting hot wastewater straight into the river." I stood stock-still, feeling the ice creak under my feet. "It's melted the ice." Emergency cooling, in a nuclear fission plant, means flooding the fuel rods with water. Lots and lots of water. All that water then has to go somewhere. I could hear the emergency pumps throbbing like a giant heart over the whistle of the wind.

We were trapped. Radioactive water ahead, Travellers on one side of us, Sixers on the other. Martin and I shot at the Travellers scrambling over the wreckage of the collapsed building, forcing their heads down. But now, through the gap, I could see the Traveller ship, a monster standing on its three duck-foot engine pods on a sheet of glassed rubble, facing the wall of the power plant.

The tank had scored some hits. A region of the hull on the starboard side was crumpled like paper. That ship would not be flying again. But that didn't mean it was no longer dangerous. People climbed on top of it, heading for the .50 turret. When that gun opened up, it would sweep us away like a steel broom.

I stared up at the wall beyond the black water, tipped back my head, and shouted at the top of my lungs, "MF! Mechanical Failure!" The wind seemed to carry my voice away. "MF, are you there, buddy? It's me! Mike!" The snow swirled into my face. "I'm sorry, MF! Can you hear me? In God's name, MF! *Help!*"

Ijiuto threw down his rifle. For an instant I thought he'd been hit. Then he ran towards the Travellers—betraying us the first chance he got. Robbie dived after him.

Abruptly, Ijiuto vanished. Robbie stopped short. A crack ran through the ice, right between his legs, scissoring them apart.

Ijiuto thrashed in the water.

A small, suitcase-shaped object flew over the wall of the power plant, trailing something beneath it.

The Travellers on top of the ship shot at it.

MF bobbed like a suitcase-shaped swallow, making himself an unpredictably moving target. He swooped low over us. The thing trailing from his chassis was a ladder, such as sea rescue crews drop from helicopters. Morshti grabbed it with all five of xis working hands. "Marty! Robbie! Climb!" I shouted. Once they were on the ladder, I seized it, hooked my knees over the second-to-last rung, and let myself hang upside-down. My rifle bashed me in the face. I snatched for Ijiuto's flailing arms, twisted my fingers into his coat, and took his weight in my shoulders as MF rose into the snow.

Why did I save Ijiuto? I should have let the bastard drown. I just didn't want to let the Travellers have him back.

MF's levitation bubble had expanded to the size of a three-storey building to lift all of us. It sheltered us from the snow like a roof. Swinging upside-down, fighting to keep my grip on Ijiuto's wet coat, feeling like my arms were pulling out of their sockets, I glimpsed the shocked faces of the Travellers on top of the ship.

One of them was Sophia.

Our eyes met for an instant.

She whipped her rifle up and fired at me.

Thank God she was such a bad shot.

MF dropped over the top of the wall. We landed in a heap on the ground among the dingy prefab buildings of the power plant. When I untangled myself, I found a bullet hole in the hood of my parka. Whoa. She came pretty close to getting me this time.

Justin stooped over us, beaming delightedly. "My friend, my friend! I knew you would come back! Have you brought us some more good luck? We sorely need it."

"Dunno about that, but I've brought you something else," I said, hauling Ijiuto to his feet.

49

THE Sixers put Morshti in chains. Ijiuto they did not, despite my pleas. They felt sorry for him because he was soaked through, and on top of that he turned out to have been grazed by a bullet. Blood trickled from the fingers of his left hand and mingled with the water dripping from his clothes. We straggled into the control room. Amid old-fashioned banks of dials and readouts, Sixer technicians were frantically working to keep the nuclear core cool. We went on down a flight of stairs too deep for human legs, into the power plant's safety bunker.

It was a peculiar room. Pillars rose from the floor here and there, ending in double-bed-sized surfaces that were chest-high on me. The Sixers had piled these "tables" with computers, hazmat garments, and dirty dishes. Cots lined one wall, some occupied by exhausted Sixers. A radiation counter, steadily beeping, beeped faster when we came in. It took me a moment to notice the walls. One wall looked like frosted glass. Around all the other walls writhed faded cloisonné murals of four-legged, long-necked, shaggy-furred Urush having sex.

MF goggled ruefully at the alien orgy. "This was an Urush temple. This was the holy of holies. Those are altars. Oh, *I* don't mind! Time passes, and times change."

"The Urush had a religion based on sex?" I said.

"Is that any stranger than your religion based upon a crucified God?"

A boom rumbled through the room. The floor vibrated.

"The Travellers are firing the ship's railgun at the curtain wall," MF said. "The Urush used to say *nothing* could get through exodiamondite. That may have been true once, but after thousands of years, everything starts to decay. I estimate they will break down the wall by the end of the day, if they do not run out of shells first. Where is the *St. Clare?*"

*

The *St Clare* was still sitting at the spaceport. The water, LOX, and LN2 tanks were full. Dolph had run pre-launch checks, and then run them again. He'd messed with the HF awhile, but he couldn't get through to me. Olthamo had lifted Burden's all-frequencies jamming protocol, but I was sitting in a former Urush temple underground. It might be true that nothing could get through exodiamondite; radio waves certainly couldn't.

With nothing to do except wait, Dolph was restless. He told me later that he'd started thinking about how he stayed behind on Yesanyase Skont before this, and the reasons why.

He put on his polar gear and trudged over to the graveyard. He visited with the Artster for a while, talking to him under his breath, telling him what was going on. His breath clouded white in the air, and as if transferred up from the frozen ground to him by some process of living memory, the old deep hunger for oblivion, the need I've never really felt and can only imagine, took hold. He started fantasizing about a little something to take the edge off. But he realized what was happening, he said. Realized that being around Artie, even in spirit, brought out the worst in him. And he further realized that he had come out here on purpose, so he'd have an excuse for getting high. He kicked the cross so hard it hurt his foot.

Then he went back to the ship.

And he went to the first-aid locker.

We didn't carry any strong medications on the ship as a rule. Shifters don't need them. But Smith, in addition to having every last ding and dent on the *St. Clare* fixed, had restocked our first-aid locker with a pharmacopoeia fit for a front-lines unit, including the latest Fleet-approved formulation of the drug we used to call shabu.

Dolph said he only took half the recommended dose, but I think it was probably more than that.

Then he went and sat in the open airlock with his feet up on the wall of the chamber, chain-smoking.

Waiting.

*

"Wonderful," MF said bitterly, when I told him the *St. Clare* was at the spaceport. "And even if we could contact Dolph, the ship cannot land here. What sort of a rescue is this?"

Martin said, "Bet Dolph could put down inside the compound. Sure, it would be risky, but he lives for that shit."

"You are referring to the *apparently* open ground beyond the cooling towers," MF said. "Look." He rolled over to the only orgy-free wall of the bunker and shone his integrated lamp straight at it.

I caught my breath. A circular area of the wall seemed to dissolve under the powerful beam. No, it became transparent, like glass, or ... what did MF say? Exodiamondite.

Suddenly, we were looking out into daylight. This bunker was actually built into the side of a shallow bowl within the compound. The falling snow obscured Sixers patrolling the curtain wall. And at the bottom of the bowl, more Sixers stood guard underneath a fancy arrowhead spaceship.

"The temple had its own launch pad," MF said. "The ship is of more recent vintage."

Hope lit me up. We might be able to use that ship to escape. Call Dolph, link up with the *St. Clare* in orbit. "Where did that ship come from?" As I spoke, I realized the answer. It was the same ship that Irene had spotted on a barge at the spaceport last time we were here.

"Justin stole it under cover of darkness," MF said. "He is a most enterprising young man." He blinked his sensor covers rapidly. "Don't get your hopes up, Captain. He will not let you have that ship."

MF had read my thoughts. "Why not?"

"Because he intends to use it himself."

Justin came back in with Pippa.

"Mike! Marty! Oh my God!" Pippa hurried over to us. Her face blazed with happiness. In the short month since we last met, she had gained a massive injection of self-confidence. Gone was the defeated, tearful IVK victim. Her hair was brushed sleek. She wore a cape-like sweatshirt over thermals and wide trousers, all evidently cut-down Sixer garments. She was at it again, restyling charity gear to her own liking, just as she had done on Gvm Uye Sachttra. *That* was the girl I saw before me now—the cheeky, precocious knife-seller from the refugee camp. Pippa had got her mojo back, and then some. A new poise infused her carriage; she looked like … a princess.

Watching Justin wrap his lower set of arms possessively around her shoulders, I realized her transformation was probably due to good sex, and lots of it.

When a boy and a girl are in love, they can't hide it even if they try. They can't keep their hands off each other, even in the direst circumstances. So Pippa and Justin petted each other's hands and toyed with one another's hair while the Travellers battered at the wall outside. Justin gestured normally with his free set of hands and talked to us, explaining how he'd cleverly stolen the spaceship, as if he and Pippa weren't practically having sex with their clothes on.

Well, he'd probably never had a girlfriend before. Sure, he was 25. But he had been groomed to rule from childhood, and spent his adulthood in a miserable marriage to an alien. No wonder he had fallen hard for this sweet girl whom we, like the chumps we were, had consigned to his protection. And Pippa herself? She'd spent much of her young life hustling to keep herself and her cousins alive. She'd known hard times, but she may never have tasted love … until she met the young king of New Abilene-Qitalhaut.

Trust me to show up and harsh their buzz.

Without trying to soften it, I told them everything: the Iron Triangle, Smith's threats, my mission to retrieve the TrZam 008. I also told Pippa that Jan and Leaf had been fostered, and were thriving. That news brought a smile to her face, but it dimmed as she stared at Ijiuto, who was sitting in the opposite corner, guarded by two Sixer toughs, dripping and miserable.

"Of course. Now I recognize him. Rafael, born of Ludmilla and Jan." I frowned; I'd thought the last Rafael in the Tree was born of Cornelia and somebody, but I let it go. "He's the New Gessyrian pretender to the throne. Gran always warned us that he might come looking for us someday. New Gessyria won the war, but they wouldn't consider their victory complete until the Old Gessyrian line was extinct. That's what she said. Oh, I wish I'd taken the threat more seriously." Pippa's lower lip suddenly pushed out. Jan and Leaf may have resented their authoritarian grandmother, but Pippa must have loved the old woman. Her eyes sparkled with tears. She picked up one of Justin's hands and rubbed her face against his broad palm, wiping the moisture away. "So he *did* come looking for us." She raised her voice and shouted in Ijiuto's direction. "Why couldn't you just leave us alone?!"

"You stole the Code," Ijiuto yelled at her, in a tone of raw fury that made his Sixer guards close in threateningly.

"No, *you* stole it," Pippa shouted. "You attacked Old Gessyria on purpose to steal the Code!"

"Your grandmother was a liar," Ijiuto shouted. "The Code was ours, and you stole it! We were only defending our intellectual property rights!" One of the Sixers hit him, and he subsided.

"Oh, don't you sound educated," Pippa said, digging her fingers into Justin's knee. She was sitting beside him on one of the cots. She shouted across the room at Ijiuto, "Defending your intellectual property rights! Is *that* how you describe a war that left fifteen million dead?"

"Fifteen million?" I whistled softly. I'd had no idea the Gessyrian civil war wreaked destruction on that scale.

"Oh yes," Pippa said. She slumped against Justin's chest. "I was born on the carrier that had just delivered a counterstrike to New Gessyria. After that, it carried the last six thousand survivors of Old Gessyria to the Cluster."

Justin told the story. Pippa must have told it to him in private, with plenty of breaks for tears and kisses, but it was too emotionally charged for her to relate to anyone else. So she just sat there, half-covering her ears, sometimes covering her eyes, and we got the tragedy of the Darkworlds filtered through the perspective and vocabulary of a Sixer. It was oddly appropriate. Justin himself, after all, was another royal heir, of another planet that had suffered through the hell of war. He knew whereof he spoke, although he'd never been to the Darkworlds, any more than Pippa had.

This was the gist of it. Five hundred years ago, in the late Age of Adaptation, a convoy of human colonists reached the system that would later be known as the Darkworlds, and they saw that it was good. Not one but *two* human-compatible planets orbited a star of 1.2 solar masses with a human-friendly radiation spectrum. The colonists made landfall on the second and slightly smaller planet, which they named Gessyria. They broke up one of their colony ships to bootstrap power generation and industry. They flourished under the guidance of their hereditary monarchy, which they had determined to be the least bad of all political systems (Justin spoke approvingly of this choice), and after fifty years or so, they planted another colony on the third and larger planet. This then became known as New Gessyria, while the original colony turned into Old Gessyria. A prince of the dynasty went out to rule the new colony as a satrapy of his father's dominion.

Anyone with minimal knowledge of history could have predicted that *that* wasn't going to end well.

But in fact, disaster struck from a different quarter. Not politics, but nature, landed the Gessyrians a one-two punch.

First of all, New Gessyria turned out to be tectonically restless. A massive volcanic eruption spewed ash into the planet's atmosphere, borking the colonists' solar power and killing their crops. They suffered through three years without a summer. They converted their remaining spaceships into power plants and synthesized food out of local resources, but that killed more of them than the bitter cold.

At almost the same time, a shower of meteors struck Old Gessyria, causing quakes and tsunamis which washed away three-quarters of the colonists, and all *their* remaining spaceships.

(Also at around the same time, fifty light years away, the colonists of San Damiano were spiraling into a life-or-death crisis. In our case, it was nothing dramatic, just a lot of little stuff—soil problems, insect problems, foot-and-mouth disease, viruses—that added up to an onrushing colony failure event. Our technocrats stared the math in the teeth and pulled the trigger on the Big Shift. Some say that they just used the crisis as an excuse for something they wanted to do anyway. The Darkworlders were not led by a smartypants club of technocrats. They were led by kings and queens, and they found a different solution.)

When the dust settled on Old Gessyria and New Gessyria, neither planet had a single working spaceship left.

They were cut off from one another by a void of 1.1 AU.

They stayed in radio contact for a while, but when the radio telescope arrays got broken up for parts, that ended, too.

Three hundred and fifty years passed.

*

One day in 3375—the year of my birth, coincidentally—Fleet ships burst out of the sky of New Gessyria. The Darkworlders were clinging on at an eighteenth-century tech level. They had started mining coal for fuel, and they dressed in clothes made from the wool of local fauna. Unknown to them, during the last three hundred years, humanity had colonized the Cluster. The Fleet was now casting back over our path from Earth to the Messier 4 Cluster, visiting older colonies that had not been heard from recently. San Damiano had been re-contacted in 3361; my parents were young adults at the time, and they never quite got over the shock, nor did most people of their generation.

Re-contact seems to have been an easier adjustment for the Darkworlders. They looked agreeably mainstream, and they played the part of supplicants with the virtuosity you would expect from people who had lived under a monarchy for four hundred years. The Fleet, and the whole constellation of government agencies and charitable NGOs based in the Heartworlds, showered them with goodies ... including spaceships. Crucially, they gave ships to the New Gessyrians first, supposing them to be in more need. The Old Gessyrians had done better during the long separation—there were fifteen million of them by this time, spread out over two continents with rail, road, and sea connections.

The first thing the New Gessyrians did with their new ships was to head over and bomb the shit out of their neighbors.

The story got a bit confused at this point. Rafael Ijiuto, who had concurred with Justin's telling so far, now yelled that Justin and Pippa had it backwards. It was the *Old* Gessyrians who had attacked *them* first.

"Whatever," I said. I was sitting on the floor, leaning against an altar-table. I'd begun to feel sick again. I was smoking vile cigarettes blagged from the Sixers to try and combat the nausea. The story so far had been punctuated by the thunder of the Travellers pounding away at the wall, while Sixers rushed in every so often to update Justin on the status of the power plant. We couldn't stay here much longer. That was very clear. Yet I was far from making up my mind what I should do. "It doesn't matter who started it. All war stories are the same. People are horrible to each other and lots of them die. Skip to the end."

"Well, that *is* the end," Justin said. "A tiny remnant of Old Gessyria escaped to the Cluster. They found refuge on Gvm Uye Sachttra, and there they lived for fifteen years, until that wretch showed up with his Travellers to destroy them."

I looked at Ijiuto. "You know, it's never stopped bugging me. *Why* did you come up with that preposterous scheme of using toy fairies to—to infect them with IVK, instead of just dropping a nuke on the refugee camp? Your people clearly have no objection to bombing civilians from orbit. And since you were hiding behind the Travellers, you would've had deniability."

Ijiuto sat up, skull-faced in the gloom. "Exactly! That's what *I* wanted to do!"

"But?"

"The Travellers refused."

"Even though you were paying them so much money?"

"Not money. Antimatter."

"Where'd you get *that?*"

Antimatter is hellishly difficult, expensive and dangerous to produce. You'd better not manufacture it on the surface of a planet if you like your planet. The Eks do it on orbitals in barren star systems. We do it on airless moons ringed with gigantic particle accelerators.

"From the Fleet," Ijiuto said, "of course. For our spaceships. But we don't *have* any more spaceships. Our last ships were lost chasing the Old Gessyrian carrier that the refugees escaped on. Back to square fucking one. We won, but it doesn't feel like winning sometimes. So there I am, sitting at home, wondering what I'm going to do about those vermin that stole our Code, and here comes the anti-matter tanker. I tell the guy, 'You might as well take that away. What are we gonna use it for? We don't have any more ships.' And the guy goes, 'So why not hire some?'"

I sat up. I sensed something important here, maybe even the key to the whole mystery …

"So I did," Ijiuto said, "and now they're sitting outside of here, trying to kill us. Demon-worshipping cretins."

On cue, another boom reverberated through the bunker. Pippa shuddered. "We'd better go," she said, pulling Justin to his feet.

"Yes, we'd better." Justin straightened his coat and looked around at the other Sixers. "Bernard, I'm leaving you in charge. Once we are gone, the Travellers will have no reason to remain. Then you'll only have to deal with the Eks …"

"Hold up, hold up," I interrupted, moving around to stand in front of them. "*Where* are you going?"

I could practically feel Justin's excitement, like the warmth from a fire, banked down behind his solemn expression. "Away."

"Together," Pippa said.

"You can't do that," I said.

"I *love* him," she said.

"I'm abdicating my throne," Justin said. "This is the only way I can save my people." But the look in his eyes gave the lie to his noble sentiments. The sheer heat coming off those two made the nuclear power plant look like a candle. They lit up the room, and I unwillingly remembered the beginning of my relationship with Sophia, when the same kind of heat had burned between us, like the gravity binding a binary star into its death spiral. I knew all about doing dumb shit for love.

50

Dolph, sitting in the starboard airlock of the *St. Clare,* watched the day darken. There were no city lights to illuminate the snow-clouds. The whole planet seemed to be sinking into a primordial night, rent by battlefield noises.

The floodlights around the perimeter of the spaceport came on. Armored Guardians patrolled the inside of the force field perimeter. Dolph noticed, with his pharmaceutically enhanced focus, that the patrols were spaced pretty far apart. One would go past, and it would be 3 minutes and 20 seconds (he timed it) before the next one appeared.

During one of these gaps in coverage, he spotted someone trudging towards the *St. Clare,* not from the gate, but from the river. The figure wore a heavy coat, and had only two arms, but it was not one of us. He could tell by the gait. It was a woman.

He waited, with his chilled finger on the trigger.

"Little pig, little pig, let me come in." The hooded figure, standing at the bottom of the ladder, turned its pale face up to him.

"Sophia." Dolph stared down the barrel of his Koiler.

"Can I come up?" She was alone. She sounded like she was in pain. She was wet—her hair hung out the hood of her coat in lank dark strands.

"Drop your weapons. Whatever you've got. Fucking do it!"

"I don't have anything. *Please,* Dolph."

Dolph didn't want the Guardians to see her hanging around the ship. "All right. Quick!"

Sophia started to climb the ladder, favoring her left side. Dolph backed out of the airlock. He dropped into the trunk corridor and aimed his Koiler at the inner hatch.

"Shut the outer hatch," he yelled when she appeared.

The airlock thunked shut. Sophia sat on the edge of the inner hatch, hunched over beneath the ceiling, looking up and down the trunk corridor. She wore an ordinary down coat, not a Traveller coat. It was sodden. Water dripped off her onto the floor. "So this is Mike's new ship."

"Not that new." Dolph pointed the Koiler at her. "Weapons."

"You mean this," Sophia said, cupping her crotch, "and these? What you see is what you get. I escaped along the river. The Sixers can't see you to shoot at you after dark. They *still* haven't got any barriers across the river where it enters the spaceport. The Guardians saw me, though; shot at me. The ice broke. That's what saved me. I dived under the ice and waited until they were gone." She showed him some cuts on her bloodless fingers.

Her lips were blue. Dolph said, "Take off those wet clothes."

"Strip-search?" Sophia grinned palely and pulled her shirt off over her head.

"You can change in one of the berths."

"Really? I might find something to use as a weapon. You'd better watch, so you can be sure I'm unarmed." She peeled off her sodden shoes, socks, trousers, and underwear.

Sophia had the body of a goddess. Close my eyes and I can still see her long thighs, those full breasts with dark nipples and aureolae, the slender waist flaring to a luscious ass. Seven years couldn't have changed her *that* much. It would have been as if a fertility deity of olden times had materialized in the *St. Clare's* trunk corridor.

"Go in there," Dolph said, motioning with the Koiler. The nearest berth happened to be his own. "Look in that locker." He directed her to take out one of his shirts and a pair of his sweats.

She winced as she closed the locker. Bruises discolored the left side of her ribs. Dolph wondered if they were fractured. That's what he was thinking about, he swore.

"Give me what I want, and I'll give you what you want," she said suddenly, holding his clothes in her hands.

"What do you want?"

"The entire freaking Cluster is after me. I've burned up my credit with everyone I know. There's more than one bounty on my head. Hide me. Get me off this goddamn planet."

"In your dreams." Dolph was thinking that he'd let her get dressed, then lock her in the admin berth. Take her home to Smith as a bonus gift. He felt a certain self-disgust, he told me, even as the plan took shape. *Good* dog …

"You don't even have to tell Mike," Sophia suggested.

"Why would I do that?"

"Because you want what Mike has." Her voice was soft. Knowing. She stepped closer to him. "You always have. You want his ship. Hey, I don't blame you. This is a *nice* ship. Ceilings are a bit low … You want his amazing ability to Shift into sixty different animal forms."

"No, I don't," Dolph said with conviction. He knew better than anyone else what I'd gone through with Chimera Syndrome.

"And you want his wife." She held up one finger, as if telling him not to say another word. Dolph stepped back, keeping the Koiler out of her reach. "*Ex*-wife, of course. That's convenient. Your faith doesn't have to get in the way."

"Ain't no such thing as ex." Dolph's heel hit the wall. He couldn't back up any further.

"So you're saying nothing's changed? Well, maybe it hasn't. I remember how you used to look at me even when Mike and I were married."

The fact is that Dolph spotted Sophia first. We met in an Ek bar, right there at the spaceport on Mittel Trevoyvox. It was him that tried to pick her up. And it was he who convinced me, at a later time, when Ek felons were shooting at us, not to leave her to find her own way home. He was *chivalrous* in those days. Not long afterwards, of course, he turned against her. He told me that she was trouble on legs. And he was absolutely right. I should have listened to him. But the fact remains, he was attracted to her at the very beginning, and I never quite managed to forget it. Even after he was best man at our wedding, even after he moved on to someone else and someone else and someone else again, I could never shake a little niggle of insecurity. When Sophia left me, it at least had the silver lining of removing that irritant from our friendship.

"I'll tell you a secret," she said. "I would've loved to do you and Mike at the same time. One of you in animal form, the other in human form. God, that would have been hot. You'd have liked it too, wouldn't you?"

Dolph told me this to illustrate how depraved she was. But it had the effect of reviving that niggle of insecurity. I'm still not sure I believe his version of what happened next. She would have been standing so close to him. She was naked. Her nipples would've been as hard as bullets in the cold air. Didn't he at least struggle with temptation? We're all human, so I don't blame him if he did.

What he *said* happened was this.

He grasped Sophia by the shoulder and drew her closer, as if he was going to kiss her. The Koiler dug into her stomach. Her eyes were wide and drowning-dark. He said, "You know what Mike has? *IVK.* He's got five years to live, because of you. So no, I wouldn't screw you if you were the last woman in the universe."

He spun her away with a contemptuous snap of his wrist. But she grabbed his arm and pulled him with her. They crashed to the floor. He reared up to flip her over, but she was faster.

That's how he said it happened. And if, in fact, it didn't go quite like that, if there was indecision, if there was drug-impaired judgement, if he forgot how dangerous she was, what does it matter?

All that matters is that one way or another, Sophia ended up with the Koiler in her hand.

Dolph picked himself up. He was going to rush her. He didn't think she'd shoot him, or maybe he just wasn't thinking that clearly.

A metal tentacle whipped around his arm, hauling him up short.

Our new maintenance bot, which had crawled soundlessly into the berth, said in its monotonous croak, "Do not move."

It raised another tentacle, brandishing an injector full of something clear, and lowered the needle to within a few centimeters of Dolph's arm.

"What's … in the injector?" Dolph said.

"Not sure," Sopha said carelessly. "I told it to pick whatever was closest to shabu. I know you used to be a fiend for that stuff."

Dolph eyeballed the dose. It looked like enough to kill a mainstream human being. Maybe not a Shifter. *Maybe.* "How?" he said at last.

Sophia laughed. "I was telling the truth: I don't have any weapons. I don't *need* any weapons, when there are poorly secured AIs around."

"But you don't have a computer, or a phone, or—"

She pointed at her head. "Wireless uplink. Yeah, I finally caved in. I'm against cybernetics on principle, but it's just so handy being able to carry my favorite exploits in my brain."

She put on Dolph's spare clothes, and wedged the Koiler into the pocket of the sweats.

"The bot was easy to crack, but it looks like I can't break into your ship's computer. You've got some outstanding encryption there." Dolph mentally gave thanks to MF for that. "I was planning to get the bot to knock you out. But since I can't access the flight controls …" She chuckled. "I guess we'll find out if Yesanyase Skont was a fluke, or if you really are that good."

She herded Dolph onto the bridge. The maintenance bot followed, and stationed itself behind Dolph's couch.

"Turn up the heat," Sophia said. "It's freezing in here." To the bot, she said, "If he makes any sudden moves, give him the whole dose."

Dolph figured she was probably bluffing, since she needed him to fly the ship, but he didn't want to find out. She perched on the arm of the left couch, pointing the Koiler at him, while he went through all the pre-launch checks again, as slowly as possible.

Sophia could pilot a spaceship, of course. But the *St. Clare's* bridge had a unique console layout, due to being built by MF for the Kroolth, and we'd further customized it to our own preferences, making it difficult for outsiders to figure out. Dolph satisfied himself that Sophia couldn't actually tell what he was doing with all the screens and switches. That gave him a potential advantage, although he couldn't think of any way to use it right now.

"Hurry up," Sophia said. "Mike'll be back any minute."

"I know how I ended up here," Dolph said. "But what about you? You used to talk about human solidarity, the search for the Divine, the rebirth of meaning." These were some of the shipboard conversations we used to have, late at night, half-drunk or completely drunk. God, we were young. We used to wrestle with what it meant that we would do bad shit for money. Sophia had had several different elaborate justifications. After she left, we stopped wrestling with it. We just did it.

"Nothing's changed," she said. "I still believe in all that stuff."

"Which stuff? You used to have a different philosophy for every day of the week."

"No, I didn't. I just hadn't put it all together yet."

"So what's the meaning of life?"

"It's *obvious.* That's why it took me so long to figure it out."

"Well?"

"How big is your cock?"

Dolph chuckled despite himself. "Blatant change of subject alert."

"No, it's really not. How big is it?"

"In human form, jackal form, or dolphin form?"

"Any of the above. Human form."

"Big as I need it to be."

"That's my point. I've never known a male Shifter who wasn't hung like a horse."

"And you've known so many of them."

"Not really, but there's been research done, believe it or not. Adult male Shifters have anomalously large penises, *even in human form.*"

I wouldn't be surprised if that were true. Show me the adolescent boy who, when he learns to Shift, doesn't try to enlarge his penis. Real animals tend to have pencil dicks, but Shiftertown is teeming with well-hung wolves, lions, and so forth. Even on San Damiano, the authenticity criteria are relaxed with a wink and a nod when it comes to boys endowing themselves with a couple extra centimeters. And mightn't it carry over a little bit into our human forms when we Shift back? I've certainly always considered myself above average, but maybe every other Shifter guy does too … and maybe we're all right. I would just like to know who the heck did that research. Sophia did not say.

"So what does that prove?" Dolph said. "Guys are vain?"

Sophia sighed. "It proves that we can be whatever we want to be. We can shape our own destinies. Shifter dick size is trivial in the grand scheme of things, but it's a proof of concept."

Dolph pulled another switch. "I'm not seeing how this fits in with plotting to murder millions of innocent people."

"You'll understand when Mike gets back."

Dolph raised his eyebrows. He had assumed she wanted to launch before we returned. He had assumed it was our *ship* she wanted to steal.

"We're waiting for him," she said. And grinned. "He's such a loyal friend. I'm sure he'll trade the TrZam 008 for your life …"

51

Justin and Pippa gathered up their luggage. They had backpacks, rope-bound bales, and duffel bags of supplies. They had planned their escape in detail … and then the Travellers had come. They couldn't have taken off with three Traveller ships in orbit. They'd have been sitting ducks.

But then I had come along and helpfully removed the Traveller ships from the equation.

"Nice ship," Martin said. He'd got MF to light up the exodiamondite wall again so he could see the arrowhead cruiser parked outside. "Military surplus? Which one of you is gonna fly it?"

He had a good point. Pippa couldn't fly a spaceship. Justin couldn't. Who did that leave?

"I'm gonna fly it," said a familiar voice.

Zane Cole walked into the room. The cuff of his right sleeve hung empty. He nodded hello to us, smirking all over his chipmunk face.

"How you gonna fly a ship with only one hand?" I said.

"That ship is a state-of-the-art passenger cruiser," Zane said. "Practically flies itself. It's all AR, anyway."

I said to Justin, "You trust this guy?"

"I'm not as naïve as you seem to think," Justin said.

"Guess it's all about the KGCs," I said.

"No," Zane said. "Actually, it isn't. I joined the Travellers for the money. But they don't make bank like you think they do. Some of those big motherships in the Core, all the micro-gravity levels are filled with burnouts and children growing carrots in freaking sewage. It's all a pose: a big performance. Look at us, we're free. Big fucking whoop. You're eating *rats* on a stolen space station orbiting a neutron star, and you pity the folks in the Temple for believing the hype?" He chuckled, and picked up his pack. "Sayonara to all that." He gave Pippa a strange look. It reminded me of the way he used to look at Sophia. Almost worshipful. "I'm ready to take a bet on something different."

"You won't get far," I said.

"Keep on believing, Starrunner."

I wheeled to face Pippa and Justin. "The Fleet is holding my family hostage." I was talking about Lucy, but I also meant Irene and Rex and their kids, and the jungle wolves, and Robbie's family and friends, and Dr. Zeb, and … and everyone. All the Shifters on Ponce de Leon would pay if I failed. Yet why would I expect Pippa and Justin to give a damn about my problems? They were young and in love. That's why I was surprised when Pippa stopped, her face crumpling like my words had hurt her.

"Can't you please try to understand, Mike? This is my only chance to be happy!"

"Oh, for fuck's sake," Robbie growled. "Happy for a few months, until IVK starts making you go like this?" He let his jaw hang, rolled his eyes up, cocked his head at an angle, and imitated an IVK cripple's palsied walk. I don't think he would have done that if he knew I had IVK, too.

"Very funny," Pippa snapped. "I don't have IVK anymore."

I tensed. "Wait a minute what did you say you don't *what?*"

Maybe her diagnosis was mistaken? But she said she didn't have it *anymore—*

"Come on, Pippa." Justin caught her hand and pulled her towards the exit of the bunker, while she kept apologizing to me, saying that she'd never known what love was, but now she did know, and nothing mattered more.

I did a lightning-speed situational appreciation. Martin, Robbie, and I were at the end of the bunker with the exodiamondite wall. Our rifles were piled on a cot two yards from me. All the Sixers were trailing after Justin, Pippa, and Zane, helping to carry their luggage, except for the two guarding Rafael Ijiuto. I edged closer to the rifles. I didn't want to do this, but what choice did I have? I would try not to hurt Justin. I would try not to kill anyone. I hand-signaled to Robbie to Shift. In the same instant, I snatched one of the rifles, threw it to Martin, and grabbed a second one for myself.

Rafael Ijiuto tore through the Sixers, body-slamming them aside.

I already had my rifle at my shoulder, so I shot him.

I guess I must have missed.

He went through Justin, and I swear to God it looked as if he *literally went through him,* disappearing through his torso and coming out the other side. Justin clapped his lower hands to his stomach with a look of complete surprise. He was now blocking my view of Ijiuto, but I saw Ijiuto's hands and arms coming out from behind him, stretching and *stretching and stretching* towards Pippa's throat—

—but Pippa was not there. She had been there a split second ago but now she was stretching and *stretching* away, bending over backwards at an impossible angle, her neck and chest elongating. She fell to the floor. Ijiuto pounced on her, scrabbling for the TrZam 008. But instead of landing on top of her, he went *through* her. For an instant their bodies actually seemed to occupy the same physical space, but I couldn't be sure, because it was hard to look at, like the blurring that you see for a couple seconds when someone Shifts, except that this went on for long moments and moments. All the Sixers stumbled away. It was a natural reaction. Reality itself seemed to be bending and blurring. Ijiuto's head reared out of Pippa's head and shoulders, his face contorted with hatred and desperation—

I shot at him again.

Yeah, I'm real creative with my solutions.

This time I *knew* I hit him in the head. But at the same time as the bullet pierced his skull, or before that, his head went blurry again. Justin plunged on top of him and hit the floor like a rugby player missing a tackle. The next I saw of Ijiuto, he was dashing out of the bunker. Blood shone red on the back of his head.

Maybe I didn't actually hit him.

Maybe the bullet just grazed his skull.

But I didn't think so. It had gone straight through him.

Now I knew how he had bailed out of a tumbling, burning Traveller ship, and landed in the Tunjle, and hiked back to civilization, without sustaining any serious injuries. All of the damage just went straight through him. He'd probably left that cut on his foot to make it more plausible.

A gray blur sped past me. Robbie chased Ijiuto out of the bunker.

Justin lifted Pippa to her feet and brushed her off. Her hand balled at her throat. The tip of the TrZam 008 peeked out of her fist.

MF rolled up to them, squawking in concern— "Pippa! Are you all right? Are you hurt?"

"I'm OK," Pippa said. "Thanks to *you,* Krasylid Athanuisp Zha." She used MF's real name, and gave him a watery smile.

Martin growled, "OK. What the *fuck* just happened?"

*

"It's called the Transcendence," Sophia said. She was now sitting in the *St. Clare's* left couch with her feet on the consoles. She'd helped herself to vodka from the dispenser. Her voice had grown a bit foggy. "It's the DNA patch to end all DNA patches. Your Big Shift scientists were on the right track, but they didn't go far enough. This is Shifting *plus.* Shifting the way it should have been."

"The Transcendence? Sounds like a religion." It had gotten hot on the bridge. Dolph was fighting sleepiness as his high wore off.

"That's exactly what it isn't," Sophia said. "You always did see everything through a religious lens."

"So what is it? Not just ye olde transhumanism with a modern twist?"

"Closer," Sophia admitted. "But the transhumanists envisaged uploading human consciousness to computers. If that were even possible, of course, the uploaded consciousness would cease to be human. It would become an AI. That's a dead end. So the solution is to attack the problem from the other side of the equation: not the brain, but the body."

"What problem?"

"The problem of mortality, of course."

"That's a problem?"

"I know you believe in life after death," Sophia said. "But you're wrong. After this life, there is nothing."

"You'll find out differently when you die," Dolph said. Like me, he was raised Catholic. Like me, he honored the teachings of Christ more in the breach than in practice. But unlike me, he retained a matter-of-fact belief in Heaven and Hell. He once put it like this: "Mike, the difference between us is that you're afraid of going to Hell. I *know* I'm going there."

Sophia said, "If you were right about that, I'd be on my way to shake hands with Old Scratch, for sure. But your premise is void, because I'm not going to die."

"Everyone dies," Dolph said. The maintenance bot was still standing behind him. The injector glinted in his peripheral vision.

"Not the royalty of the Darkworlds," Sophia said. "The oldest of them are something like five hundred. Or I should say, they used to be. The Fleet made damn sure they got whacked in the civil war between the Gessyrias. The Transcendent are capable of unlimited rejuvenation and self-healing, but that can't save you if some shithead drops a nuke on your house. They should have been more careful. All the same, a handful of them survived the war. That guy I was working for, Rafael Ijiuto? How old would you say he looks?"

Dolph was silent for a moment. "Twenty-six, twenty-seven?"

"Right," Sophia said. "He's actually two hundred and thirty years old. And he still chooses to look like *that.* I guess it's a homage to his ancestors. Me, when I get the Transcendence, I'm going to lose these love handles and get 36DD tits."

"Wouldn't surgery be easier?"

"You're missing the point."

"Your tits are fine the way they are."

"You didn't want to fuck me, though."

There was another silence. On the external feed screen, one view of falling snow followed another. The drifts around the *St. Clare's* engine pods were getting deep.

52

"THERE are only two of us left in the universe," Pippa said. She was standing in the protective cage of Justin's arms, drinking broth from a dirty mug. She looked drained from her tussle with Ijiuto, but that new confidence radiated out through her skin, stronger than ever. I'd thought it was the look of royalty. It was actually the look of the Transcendent.

"What about Jan and Leaf?" I said. "Are they Transcendent, too?"

"They have a lot of the Code in their DNA, but not all of it. Rafael and me are the only ones with the whole Code. I always knew that, but Gran never told me what the Code *was.* I guess she thought it was safer for me not to know. Maybe she was planning to tell me when I got older."

"Don't cry," Justin said.

"I'm not crying. I just never *knew.* Until ..."

"Until I told her," creaked MF, swaying on his wheels. "I told her everything."

I stared at the bot. "You said this shit, the Transcendence, could destroy humanity. You said Pippa should be killed." Justin growled and pulled Pippa closer. My attention stayed on MF. "Why in the hell would you turn around and tell her how to use it?"

"I had to make it up to her somehow," MF wailed.

"Make it up to her for what?" Robbie said.

I caught my breath, remembering MF's betrayal on board the *St. Clare.* He, Martin, and Irene had taken the TrZam 008 from Pippa by force. Afterwards, he must have felt bad enough about it that he decided to make it up to her. Maybe that's even why he stayed on Mittel Trevoyvox in the first place. I'd always known he was smarter … more human … than most AIs.

Human enough to make terrible decisions.

"Guess I owe you an apology, too, Pippa," Martin said.

She smiled at him over the rim of her mug. "It's fine. It's forgotten. I thought the crown jewels were the important thing, but actually, I had the whole Code in my head all along. I just didn't know what it was … until Krasylid Athanuisp Zha explained."

She patted the top of the bot's housing affectionately. He goggled up at her with an adoring light in his sensors. I suspected his decision had also been based, in part, on his chronic weakness for cute girls.

"Now that I know what it does," she went on, "I'm going to fix Justin, too. I might be going to live forever, but what would be the point, without him? And he's not going to live past fifty without help. He has an enlarged heart, high blood pressure—Sixer DNA is just *terrible.* But I can fix him."

"I was going to reverse-engineer the genetic defects out of my people," Justin said. "But the Transcendence is more elegant and subtle than modern gene-modding technology. I'll be the guinea pig. If it works on me, we'll return and offer the same treatment to everyone."

"If *only* the Eks hadn't destroyed the laboratory," Pippa lamented.

"It was the Eks?" I said.

"Oh yes," Justin said. "They bombed the MTEV building from orbit. Olthamo must have found evidence of my purchases when he went through Burden's files. The Eks disapprove very strongly of genetic engineering."

I shot MF a look. "Well, the cat's out of the bag now," I said, wondering how this would play with Smith. Actually, I knew how it would play with Smith. It didn't bear thinking about.

"We really have to go," Justin said.

Pippa nodded. "We need to find a new lab, so we can build the patch and program it into a rewriter virus. That's why we're leaving, Mike. You do understand, don't you?"

"Wait," I said. "Go back to the IVK thing. You … healed yourself? It's *gone?*"

"Yes. I just had to Transcend and then come back the way I wanted to be. It was *easy!*" She twirled around and headed for the door.

I went after her. Justin tried to stop me. Martin grabbed his arms.

"Pippa. The TrZam 008." I could not find the right words. "If I don't destroy it, and deliver the pieces to the Fleet, they're going to kill my friends. They'll take my daughter away. I … please …" I didn't have to fake the desperation in my voice or on my face.

Pippa looked at me thoughtfully, and then lifted the TrZam 008 over her head and placed it in my hand. "OK," she said. "I don't really need it. I have the whole Code memorized, anyway."

She left. Justin left. The whole lot of them left. Even MF went with them.

I stood with the TrZam 008 in my hand, quietly thinking for a moment.

"Gimme that," Martin said.

"Huh?"

"Anyone finds it on us, we're fucked."

"I know what you're going to do," I said. "I'll do it. Watch the door." I shut my eyes tight for a second, concentrating.

Then I held the TrZam up above my face.

And began to Shift.

Into a snake.

My head flattened. My neck elongated. I'd never tried this before, but I'd seen Martin do it hundreds of times. How hard could it be? I held the image of a python just like Martin in my mind. My shoulders sloped into my neck …

It's normal to start Shifting from the head down. That's how all the best Shifters do it. The difference was, this time, I had to stop my Shift just south of my heart. Amidst the normal pain of Shifting, I concentrated fiercely on controlling this new form, *not* letting it go any further down than my esophagus, and—

Just before my arms would have started to weld to my sides, I dropped the TrZam 008 into my snake's gaping jaws.

And swallowed.

I felt every link of the chain as it was going down. Tasted like old-fashioned money.

I took a breath, and reversed my Shift. My shoulders filled out my clothes again. My neck shrank. My head bulged back to its rightful size. An inhuman hiss escaped my lips as they retreated into my reforming jaw.

I sat down—collapsed, actually—on one of the cots. I felt like I had just woken up from one of my Chimera Syndrome dreams, where I'm Shifting uncontrollably into grotesque and unnatural forms, and can't Shift back, even if I try. It shook my confidence in my own humanity. I clasped my hands over my stomach.

Martin stared at me. He had taken several steps back. "That was the fucking ugliest thing I ever saw."

"I was just copying you," I said.

"Cap'n, that wasn't no python. That was a chi …" Martin trailed off in the middle of the word. "Chimera."

I smiled lopsidedly. "Give that snake a gold star." It's amazing how people don't want to see what's in front of their eyes. Martin had known I had more animal forms than anyone he ever met, but I had had to Shift into a chimera right in front of him before the lightbulb went off. "I'm a Chimera Syndrome survivor. Comes in handy sometimes."

I rubbed my stomach. I could feel the TrZam 008 in there, not painful but uncomfortable. On the bright side, I no longer felt nauseated.

"You know how long that's gonna work," Martin said.

"Yeah. Until I Shift again." The next time I Shifted, the alien object would fall right out of my body.

"I was gonna say until you take a dump."

"Good thing those meds got me constipated." I went over and cupped my hands against the exodiamondite wall, trying to see out.

Without warning, the wall moved, the solid surface under my hands rippling and contracting. An arch-shaped opening gaped in the middle of it. MF rolled amidst a gust of cold wind and snow. The exodiamondite stuff must have been in some way similar to the mysterious material that MF's own chassis was made of. He rolled to a stop before us.

"Thought you were going with them," I said. Through the opening, I could see that all the ship's pilot lights were on. Air-breathing jet engines whined, revving up for a vertical takeoff.

"I do not want to go where they are going."

"Where *are* they going?"

MF wouldn't answer. I figured I could bribe it out of him later. Right now, we had to find Robbie and get out of here.

"Come on, Marty." I pulled him out into the snow. "Gotta call Dolph."

Now that we were in the open air, the HF worked.

I got through to the bridge of the *St. Clare.*

I did not know that Sophia was sitting beside Dolph with a gun to his head.

*

"Got the TrZam 008."

My jubilant voice crackled out of the HF. Sophia grinned in silent glee. Dolph closed his eyes.

She ground the muzzle of the Koiler against his head, prompting him to reply. "That's great," he said.

Sophia mouthed in his ear, "I'll come and pick you up."

Dolph wished he had never heard of the fucking TrZam 008. He had known from the beginning that it would destroy us. It had torn the crew apart when we had only thought that it might be worth a lot of money. The truth, according to Sophia, was immeasurably worse. Words rose to the tip of his tongue: *Destroy it.*

Impatient with his silence, Sophia frowned. The maintenance bot leaned over Dolph's couch and pinned his right arm to the armrest. Dolph was so skinny that his veins popped out even when there wasn't a robotic tentacle wrapped around his bicep like a tourniquet. The injector slid into his cubital vein and released a small dose of newfangled shabu equivalent.

Within instants, a headrush of pharmaceutical calm took the edge off Dolph's anguish. He relaxed, despite the gun still pressed to his head.

"Dolph? You there?" I said from the radio.

"I'll come and pick you up," Sophia whispered again.

"I'll come and pick you up," Dolph said. The drug clarified his priorities. He would think of something as soon as he retrieved me, Martin, and Robbie. "Where are you?"

*

I thought his responses sounded a bit flat. *Off,* somehow. But I let it go. I was squatting in the snow, icy wind slicing my face, and I didn't like the noises I was hearing from the other side of the compound. Grinding crashes, and screams. "At the power plant," I said. "Situation's looking a bit precarious. I got a feeling the Travellers are about to break in. Martin and MF are with me, but we lost Robbie, and I don't know how long it's gonna take to find him. So, listen, there's a ship here. It's about ready to take off—"

I was going to tell him that after the other ship took off, there would be room for him to put the *St. Clare* down inside the compound. But I got no further.

A deafening boom resounded through the air, followed by the unmistakable noise of the Travellers' .50 cal ship gun.

"Uh oh," Martin said. "Sounds like the Travellers just tested that exodiamondite wall to destruction."

I stood up to get a better view. The cooling towers loomed between us and the wall on that side of the compound. Except there was no more wall. Snow blew through a jagged gap. Floodlights mounted on the Traveller ship speared between the cooling towers, spotlighting Sixers—and a few Eks—running desperately towards us.

Out on the launch pad, the Sixer technicians scattered away from Pippa and Justin's ship.

"Fuck!" I shouted. "Back into the bunker!" I grabbed the HF. Martin and I piled back through the arch-like opening in the exodiamondite wall.

The arrowhead cruiser took off. Its launch plume lit up the whole compound. After reaching VTOL altitude, the ship reared to a steep angle and burned into the clouds, lighting them up from inside for a moment like dawn. I remembered the nuclear dawn Dolph had jokingly promised me if we didn't make it back. "Sayonara," I murmured.

"Barricade the door and wait?" Martin said.

"Can't. We gotta find Robbie."

We left the bunker, carrying our rifles. MF clambered effortfully behind us, using his grippers to swing himself from stair to stair. He couldn't fly, as there wasn't room for his levitation bubble in this enclosed space.

Halfway up the stairs, we heard shouting from above, and gunfire. A Sixer ran down towards us. Suddenly he stumbled and fell headlong. I jumped out of the way, aiming my rifle up the stairs—

—at Jonathan Burden.

I *knew* that fucker wouldn't be far away.

I shot at him. Missed.

Return fire from the Travellers forced us back down the stairs. We sprinted towards the arch in the far wall—

—and came face to face with *more* Travellers. Wild-haired, wild-eyed, covered with snow, they were too surprised to shoot at us. I dropped one of them as we fell back into the bunker.

Trapped!

"Force field," Martin bellowed. He yanked me closer to MF. The bot initiated his force field, crushing us together inside the slick, shimmering barrier, just in time. Travellers streamed into the bunker from both directions. They hammered on the force field, shot at it, and spit on it, while begging their fiendish gods at the tops of their voices to destroy us. A madness was on them. Looking at their faces, mere inches away, I felt a touch of otherworldly fear. Their rage seemed more than natural.

At last the bedlam died down. The Travellers fell back as Burden strolled into the bunker.

My fear ebbed. Burden was no berserking maniac. For a Traveller, he was practically a normal guy.

"We really must stop meeting like this." He was wearing his Traveller coat. He poked the force field with his .45, right in front of my face. "Where's the TrZam 008?"

He didn't know I had it in my stomach.

"Gone," I said, gesturing upwards with my chin. Let him think Pippa took it with her.

"Nice try, Starrunner. Thing is, I don't have you down as the too stupid to live type. You're not dumb enough to let it slip through your fingers. And I'm not dumb enough to believe you did. So where is it?"

Any wiseass response I may have thought of died on my lips when I saw who had just been carried into the bunker.

Robbie, still in wolf form. Blood drenched the fur of his chest and side. The Travellers dropped him on the floor like a sack.

Behind them came Rafael Ijiuto, grubby and bloody, but grinning.

53

"That was a ship launch," Dolph said, zooming in on the radar alert that had just popped up on the bridge of the *St. Clare.* "It took off from the power plant. Must be the ship Mike mentioned—"

"That's *my* ship!" Sophia said.

"Your ship?"

"I didn't get here from Valdivia on foot," she snapped. "I stole a ship. Left it here. Burden was supposed to get rid of it." She swung her feet to the floor, leaning forwards to the screen. "The trouble with him is he's deeply unserious. He always has been. Life is a joke to him. So he hung onto the ship, looking for a buyer, and while his back was turned, the Sixers lifted it. The question is, who's flying it now?"

She didn't think of Zane, because she thought we'd killed him. Dolph had not corrected her. He was a little ashamed that we *hadn't.*

"It must be Mike."

That's what Dolph hoped. If I'd managed to launch with the TrZam 008, the odds of it falling into Sophia's hands had just dropped precipitously.

She clearly knew that, too. "Launch," she commanded him. "Tell that Olthamo creep you're going to intercept it."

Olthamo didn't entirely trust Dolph. He instructed one of the Guardian ships at the spaceport to launch, as well.

The *St. Clare* got off the ground first. While Dolph worked the controls, Sophia repeatedly pinged the ship that had just launched.

Dolph figured that if I answered, Sophia was going to pass the comms to him and make him set up a rendezvous in orbit. It puzzled and worried him that the ship did not respond at all.

*

That ship, which Sophia had called "her" ship—the one she had stolen on Valdivia, and flown to Mittel Trevoyvox—was quite the special little craft. Its name, I later learned, was the *Minotaur.* Zane had described it as a passenger cruiser. Martin had thought it might be military. It was both those things, and more. Specifically, the *Minotaur* had advanced all-aspect stealth. Its arrowhead form factor and majority-composite build gave it a radar cross-section so small that it vanished off Dolph's screens before he reached orbit. On-board—Sophia told him about this, in agitated fits and starts—the *Minotaur* had a powerful passive sensor suite that utilized probability theory to find enemies without actively tracking them. It could even hide *while burning,* by temporarily cooling its heat shields to the temperature of cosmic radiation, and not using its drive. Instead, it used its integrated railgun as a mass driver to push cold gas out the back. Cold, in space, means undetectable. Apply an exhaust field to that, and you can build up a fair bit of acceleration.

So when they got into orbit, Dolph and Sophia couldn't see the *Minotaur* anywhere.

The Guardian ship burned into orbit and began to swing its radar all over the heavens. *Their* orders were simply to let no one escape from Mittel Trevoyvox alive.

*

Was Robbie breathing? I pressed my face to the force field, trying to see past the Travellers who were blocking my line of sight.

"I cannot sustain the field much longer," MF squeaked. "Oh, why doesn't Dolph come?"

I made out a faint, familiar crackle of thunder, followed by a sonic boom. Then another one. I identified the noise of ship launches, and prayed that one of them was the *St. Clare.* Little did I know that it was, but the *St. Clare* was not coming to save us.

Burden left the bunker, saying there was something going on with the core of the power plant. He took half the Travellers and left the rest to guard us.

Quieter now, they sat, glowered, smoked. Snow blew in through the arch in the exodiamondite wall. The bunker was getting colder. My energy ebbed with every minute of inaction. I rested my fingers on my stomach, pressing on the place where I could feel the TrZam 008, telling myself to stay alert.

"Force fields don't keep out radiation, you know," Martin was saying gloomily when the field gave way, spilling us onto our asses.

"Sorry," MF wailed. "Sorryyyy!" The word ended in a dying squeak. He rolled onto his back and lay there with his grippers in the air like a dead beetle. He had used up a lot of his reserves flying us over the compound wall, and although he had an RTG inside his chassis, he couldn't store an infinite amount of charge.

I didn't have time to worry about him. The Travellers fell on us. Martin and I fought back, trying to reach Robbie, but it was hopeless. The Travellers punched and kicked us to the floor. The only silver lining was that in Burden's absence, they didn't dare to hurt us too badly.

I wound up face-down on the floor, dribbling blood. I had lost an upper incisor to a Traveller's brass-knuckled punch, and my whole jaw throbbed with pain. I could hear Martin groaning. If I so much as turned my head to try to assess Robbie's condition, I got a boot in the ribs.

Vaguely, I wondered where Sophia was. It seemed odd that she hadn't come to have another go at me. Were she to aim at me now, even she couldn't miss. Had she been killed in the fighting?

Suddenly, the roar of ship engines tore through the ravaged silence. Closer, this time. *Much* closer.

The exodiamondite wall lit up. The light of a ship's plasma jets cast the shadows of Travellers starkly across the floor.

While they were distracted, I crawled to Robbie. Lowering my face to his muzzle, I felt faint warmth brush my cheek.

Alive. Thank God. Alive, but maybe not for much longer. I took his head in my hands and shook it. "Robbie, wake up. Wake up, you dumb wolf. Wake up!"

The ground jumped under us.

Outside, a swag-bellied, hog-nosed silhouette dwarfed the compound wall. It was one of the biggest spaceships I had ever seen land on the surface of a planet.

Ramps hinged down. Armored figures pounded across the ground. Muzzle flash stuttered, and lasers painted phosphorescent smears in the falling snow.

The Travellers in the bunker jammed their guns against our heads, screaming that they'd blow our brains out. It never takes much to make a Traveller carry out *that* threat. I closed my eyes and tried to picture Lucy on the beach, in the sunshine, sand crusting her arms and legs, laughing up at me. I wanted to be thinking of her when I died, even though she would never know it.

The memory fragmented into unbelievable agony. My skin was on fire. The Travellers who had hold of me let go, screaming. I writhed, clawing at my arms, rolling on the floor, burning in a Babylonian inferno.

The pain vanished. Just like that. Gone.

It had been so intense that its absence felt downright blissful.

Running footsteps.

Shouts.

I pushed myself up into a sitting position.

Fleet Marines in body armor and full-face helmets barrelled into the bunker. They handcuffed the Travellers.

I slowly raised my hands over my head. Martin did the same.

"Take the microwave blaster with you, Lieutenant," a familiar voice said. "Might be more of them around."

Major General Smith, in Fleet uniform, with his fake captain's bars in place, strolled into the bunker.

Beside him—minus his Traveller coat, with a Fleet bulletproof vest buckled over his blacks—walked Jonathan Burden, free and easy as a bird in spring.

*

My mouth hung open. Forgetting about keeping my hands up, I absently wiped a dribble of blood from my chin. A Marine handed me a wad of gauze.

Smith—and Burden?

Burden—and Smith?

Martin hoarsely said what I was thinking: "Which of 'em's the traitor?"

Smith overheard, and laughed. "Neither of us." He threw his arm over Burden's shoulders and gave him a big old shake, knuckling his scalp. "Jon is one of the Iron Triangle's top undercover agents. He's spent years infiltrating the Traveller organization."

"Such as it is," Burden said. "Sorry I had to kick you in the face … and shoot at you … and tear-gas you … and whatever else I may have forgotten at the moment. Vital to keep up appearances." He directed a malicious grin at the Travellers lying on the floor in handcuffs. They looked stunned. They had believed in him. They had followed him into battle. "Fear not," Burden said almost gently. "The Fleet doesn't blow people's brains out. It just *dumps them on penal planets to get slaughtered by some other motherfuckers!*" On the last words his voice rose to a manic Traveller shout. They cringed—as much out of force of habit, perhaps, as fear.

I said urgently, "Can I attend to my colleague?" The Marines were already giving Robbie first aid, but they hadn't come prepared to treat a wolf. On my plea, they injected him with something that made him wake up. His eyes opened, pain-clouded. I shook him by the scruff and shouted, "Shift back! Robbie, Shift back! That's an order!"

He found the energy somewhere. Twist and blur, shiver and bulge. A flailing leg passed through my hand with an electrical tingle. Shifting is spooky shit. Fur melted into pale skin, tail vanished, and there lay a naked man with a bullet wound in the side of his stomach.

The Marines got to work with their portable surgical robots.

I wobbled to my feet. I badly needed a drink. But I didn't get one. What I got was Smith invading my personal space, breathing his minty breath on me, and curling his nanotech-tipped fingers into the hollow of my collarbone. It was an obscenely intimate touch, and the curl of his lips said he knew it. He kept his razor nails sheathed—for now. "So where's the TrZam 008?" he breathed. "Where's Pippa Khratz?"

Behind me, Burden said, "We need to boost. These idiots killed the technicians who were cooling the plant. Not only that, but they damaged the emergency pumps. It's going to melt down in a matter of hours."

"Well, Starrunner? Where is she?"

I stood unmoving, looking anywhere but into Smith's face. Martin was kneeling over MF, trying to reboot him. Burden stalked around the bunker with a cigarette hanging off his lip, verbally abusing the prisoners. Fear forced me to weigh the possible consequences if I lied about the TrZam 008 and got caught out later. Sheer cussed obstinacy made me roll the dice.

"She's gone," I said, meeting Smith's eyes at last. "Seriously, you didn't see? They took off in a funky little arrowhead ship that the Sixers stole from the spaceport."

Smith let go of me. "The *Minotaur!*" he yelled to Burden. "They took the fucking *Minotaur!*" He rounded on me again. I took an inadvertent step back. Fury flushed his face and corded the muscles in his neck. "You let her go," he grated. "You're going to pay for this."

"Don't worry," Burden said to me. "The worst he can do to you is dump you on a penal planet. Somewhere like, er … here."

"Fine with me." The new voice belonged to an Ek. It was Morshti. "I will dismember them and use their skulls for drinking goblets."

"Thanks," Burden snapped. "Now he can't, under the applicable interspecies convention. Clear and present danger to their lives. For a queen, you're not much of a politician, are you?"

"A queen need not be a politician," Morshti said indifferently. "Xe need only be a killer."

Eks milled through the bunker. Morshti boomed at them in the Ek language. Burden licked his lips. "All right, they're taking over the emergency cooling. They say they can fix the pumps … Try to find some mercy in your heart for the Sixers, won't you, Morshti?"

"I shall," Morshti said, "as long as they obey me. That is all I ever wanted, you know."

More Marines appeared. They hustled us out into the snow, carrying Robbie on a stretcher. Two hulking privates lugged MF. The Fleet troopship *Rogozhin* loomed over us, its warning lights flashing against the clouds. Robbie, Martin, and I were thrown into the back of the bridge like so much trash, with the TrZam 008 still safely hidden in my stomach.

54

THE *Minotaur* had fallen away from Mittel Trevoyvox as silently as a meteorite, leaving no trace behind.

Another Guardian ship burned into orbit and joined the search, scanning the volume around Mittel Trevoyvox for any faint smudge of heat that would betray the little ship's trajectory. Dolph set the *St. Clare's* sensors to perform a full-sky sweep, too. "This could take hours," he told Sophia. "Might as well relax."

Not that *he* could relax, with his heart racing and the maintenance bot still floating behind him like an angel of death. He lit a cigarette —to hell with no smoking on board.

"Looks like Mike ditched you," Sophia said.

"Naw," Dolph said. "He wouldn't do that."

"Nothing lasts forever. Sometimes we have to let go of old attachments to achieve a better understanding of self." Sophia clicked her tongue. "You haven't changed since we first met! You're stuck in a rut. You and Mike enable each other … to never change."

Dolph did not respond. The sky stayed empty. The *St. Clare* orbited around the planet and began to orbit around it again. Dolph's cigarette smoke collected around the two in a gray sphere. Sophia waved at it in annoyance.

"Look at you," she said. "You used to have ideals. You used to talk about helping human beings. Bringing bad guys to account. I never worked out how you squared that with taking money from bad guys, but—"

"You're right," Dolph said. "I couldn't square it, either. I gave up trying."

"That's … sad."

Dolph shrugged.

"You should try meditation."

"I prefer beer and cigarettes."

"And getting high." Her contempt stung him. "Nothing blocks out the voice of the Divine like drugs. Guess that's why you do it."

"The Divine? Which one would that be? Loki? Cthulthu?"

"Actually, my personal spirit guide is Cipactli." The face of Cipactli flickered on Sophia's cheek, grinning and vanishing. "She's always hungry, and she has an open mouth on every joint of her body so that she can eat more. She bit off the foot of the war god."

Dolph put out his cigarette. "You're full of shit, Sophia," he said. "You abandoned your own daughter. Nothing you say counts for a damn thing against that."

Sophia's tone did not change, and yet a new, chilly menace imbued her voice. "How about you quit judging me?"

"Facts are facts."

"The problem with that apparently inarguable statement," Sophia said, "is that you don't *know* the facts."

"I know you ditched Mike and Lucy to shack up with Zane Cole on a Traveller ship."

"Et voila. You don't know anything. Zane was just a passing … *thing.*"

"What was it about, then? The money? The camaraderie? The thrill of high-risk operations? Or it gave you an illusion of being on the right side of history?" Dolph listed all the things that had motivated *him* over the years, not necessarily in that order. He left out only one, in my opinion: doing the right thing.

"Funny you should mention the right side of history," Sophia said. "I know something about history. With that perspective, it's possible to see that humanity is in crisis. We appear to be doing great—look how many colony planets we have! But the Eks are blocking our expansion beyond the Cluster. And at the same time, we're stagnating technologically. When we met the Eks—the first alien species we couldn't lick with one hand tied behind our backs—we stopped innovating, and circled our wagons. Fifty percent of all human investment in the Cluster now goes into *entertainment.*" She said it like a bad word. "Lifespans are declining. More colonies are failing than are being founded. Something's got to give."

"So?"

"So, I thought I was defending humanity against our ideological traitors within. The Temple, you know. *That* would be a cause worth fighting for."

Dolph shook his head and chuckled.

"Yeah," Sophia said. "I was wrong. But it was a stage I needed to go through." She suddenly rocked forward. "What's that?"

Dolph glanced at the screen showing the full-sky scan. Sophia had sharp eyes. The sensors had picked up some faint smudges of heat beyond Mittel Trevoyvox's lumpy little moon.

"Assuming that's not some unrelated outgassing event," Dolph said, "they ran cold, using a sky-high exhaust multiplier, for about two hundred thousand kilometers. Then they switched to the plasma drive for a few minutes to boost their acceleration before entering the skip field."

"Why would they go *that* way? What's out there?"

The *Minotaur* had burned towards the edge of the Cluster. Dolph shrugged.

"Guess we'll find out. Plot a course based on those points, and program our FTL burn."

Dolph didn't move. Sophia got impatient.

"Mike's probably *expecting* us. Well, he won't be expecting me. But I'm sure I can talk him around." She stashed the gun down the side of her couch, loosened her straps, and floated over to put her arm around Dolph. "I hate to see you hurting like this. I want to see you better. I want to set you free."

Dolph realized it didn't matter if I was on that ship or not. He had to do the right thing, anyway. He caressed Sophia's arm, and murmured into her hair, "You know me. I'm up for anything, if there's money in it."

She didn't really know him at all. She didn't know how the pull of money had weakened over the years, until it repulsed him rather than the opposite, and the promise of fuck-you money felt like an actual threat.

With a satisfied laugh, she said, "If we succeed, you'll be able to have anything you want. What do you want most in the universe? You'll get it."

"Hmm," Dolph said. "That's a toughie." He dropped a kiss on her cheek. Then he loaded the *Minotaur's* trajectory data into the flight computer and began to program an identical course.

*

The Marines made us all get into spacesuits. Even Robbie had to wear one. They said the compression would be good for his wound, which wasn't serious, anyway, according to them. The Marines do not consider a wound to be serious unless you're bleeding out. When we stepped on board the *Rogozhin,* we had stepped into a different universe: the hardcore universe I remembered from basic training. In the private sector, it is not uncommon to launch to orbit wearing a wifebeater and jeans. (Guilty.) In the Fleet, you'll put on the pressure garment with retractable helmet, which feels like being shrink-wrapped, and the life-support backpack that weighs fifteen kilos, and you'll like it, soldier.

We didn't have to wear the separate flexible armor, because after all, we *weren't* soldiers. But we weren't exactly prisoners, either. The Marines looked at us the same way they looked at Smith and Burden, with a combination of distrust, fear, and contempt. That tipped me off. I realized that we wore the same invisible aura as Smith and Burden, the sheen of squirrelly business. The *Rogozhin's* hive mind had pegged us for spooks.

I'd have laughed, if not for the TrZam 008 in my stomach.

My whole being was now focused on that little knife-shaped device, and possible strategies to hide it.

Yet worries kept intruding into my mind. What had happened to Dolph? Where was the *St. Clare?*

We took couches at the back of the bridge. *Couches*—they were bare-bones jumpseats. The *Rogozhin*, a Century-class troopship, carrying two platoons of Marines plus all their warfighting kit, was mostly bridge. If you have a dozen staff officers and non-coms collaborating on operations, it makes sense to seat them all in the same space, and by that time you've already designed your ship as a sandwich, with crew quarters above the spine and storage and magazines below, so you may as well take out the rest of the non-structural partitions upstairs and have everyone in one big room: eating, resting, talking, manning the instruments. Good for unit cohesion. The guys flying the ship are immersed in their AR environments, anyway, so they're immune to distraction.

The commander of the ship—Smith—did have an office of his own, all the way forward, behind the ship's snout-like sensor blister. He summoned me in there as soon as we got into orbit.

I navigated forward from handhold to handhold, staying out of the Marines' way, feeling as sick as a dog, praying to God that I wouldn't puke the TrZam 008 up right in front of him.

*

Sophia pushed forward in her straps. "What's that? Looks like someone else just launched."

Dolph didn't look up for a moment. While programming his FTL burn, he had been covertly programming another set of commands into the computer. He pushed the last keys and swept the display out of his AR view. Expressionless, he switched over to the radar. "Yup, that's a ship."

The spark on the radar rose at a steep angle. Dolph ran calculations. The other ship would reach orbit before the *St. Clare* achieved optimal FTL burn positioning. He felt a glimmer of hope, although he didn't know what ship this might be; probably just more Eks.

Sophia bent over the comms. "Unknown ship, identify yourself."

Dolph couldn't hear the response. But he saw Sophia's expression of shocked recognition. "Yes, it's me. What? *No.*"

The person on the other end talked for a minute. Sophia's face grew tight and angry.

"No," she said. "In fact, screw you." She cut the connection. "It's the Fleet. Fuck, fuck, fuck."

"Can't outrun that," Dolph said, suppressing a smile. He remembered how the *Williencourt* had overhauled the *St. Clare* in the Yesanyase Skont system. The *Rogozhin,* three times the *Williencourt's* size, had an even more powerful drive. "In FTL mode, this is the fastest ship in the Cluster. STL, she's just a heavy old freighter. They'll either catch us … or follow us all the way there." He thought for a minute. "Or blow us to shit."

"Yeah. Put that burn on hold."

Dolph touched the keys. He left his secret contingency plan in place.

"Go higher and burn retrograde."

"What?"

"You heard me."

Dolph knew exactly what this maneuver portended. Sophia wanted to loiter in a higher orbit until the Fleet ship rose into the *St. Clare's* crosshairs. "You can't shoot them."

"Why?"

"Because I'm not gonna authorize you to use the weapons systems."

Sophia's smile didn't change. "Oh, I think you will," she said. "Or I'll get the robot to give you a fatal dose. The burn's already programmed; all I have to do is press your finger on the go button. I'll have the rest of the journey to break your encryption. But I'm going to blow these fuckers to shit first, either way."

55

WHEN I entered Smith's office, I was expecting to be yelled at, though I didn't think he would risk torturing me on a ship full of Marines. However, he seemed oddly conciliatory. The fire-breathing fury had passed. He pushed his sleeves up to his elbows and ran a hand through his bristly hair. It's hard to maintain military formality in freefall. Smith floated on one side of the desk that stuck out from a wall full of screens, using the toe-straps. I floated as far away from him as possible, tonguing the gap where I was missing a tooth. The shoebox-sized space reeked of mint, with undernotes of ozone and barracks funk.

"We need to discuss your wife," Smith said.

"Ex-wife," I said.

"Right," Smith said. "Just how ex is she?"

"I saw her back there," I said. "She shot at me. That's how we relate these days."

"Hate can be an aphrodisiac," Smith suggested.

"Not for me." I realized that he thought Sophia and I might be in cahoots. I was angry, frightened, and feeling sick. "What are you trying to imply?"

Burden squeezed into the office, defusing the confrontation. He was sucking on a beverage foilpack. He lobbed identical packs to me and Smith, and lounged near the ceiling. "We talking about Sophs? She lost her virginity to me when we were post-grads at Montemayor

University. Maybe she never told you about that." He chuckled. "She was a late bloomer."

"So were you," Smith said, smiling indulgently at him.

"Sure. I had no time for relationships back then. I was all about the philosophy of science. We used to talk all night in the coffee shops, or walking down by the Don. We were gonna fix the Cluster together. We were gonna fix *humanity.* Talk about youthful fatuity. The three of us—me, Aki, and Sophs—we had it all worked out."

My mouth hung open. I remembered my own words to Lucy, when I told her about her mother's privileged past: *the top universities in the Cluster graduate Travellers and politicians in equal numbers …* and I remembered those booze-fuelled philosophical conversations on board our ship, when Dolph, Sophia, and I would try to convince each other that we weren't going to hell. She must have found those sessions pitifully shallow, compared to the erudite conversation of her past philosophical sparring partners.

Burden and Smith.

"We were the Fearsome Threesome," Smith said with a reminiscent smile. "We hit a speed bump when Jon and Sophs started screwing. But then they invited me to join in, so all was good again." I caught a tiny twist in Burden's lips. I would bet that hadn't been *his* idea. One would go along with a lot of things in order not to lose Sophia … as I knew too well. But in that moment, I felt like I was the only person in the room who had really broken free of her. These revelations only increased my incredulity that she had had it all, *twice over,* and thrown it all away.

"When we graduated," Burden said, "Akira and I joined the Fleet." So Smith's first name was Akira. "Not like you did, Starrunner. No PTs and dawn patrols for Montemayor University graduates. We were on the fast track, straight to the top. It wasn't long before the Iron Triangle recruited us both. Meanwhile, Sophs went off on a Wanderjahr that turned into an extended criminal jaunt through the Cluster. The amazing thing is that she stayed off the Travellers' radar as long as she did. When they recruited her, did they try to recruit you, as well?"

I caught the implication of the deceptively casual question. "Yes." Honesty was the best policy here. "They did." I remembered that argument with Zane in a Mag-Ingat parking lot. "I told them to go to hell, and if she was so dead set on it, she could go with them."

"Uh huh, guess she didn't tell you," Smith said. "She wavered for a long time. She was interested in the Traveller lifestyle and ideology, but she couldn't find a sound philosophical basis for taking the oath."

I smiled bleakly. Guess Lucy and I didn't figure into her decision at all.

"She contacted me to discuss it. By that time I was the top HUMINT specialist in the Fleet Clandestine Service. Jon was already working undercover in the Traveller organization. I looped him into the discussion, and we worked out a plan for Sophia to join the Travellers on the same basis."

"As an undercover agent?!" I said.

"She became my best agent ever." Smith nudged Burden. "She always did have you outclassed!"

My head was spinning. "Sophia works for the Iron Triangle?!"

"She did," Burden said.

I did not pick up on the tense. "She was working for you all along?!" I sounded like an idiot. I felt like an idiot. Had I ever known anything about the woman? Had she shared *anything* with me apart from her body? I needed a drink. I looked at the foil pack in my hand. It said *Alcoholic Beverage.* Turned out to be a premixed gin and tonic. It tasted like crap, but it kickstarted my brain. "Was she still working for you," I said, "when she tried to infect every man, woman, and child in Mag-Ingat with IVK?"

"No," Smith said. "By that time, she had gone rogue."

"I actually don't see it that way," Burden said. "I think she thought she was still following orders."

"I would *never* have given orders to launch bio-weapons on Ponce de Leon!"

"I know that. But she didn't know it. She thought she was doing what you wanted, or …" Burden shrugged.

"It wouldn't have been that hard for her to check," Smith snapped. "In my opinion, she wanted to see what it would feel like to murder millions of people."

"The original plan was only to murder thousands, yeah?" I said. "Every man, woman, and child on Gvm Uye Sachttra."

Smith did not pick up on my sarcasm. "Correct," he said curtly. Burden did.

"If you ask me, that's what broke her," he said. "Deliberately infecting an entire population with IVK? Undercover work starts to look less glamorous and fulfilling when that's the kind of thing being asked of you."

"It was approved at the highest level," Smith said. "The Transcendence has to be eliminated. It's the most serious threat we've ever encountered. You know that."

I marvelled at the onion-like layers of intrigue and malice. "You used Rafael Ijiuto's grudge against his cousins. You gave him enough antimatter to pay mercenaries, and provided the mercenaries, too." *That* explained the choice of IVK as a weapon. Nothing could have *less* suggested Fleet involvement. The whole plot had been designed to maximize deniability. "And I guess, once Pippa was eliminated, it would be Ijiuto's turn. Right?"

"We still need him for now," Smith grunted. "He says he knows where they've gone."

"Commander," a voice said on the intercom. "Ship at our two o'clock high."

Smith's heads-up screen flashed. I snuck a glance at it as he shoved me out of the office.

The sight winded me. It was the *St. Clare.*

*

Sophia bent over the weapons console, finessing the targeting controls. She was using the optical telescope to target the *Rogozhin,* not the targeting laser, so that we wouldn't know we were being targeted. The tradeoff was a less stable targeting solution. That's why she was taking it slow, drifting closer and closer to us in a nearly matched orbit, and that's why I, on the *Rogozhin,* had been able to clearly see the unique plesiosaur silhouette on Smith's heads-up screen.

"They're assholes," she said to Dolph. "I mean, they're my oldest friends. But they're also assholes."

She had ended their verbal scuffle over the weapons systems by telling Dolph about her history as an Iron Triangle agent. She also told him that the commander of the *Rogozhin* was none other than Major General Akira Smith. That changed Dolph's mind about blowing the *Rogozhin* away. He considered that Smith deserved to die. He had no idea that Martin, Robbie, MF, and I were on the ship, too.

All the same, he felt terrible about the troopship's complement of Marines. "Target the bridge, not the drive," he told Sophia. "Give the grunts a chance to reach the lifeboats."

"Oh," Sophia said, "because they're just following orders, which makes them innocent?"

"Close enough."

"I already killed four Marines on Valdivia, and funnily enough, I don't feel bad about it."

"What happened on Valdivia?"

Sophia raised her face from the optical telescope. "All right, we're just waiting for them to come closer now. So, Valdivia. It was my debrief after the Ponce de Leon fiasco. Aki didn't come himself, of course. It was this woman called Ingrid. Your typical fanatical female groupie. Aki attracts those like navel lint. She started ticking me off in her usual high and mighty style. She said Aki wasn't happy with what I did on Ponce de Leon. I said, a) I failed anyway, and b) if the Transcendence is as bad as I've been told, doesn't that justify doing whatever it takes to destroy it? And actually, I said, what is the Transcendence, anyway? Has anyone figured that out yet?"

"You didn't know?"

"No one knew. I'd stolen some DNA from Ijiuto, way back at the beginning of the op, and had it analyzed, but we still couldn't figure out exactly what we were dealing with. It looked like an extreme longevity mod. That made it a priority target for technology control operations. But there were suggestions that it might be something more than that ... Anyway, when I asked that question, Ingrid's eyes got all shiny. She said that after the Ponce de Leon fiasco, Aki had taken the gloves off. He'd got at Ijiuto in police custody and interrogated him."

Dolph could picture that interrogation. He almost felt sorry for ol' Rafe.

"Ijiuto spilled everything. This is still Ingrid talking. The Transcendence turns out to be Shifting *plus.* What Shifting could have been, but isn't." Sophia had her targeting solution. She powered up the railgun. The familiar whine seeped through the ship. "Picture it. We're standing in a circle of scorched grass, way out in the Trevasse, at night. Her ship looms over us. Her Marine escort are standing with their backs to us, with their helmets sealed and white noise playing in their ears, 'cause they're not allowed to hear this stuff. You feel tiny out there, you know? The sky is *huge.* I'm looking up at all those stars, which I've had to accept that I'll never reach. And stupid little team player Ingrid says, this is immortality in a DNA patch. It could destroy humanity as we know it. Blah, blah, blah. And I just kind of snapped. I said to her, I just came this close to committing genocide to eliminate this mod. But you know what? I accept that I was wrong. Oh good, she says. It's great that you're acknowledging your mistakes. And I say, yeah. I was wrong to try to eliminate it. Immortality in a DNA patch? I *want* that."

The lights dipped and came back up.

"So I killed her. The Marines, too. Shot them in the back. Those dumb jocks never knew what hit them. Then I took their ship and went looking for the Transcendence."

She fired the railgun at the *Rogozhin.*

"Goodbye, Aki. Goodbye, Jon. See you in Hell. Except not, because I'm not going there. Ever."

56

The *Rogozhin's* all-hands klaxon sounded. Halfway back to my seat, I froze, fingers locked around a handhold. "Incoming. Incoming." The ship shivered like an animal in its sleep. If that was a hit, we'd be dead, so I knew the point defenses had destroyed the incoming missile. There had been so little warning that the attacker must be right on top of us.

"Who's attacking us?" I yelled. "Is it the Travellers?"

Smith flew out of his office. His face was purple. "It's *your* fucking ship! You gotta talk to her!"

"To who?"

"To your wife!"

It fell into place. The *St. Clare* was attacking us. *Sophia* was attacking us. She was on the bridge of the *St. Clare.*

"Dolph?" I said numbly.

"Figure she flipped him," Smith said.

Burden took my arm in a friendly grip. "She tried to flip me, too," he murmured, amidst the organized chaos of officers separating to their battle stations. "I played along for a while, trying to bring her back into the fold, but you see how well *that* worked. You try." He maneuvered me in front of a comms station.

I slid my feet into the toe straps. The deck quaked. The *Rogozhin* was returning fire.

Half-convinced that I was talking to the void, I said, *"St. Clare,* come in. This is Mike Starrunner on the *Rogozhin."*

"Mike." Sophia's voice wafted out of the comms headset. "They turned you, huh?"

Smith listened in on another headset, a vertical line deepening between his eyebrows.

"Let me speak to Dolph," I said.

On the bridge of the *St. Clare,* Dolph was fighting to reach the comms, yelling my name, while the maintenance bot restrained him with its tentacles. But Sophia was using the headset with atmospheric noise cancellation, so all I heard was her voice. "Dolph says no. You rolled over for the Iron Triangle, Mike. You're dead to him."

"I had no choice!"

"There's always a choice. You fucking idiot." Now I could hear Sophia's fury. "Why would you give the TrZam 008 to *them?* They'll only destroy it! Jesus Christ, what a fucking waste!"

Smith frowned suspiciously at me.

Oh, shit.

"You used to at least have balls," Sophia raged. "Now you're sucking Aki's dick. Why not? Everyone else does."

"I don't have the thing!" I was trying not to look at Smith and Burden. "Pippa and Justin got away, and they took it with them." My lies sounded limp and implausible.

"Oh, so I guess I should just lie down and die," Sophia shouted, "like every other human being in history? You fucking wish. If I can't have the Transcendence, you can't, either."

Screens lit up all over the bridge. The klaxon blared.

Let no one say that space battles are decided by Newtonian physics. The *Rogozhin* could have swatted the *St. Clare* out of the sky at any time in the last half hour. But Smith and Burden had not wanted to kill their old friend. They had half-assed it with warning shots, which Sophia took as a sign of weakness. They had tried to talk her down.

And now we were reaping the consequences. I fumbled the stability harness attached to the comms station over my shoulders—

The deck jumped up and smacked me. An explosion of darkness swallowed the front half of the bridge. I had not finished fastening my harness. It tore off me, wrenching my left shoulder. As I flipped out of control through the air, I glimpsed a fire where the forward bulkheads used to be. But this fire burned cold and white. It was the Core, peeking through the twisted remnant of the front end of the truss.

A blizzard of loose papers and electronics and furniture whirled around me. As the decompression boom hit, I slapped my helmet seal shut. Gasping in the sudden silence of my helmet, I tumbled helplessly out of the sheared-off stump of the *Rogozhin's* hull, while pieces of the ship spread out in a ragged corona across the bright clouds of Mittel Trevoyvox's dayside.

*

Dolph shouted, "That was Mike!"

"So?" Sophia said.

"Mike was on that ship!"

"So?"

"You killed him!" Standing off from the wreck of the *Rogozhin* at a distance of five klicks, Dolph maxed out the zoom on the optical feed. Debris sprayed into the void. Some of those clumps of pixels were people. One of them was me. Horror overwhelmed him. He had sat there and let me and Martin and Robbie die. "Lucy," Dolph croaked. It was hitting him in waves. If I was dead, he was responsible for Lucy, as he'd promised.

"Oh yeah," Sophia said indifferently. "We'll pick her up after we get the Transcendence."

Dolph realized in that moment, he told me, what it must feel like to be a father. It put the situation into perspective. Nothing now mattered more than that little girl back on Ponce de Leon. Self-destruction was no longer an option. He had to survive to get back to her. And even more importantly, he had to make sure that she had a universe to grow up in.

"Guardians will show up soon," Sophia said. "Let's get out of here."

I would've been tempted. I won't lie. I would have seen visions of having it all, again. Sophia could always make me feel that way.

But Dolph was a better man than me. He smiled at Sophia … and enabled the override sequence he'd covertly programmed into the ship's computer.

It took Sophia a minute's frenzied rummaging through the torrent of error messages that ensued to see what he'd done.

"Oh. Oh, Dolph."

She sank into her couch and gestured dully.

The maintenance bot pounced on Dolph and plunged its injector into his neck.

*

It took me endless seconds to straighten out my spin. The Marine suit's mobility system had wrist panel controls to vector the cold gas jets integrated into the life support backpack. Once I had my orientation under control, I flew back to the wreck of the *Rogozhin,* shouting, "Marty! Robbie! MF! Come in!"

It was hopeless. Crosstalk drowned the suit radio frequencies. The survivors must have numbered twenty or more, and they were all trying to reach the lifeboats. Several spacesuits, Fleet-blue like my own, clustered under the *Rogozhin's* belly, crawling in and out like rats raiding the garbage. An oval lifeboat dropped out of the ship, scattering the survivors, and spurted away.

"Who was that?" voices shouted.

I didn't know or care. I just wanted to find Martin and Robbie. Instead, a flurry of snow found me. It blew out of nowhere, spattered on my faceplate, and dispersed past me. I wiped my faceplate and stupidly gaped at the powdery white residue on my glove. Snow? In *space?*

I looked up.

The *St. Clare's* silver belly shone in the sunlight.

Hope ignited. I wasn't thinking about Sophia anymore. I just wanted to get back to my ship. I'd tell Dolph what happened, make him understand that the Iron Triangle hadn't really flipped me.

"Marty! Robbie!" I bawled into the radio. I couldn't leave them—

A rooster tail of blue flame crossed the terminator of Mittel Trevoyvox, and faded to plasma wisps as another ship decelerated to match the *Rogozhin's* orbital velocity.

Fleet markings glittered on the raked-back wing of an atmosphere-capable picket ship. Smith's backup had arrived. The survivors flocked towards the newcomer. A second delta-wing vectored in as I watched. Loud orders and Fleet jargon overflowed the suit radio frequencies. It was no use shouting for Martin and Robbie anymore. Nor did I have any hope of visually distinguishing them from the other blue suits.

A third ship dived in. This one swept past without stopping.

The second Fleet delta-wing fireballed.

The explosion caught the hulk of the *Rogozhin,* and tore the two ships apart, the delta-wing burning—must've hit the LOX tanks—the *Rogozhin* limned by curling blue lines of fire, consistent with electric arcs sparked by contact of the attacker's exhaust plume with the hull.

The light of the explosion cast a fleeting glow on the attacker as it fled into the darkness.

Revealing the stylized pictures of maneating gods on its hull.

The Travellers' reinforcements had been lying in wait for the Fleet.

The delta-wing's antimatter containment exploded in a white-hot star so bright, it blinded me for a moment. My vision came back, blurry, as microscopic pieces of debris sleeted past me. I had been far enough from the antimatter explosion. I was not dead. I couldn't say the same with any certainty for the spacesuits tumbling past amidst the debris.

One of them was shaped funny. Its legs seemed too short. The feet of its spacesuit flapped.

I seized it by the arm, twisted its faceplate to the sun.

The face of a terrified wolf looked out at me.

Robbie had Shifted inside his spacesuit, an instinctive response to danger. His jaws moved, but I couldn't hear him. He had been closer to the explosion. It had fried his comms.

"Die, motherfuckers, DIE!"

A single Fleet spacesuit clung on top of the *Rogozhin's* hulk, riding the handlebar-style controls of the troopship's Gauss gun. The muzzle flashed, spurting lead.

"Marty!" I yelled, waving. "Leave it!"

A second Traveller ship, diving in for the kill, met the stream of hot lead from the Gauss, and went into a tumble.

"Run, you dumbass!" Martin howled at me. "Don't let them have it!"

I sobbed out curses, gripped Robbie by a suit-swaddled forepaw, and oriented us towards the *St. Clare.* As we flew across the void, accelerating from a relative standstill, another, and yet another, Traveller ship swooped down. They clearly perceived their opposition to be limited, and hoped to claim their prize: the undamaged Fleet delta-wing. Acolytes in black spacesuits jumped out of the airlocks and went hand-to-hand with the surviving Marines.

They hadn't seen us. We were two klicks from the mayhem around the wreck of the *Rogozhin.* We just looked like drifting corpses. In fact, there was another one, close behind us …

"Starrunner! Give me the TrZam 008!"

Smith.

Heck with playing dead. I opened the throttle of my mobility thrusters all the way.

The *St. Clare* came closer.

But so did Smith.

He was cutting the corner. He'd reach the ship at the same time we did.

I switched my grip on Robbie's suit to the other hand, putting myself between Smith and the young wolf.

The *St Clare's* head grinned down at us, in a sort of curtsey that turned into a slow somersault.

Why was she tumbling?

And what were those glittering specks clinging to her flanks?

"Stop! Starrunner! Stop or I shoot!"

Smith was right beside me. His faceplate was in shadow, so it looked like he had only half a head.

He aimed a machine pistol at me.

Those babies have no issues working in vacuum.

I was only a hundred meters from the airlock of the *St. Clare.* Maybe thirty seconds. My breath rasped heavily. I could smell my own sweat. I was a prey animal running for cover, with my prize in my stomach.

But there is no cover in space.

Smith shot me.

The bullet tore through my spacesuit and the meat of my left calf.

Pain flared up my nerves.

A mechanical voice said urgently, "Decompression alert! Decompression alert!"

Smith shot again.

The bullet struck me in the back, but by that time I was Shifting.

You can't hit what isn't there.

A typical Shift, for me, takes fifteen seconds. There are a few seconds in the middle of that process, maybe five, when the man has gone away but the animal isn't there yet. That's when we go blurry. We are here but not here: our minds are here, but our bodies are in a state of quantum uncertainty, waiting for the probabilities to be resolved. The way they teach it to us in school on San Damiano is that on the quantum level, everything's made of energy. A human being is essentially a being of energy and vibration, radiating a unique energy signature. That unique signature is the part that never goes away. Everything else can. Mass can be converted into pure energy. So in the middle of a Shift, we are energy without mass.

And as Rafael Ijiuto had demonstrated in the bunker, a bullet can't hit that.

So I Shifted, and at the moment when my wolf's chest pushed out against the human-shaped pressure garment, I Shifted again.

Bullets punctured my suit and helmet. I *felt* them go through me —the oddest feeling, like a ghost walking on my grave, not painful. The air rushed out of my wrecked helmet. I was in vacuum.

But energy doesn't need to breathe.

I Shifted again.

Tiger.

Jaguar.

I even did my zorilla, I think.

Lion.

Bear.

Sabertooth tiger.

Then back to wolf again.

I hit the side of the *St. Clare,* tumbling. The port side airlock was a mile away. I had no hands to crawl with. I had no feet. Robbie, back in human form, grabbed a handful of my shredded spacesuit and towed me to the airlock, while the appendage inside his grasp changed from a hand, to a paw, to a hoof.

The airlock slid open.

Someone wearing my own spacesuit somersaulted out and flew away.

Robbie pushed me into the airlock, crawled in after me, and slammed the hatch in Smith's face.

I fell into the trunk corridor, still Shifting. I had passed the point where I could control it. This was what used to happen to me when I was a kid. I'd start Shifting, and I wouldn't be able to stop. It takes on its own momentum, and with every additional form, you leave your humanity farther and farther behind. That's how Chimera Syndrome kids die.

I've recovered, I always insisted.

But it wasn't true. I had only learned to live with CS. Learned to control it. And now, by voluntarily embracing it again, I had plunged back into the nightmare.

I floated in the trunk corridor of the *St. Clare,* but for all I knew, I might have been lying on the forest floor on the hillside behind my parents' house on San Damiano. The air felt like a bed of dry leaves. Distantly, I felt hands pulling my spacesuit off, just like they used to pull my clothes off in the old days, so that I would not get trapped inside them and get even more panicky. I twisted and snapped at the interfering hands with jaws that no longer resembled any terrestrial animal's. I had a snake's tail, a lion's claws, a walrus's body, a leopard's head. All of it was me and yet none of it was me. None of it was human.

"Mike!"

The voice had been shouting at me for a while, but I couldn't answer. I couldn't do anything except Shift. It was like endlessly falling.

"Mike!"

Fuck off, douche. Nothing is permanent, anyway. Everything is made of energy. Let me fall.

"Mike, hold on. Hold on. *HOLD ON!*"

Hands dug into the tops of my arms. My shoulders sloped, hunched, bulged through random permutations of flesh and fur and scales, and yet the hands held on. They grasped my scapula and clavicle, as the bones themselves melted away and came back in different shapes. It was the strangest feeling, and yet not unpleasant. It held my attention, whether I liked it or not. It broke my endless fall.

"Hold on," I rasped, a command to myself, and to him. "Hold on."

The trees turned into walls. The autumn foliage turned into rust-colored splotches of blood on the ceiling of the trunk corridor. The hands relaxed their grasp. I looked into Dolph's face, just like in the old days. His pupils were so dilated there was only the thinnest rim of brown around them.

"She didn't know what a Shifter can handle," he said.

"They didn't flip me," I said.

"I know."

57

THE *St. Clare's* auxiliaries burned for a split second, stabilizing our tumble. I lifted my hands off the controls. "You didn't leave me much to work with," I whispered wryly.

Before he collapsed, Dolph had told me that he'd dumped 90% of our reaction mass overboard. That's what I'd seen sticking to the *St. Clare's* sides. That's where the strange flurry of snow in space came from. Sophia had tried to make Dolph pursue the *Minotaur* out to the edge of the Cluster … but instead, he had made sure that the *St. Clare* couldn't go anywhere.

He had saved the Cluster.

I just hoped he had not doomed us.

I left the bridge, trailing my fingertips along the ceiling, and floated into Dolph's berth.

Robbie, in wolf form, lifted his head. "He Shifted in his sleep."

I could see that for myself. Dolph floated in jackal form in the air, limbs weakly splayed. White rims showed under his half-closed eyelids. At Sophia's command, the maintenance bot had injected him with a dose of new-formulation shabu that would have killed a mainstream human. Dolph had somehow managed to stay functional long enough to intervene in my CS episode. After that, though, his willpower had given out and he'd lost consciousness.

I'd disabled the maintenance bot.

There was nothing we could do for Dolph except stay with him, monitor his pulse, and pray. I believed he was out of danger, but it sounded like he may have had a seizure in his sleep. Because he was a Shifter, the seizure had come out as a Shift.

Robbie floated beside Dolph, holding him down with his forelegs, licking Dolph's face with his long, pink tongue.

"It helps to bring 'em around," he said, in between licks.

"We used to do the same thing in the army," I said. On scouting missions deep behind the Necro frontlines, we had lived as animals for days on end. Animals bond by grooming each other; they lick and nibble each other's faces, and curl up together to sleep. It was against regs, but I ended up allowing it in my platoon because it clearly helped my soldiers to deal with their anxiety and fear. "How do you know about that?"

"Where I come from, overdoses ain't all that uncommon."

I flexed my fingers and toes, and Shifted. Now two gray wolves floated in the berth, one younger and heavier, one older and rangier. I nuzzled up to Dolph on the other side from Robbie and gently rasped my tongue over his muzzle and around his closed eyes. My tongue picked up flecks of ship dust and grit from his fur, which I spat out. It did me more good than it was arguably doing him, bringing a sense of peace. I caught myself thinking how lucky we were to be Shifters. Comforts were available to us that you'd never experience in human form. The Darkworlders may have kicked our asses in the genetic engineering arms race, but the Transcendence could surely never measure up to the simple relief of being an animal now and then.

If only I could just … just goddamn *live* …

The TrZam 008 floated around my wolf's neck, the chain buried in my fur.

It had fallen out of my body when I started Shifting, and wound up lodged in my cracked, deformed helmet. I'd examined the spacesuit on my way to the bridge. The thing was so full of holes, I should have been Swiss cheese. As I shook it out, the TrZam 008 had drifted into my hand.

I had hung the chain around my neck the way Pippa used to wear it, as if it were mine.

Robbie saw it. He said, "Don't look any the worse for wear."

"I guess it's lasted a thousand years so far."

His muzzle wrinkled. "You know, that bugs me. These Darkworlders were doing their thing five hundred years ago, give or take. So how'd they record their Code on a thumb drive from a civilization that vanished five hundred years before *that?*"

I stopped licking. Stared at him across Dolph's head. "You know, that's a very good point."

A few moments later, I said, "Maybe they found some Urush technology that was still in working order."

"And they figured out how to operate it?"

"Well, we did," I said. "Just bribe it with porn from time to time …"

Robbie laughed. I smiled slightly, missing MF more than ever. If he were here, I would have someone to share the responsibility for the decision I must take.

The comms sounded an incoming transmission chime.

"That'll be MF again." I flew to the bridge and punched the radio on with a claw.

MF was on the *Harnith Po.* A Guardian dreadnaught had joined the fray, better late than never, I guess, and chased the Travellers away. In typical Ek style, it had blasted them from a distance of 3,000 klicks with its big guns, and then tiptoed cautiously down into low orbit to hunt for survivors.

It had found a few, including MF and Martin.

The screen showed MF standing on the deck of the *Harnith Po.* Yes, standing. The dreadnaught loomed against the stars like a double-pointed gem, shaped like two cones with their large ends joined together by a central cylindrical segment. 1.5 klicks from end to end, it was so big that the central segment could rotate to simulate gravity. A nice benefit for the higher-caste officers, and right now, the prisoners.

Guests?

Allied personnel?

I really wanted a bit more clarity there.

"Well, Mike?" MF squeaked. "Have you made up your mind?"

"Yes, and no." Behind MF, I could see Martin, on his knees, hands cuffed behind his back. Because they knew he was a Shifter, an enormous Ek stood over him with a taser, as well. But his glowering expression projected defiance, not defeat.

I could also see Smith. *He* wasn't handcuffed. He stood with his arms folded, nose wrinkled in disgust, although that may just have been the smell on board the *Harnith Po.*

I said, "What are the views of the *Harnith Po's* commander on … this?" I moved so they could see the TrZam 008 nestling in my neck fur.

An Ek shoved MF out of the way. Ze had *eight* arms. That alone told me ze was the commander of the dreadnaught, even without the mixed salad of gemstones adorning zis uniform.

"My views," ze boomed, in an almost indecipherable Ek accent, "are as follows. The Fleet are our allies. Together, we ensure the safety of all sapient species in the Cluster. Major General Smith is my brother in arms."

Major General—so they knew Smith's true affiliation.

"My views on the so-called Transcendence, therefore, are identical to his."

That helped a lot.

"I will add only this. My ship's guns are much bigger than yours."

The Ek commander stepped away, and I cast my eyes over the composite external feed. We were orbiting Mittel Trevoyvox at an altitude of 140 kilometers. That's about as low as I could go without committing to a de-orbit burn. The *St. Clare* was currently over the nightside. The *Harnith Po* was a dot over the terminator, 11,000 klicks behind us. The Ek commander talked a good game, but he was staying out of easy range of my guns.

There was nothing else in orbit, except for wreckage whirling high above, where the *Rogozhin* and several other ships had died.

Smith stepped forward. His eyes seemed to burn through the screen like lasers. "Burden defected."

"Huh?"

"Before the *Harnith Po* joined the fight, it looked like we were going to be overwhelmed." Smith chewed on his lower lip. I guess there was no chaw on the dreadnaught. "Burden seized command of the *Alcazar* and declared his allegiance to the Travellers."

"The *Alcazar,*" I said. "The other delta-wing?"

"Yes. It won't be improved by pictures of prehistoric gods. Nothing is."

"Well, damn," I said. "Guess you *can't* work with the Travellers for years, pretending to be one of them, and acting out their ethos, without soaking it up some."

"I can't even see who you are through all that fur," Smith said.

"It's me." I frowned. "And Sophia?"

I knew that she had escaped from the *St. Clare,* in my spacesuit. That was who we'd seen exiting the airlock. She hadn't stayed to make sure Dolph was dead. She was only interested in going after the Transcendence.

"Need you ask? Jon picked her up. He took her with him. Those two ..." Smith's voice faded. I almost felt sorry for the man. He was reliving the decades-old betrayal by his two best friends. "He also picked up Ijiuto."

"That's bad news," I said.

"You're telling me. The *Alcazar* is nearly as fast as the *Minotaur.*"

Smith wasn't saying so, but I could put two and two together as well as the next person. We had lost.

As Pippa had said, the TrZam 008 was not the only place the Transcendence code existed. She also had it in her head. And Sophia knew where Pippa and Justin had gone, to a near approximation, thanks to the *St. Clare's* scan … and Rafael Ijiuto.

Now, a trajectory is not the same thing as a destination. And course changes are possible even during FTL. But based on that initial trajectory, and the *Minotaur's* reaction mass and life support specs, Sophia would be able to narrow it down to a relative handful of worlds.

Then she and Burden would just have to search all of them.

I'd be the last person to underestimate that pair, especially with the firepower of the Traveller organization at their backs. The odds were good, in my estimation, that they'd locate the runaways before the Fleet could.

Then the genie, as Smith put it, would really be out of the bottle. All hell would break loose.

"So," I said, twisting my neck to make the TrZam 008 float free on its chain, "I guess this doesn't really matter anymore."

Smith's eyes tracked its movement on the screen. "Your mission has not changed," he grated. "Recover the device, and *destroy it.*"

He was clinging to the mission as a bulwark against reality. He was wrong, and I was right. The little device no longer mattered … except to me.

Here around my neck I held the cure for IVK. Not a possible cure, a *proven* one. If, by guile or persuasion, I could retrieve MF and make him read it for me … if I could get home and get to Dr. Tierney's lab … no, Dr. Tierney had been arrested. *Any* genetic engineering lab, then …

The sword hanging over my head would be lifted.

I'd have my life back.

I would live to see Lucy grow up.

I had never wanted anything so much in my life as what I now held in my hand.

Smith didn't like my silence. He said brusquely, "You have no options! You're virtually out of reaction mass. You could attempt a landing. On Mittel Trevoyvox. What then?"

I could run. Hide. Try to make it back to New Abilene-Qitalhaut. Pray that Justin's genetic engineering lab wasn't ruined beyond repair.

Pray that the *Harnith Po* didn't shoot me down as I de-orbited.

With Dolph and Robbie, who did *not* have IVK, as helpless passengers.

Martin abruptly shouted, "Fuck's sake, Mike! How many times I gotta tell you? *Don't let them have it!*"

His Ek guard silenced him by clouting him in the face.

"Either give it up," Smith growled, as I floated paralyzed by indecision, "or we shoot you down here and now!" He leaned in close to the screen. "The device gets destroyed either way. But *my* way, you get to go home to your daughter. *Your* way, you don't … or maybe you do, but she won't be there anymore. Your choice."

My choice.

I made it.

58

HALF an hour later, the *Harnith Po* overhauled the *St. Clare.* I eased up to the docking area on the Ek dreadnaught's slowly spinning cental segment. Magnetic grapples shot out, clamping the *St. Clare* in place. The heavy thunks that travelled through the hull sounded like a trap closing.

From the bridge, I watched a flexible transit tube extrude from the Ek ship's truck-sized crew airlock. It narrowed at the end, like an elephant's trunk, and fastened itself over my starboard airlock.

Robbie joined me in the arterial corridor as we waited for the seal to be completed. Both of us were back in human form, dressed in whatever rags we could find.

The external pressure light turned green. I crawled into the airlock chamber and opened the outer hatch.

I had my .22 in my other hand.

Warm air rushed in. Smells of plastic, disinfectant, and Ek.

I pointed the .22 at the person in front of me.

Smith.

"The device," he said, steadily. His own weapon stayed holstered. Credit where it's due, the man was no coward.

"You're gonna have to come and get it," I said. "And bring my crew."

He'd anticipated this. He edged aside in the tube, and Martin floated past him, scowling and subdued, with a rainbow-hued black eye and a bandage on his bald dome. MF came next, goggling hopelessly at me.

Robbie held one of our Fleet rifles on Smith as he descended into the trunk corridor. I let one Marine follow him, but shut the hatch on the rest of the Eks and humans in the transit tube. "One, no more."

"It's almost like you don't trust me," Smith said.

"No shit," I said. "This way." Grabbing Martin, I led the two Fleet officers back to the engineering deck. Robbie brought up the rear with the rifle.

Back amidst the tangle of coolant pipes, I flipped on the lighting. Martin seldom turned the lights up back here, probably to hide how filthy he let the engineering deck get. It even shocked me. There was *moss* growing on the walls. The AM containment ring took up most of the space. I led Smith and his companion to the other side of the deck, which was Martin's workshop.

We had the basic tools necessary for in-flight repairs: a hydraulic press, a small sintering furnace, and a lathe.

"Power her up, Marty," I said, motioning at the lathe.

As the machine whined up, I took the TrZam 008 out of my pocket and fixed it into the work piece holder.

Smith's eyes followed it hungrily.

Last chance.

I drove that thought from my mind. I'd already used up my last chance, on the day when I killed Timmy Akhatli.

I sealed the transparent hood of the lathe to collect the scurf—and then paused. "Water."

"What?"

"I want water. Tell your Ek friends to hook up their hoses and give me enough water to get home."

Smith sighed, but he spoke into his suit radio. We all waited in silence until Martin confirmed that the *Harnith Po* was pumping water into our tanks.

"Some extra LOX wouldn't hurt, either," I said. "And food. I guess it'll be Ek stuff. We won't die of it."

"What's the idea, Starrunner?"

"Let's just say I don't trust you."

"All right, you can have your consumables." He gave the order and then growled, "Get on with it."

I made him wait until the consumables were on board. Then I started the TrZam 008 spinning, and moved the tool bit up to it.

"Start filming," Smith said to the Marine.

"Yes, sir."

The tool bit dug into the ancient device. The TrZam 008 may have lasted a thousand years, but it couldn't stand up to the high-speed steel cutting tool. Shavings spat off in short spirals. MF moaned and flew away to hide in the corner behind the AM ring. Even though he feared the Transcendence, I guess it still hurt to see something as old as himself destroyed.

Over the whining of the lathe, I said to Smith, "I guess I got you wrong."

"Huh?" His gaze was fixed on the crinkles of Urush metal hitting the inside of the hood.

"I thought maybe you didn't really want it destroyed. Thought maybe you wanted it for yourself."

He flashed a rictus-like smile. "You're getting me mixed up with Jon and Sophs. They've decided their personal interests are more important than humanity. They've sacrificed their *own* humanity, whether they know it or not. But I swore a goddamn oath, with my hand on the Bible, and I will never waver in my commitment to protect our species." His hands were raw balls of knuckles.

"Sorry," I said.

"Sorry?"

The lathe stopped spinning. The TrZam 008 was a half-centimeter stump. It turned out to be black inside.

A series of heavy clunks vibrated the ship, followed by a slight but distinct sensation of thrust.

Smith and the Marine grabbed handholds, swearing.

"You're coming home with us," I said. "Just in case you had any ideas about, oh … blowing us away as soon as you got back to the *Harnith Po.* Or anything like that."

I figured that with the mission complete, we would be dispensable. I wanted a chance to change Smith's mind about that. Maybe kidnapping him wasn't the best way to go about it, but as he had said himself, I was out of options.

I flew forward and hit the intercom. "How's it looking?"

"Couple more klicks of separation," Dolph said from the bridge, "and then we burn for home."

He had come around while we were on our way to the rendezvous with the *Harnith Po.* Face-licking really does work, if only because the lickee gets tired of being slobbered on. When I explained what we needed to do, he'd agreed, and taken a couple of stim pills to get his edge back. I'd hated to see that, but I needed him firing on all cylinders right now.

"I'm sending Smith forward," I said. "He's gonna come on the bridge and say bye-bye to the Eks."

"Roger."

Smith was so rigid with fury, he looked like he might explode. "I suppose you'll want us to surrender our weapons," he gritted.

I was going to say yes. He was in my power now, and I had a mind to rub his face in it. he deserved a little taste of his own medicine. But I recognized the impulse and fought against it. I was still trying to be a better person. "No. Keep 'em. I'm putting you on your honor." I stuck out my hand.

He glowered at me instead of shaking it, and left the engineering deck with his stunned-looking subordinate in tow.

I followed them to the pressure door, saying, "MF, come with me. I have to trust 'em, but I still want to keep an eye on 'em for a while."

A suppressed shriek emanated from MF's corner, followed by the sound of metal smashing on metal.

I flew back with Martin to see what he was doing.

Clinging onto one of the AM ring's electromagnets for stability, MF held the new maintenance bot in two grippers. He bashed it against the side of the AM ring. Shrieked. Bashed it again. Its tentacles flopped loose. Its chassis was stove in.

"I already disabled that," I said. In fact, I had shot it with Dolph's Koiler.

"You took *my* job!" MF screeched at the bot's broken corpse, flailing it against the ring again. "Take *that!* And *that!*"

Martin touched my arm. We moved away.

"He's angry with it for hurting Dolph," Martin whispered. "Figure he's also upset about you destroying the device, but he knows that's irrational, so he's taking it out on the bot instead." Martin sighed. "Figure he's upset about … everything."

MF caught up with me in the trunk corridor. He blinked his optical sensors shamefacedly. "I apologize, Captain."

"It's all right." I could hear Smith on the bridge, talking tersely to the Eks.

"I apologize … for leaving the *St. Clare.* That was the mistake which led to … to all this. I should have stayed quietly on board and watched my movies."

I half-smiled. "You're capable of a lot more than that, bot. And I'll make you prove it before we're done."

We floated at the back of the bridge and listened in as Smith completed his transmission to the Eks. Speaking in English, for our benefit, he explained that he would be returning to Ponce de Leon on the *St. Clare,* and that other Fleet ships would shortly arrive in the Mittel

Trevoyvox volume to wind up the operation. "Smith out." He floated up to face me.

"Well done," I said. "You stuck to the script."

"What now?"

I shrugged. "It's a two-week journey. Make yourselves at home. You don't bother us, and we won't bother you."

The Marine introduced himself as Kwok, and said he wouldn't mind getting a poker table together.

"Maybe," I said. "Later."

They drifted away. Dolph said, "We should lock 'em up."

"I learned my lesson on that," I said. "Locking Ijiuto up was a big mistake. We had a chance to talk to him, get him talking to us, maybe even form a rapport. We could have found out about the Transcendence *before* it blindsided us on Mittel Trevoyvox. I didn't want to make friends with the guy, but there was no need to make him hate us. I don't want to repeat the same mistake … especially since Smith is still a big-shot Iron Triangle officer."

"Not for much longer, I bet," Dolph said.

"Dunno about that. It's the Fleet. Bad guys fail upwards." I sighed. "So for the next two weeks, our mission is to make him not hate us."

Dolph said under his breath, *"Good* dog."

"What?" I'd heard what he said.

"Nothing."

I studied him. "You're still all messed up. Shift." I led by example, stripping and Shifting into my wolf right there.

"Someone needs to stay on the bridge," Dolph said.

"I got it," MF squeaked.

"You could fly this bird without us, couldn't you, bot?" Dolph said.

"I could," MF admitted. "But I do not want to. It is nice to have friends."

"Aw," Dolph said. "You're gonna make me bawl."

I felt a bit sentimental, too. But wolves do not cry.

Dolph Shifted into his jackal, and we drifted down to the lounge, where Robbie was in wolf form, eating tandoori chicken out of the packet. Smith and Kwok floated amidst the exercise equipment like they didn't know what to do with themselves.

We paid them no mind. They would have to get used to our ways.

"Dammit," I said. "I forgot to get a present for Lucy."

That's when Dolph told me what he had realized about fatherhood, the way it reshapes your priorities. He told it haltingly, a bit embarrassed, as if he didn't have a right to the insight now that I was back. But I felt chastised as I listened. A reluctant new awareness settled in, of stakes larger than my personal fate.

"We're gonna have to save the Cluster, aren't we?" I said. "Whatever it takes."

THE STORY CONTINUES IN *ENEMY PLANET,*

BOOK 3 OF A CAULDRON OF STARS.

Congratulations, you have unlocked a free gift!

Go to this link to receive a bonus novella from the Clusterverse archives, exclusively for readers who've finished *Lethal Cargo*:

`http://felixrsavage.com/clusterverse-story`

ACKNOWLEDGEMENTS

I'm deeply grateful for multiple brainstorming sessions with `WalterBlaire`, whose books I heartily recommend to all sci-fi readers! This book also benefited from the expertise and suggestions of `BillPatterson`; Dr. Martin "X-Ray Eyes" Miller; Christopher Andersen; Jerry Larson; AJM; and Ben Aupperlee. Any remaining mistakes are my own.

READ MORE BY FELIX R. SAVAGE

An exuberant storyteller with a demented imagination, Felix R. Savage specializes in creating worlds so exciting, you'll never want to leave.

Join the Savage Stories newsletter to receive a starter library of FIVE free subscriber exclusive books:

www.felixrsavage.com/subscribe

A CAULDRON OF STARS

Space Opera Adventure

Far in the future, in the distant Messier 4 cluster, humanity coexists with the legalistic Ekschetlan Empire, a host of lesser alien species ... and an age-old mystery that could shatter the balance of power. The long, uneasy peace is about to boil over into war.

A foiled terrorist incident on a backwater planet lights the fuse ... and drags freighter captain Mike Starrunner and his crew into an intrigue spanning thousands of light years, with all the wealth and power of the Cluster at stake.

LethalCargo

DirtyJob

\hspace{0pt}…\hspace{0pt}andmoretocome!

EARTH'S LAST GAMBIT

A Quartet of Present-Day Science Fiction Technothrillers

Ripped from the headlines: an alien spaceship is orbiting Europa. Relying only on existing technology, a handful of elite astronauts must confront the threat to Earth's future, on their own, millions of miles from home.

Can the chosen few overcome technological limitations and their own weaknesses and flaws? Will Earth's Last Gambit win survival for the human race?

EXTINCTION PROTOCOL

Hard Science Fiction With a Chilling Twist

Humanity has reached out into the stars - and found a ruthless enemy.

It took us two hundred years to establish fifteen colonies on the closest habitable planets to Earth. It took the Ghosts only 20 years to destroy them. Navy pilot Colm Mackenzie is no stranger to the Ghosts. He has witnessed first-hand the mayhem and tragedy they leave in their wake. No one knows where they came from, or how they travel, or what they want. They know only one thing for sure:

Ghosts leave no survivors.

\textit{SaveFromWrath}(shortstory,subscriberexclusive)

TheChemicalMage

TheNuclearDruid

THE SOL SYSTEM RENEGADES SERIES

Near-Future Hard Science Fiction

In the year 2288, humanity stands at a crossroads between space colonization and extinction. Packed with excitement, heartbreak, and unforgettable characters, the Sol System Renegades series tells a sweeping tale of struggle and deliverance.

KeepOffTheGrass(shortoriginstory)

Crapkiller(prequelnovella,subscriberexclusive)

1.TheGalapagosIncident

2.TheVestaConspiracy

3.TheMercuryRebellion

AVeryMerryZero-GravityChristmas(shortstory)

4.TheLunaDeception

5.ThePhobosManeuver

6.TheMarsShock

7.TheCallistoGambit

VOID DRAGON HUNTERS

Military Sci-Fi with Space Dragons

In 2160, a Void Dragon ate the sun.

In 2322, eight-year-old Jay Scattergood found a Void Dragon egg in his garden.

Humanity survived the death of the sun, but now we're under attack by the Offense. These intelligent, aggressive aliens will do whatever it takes to destroy humanity and take Earth for themselves.

Our last hope against the alien aggressors is Jay Scattergood ... and his baby Void Dragon, Tancred.

THE RELUCTANT ADVENTURES OF FLETCHER CONNOLLY ON THE INTERSTELLAR RAILROAD

Near-Future Non-Hard Science Fiction

An Irishman in space. Untold hoards of alien technological relics waiting to be discovered. What could possibly go wrong?

\textit{RubbishWithNames}(prequelstory, subscriberexclusive)

SkintIdjit

IntergalacticBogtrotter

BanjaxedCeili

SupermassiveBlackguard

Made in the USA
Middletown, DE
19 September 2019